D1626478

COMMANDER

COMMANDER

Paul Fraser Collard

HEADLINE

First published in Great Britain in 2021 by
HEADLINE PUBLISHING GROUP

1

Cataloguing in Publication Data is available from the British Library

ISBN 978 1 4722 6347 6

Typeset in Sabon by Avon DataSet Ltd, Arden Court, Alcester, Warwickshire

Printed and bound in Great Britain by Clays Ltd, Elcograf S.p.A.

HEADLINE PUBLISHING GROUP
An Hachette UK Company
Carmelite House
50 Victoria Embankment
London EC4Y 0DZ

www.headline.co.uk
www.hachette.co.uk

For Jay Schreyer

Glossary

———◆·◆·◆———

afandi	master or sir (Egyptian Arabic)
ajnabi	stranger, barbarian (Arabic)
arrack	native liquor/spirit
baladi bar	traditional Cairo bar
barracoon	enclosure for the confinement of slaves
branleurs	wankers (French)
ça me fait chier	that pisses me off (French)
casse-toi, pauvre con	piss off, you fool (French)
cataract	white-water rapids
crapaud	toad (French) – British army slang for the French
dahabiya	flat-bottomed, twin-masted sailing house-boat
dragoman	servant who acted as guide, interpreter, translator and organiser for visitors to Egypt
je m'en fous	I don't give a fuck (French)
firman	edict
galabia	traditional loose-fitting Egyptian robe worn by both males and females
macadam	road surface made of tiny stones

Manchester goods	trade goods made in Manchester, England, usually cotton or wool
pagdi	turban, cloth or scarf wrapped around a hat
pandy	colloquial name for sepoy mutineers, derived from the name of Mangal Pandy of the 34th Bengal Native Infantry
putain	whore (French)
rosbif	roast beef (French) – French slang for the British
sloop	small single-masted sailing boat
tarboosh	fez
tob	long length of cloth worn as an outer garment
sawars	native cavalry troops, Indian Army
sepoy	native soldier in the service of the East India Company army
Zouave	French light infantry first raised in North Africa

EGYPT AND THE SUDAN 1869-1870

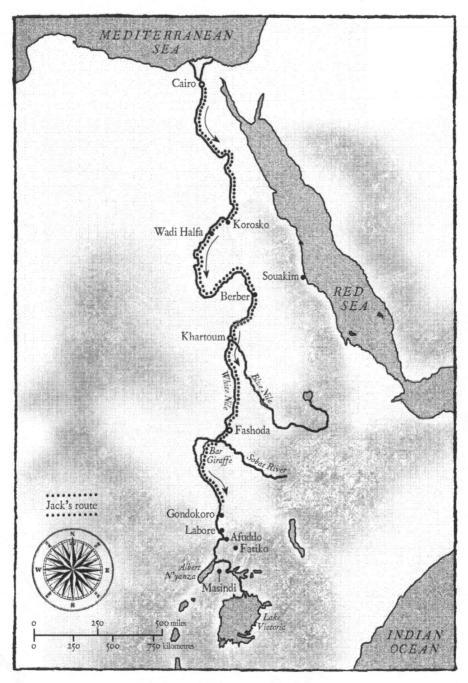

MEDITERRANEAN SEA

Cairo

Wadi Halfa   Korosko

Souakim

Berber

RED SEA

Khartoum

White Nile   *Blue Nile*

Fashoda

Bar Giraffe   *Sobat River*

Gondokoro

Labore   Afuddo
          • Fatiko

Albert N'yanza
Masindi

Lake Victoria

INDIAN OCEAN

•••••••• Jack's route
••••••••

N

W   E

S

0   250   500 miles

0   250   500   750 kilometres

The main objects of the enterprise are, after crushing the Slave Trade:

1. To annex to the Egyptian Empire the Equatorial Nile Basin.
2. To establish a powerful government throughout all these tribes now warring with each other.
3. To introduce the cultivation of cotton on an extensive scale, so that the natives shall have a valuable production to exchange for Manchester goods, etc.
4. To open to navigation the two great Lakes of the Nile.
5. To establish a chain of trading stations throughout the country to be annexed.

Letter from Sir Samuel White Baker to his friend,
Lord Wharncliffe

Chapter One

Near Gondokoro, southern Sudan, December 1868

The herd never stood a chance.

The hunters had scouted the area the day before, the guides they had employed tracking the herd's spoor and bringing the men with the guns into position so that they could strike at first light.

They had done this before. Many times. They numbered over thirty – men from every corner of the globe. Syrians, Copts, Turks, Russians, Americans and Franks. Robbers and villains. Crooks, swindlers and murderers. Penniless adventurers and tuppenny cut-throats. All drawn to the lucrative trade that could make a man a year's pay for just a few short months' work. They flocked to Khartoum like flies to a dung heap, the town at the heart of the East African ivory trade a hive of activity once the hunting season started in late December. There they were recruited into the hunting parties that would head south, following the White Nile then turning inland.

They did not come alone. Other parties left Khartoum in the first months of the new year. These men were journeying further south and west than those hunting for ivory, their prey not the enormous beasts that roamed the hinterland near the Nile but the young men, women and children who could be sold into the slave trade that was thriving in East Africa now that the Atlantic traffic had been curtailed. Both were lucrative businesses, the dealings in ivory and the commerce in human flesh, drawing men from all over the globe, every one of them enticed by the easy lucre that could be garnered from ravaging the vast tracts of land far to the south of civilisation. These hinterlands were ruled not by the principles of law and government but by the old rules, set by any man strong enough to control the territory that would yield the commodities the world demanded. These were the places where the power of the gun outweighed the power of law; the domain of men who cared nothing for the destruction that they wrought on the people and animals that called the wilderness home.

Leading the hunters was the Frenchman. He was the man who had borrowed the money to put the hunting party together, a loan that was to be repaid in ivory at fifty per cent of its market value, the men with the means to finance such an expedition able to charge a premium as they had no shortage of willing borrowers. Even with such an exorbitant rate of interest, the Frenchman still expected to make a small fortune. Demand for ivory had never been stronger. Whether it be for the fashionable clubs of the major cities of Europe, where it was used to produce the billiard balls and the piano keys that would entertain the gentlemen able to afford entry into the most salubrious of establishments, or for the handles of the fans wafted so decorously by the women those same men left at home, ivory was worth its weight in gold. And worth the trouble, and the cost, of journeying far into the badlands, where only the strongest would thrive.

The Frenchman led the men onto the rising ground the local tribesmen he had employed as their guides had chosen, just as the first rays of the morning's sunlight were pushing away the greys and browns of night, filling the forest glade with shadows and warming the sky with a beguiling cocktail of colour that belied the carnage to come.

There were ten elephants in the herd. All were females. Around their legs were half a dozen calves, the youngsters starting the day frolicking back and forth, trunks raised in challenge to their playmates, their small frames galloping past the slow-moving body of the herd's matriarch, who was clearly not at all amused by their antics, her disdain shown in the warning she trumpeted at the boisterous youths. As the light of the sun warmed the shadow-drenched land, the herd started to feed, the great beasts moving with the languid pace of the newly awoken, their breakfast of ripe lalobes from the heglik tree a fine treat for the start of another day. The females in the herd cared nothing for the effort of sourcing the rich fruit, nor the pain of the headbutt they administered to the solid trunk to shake the date-sized lalobes from the branches at least thirty feet above their heads.

The Frenchman lay at the centre of the line of hunters as the herd began to feed, the sun warming his back, the skin on his face tingling as the breeze washed over it. They were perfectly positioned, the wind keeping their scent away from the elephants and the raised position giving them an easy shot at targets not much more than a hundred and fifty paces distant.

As he lay there, he heard a low rumbling sound, like distant thunder. He smiled, recognising the sound for what it was, the noise coming from the enormous bellies and bowels of the animals he would shortly slaughter. With the grumble of hunger came the thump of heavy feet as the adults in the herd started to move around the glade.

It was almost time.

The Frenchman assessed the tusks of the ten females destined to die before the sun had fully risen into the sky. All would add to his haul, a haul that would fetch him a fortune when he got it back to Khartoum at the end of the season. The tusks of the nine younger females could not weigh much more than fifty pounds apiece, but that was still more than enough to repay the effort of a few hours' work. The matriarch was different. She had to be at least fifty years old, and her tusks were the warm colour of clay. The Frenchman watched the ancient female as she took stock of her surroundings, a sure sign she was preparing to move the herd along. Each of her tusks had to be around sixty to seventy pounds in weight, far less than those that could be hacked from a fully grown bull, but still enough to make him smile. Yet as fine as they were, they would be but a minor addition to the stock he had amassed already, some from herds just like this one that he and his men had hunted for themselves, others either traded or taken from the scattered tribes that still clung to life close to the Nile. Soon he would forget which animal they had belonged to, their history and her story lost amidst the tales of so many.

'Make ready,' he hissed to the others in the shooting party. The Frenchman himself was not carrying a weapon, but there were ten men armed with elephant guns made by the finest gun manufacturers of Europe – Holland, Dickson of Edinburgh, Rigby, Gibbs, Webley, Reilly and Purdey, some single-shot smoothbores, others double-shot. Most were muzzle loaders, just a few the more modern breech loaders. With each man were two gun bearers, the lowest-paid of the Frenchman's gang, there to relay weapons and reload, then to help hack the ivory from the corpses those guns would create before carrying it to the Frenchman's encampment. The rest of his men waited behind the ridge, some mounted ready to give chase after any wounded elephant that bolted, others controlling the hunting dogs that would be released in the aftermath of the shooting to corral and contain as many of the wounded beasts as they could.

Around him, the men lined up their first shot, taking their time, making sure.

Then the herd sensed their presence.

The Frenchman did not know how they had been spotted, but there was no time to dwell. The females started to circle, facing into the wind then away from it, trunks swinging as they tasted danger in the air.

'Fire!' The Frenchman shouted the command. The time for stealth was over.

It was an easy shot, one a child could make. Every man with a gun was an experienced hunter who had done this a hundred times.

Not one of them missed.

Heavy bullets seared through the early-morning air, the sound of each fierce retort punching into the ears of every man in the Frenchman's gang.

All hell broke loose.

Trumpets of alarm. Shrieks of pain. Fear. Panic. Distress.

Some of the herd were hit in the head, heavy rounds driven by fine-grained black powder gouging deep before hitting the hard bone of the skull. Others struck the elephants in the shoulder, the fast-moving projectiles cutting into the softer flesh and tearing far into their bodies.

Yet not one elephant fell. The elephant guns fired heavy-gauge lead shot, but even such bullets moving at close to one and a half thousand feet a second were not powerful enough to kill the enormous creatures by themselves.

The gun bearers handed forward second guns kept ready for this moment, then reloaded the now emptied first guns as fast as they could, hands and fingers moving through the process with skill honed by hours upon hours of practice.

The herd started to run. With blood streaming from their wounds, they tried to flee from the deadly storm that had torn into them. Not one made it more than four or five yards before the hunters' second shots punched into their flesh.

Four females fell, great bodies thumping hard onto the forest floor.

The rest ran on.

'Go! Go! Go!'

At the Frenchman's command, the men at the base of the ridge rushed forward. Horses snorting. Dogs barking. Men shouting. All added to the chaos of the moment, the sounds mixing with the terrified screams of the herd as they tried to escape the ambush.

The men with the guns rose from the ground, the need to hide away long gone now. More shots were fired as freshly reloaded guns were handed forward. More animals fell, bodies tumbling into the dirt. Blood flowing into the tangled greenery on the forest floor.

The matriarch had heard the sounds of gunfire before. She knew the threat it posed to her family. She raised her trunk high as she trumpeted into the sky to encourage those that could to follow, then ran hard, fast, thrashing through the undergrowth, three females and half a dozen calves doing their best to stick with her. Every adult beast was bleeding, grey skin slathered with red.

The dogs and the horses chased them down.

None of the herd would be allowed to escape.

The men on horseback started to fire; revolvers, shotguns and carbines shooting fast. Even the lighter bullets struck the wounded animals hard, slowing them, hurting them. With dogs and horses chasing them down and heading them off, the herd had no choice but to turn back.

It brought them back into the range of the hunters with the guns.

Shots came at them the moment they turned. More bullets struck them, gouging, tearing, cutting deep.

The last of the young females went down, her despairing trumpet of agony ending abruptly as she died a bloody, vicious death.

Only the matriarch still stood.

She came to a halt, blowing hard, blood flowing freely from the dozen rents in her flesh. She stared at the men, horses and dogs that surrounded her, shaking her great head as she tried to understand the end that Fate had decreed for her.

The Frenchman came closer, pace slowing as he closed on the last elephant standing.

He stopped then, looking at her in admiration. She was a magnificent creature that inspired awe even in the fast-beating heart of the man who would soon order her death.

'Here.' A breathless voice announced the arrival of one of his men at his side.

'Are you loaded?' The Frenchman's voice rasped as he snapped the terse question.

'Yes.'

'Then get ready.'

The two men were no more than twenty yards from the huge beast they had hunted down.

The matriarch stood still, eyes moist, a single fat tear running down the side of her head where it mixed with the blood flowing from the deep crevices the hunters' bullets had carved into her skin. She stared back at the two men. Beast facing her hunters.

'Kill her.' The command left the Frenchman's lips in barely more than a whisper.

The man at his side pulled the trigger.

He could not miss. The heavy round punched into the matriarch's forehead, blowing out her brain, and she dropped like a stone.

It was over.

'Make sure they are all dead.' The Frenchman spoke in English, directing his men to the line of bodies ahead. Few of the elephants had been killed outright. Most of them still moved, bodies heaving and twisting where they had fallen.

His men swarmed forward. All understood what had been said. It was the sole prerequisite for being included in the Frenchman's party, the language the only one shared between the polyglot group. Otherwise, all a man needed was a pair of working arms and legs, and a conscience not troubled by killing.

The Frenchman followed his men until he stood over the body of the matriarch. She was quite dead, but that did not stop the flow of blood that poured into the warm soil from the dozen rents in her flesh. The Frenchman cared nothing for the sight of so much blood; he had seen enough in his life for it not to offend. He had eyes only for the animal's tusks, and he tutted as he saw a fat crevice running the length of one of the pair. Its value had been halved in an instant. And that did offend.

Around him his men were doing as he had ordered. Any elephant left alive was killed where it lay. Shots came one after the other, the sickening thump of bullet striking flesh sounding clearly.

'Herman.' The Frenchman summoned one of his men, a German from Munich who was the best shot amongst them and who would do whatever he was told, no matter what.

'*Ja?*'

'Get the blacks. Make a start.'

The German did not so much as twitch at the curt command. '*Ja, stimmt.*' He turned to do his master's bidding.

'And kill those noisy bastards.' The Frenchman gestured to the calves, which were whimpering forlornly as they thumped their trunks against the corpses of their freshly slaughtered mothers, their distress both loud and pitiful.

'*Jawohl.*'

The Frenchman nodded as the German went to do as he was told. It would take a good fifteen minutes for the main body of his party to be brought forward, the tribesmen with the hatchets and butchers' knives who would hack the tusks from sockets of bone; these men had been left far from the ambush lest they warn the herd of the presence of the killing party.

He checked around one last time, making sure there was no danger that he had missed. The corpses were already attracting attention, the vultures and the marabou gathering ready to feast on the bones and flesh that would be left behind, drawn to the smell of blood that would taint the air for miles around. His men would have to work quickly. He wanted the job done long before night fell.

Herman directed some of them to kill the calves. Laughter followed as a couple of the calves tried to flee at the last, the men making a game of shooting them down. The Frenchman paid it no heed. His men had done well. They deserved a little fun. And it would not last long. They were good shots.

As he stood there, he carefully removed the single black glove from the wooden hand that had replaced the one he had lost in Mexico. As ever, the stump was hurting. He unbuckled the wooden prosthetic, then slid it from the leather cup that covered his arm from wrist to elbow. Tucking it under his arm, he used his right hand to massage his left forearm, his fingers kneading the aching flesh, not caring that some of his men looked his way. He never hid his disfigurement. It was a part of who he was now. He had nothing to hide. From anyone.

Only when his arm had stopped paining him did he push the carved wooden hand back onto the leather cup. It took but a moment to buckle the straps that held it in place, the fingers of his right hand well practised at the action. Then he slipped the glove back on, taking time to adjust the articulated fingers so they formed a fist.

Job done, he went to find some coffee. He would play no part in the butchery that was to follow. His men would make sure the tusks were removed and made ready for the journey back to their encampment. The rest of the animals would be left. He had no use for dead flesh. It could not be sold and so it would be abandoned. Eventually the carrion feeders would strip the flesh from the bones, the skeletons left as a lasting memorial to a herd that had been in the wrong place at the wrong time.

Life did not matter. Not here. And not when it belonged to animals like those that had died that morning. He was no more moved by their plight than he was by the fate of the cattle led each morning to the butcher's yard. The only thing that mattered was their price, and that morning had yielded him a fine haul.

The sun had still not fully risen over the forest, yet it had already been a good day.

Chapter Two

Cairo, Egypt, 17 March 1869

Ezbekiyeh Square bustled with life. It was a little after six in the evening, and locals swarmed across the plaza in enormous numbers, each one moving with purpose now that the sun was setting and the cooler air of evening was making itself felt across the great city. The noise was incredible. The call to Maghrib prayers echoed from tall minarets, whilst in the square itself, hundreds of voices clamoured for attention.

The wealthier merchants were standing by their carts, goods displayed proudly for all to see, whilst poorer street vendors spread their meagre wares on the ground. Both groups were working the crowd, their bold claims and vague promises shouted with the same confidence and swagger no matter the status of the seller. Water carriers were there in numbers, heavy clay amphorae clamped tight to their backs in tight wicker sheaths, the tin cups that hung down onto their chests clanging as they clashed together, their cries adding to the clamour. Boys led donkeys through the throng, high-pitched voices competing with one another as they tried to sell their beasts' backs for a few piastres. With them came men carrying snakes, carpets, bags full of fish, baskets of bread or any other of the thousand commodities that were demanded by the denizens of the city.

The few Europeans in the crowd stood out, the sombre greys and blacks of their tailored clothing so very noticeable amidst the pale galabia of the locals. These ubiquitous long robes came in dozens of shades, from whites, creams and greys to the palest blue of a winter sky. Men wearing turbans added a splash of colour to the scene, those who favoured a brightly coloured yellow or red cloth in place of a simple brown cap or battered red fez bringing a gaudy warmth to the beguiling palette of colours.

The consul general's agent wrapped his shawl tighter over his borrowed galabia as he paused at the corner of Boulevard Halim, close to the side entrance of Shepheard's Hotel. He stood still, a living statue, eyes scanning the great horde ahead. He was early, and so he would have to wait. He leaned against the wall of the hotel, counting off the seconds whilst taking time to survey the crowd. He was searching for danger, for a sign that someone in the great crowd was aware of his presence. He had learned to be cautious. He might no longer be on the battlefield, but that did not mean he was safe. Even here, surrounded by a thousand people, he knew he could be in danger. He would not be being paid if he were not.

Enough time passed. He moved on, walking into the great square that was the beating heart of the vibrant city of Cairo. The whole area had been cleared over the course of the last few months, the canal that had been dug in a futile attempt to prevent it flooding during the annual inundation now filled in, the bruised earth still clearly visible beyond the macadamed surface of the main road that ran straight through the plaza's centre. The houses of the Copt quarter, which had once butted up to its northern flank, had been torn down, to be replaced by empty building plots.

The Khedive of all Egypt, Ismail Pasha, was said to have grand plans for the centre of his greatest city, just as he had grand plans for the whole of his country. Like so much of Cairo, the square was to be redesigned and modernised, a beautiful French pleasure garden planned for its centre, whilst new cafés and a theatre would be built to entertain and please all those who were drawn to the city now that the Suez Canal was soon to be opened. The country was at the start of a new age of prosperity, one that had been secured by the great waterway that would connect the Mediterranean to the Red Sea.

The agent strode into the throng, taking his place as just one more local amidst many. He was following his instructions to the letter, just as he had promised he would. He had built his fledgling reputation on his ability to do exactly as he was instructed, completing whatever mission he was given no matter what it took. He had only been in Cairo for six short months, but already Colonel Stanton, the consul general, knew who to send for when something had to be done, especially when that something needed an unofficial, and completely deniable, solution.

A party of Egyptian soldiers ambled through the crowd. They wore bright white trousers and tightly cut hip-length jackets with a single row of brass buttons down the front. Like all Egyptian soldiers, they sported red fezzes with jaunty little tassels that flicked back and forth as they moved. Their smart uniforms marked them out, but it was their loud voices and laughter that eased their passage through the locals, the men, women and children who found themselves in the soldiers' path moving out of their way with alacrity. The agent ran his eyes over the soldiers' faces as he passed, checking for any hint of familiarity before averting his gaze and letting them go by. He had only seen his contact once before, a clandestine rendez-vous in the street behind the British mission two days before. Yet it would be enough for him to recognise the man. It would have to be. For there could be no failure. The consul general's message had to be delivered.

The agent slowed his pace as he made it to the heart of the square, but his eyes were never still as he searched every face coming towards him. It was time to be patient, and to wait for the moment when he located the man he had been sent to hunt down. He made sure to match his posture to those around him, mimicking their gait and the slow shuffle of their sandalled feet. He did not fear the presence of the soldiers. He had fought men like them too many times to count. The Beaumont–Adams five-shot revolver he carried underneath his galabia was loaded and ready for use. He could draw it in an instant, a slit cut into the right hip of his robes for just that purpose. He did not doubt that if he had to fight, he would win. For he would kill without a qualm. No matter the consequences. No matter the cost.

He pressed on behind a man carrying a basket filled with *eish baladi*, the bread that was served at nearly every meal, as much a utensil as it was a filling part of the repast. It was easy enough to follow the baker then angle his path so that he curved back around until the setting sun was in his face as he headed towards the western side of the square.

Time was passing slowly, yet the agent felt no sense of impatience. The moment for action would arrive only when Fate was ready, whether he wished it to come quicker or not. Nothing could change the future. Only Fate could do that. She had been his mistress for well over a decade. He had placed his life in her hands the moment he had stolen a British officer's scarlet uniform and taken it for his own. She had led him from one continent to another, first to the battlefield at the Alma River in the Crimea, then to the east to fight in India and Persia.

He had once believed that he had discovered himself in those early years. He had learned what it was to lead men in war, and what it took to survive. He had thrived, learning his skills then applying them in the bloody maelstrom of battle. These had been the years when he had believed himself to be a warrior and a commander. There had been pride then, stubborn, hard-earned, bloody-minded pride. Pride that had led him back to Europe and the slaughter at Solferino. Much of that pride had been left behind amidst the silent mountains of corpses that had filled the tiny villages of northern Italy, but Fate had not let him find peace. She had taken him further afield, and he had voyaged to the United States of America, where he had thrown himself into the dreadful destruction of the civil war that had torn the young country apart, once again leading men into battle before striking out on a lonelier path on his own. It had been in America that he had discovered that much of what he believed he had learned about himself was wrong. He was no warrior. He was nothing more than a killer with a gun and a sword. His survival was in Fate's hands, not his own.

Another group of soldiers came towards him. Once again the consul general's agent surveyed each face in turn. None matched the image he carried in his head. He was about to move on when he saw an officer trailing after the soldiers. In place of the bright white uniform of the men, the officer wore a longer tail coat in dark blue, paired with dark blue trousers. On the jacket's shoulders were heavy gold-fringed epaulettes, but it was not the gaudy demarcation of the man's rank that caught the agent's attention. It was the moustachioed face under the red fez. A face he had seen before. The face of the man he had come to find.

The agent's steps did not falter as he located his target. He shuffled on, eyes cast downwards, giving nothing away even as his heart beat faster. He let the officer and the soldiers get away from him before he changed course, sliding past two men carrying a huge rolled carpet then heading back the way he had come, sun warm on the back of his head.

A dozen or more people now separated him from the officer in his fine blue uniform. Enough to screen his presence as he began to follow, but not so many that he would lose sight of his target.

As he watched, the officer broke away from the soldiers and turned right, heading towards the southern side of the square, where the impressive house and gardens of Ahmed Pasha Taher looked out over the open space. The agent followed, making sure to hang back. The officer paused just once, turning to glance hurriedly over his shoulder, as if he felt the presence of someone behind him. Yet the moment passed quickly, and he pressed on through the crowd that was already starting to thin now that the chill in the air was making itself felt as the sun sank lower into the far horizon.

There were many tight, narrow streets on the southern side of the square. The officer entered the nearest, pace unaltered as he left the open space behind. For the first time, the agent hesitated. The locals who had screened him from view had dispersed. Now there was no one between him and the officer. To follow was to risk discovery, but there was nothing else for it, not if the message was to be delivered, and so the agent lowered his chin and pressed on.

The houses on either side of the street huddled close, upper storeys projecting out over the narrow roadway, sealing off the light and casting everything below into shadow. It was noticeably cooler here. The agent felt it keenly, the skin on his face tingling. He glanced up. The tiny sliver of sky that he could see beyond the encroaching buildings was getting dark.

Ahead, the officer increased his pace, as if the cold was urging him to his destination. The agent followed, eyes fixed on his target's back. He kept them there as they walked further from the square, following the street for no more than a dozen yards before the officer turned into an alley even narrower than the first. Locals flowed both ways, voices filling the narrow space with noise. The agent paid the babble no heed, mind focused on his target and nothing more.

The two men kept moving, as if locked together by an invisible tether. The agent lost his bearings within the first five minutes. The labyrinth of streets on this side of town was impossible to navigate for anyone who had not been born here. In many ways, it reminded him of the cramped alleys of Whitechapel, in London's East End. Away from the main thoroughfares, a newcomer to the city would find themselves lost in moments. But that did not matter this night, and he did not spare a thought to finding a way out of the maze. That was for later. For when his mission was done.

Then the officer turned.

It was not for long. But it was just long enough for him to see the agent. For one long, drawn-out moment, the two men stared at one another, their eyes meeting for the span of a dozen heart-beats.

The officer began to run.

'Shit.' There was time for the agent to hiss the single word before he increased his own pace to match that of his quarry.

The chase was on.

Chapter Three

———◆◆◆———

The agent pushed his way through the crowd, elbows working hard to force a passage whilst trying to keep his eyes on the officer, who was fast disappearing from sight. It was hard going. Men shouted at him, faces creasing in sudden anger as he fought to shove past. He paid them no heed, ignoring hands that clawed at him or thumped against his shoulders as he bundled his way by.

The alley bent sharply to the right, then opened onto a small square. After the tight, claustrophobic confines of the last hundred yards, it should have come as a welcome respite. At the centre was a small oblong fountain, a thin jet of water gushing out of each face and falling into a surrounding pool. On another day, it would make for a pleasant place to rest a while, the cooling water a boon in the usually boiling-hot city. But not on that crisp March evening.

The agent reached the square just in time to see the officer pause by the fountain. For a second time he looked back, eyes narrowing as he spotted the man on his tail, assessing the threat he faced.

Two soldiers sat near the fountain, bottoms perched on the

very edge of the retaining wall of the pool. Both started to rise as the officer's presence was noted. A rapid burst of Arabic greeted them as they came to a slow attention. At once, both men's heads turned towards the agent. More orders followed, a raised hand and a pointed index finger leaving no doubt that he was the target of the quick-fire instructions.

The agent saw the two soldiers turn to face him. Neither looked like much, not to a man who had fought the Persian Fars at Khoosh-Ab, or who stood on the slopes of the Bull Run river as the Confederate army gutted the blue-coated ranks of the Union column that had come so close to turning their flank and securing the north their first victory of the war. Yet they still provided an obstacle, one he would have to brush aside.

The officer shouted one last word of command, then scurried away, leaving the two men to do as they had been told. Both stepped forward, placing themselves directly in the agent's path.

'Stand aside.' The agent gave the first command of his own as he kept his eyes on the back of the departing officer, marking his path as best he could. He did not expect to be understood. Most locals spoke some French, the language of choice for the khedive, but the agent knew little more than a handful of words. Few spoke English. He would have to make them obey him a different way. One understood the world over.

Arabic came back at him as the two men moved to stand on one side of the fountain. Neither one was taller than the agent, who stood just shy of six feet, and both were slight of build. Gestures followed their words, short, sharp waves of the hand that made it clear that the agent should turn and go back the way he had come.

It was an instruction he would never obey.

He did not hesitate. There was no time for that, not if the target was to be caught. He came forward, quick, short steps taking him directly towards the two soldiers. The one on the left raised his hands with palms held out to stop the man the officer had commanded him to hold at bay. The agent kept coming, left arm sweeping away the soldier's hands whilst he curled his right hand into a fist. The moment the soldier's arms were knocked to one side, he lashed out, the punch moving quicker than the eye could track. It connected with the very point of the soldier's chin, the blow powerful enough to snap his head back as if it were held on his shoulders with a spring.

The soldier staggered, then crumpled, senses gone, hitting the ground on his backside then lolling back so that he was laid out on the ground as neatly as if he had just gone to sleep.

The second soldier's eyes widened in a moment of horrified shock as his comrade was knocked on his arse. He had no time to do anything but stare as the agent twisted on the spot, using the momentum of his swinging right arm to turn him around and leave him facing the astonished soldier. As soon as the two men were eyeballing one another, the agent stepped forward, then slammed his forehead into the soldier's face. It was a brutal blow, one that came straight from the dark back streets of London's East End, and it pulped the man's nose, flooding his face with blood.

The agent kept moving forward, even as his own head rang with the force of the butt. He grabbed the front of the soldier's white jacket, pulling him forward. There was time to see the blood-splattered face loom towards him before he twisted around, rolling the man over his hip then pushing hard. He tumbled over the low retaining wall of the pool, hitting the water with a splash, then flailing his arms as he tried and failed to keep his head above water.

The fight, if it was to be called that, was over in more than two dozen seconds, the agent already moving away as he went after the man he had been sent to find.

It would take more than two off-duty soldiers to slow him down.

As he jogged down the alley, he was starting to breathe harder, the nippy air rasping in his throat. Despite the chill, he could feel sweat running down his spine and into the waistband of his drawers. Yet the galabia he had chosen was perfect for the chase, the flowing garment leaving his limbs free, a cooling rush of air around his ankles as he ran.

He saw the officer almost the moment he left the square behind. Clearly he had expected the two soldiers to delay the man chasing him down, and so he had slowed to a walk. He would pay a price for such complacency.

The agent increased his pace. The officer turned at the sound of fast-moving footsteps behind him, but he was too late to react. The agent grabbed his lapels then hauled him forward until the two men's faces were no more than an inch apart.

'I want a word with you, chum,' he hissed. He dragged the officer to one side of the alley, turning him around as he did so. Then, holding him tight, he frogmarched him through an archway that led down the side of a tall town house that loomed over the alley.

It was darker here, and the agent pushed the officer ahead of him, holding tight to his jacket. A fine wooden doorway stood at the far end of the alley, the frame beautifully carved into an intricate pattern. The door itself was shut tight, and it served perfectly for the agent as he thrust the officer forward, twisting him around then pushing his back against the door so that he hit it with a solid thump.

'You know who I am?' He fired the question at the officer, who tugged down his jacket where it had been ruffled by the agent's rough handling.

Unintelligible Arabic came back at him, the officer's face twisting with distaste as he addressed the man standing in front of him. The agent cut him off in mid-stream.

'Stow it, chum. Speak the Queen's English. I know you can.' He felt something on his face and swiped the back of his hand across his cheek. It came away streaked with blood. It was not his. It belonged to the unfortunate recipient of the headbutt he had thrown. He left the rest where it was. It would serve as warning to the man standing in front of him, a visceral pointer to the fate he would suffer should he resist.

More acerbic Arabic followed, the officer starting to raise his voice. The agent shook his head, but the officer kept talking, the words coming fast and loud and in a tone sure to attract attention. He had to be stopped, so the agent threw his right hand forward, clamping it over the officer's mouth.

'I said stow it.' He snapped the command before easing forward so that he was pressed even closer to the man in front of him. 'Let's try this again.' There was no hiding the menace in his voice or the threat in his hard grey eyes. 'Do you know who I am?'

The officer's own eyes widened over the hand that was crushing his lower face. Understanding dawned. There was fear in his expression. Real fear. He nodded, the action awkward with his head held tight.

'Good. Now I'm going to move my hand. If you so much as

breathe too loud, I'll rip your head off and piss down the hole. You understand me?'

Again the officer nodded, this time repeating the gesture over and over to make sure it was understood.

The agent took half a step back, removing his hand as he did so. He watched the officer carefully, waiting for any disobedience. There was none.

'Good.' He took a second to glance over his shoulder. The alley was empty. All was as it should be. It was time to deliver the message he had been instructed to give.

His right hand moved quickly, sliding through the slit in his robe, and he drew the revolver smoothly, keeping it out of the officer's sight line. The weapon was heavy in his grip, yet its weight was reassuring. It completed him.

'So, my good friend Colonel Stanton gave you clear instructions, and from what I understand, he paid you to do a job. A job that included you writing him a little list. Now I want that list. The one you promised. The one you were paid to deliver.' He kept his voice low, so as not to attract attention from any passers-by.

'I don't have it.' The words were spoken with a guttural accent, but they were clear enough.

'So you do speak English,' the agent snorted.

'When I must.' There was disdain in the officer's tone, but it was wrapped in fear.

'Good. Then we won't misunderstand one another. I want the list.'

'I don't have it.'

'Why?'

'It is not so easy to do this thing.'

'Bullshit.' The agent slowly raised his right hand, revealing the revolver. He did not threaten the officer with it. He didn't have to. The officer saw it. He knew what it meant.

'Tomorrow. I will deliver it tomorrow. Or the day after.'

'No, that's not how this goes.' The agent shook his head slowly. 'I want it now.'

The officer opened his mouth to protest once again, but whatever words he had planned to utter were lost as he looked straight into the agent's unrelenting stare.

'Give it to me now.' The agent held out his left hand. The consul general had said the man would be carrying the list. The refusal to hand it over was a delaying tactic, nothing more. The officer would stall, then ask for more money. But Stanton would not be played. The agent was not to leave without the list. No matter what it took.

The officer hesitated for a second, then slipped his hand into a pocket, producing a small black leather notebook that he held out towards the agent.

'There, that wasn't so hard.' The agent took the notebook in his left hand. He had no idea what the list contained. He did not need to know, and he knew he would never find out. Such was the way with his current employment. He was not paid to ask questions, just to carry out the instructions he was given. Nothing more. Nothing less.

'Now. If you make a fuss, I'll fuck you up. You understand?' For the first time, a hint of a smile played over the agent's face.

The officer's mouth opened as though to reply, but whatever words he had for the agent died as he considered the hard-faced man in front of him. His mouth closed and he nodded.

'Good. Now you walk your chalk. Make a ruckus and I swear I'll shoot you down where you stand.' Having delivered his last instruction, the agent stood to one side, making space so that the officer could leave.

For his part, the officer needed no urging. He moved at once, easing past the agent, careful not to let their bodies touch, then scurried away without so much as a backwards glance.

The agent let him go. Only when he had disappeared out of sight did he let out a sigh. It had been easy. Too easy. He was almost disappointed. It would have been interesting had he been forced to be more persuasive. He slid the revolver back under his galabia, settling it into the holster he wore around his waist. The two soldiers had been something of a distraction and had added a little spice to the night's chase. But the fight had been over in the blink of an eye. Neither of them had offered a challenge, not to a man who had killed more times than he could recall.

He let out another sigh, then started on the long walk back to his suite of rooms at the Hotel d'Albion. He would deliver the list to his master the following evening, just as he had been instructed.

Maybe his next mission would present him with the excitement he craved.

Until then, he would have to wait.

He would have to be patient.

And Jack Lark knew himself well enough to know that patience was not one of his greatest virtues.

It never had been.

Chapter Four

———◦•◦•◦———

The banquet was hosted by Ferdinand de Lesseps, the French diplomat-cum-developer who had taken the lead role in the building of the Suez Canal, which was finally nearing completion after nearly a decade of construction. De Lesseps had taken over the entire terrace of Shepheard's Hotel, as well as the ballroom and half the foyer. He would not let it be said that he was anything but a generous man, and he wanted to ensure that the visiting Prince and Princess of Wales would not leave Cairo with anything but the best impression of his hospitality.

Jack walked to the edge of the terrace, doing his best not to sigh. He had no desire to be at the glittering reception. Hobnobbing with the powerful men who ran the city was not his thing, and he wished his boss had chosen a different venue for their meeting. Yet the consul general was a busy man and his day had been spent out of town, which meant this was the first opportunity for his agent to report on his latest mission.

The khedive might spend his time tucked half inside the pocket of the French, but that did not deter the British from trying their best to undermine their ally and to exert an ever-growing influence on the ruler of Egypt. The forthcoming opening of the Suez Canal only made that ambition more important, and Colonel Edward Stanton, the consul general, would not tolerate any delay regarding his various plans and schemes to increase British sway in Egypt. It had been Stanton's impatience that had sent his agent into the night to find the Egyptian colonel who had failed to deliver the goods that had been promised.

Jack surveyed the crowd. It was disappointingly familiar, even though it was the first such event he had attended in Cairo. No matter that he did not recognise a single face; he had been to enough such events over the years to know what sort of people would be here.

The men wore formal tail coats over black trousers, the sombre colour dominating every space. The few women present sported extravagant evening gowns in muted pastels decorated with every imaginable type of frill, flounce and bow. The dresses were often swathed in large overskirts made from some sort of gauze, the dense covering almost hiding the colour of the silk beneath. The women wore their hair curled behind their heads in a chignon, decorated either with an eclectic collection of ribbons woven around the coiled tresses, or with a peacock or ostrich feather tucked deep into the tight curls. A few were pretty enough to attract Jack's attention, but most were older, their heavily powdered faces contorted into rictus smiles of exquisite pleasure that sat at odds with eyes that darted around the throng, surveying the crowd to see who was talking to who and who was wearing what.

Jack waited on the fringe of the gathering, trying in vain to spot his master.

'*Monsieur?*' A waiter wearing an immaculate white galabia

proffered a silver platter on which sat tall flutes of champagne.

Jack glanced at the champagne and shook his head. He had no taste for the ludicrously expensive tipple.

'Would *monsieur* care for something else, perhaps?' The waiter was not deterred.

'Have you got any Allsopp's?'

The waiter smiled. 'Of course, *monsieur*. We have their pale ale on draught.'

'Perfect. Thank you.' Jack caught a hint of a smile on the waiter's face. 'I'll wait here.'

'Very good, *monsieur*.' The waiter bobbed his head and backed away.

Jack half smiled. Things were looking up. Securing a beer was a good start. He took a long, slow breath, summoning some energy as he planned for what was to come. He would wait until his beer arrived, then he would begin to work around the rooms looking for Stanton. When he had reported in and delivered the notebook, he would attack the buffet then be on his toes. There was a fine spread laid out, de Lesseps sparing no expense: platters of hashed meat wrapped in cabbage leaves next to heavy black dishes filled with mutton that the guests would eat with their fingers, the meat cooked for so long that it would pull apart with ease. A neat pile of fine white linen napkins stood next to the cauldrons of meat ready for the guests to wipe their hands clean. Other dishes awaited: sausages filled with garlic alongside bowls of chicken broth thickened with rice. For those favouring something sweet, there were pastries of every type, dozens of small bowls of almonds and cherries, and small dishes filled with tapioca flavoured with rose water dressed with more almonds that had been crushed to little more than a fine powder. It would make a good meal for a man of limited means, and Jack vowed to make sure he ate his fill before leaving with a good stash of the tasty pastries squirrelled away inside one of Shepheard's napkins.

'Your pale ale, *monsieur*.' The waiter had returned. He carried a fresh silver platter bearing a single tall cut-crystal glass filled with golden beer. The glass was misted, a promise that the beer had been chilled.

'Thank you.' Jack took the glass, noting its cool touch. For the first time in a long time, he smiled widely, before raising the beer to his lips and taking a hefty draught. It tasted like heaven.

He stopped himself before he could drain the glass in one go. He might not want to be there, but he should at least deport himself with reasonable manners. He had learned in the officers' mess how a gentleman should act, his stint as an orderly giving him ample opportunity to study his betters. It had taken time to learn their ways, but that first grounding had served him in good stead over the years. He would never be at home in their world, but he had long ago learned how to look comfortable in any surroundings, and how to fake it so that it appeared to anyone who should look at him that he belonged there.

It was time to get on with it. He nodded his thanks to the waiter, then moved along the edge of the terrace, making sure not to make eye contact with any of the faces that glanced his way. He was no good at small talk, and he would do his best to avoid conversation with anyone but Stanton.

It took five long minutes to discover that Stanton was not on the terrace. With his half-drunk beer in hand, Jack moved inside. Twice his search was interrupted. The first time was by a fat, jowly man with a sweaty face who staggered away from the terrace to swipe a fresh flute of champagne from a nearby waiter. The two came close to an uncomfortable collision, one that was only narrowly avoided by Jack stopping on a sixpence. He moved on before the man could apologise, his quick feet saving him from both a painful impact and an even more painful exchange.

The second person to delay his progress was a handsome woman dressed in a muted pink gown swathed in cream muslin. She quite deliberately stepped into his path so that he had no choice but to stop and force a hasty smile onto his face.

'Good evening, I do not think we have been introduced.' She looked at him with hooded eyes as she laid her lure.

'No, we have not.' Jack's reply was curt to the point of being rude. But he did not care. He had never been one for niceties.

He made to step around her, moving as quickly as he could. To his annoyance, she sidestepped nimbly, blocking his escape.

'Are you a friend of the Frenchman de Lesseps?'

Jack's attempt at a smile faded as he was forced to contemplate the lady in front of him. She was slim to the point of stringiness, her scrawny frame making it clear she consumed little more than air and champagne. Her face was long and slender, with a tiny puckered mouth and quick blue eyes that ran over his body in the span of a single heartbeat. He knew her type at once. She would be the bored wife of an official, or perhaps a merchant, her life spent bossing servants around and entertaining other bored wives by providing afternoon tea, or perhaps sharing a hand of bridge.

He did not doubt that there was every chance she might consider his battered charms intriguing. There had been enough women in his life to know that some found them appealing. He did not look like other men, he knew that. His face bore the marks of the life he had led. A raised scar ran across his left cheek until it disappeared beneath the beard he had grown for the sole purpose of hiding as much of the blemish as he could. His body bore many more scars, some on display but most hidden from view. He was also leaner than nearly all the men present that evening. He had put on a few pounds since the previous year's campaign in Abyssinia, but it would take longer than that to develop the sort of exuberant belly sported by almost every other man he could see. Not that he could claim all the credit for that. He was as lacking in willpower as any other man of his age when faced with sweet treats, and he drank more beer than was good for him, but at least his lack of funds did a fair job of preventing him from most types of overindulgence.

He liked the way he looked now. It was vanity, he knew that, but he did not care. He would never allow himself to become fat and lazy like the men in that room. He did not crave comfort and leisure. He wanted something more. Something that was not found in the comfortable surroundings of hotels or clubs, or in the stifling presence of the inbred and wealthy.

'No.' The short answer would be all he gave her. He feinted a pace to the left, waiting for her to mirror his movement, then stepped quickly to the right, leaving her behind. He did not linger, even as he heard her disappointed half-stifled cry as he escaped her clutches.

The ballroom was just as busy as the terrace. A sea of flushed and sweaty faces greeted him, along with the noise of a hundred people all speaking at once. He had no desire to enter the room, but to his relief he spotted Stanton standing on the fringes of the throng, his head bowed as he spoke to a much shorter man. Their conversation was intense, neither one of them revealing any sign of pleasure at the exchange. Stanton might be at the social gathering of the season, but that would never stop him working.

Jack moved towards his boss, taking care not to get too close to anyone who might feel the need to draw him into a conversation. When he was a few yards away, he paused, waiting in the shadows until Stanton spotted his arrival. It did not take long. The consul general nodded once to acknowledge his presence, then carried on with his conversation, leaving Jack to stand there.

Jack did not mind waiting. Especially when he had a beer in his hand that needed drinking.

Chapter Five

————◆·◆·◆————

'*L*ark!'

Jack's beer was long gone by the time Stanton summoned him. He stepped forward at once, joining the two men who had been in deep conversation for the best part of fifteen minutes.

'What happened?' Stanton fired the question at him, making no attempt to introduce him to the shorter man.

'I found him.' Jack glanced towards Stanton's companion, but the man was already leaving.

Jack liked the consul general. A former Royal Engineer, he was a bluff, no-nonsense fellow, amiable enough and scrupulously fair. He was also no fool – he would not be in his current role if he were – and that made a refreshing change. Jack had endured enough crass officials over the years.

'And?'

'I got it.'

'Good.' Stanton was a tall man and he had to look down even at Jack. 'Well, where is it, man?'

Jack slipped a hand into the pocket of his frock coat and pulled out the notebook. He held it out to Stanton, who snatched it away then buried it deep into a pocket of his own.

'Don't show the whole damn world,' Stanton snapped, then drained the last of his champagne. 'Now tell me where you got that bloody beer.'

'You just have to ask for one.'

'Then get me one; you look like you need another yourself.' Stanton raised an eyebrow. 'Do you still not feel the need to address me as sir?'

'Do you need me to?' Jack smiled, knowing it would likely infuriate rather than cajole.

'Well, I am your superior. It is customary, is it not?'

'I probably should then.' Once Jack would not have hesitated to call Stanton by the honorific. But he had been younger then. Keener. Ambitious, even. It was not who he was. Not any more.

'And?'

'I'll try to remember.' Jack paused. '*Sir.*'

'Better.' Stanton laughed at the tone Jack wrapped the word in. 'You are a damned rogue, Lark.'

'So people have said.' Jack offered a half-smile. 'Isn't that why you employed me?'

'Perhaps. You are an enigmatic fellow. I think that's why I like you.'

'I'm glad to hear it.'

Stanton might have said more, but his attention was taken by a sudden movement on the far side of the ballroom. 'Good grief, you'd think we were in a bloody harem.'

Jack turned to see what had captured the colonel's attention. The evening's entertainment was about to start. A troupe of around twenty dancing girls had followed the same number of musicians into the ballroom. Each dancer was draped in a flimsy concoction of sheer silk that barely covered her decency. Half wore yellow fabric embroidered with silver, whilst the rest wore the same scanty outfit but made from black satin embroidered with gold. Stomachs, arms and legs were covered with a thin veil of silvered gauze, and each girl wore at least a dozen golden bangles that matched an elegant gold necklace with a single round emerald pendant that was clasped tight around her neck. Every man in the room latched onto the dancers, eyes homing in on the toned, lithe figures moving to the centre of the ballroom.

'What the devil will the princess make of all that?' Stanton sounded genuinely affronted. 'That damned frog. He really has no idea. Honestly.'

'The princess?' Jack was content enough to watch the dancing girls as they lined up, the guests gently ushered out of the way to make room for the performance that was to come.

'The Princess of Wales, Lark. This whole affair is in her honour. And her husband's, of course.' Stanton spoke from the corner of his mouth, eyes fixed on the dancing girls.

'They're here?' Jack looked around the ballroom, trying to spot the future king and his wife.

'Somewhere. Although quite what they will make of such a vulgar display, I have no idea.'

Jack could not help grinning as he saw that for all his disapproving protestations, Stanton was as captivated as every other man in the room.

The musicians took up position in one corner. All were men, and not one received even a hundredth of the attention given to every dancer. They wore smart navy frock coats with a single line of gold buttons down the front, paired with match-ing trousers. At least half carried silvered flutes or brightly polished cornets, whilst the rest wielded guitars or violins. It took them less than a minute to settle. To no visible command, they started to play.

The delicate sound washed around the ballroom. The crowd hushed, their conversations replaced by the beguiling melody that rose and fell. As one, the dancers tensed, heads bowed, muscles held taut and ready.

The music increased in tempo. It was no jig or polka, the tune as foreign as any Jack had heard. Then it stopped. The silence was complete.

Then the dancers moved. The music came with them, the melody matching their rhythm. Their bodies swayed this way and that, as if their limbs were unconnected and independent of the others. Their movements were graceful yet somehow sinewy, the dancers contorting and stretching as they started to spread out, their bodies filling every available space on the dance floor.

'Well I never,' Stanton breathed.

For his part, Jack looked away. Once, he had sat at the table of honour at a feast thrown by a maharajah. The dancers that day had worn even less than those performing for the British prince and princess, and they had mesmerised him with movements that were far more wild and earthy than the controlled routine on display in front of him now. He had stared in rapt fascination, just as nearly every man in the ballroom tonight was staring at the lissom dancers as they gyrated across the floor.

Instead, he turned his attention to the crowd. Whilst the men leered at the girls, eyes following their every movement, the few women present greeted the display with forced smiles, their own eyes turning towards their husbands before narrowing in dismay at their reaction to the young dancers.

'Is this not to your taste, Lark?' Stanton had torn his attention from the troupe for a moment to glance at the man he employed as his agent.

'No.'

'No one does vulgarity as well as a Frenchman.' The consul general tried and failed to sound disapproving. 'You think your wife would approve? I know mine would most certainly not.'

'I have no wife.'

'Your woman, then.'

'I have no one.' Jack kept his answers brief. He had no desire to speak of his private life. He was alone now and was happy to be so. There had been enough women over the years. All had left, one way or another. Yet each one still dwelt in his mind, the memories and the what-might-have-beens often in his thoughts.

Things would have been very different if the first woman he had loved, a girl his own age called Molly, had not been killed. Would he be happier if that tragedy had not sent him on a very different course? Had they married, his army career would likely have been spent in a series of garrison towns across the British Isles, or perhaps somewhere in the far-flung reaches of the British Empire. Would he have been fulfilled in that life? Or frustrated by its limited horizons? His existence thus far had been many things, but it had rarely been dull. Would he have forgone all the pain of the path he had chosen in exchange for the ordinary life he should have led?

The question nagged at him more often now. And he had plenty of time to think on it. He lived alone, and save for the tasks set by Stanton, he had little to do. He passed his time reading the London papers and exploring Cairo. He had seen all the sights, the seemingly never-ending list of tombs and antiquities no longer holding much appeal now he had visited them all more than once. He had journeyed down the Nile as far as the First Cataract, and he had joined European tourists on an excursion to Heliopolis, where he had marvelled at the obelisk of Osirtasen I. Like so many others before him, he had ridden the four miles from Cairo to Mohammed Ali's palace and the gardens of Shoobra. Then there were the pyramids at Giza, the stepped pyramid at Sakkara and the remains of the ancient Egyptian capital, Memphis.

These remnants from the ancient world had fascinated him for a while. But even the appeal of the past had paled as weeks had dragged into months. Now he was growing bored, and even the tasks Stanton set him were starting to become dull and routine. Most required him to be little more than a messenger boy, his time spent delivering or retrieving letters from the network of agents Stanton maintained throughout the city. There was little danger, his discovery likely to cause the British authorities embarrassment rather than anything more disastrous. A few times he had been tasked with delivering a more personal message, one that usually came with a threat of violence. But it had never been more than a threat. More often than not, his missions had been little more than one anticlimax after another.

The music finished, the dancers still at last. Their barely covered chests heaved with the exertion and the room burst into a polite round of applause, the men clapping with a great deal more enthusiasm than the women present.

'Ah, good. At least de Lesseps knows when to serve coffee.' Stanton glanced once more at the dancers as they filed out. The band played on, their music slowing and becoming gentler after the strident tones of the dance.

Dozens of servants flowed around the room carrying silver platters covered with black velvet cloths embroidered with emeralds and pearls. Every platter bore a large number of drinking vessels no bigger than an eggcup, each one containing a liquid so dark that it was an inky black.

'Coffee, Lark?' Stanton reached for a cup from a passing waiter, his free hand held ready to take one for Jack.

'No, thank you.' Jack had no taste for the bitter liquid.

'You are probably wise. I prefer tea myself, but there is no way in hell we can expect the frog to know how to serve it properly, so I suspect we are better off being spared the attempt.'

'Indeed.' Jack straightened his back. It always ached by this hour of the day. It was time to make an excuse and head for the buffet. He had delivered the notebook to his master. Nothing else was keeping him there.

'You look like a hound waiting to be let off the leash.' Stanton raised his eyebrows over the rim of the tiny coffee cup, which looked incongruous in his large hands. 'You want to be off, I'll wager.'

'Something like that.'

'Well, you can't. I hate these bloody things as much as you plainly do, and now you're here, you can damned well keep me company.'

Jack did his best to keep his expression neutral. The pit of his spine was beginning to hurt with a vengeance, and he wanted nothing more than to return to the cool quiet of his hotel suite and enjoy some peace. It appeared that ambition was to be denied, at least until he could shake off Stanton's attention and slip away, something he would do at the earliest opportunity. 'I'd be delighted,' he lied smoothly.

'No, you wouldn't, but I pay your wages so you will just have to endure, as must I.' Stanton snorted. 'Sometimes I wish I'd stayed in the army. What about you, Lark?'

Jack's neutral expression was unchanged. He had told Stanton a tale that was partly based on truth. He had admitted to fighting in the Crimea, just as he had spoken of his time in India and Persia. From there he had been vague, revealing nothing of his time with the French Foreign Legion in Italy, or the years spent in the United States, where he had fought wearing both blue and grey before heading south with a convoy of cotton destined for Mexico. He had picked up the tale of his career with his time in Abyssinia, the months spent with Napier's expeditionary force a fitting conclusion to his abbreviated story.

'No.' It was an honest answer. He missed much about the British Army. The camaraderie he had enjoyed during his years as an ordinary redcoat had stuck with him, and there was nothing he had ever found that matched the thrill of being in command of a group of soldiers. But little else of the life appealed. He was his own man now, beholden to no one but himself. Serving the aims of the British government was not for him, not any more. At least not officially. His current unofficial role suited him well enough, even if it left him somewhat underemployed.

'You are probably right, Lark.' Stanton did not sound convinced. 'Army life can be damned hard, and damned dull too.' He sucked down a deep breath. 'Ah, now this will make our next hour or so more interesting than it might otherwise have been.' He had spotted someone in the crowd, someone interesting enough to raise a smile beneath his heavy moustache. 'There is a fellow I think you would enjoy meeting.' He beamed widely, then plunged into the throng that was beginning to reclaim the centre of the ballroom, leaving Jack to follow dutifully in his wake.

Chapter Six

―――――•◦•◆•◦•――――

Stanton worked his way through the crowd, Jack happy to trail in his wake. Enough people recognised the consul general, forcing him to nod and smile at several other guests as he made his way to the far side of the packed ballroom, where a gentleman stood smoking a cigarette encased in a delicately carved ivory holder.

'Sir Sam!' Stanton called out in greeting when still well short of his target.

As the man turned, he smiled, clearly pleased to see the consul general bearing down on him. It gave Jack the opportunity to study the fellow he was to be introduced to.

Stanton's acquaintance was slightly shorter than himself. He had the tanned and weathered complexion of a man who had spent the vast majority of his time outdoors, under light brown hair cut short and smoothed across his head so that it lay flat and neat against his scalp. His eyes were a bright but pale blue, and he had a curly beard a good eight or nine inches long. Jack got the immediate impression that he was no ordinary official. There was something in his gaze that spoke of someone more used to operating in the wider world, far from the comfort of a city like Cairo. He recognised the look easily, for he saw it every time he stared into the mirror.

'Good evening, Stanton,' Sir Sam called out in welcome as he offered his hand. 'I cannot tell you how glad I am to see a friendly face.'

'As am I. It makes this infernal nonsense somehow bearable.' Stanton shook Sir Sam's hand warmly, then immediately ushered Jack into the conversation. 'Here is someone I think you will enjoy meeting, Sir Sam, one of my more interesting and enterprising fellows. Jack, this is Sir Samuel White Baker. Sir Sam, this is Mr Jack Lark.'

'Well met, Mr Lark.'

'I am pleased to meet you.' Jack offered a respectful greeting as he shook hands with Stanton's titled associate. The other man's grip was firm to the point of being painful.

'May I ask what you do for the consul general?' Sir Sam fixed him with a piercing stare, attention focused completely on the man he had just met.

'I'm his messenger boy.' Jack spoke with an ironic smile.

'Messenger boy?' Sir Sam looked quizzically at Stanton.

'You will appreciate, Sir Sam, that there are times when one must engage unofficial channels in pursuit of one's aims.' Stanton smiled rather wolfishly. 'Jack is one of those channels.'

'I see.' Sir Sam grinned. 'So I take it you are a man of action, Mr Lark.'

'Something like that.' Jack understood the byplay between the two men well enough. Sir Sam and Stanton trusted one another, that much was clear, and there was an easy bonhomie to their relationship. 'May I ask what brings you to Cairo?'

'I am with the prince and princess. I was honoured to be their guide on their recent sightseeing trip down the Nile.

We only went as far as the Second Cataract, but there was enough to see to make it interesting for them both.'

'Sir Sam is something of an expert on the region.' Stanton leaned forward to speak to Jack. 'What better man to guide the prince and princess along the upper reaches of the Nile than the man who discovered the Lut an N'zige lake and who confirmed that it is the most likely source of the Nile, just as Speke and Grant believed.'

'The Lut an N'zige lake?' Jack was not sure he had ever heard of it, but he certainly recognised the names of the famous explorers from the London papers that he read as soon as they arrived in Cairo, and he was immediately intrigued. It was not every day he met one of the men who was brave enough – or perhaps foolhardy was a better word – to disappear into the great swathes of unknown territory that covered so much of the African continent.

'You may know it as Lake Albert, or perhaps the Albert N'yanza.' Sir Sam had showed no sense of embarrassment as Stanton outlined his success. 'Its discovery is as nothing when compared to what Speke and Grant achieved themselves. Discovering the source of the Nile, well, anything pales against that, although I suspect dear Dr Livingstone may disagree, as he so often does.' He chuckled to make it clear he was not to be taken too seriously.

Jack racked his brains and managed to recall reading something of the lake's discovery just a few years before. He was genuinely impressed. Venturing into the uncharted regions of Africa was no easy task, and was fraught with danger. It was certainly not something he fancied doing himself.

'I confess there was not so much excitement on this most recent expedition.' Sir Sam was watching Jack closely, and would surely have noticed the understanding dawn in his eyes as he realised who he was speaking to. 'We hunted a crocodile or two, but nothing more exciting than that. The bigger prey is much further to the south, beyond Gondokoro. The prince is a keen hunter and is forever talking of stalking a bull elephant, although,' he lowered his tone to a conspiratorial level, 'I am afraid to say the man is not a natural shot.' He made it sound as though it was one of the gravest charges he could level at another man.

'The prince and princess were fortunate indeed to secure your services, Sir Sam.' Stanton felt no need to lower his own voice. 'Especially given your new elevated status.'

'Come now, Stanton. I was honoured to be asked to serve.'

'And I still say he's lucky to have you.' Stanton turned to Jack. 'The khedive has engaged Sir Sam to lead an expedition into the Equatorial basin of the Nile. Why, he has even granted him the title of pasha. He is the very first Briton to earn that honour.'

'It is just a title, Stanton.' Despite the demure comment, Sir Sam was clearly pleased to hear Stanton announce the news.

'Aye, and it comes with a ten-thousand-pound salary. I'll warrant Lady Baker is pleased with that. Will Florence be joining you on this expedition?'

'That is yet to be decided.' Sir Sam was evasive.

'I am sure she will want to.' Stanton glanced at Jack again. 'Sir Sam's wife is something of a legend. She accompanied him on his expedition to Lake Albert, enduring every hardship along the way. She is the most remarkable woman.'

'She is indeed. I am fortunate to call her my wife.' Sir Sam could not hide his pride.

'Is she with you now?' Stanton asked.

'No, she remains at Hedenham Hall. After the queen refused to allow her to be presented at court, we thought it best not to put the prince and princess in an awkward position. We would not want to embarrass either of their royal highnesses.'

'That is very dignified of you.' Stanton's brow furrowed at the mention of the episode. 'I still do not understand that situation. I do not understand it at all.'

'I do.' Sir Sam's chin lifted. He was clearly not embarrassed about the tale. 'I first met my wife at a slave market, where she was among the wares on sale, as well you know, Stanton. Our queen does not approve of the way we found one another.'

Jack did his best to keep his face neutral. The two men were talking openly of something that sounded rather scandalous. It spoke well of Sir Sam's character that he did not dissemble and had addressed the issue head on, when Jack felt sure that most other men of his class would have done all they could to brush the queen's deliberate snub under the carpet.

'The market was in the town of Viden, on the lower Danube, Mr Lark. It was early in fifty-nine.' Sir Sam fixed his stare on Jack as he offered a fuller explanation. 'There were atrocities and slaughter all over the damned place, with refugees and displaced people going in every direction. Poor Florence had been orphaned in the conflict, her father and brother killed before her very eyes. She had been taken captive by the foulest of men, who had placed her for sale as though she was no more than a piece of furniture. I tell you now, just the thought of that moment makes my blood boil. I had no choice but to intervene. I outbid everyone that day, even the local pasha, a blackguard if ever there was one. As soon as I had paid up, we made a run for the border. We only just made it, too. It was a damned close thing, I can tell you. From that day on, we have been practically inseparable.'

Jack did not know what to say. The story did go some way to explaining why Sir Sam's wife would not be suitable to meet the queen. It was hardly a typical courtship, and he could well imagine that the haughty British establishment had no idea how to treat an ex-almost-slave who happened to be married to one of the country's most famous explorers.

'It is an incredible tale.' The drab reply was the best he could come up with.

Sir Sam's eyes narrowed. 'It looks to me as though you may very well have some stories of your own to tell, Mr Lark.'

Jack's hand instinctively lifted to touch the scar on his face. 'I was a soldier. I took this at Delhi.'

Sir Sam nodded. 'I was at Kustanje at the time. Building a railway, if you can believe. But I read of the mutiny. Were you with Nicolson then?'

'I was.' Jack felt the memories stir. He had served as an aide to General Nicolson and had been with him when he was killed. It was not a recollection he wished to release from the dark recesses of his mind, where it lived with the ghosts of other battles fought. He controlled them all, keeping them at bay. But they were always with him. They made him what he was.

Sir Sam looked sombre. 'It was a sad day for the Empire the day he fell.'

Jack did his best to nod. He did not agree. Hundreds had died that day, just as hundreds had died before and after. In the face of so much slaughter and suffering, one man's death meant nothing, no matter his title or reputation. But this was not the time or place to express such a statement. Playing a role had always served him well, but it left little room for offering genuine opinion.

'As a serving man, what make you of this latest debacle?' Sir Sam asked the question rather pointedly.

'Debacle?'

'Abyssinia, Mr Lark. The esteemed General Napier's exped-ition to secure the release of a handful of fools.'

Jack noted Sir Sam's choice of words. Napier had achieved the aims of his mission, recovering the prisoners taken by the Emperor of Abyssinia, the 'Gorilla King' himself. The emperor, Tewodros, had taken his own life in the moments before his mountain stronghold at Magdala had fallen. Jack had witnessed him shove a pistol into his own mouth and pull the trigger. 'I was there.' The words came out flat.

'Then you must agree that the affair was handled most monstrously.'

'What do you mean?' Jack tried to keep his tone light. It was not easy. He had no time for armchair generals.

'Come now, Mr Lark. What did the expedition cost? Eight million pounds? Nine? All for what?' Sir Sam gave him no chance to answer. 'It was nothing but a colossal waste of money. The very same aim could have been achieved by a small expedition of around one thousand men advancing on Magdala via Suakim. I told Horseguards the same. I even presented a detailed proposition to the old fools. But they wouldn't hear of it. I mean, why would they listen to the only man in the whole of England who had any knowledge of the damned place?'

Jack was suddenly intrigued. He had been drawn to the campaign in part due to the massive expenditure that had been devoted to Napier's plan. Sir Sam's idea was an interesting notion. In the end, the army Napier had marched across four hundred miles of mountainous terrain had defeated Tewodros's force with ease, the men who had flocked to their emperor's banner armed with little more than ancient muskets, swords, spears and shields. They had not stood a chance against the modern rifled muskets and Snider rifles carried by the British expeditionary force. Jack could well see how a smaller force, moving quickly, could have achieved the same result. He could also understand why it had not been an attractive option for the powers back in London. Tackling Tewodros had been about more than simply recovering the European prisoners he had taken.

'I think you might be right. But perhaps that would not have set the example that was needed.' He ventured his opinion cautiously. He was interested to see how Sir Sam would react. Many men in his position could not bear to be gainsaid, even to the slightest degree.

'How so?' Sir Sam's eyes narrowed, but he still encouraged Jack to carry on.

'Recovering the prisoners was important, I do not deny that. But it was even more important to show the rest of the world that we can project our influence anywhere on the globe. No matter where that might be.'

'That is very interesting, Mr Lark. Very interesting indeed. I do not disagree. It is certainly a powerful argument. But a penny on income tax, just to show the world what they already know, that to flout our will is to court disaster?' There was respect in Sir Sam's reply. 'I take it from your answer that you were on Napier's staff?'

'Good God, no.' Jack scoffed at the idea before he could help it. 'I was with the intelligence department.'

'Then perhaps you knew of this Watson fellow. The man

who wrote that book about sneaking into Magdala on the eve of the battle. I read it shortly after it was published, a month or so ago.'

This time Jack managed to bite his tongue. He knew Horatio Watson better than any man alive. 'I had the pleasure of meeting him once,' he lied with well-practised ease.

'He mentions in the book having a companion, but never names him.' Sir Sam was watching Jack closely. 'An experienced soldier, or so he says. His "scarred veteran", he calls him. From the description of this fellow, why, he could be talking about you, Mr Lark.'

It was a perceptive remark, but Jack had no intention of revealing the truth. 'That is indeed a mystery. I have no idea who that might be.'

Sir Sam smiled a knowing smile. 'Mr Lark, I wonder if I might make you a proposition. I shall have need of resourceful men on my expedition for the khedive. I believe you might fit the bill rather nicely. I wonder if perhaps Colonel Stanton could spare you for a while.'

'Now come, Sir Sam. I cannot allow you to poach my best man,' Stanton interjected, but there was no rancour in his words.

'I am sure you can find others to deliver your messages, Stanton. Perhaps we can leave the decision to Mr Lark.' Sir Sam refocused his attention on Jack. 'What say you, Mr Lark? I shall be returning to England with the prince and princess now that their excursion is completed, but I shall need men here. There is a great deal to be done before the expedition can proceed.'

Jack glanced across at Stanton, but the colonel's expression was neutral. 'I would need to know more of what you plan.'

He was delaying the moment when he would have to give his answer.

'You shall. I would not expect you to decide now. But would you be interested?'

Still Jack hesitated. To say yes would be to commit himself to a new future. One that might be dangerous, and that would send him far from any place he knew. He smiled. Fate was with him. She had led him to this point and had presented a new opportunity.

There was no decision to be made. Not really. There never was.

'Yes. Yes, I'd be interested.' He spoke the words clearly.

And so it began again.

Chapter Seven

---•◦•---

Shepheard's Hotel, Cairo, 19 March 1869

J ack was escorted to Sir Sam's suite of rooms by a busboy dressed in a monogrammed white galabia paired
with a burgundy fez. Jack himself had dressed smartly
in his one good suit, a solemn three-piece woollen number,
paired with collared white shirt and navy necktie. He hoped it
was the right choice, although in truth it was the only suitable
option he possessed.

The lad, no more than fourteen years old, stood back at the
door that led into the suite, a hopeful look on his face. He was
not to be disappointed, as Jack removed a good handful of
piastres from his pocket and pressed them into the lad's sweaty
palm before rapping smartly on the door.

He waited there whilst the busboy shuffled away. He was
still waiting three minutes later. He had just resolved to knock
once again when the door was finally opened.

'Are you Lark?' The question was snapped by a young man
with a thin face on which sat a precise set of mutton-chop
whiskers under black hair that had been brushed back from the

forehead so that it sat in a large wave on the top of his head. Jack was relieved to see the man was wearing a three-piece suit, although one made of pale cream linen rather than heavy dark wool.

'I am.' He did his best to offer an approximation of a smile.

The younger man said nothing, but he swung open the door and gestured for Jack to enter before calling out in a loud upper-class drawl, 'Mr Lark to see you, sir.'

Jack stepped over the threshold and entered the suite. The sitting room was bright and airy, the doors to a large terrace thrown open so that a brisk morning breeze wafted through. Several closed doors led from the room; bedrooms, Jack presumed. Only one was open, and he looked in to see Sir Sam seated at a fine mahogany desk busily writing a letter.

'I shall be there directly, Mr Lark.' He glanced up for the briefest of moments before directing his attention back to the missive he was working on.

Jack walked across to the doors that led onto the terrace and took in the fine view of the city. It was cold to the point of being icy, the draught billowing through strong enough to make the skin on his face tingle. Clearly Sir Sam did not mind the cold.

'Offer the man some tea, Julian,' came a command from the study.

'Of course, sir.' The young gentleman who had greeted Jack had been busying himself with a pile of papers that sat on a small coffee table in front of a pair of fine settees covered in pale green linen. 'Would you care for some tea, Mr Lark?' There was an icy undertone to the offer, one that perfectly matched the chilled air in the suite.

'That would be kind, but only if it is not too much trouble.' Jack was on his best behaviour. He wanted the job Sir Sam had offered. It was time to move on. If that meant he had to be pleasant to this callow prick, it was a small price to pay.

'Oh, it is no trouble. If it were, I would not have bally well offered, old boy.' His boorish host gave the waspish answer as he approached a sideboard and began to pour tea into a white bone-china cup. 'Milk and sugar?'

'Just a dash of milk, please.'

'Naturally.' The younger man added the barest whisper of milk, then handed the cup and saucer to Jack. 'I expect it's a little tepid by now.'

'Thank you.' The tea looked desperately insipid and was stone cold.

'Oh, the pleasure is all mine, old boy.'

Jack held his gaze. There was something of a resemblance to Sir Sam. Julian had the same pale blue eyes, but where Sir Sam's blazed with intensity, his were somehow lacking any trace of the same fire. But it was an indication that the two men were likely related, and so Jack made a note to tread carefully. Ties of blood were strong, even if they tied a dynamic man like Sir Sam to a crass young fool like the one standing in front of him.

'I do not have long this morning, I am afraid, Mr Lark.'

Jack's inspection of Sir Sam's aide was brought to an abrupt close as the man himself swept out of the study. He was dressed identically to Julian, in a well-cut but loose-fitting linen suit. To Jack's eye, it looked a little rumpled. Clearly Sir Sam was not overly concerned with his appearance.

'I am due at the palace before nine. The prince and princess are visiting the Place of the Citadel this morning to see the pilgrims setting off to Mecca with that holy carpet of theirs. But I am glad you have come.' Sir Sam spoke quickly before handing Julian the letter he was holding. 'Ensure this is sent to the khedive. He must have it today.'

'Yes, sir.' His aide took the letter with a firm nod acknowledging the instruction.

'Did you introduce yourself to Mr Lark?'

'I didn't have the time, sir. I was too busy making tea.'

Sir Sam barked a short, sharp laugh at the touchy reply. 'Mr Lark, this is my nephew and aide-de-camp, Lieutenant Julian Baker of the Royal Navy. Do not let his sour manner put you off. You two will be working closely together in the coming weeks. I shall be returning to England with the prince and princess when their tour is complete. If you accept my invitation of employment, I shall be trusting the two of you and my dragoman, Mr Marcopolo, to put everything in place for our expedition whilst I am gone.'

'Mr Marcopolo?' Jack raised an eyebrow at the odd name.

'The finest dragoman in all Cairo. I have worked with him before. There is nothing he cannot procure.'

'If you do not mind a good portion of the expenditure going no further than the man's own pockets,' Julian said sharply.

'That is how things are done here, as well you know,' Sir Sam snapped. 'Now, I do not have long.' He directed his full attention towards Jack. 'I shall assume by your presence here this morning that you are still interested in my offer.'

'I am.' Jack stood a little straighter.

'Good. I shall leave you to spend the day with Julian. The preparations are well in hand. If we are to be able to traverse the cataracts successfully, we must be away before the end of June, so we do not have the luxury of time.'

'I understand.'

Sir Sam nodded. 'We are trusted with a mission of the greatest significance, Mr Lark. We must not fail.' He adopted a grave expression. 'Opening the Nile basin to trade is of paramount importance. For far too long it has been the domain of despots and desperados. They ravage the land, plundering it for whatever they can take, with no thought to the consequences. The tribes closest to the river have been quite decimated by the wretched slavers, to say nothing of the damage done to the wildlife in those parts. The ivory traders are the worst. They think nothing of butchering an entire herd. The balance of the ecosystem is being destroyed by men with no mind for anything other than turning a profit. That cannot be allowed to go on.

'What do you know of the slave trade in these parts, Lark?'

'Nothing,' Jack replied honestly. 'I am aware of the trade to the Americas, although I believe that was ended by our own parliament some time ago.'

'You are correct. The Wilberforce Act early this century did indeed make the transport of slaves illegal on British ships and in British ports.' Sir Sam smiled, clearly pleased with Jack's answer. 'Indeed, subsequent acts forbade slavery throughout the British Empire and its colonies. I would say we have been tireless in our efforts to put into effect treaties with every other nation involved in the dastardly trade. However, we have not been entirely successful, especially hereabouts. Oh, I know we have pushed restrictive agreements on foreign rulers like the Sultan of Muscat, forbidding slaves on their ships and allowing for inspections by the Royal Navy. We have even gone so far as to establish a vice admiralty court in Zanzibar to adjudicate over any dhows caught with slaves on board. But we all know that this is little more than a damnable sham!' His anger was quick and hot.

'How so?' Jack had his own opinions on the subject, ones that had taken root in America, where he had fallen in love with a woman fleeing slavery in the southern states. Rose had escaped and made her way to the north. She was the bravest person Jack had ever met – and the most resourceful. For a brief second, his thoughts drifted to the clandestine network of people who had helped her to freedom, the underground railroad. He owed them his life, too.

'Quite simply, the resources allocated to the endeavour are measly.'

'I cannot imagine what they expect the navy to do.' Julian joined the conversation. 'There are far too few ships assigned to the task, and the officers chosen are simply ineffective. If I were to be given command of such a mission, I—'

'Why, it is little more than a pretence.' Sir Sam cut his nephew off. 'Slavery is still perfectly legal within the territories of the Sultan of Zanzibar, and that devil knows which side his bread is buttered. He is a strong ally of ours, providing military support and a stabilising influence in the region, something that we hold most dear. I should not have to tell an old India hand like yourself how important that is, what with the most critical shipping routes to India going directly across his territory. The sultan never fails to offer Her Majesty's Government every support, and old Gladstone won't hear a word said against him.' He snorted. 'Of course, he has signed a few treaties to keep us sweet. He has agreed to stop selling slaves to European or American vessels, and he has prohibited traffic outside of his dominions and dependencies. But the trade is left unhindered and unfettered within his own territory, and that means that most of the Persian Gulf and the eastern African coast is free to pursue it. Everyone turns a blind eye to that rather salient fact.'

He took a breath, then carried on. 'The only way to curtail the trade is by taking control of the Equatorial Nile basin and opening it to European influence and trade. When that aim is achieved, we can act to improve the whole damn place, introducing religion, education and infrastructure. It will also allow us to tackle those other devils who plunder the land and put an end to their nefarious activities. Whether that happens through annexation or through ruling the whole damn area through military occupation and despotism matters not one jot. Nor is it of any consequence whether the annexing power be European or local.

'I spoke to the khedive's foreign minister back in June last, and I am pleased to say that he agreed with me in every regard. The khedive has the best opportunity to act on this notion, and I am glad that he has taken the bull by the horns and made plans to annex the area to his kingdom. Oh, I am painfully aware that some damnable croakers are trumpeting that this means the end of Christianity in the Nile basin, but I do not give that any credence whatsoever. And Gladstone and the others can bleat all they want. I know not to count on them for support, and nor shall I have any need of it. I made it all the way to Lake Albert without any assistance beyond what I could provide for myself, and I see no reason why I shall not succeed in this venture now that I have the full backing of the khedive.'

He paused to look at a small silver pocket watch. 'But enough. I am late and that will not do. Mr Lark, I shall leave you to Julian's care. He can show you the preparations such as they are, and introduce you to Mr Marcopolo too. Then we shall discuss your position in the enterprise at greater length.'

'Very good.' Jack had listened with interest. It was clear that the expedition had powerful backing. There was much more for him to learn, but he could feel the beginning of some sense of anticipation. There was no doubt in his mind that this opportunity would give him the purpose he craved. He knew what lived in his soul, the good and the bad. There was much that was ugly and dark, and he understood it all, just as he understood his need for more than his current life was providing.

'Ah, Anna! Good morning.' Sir Sam greeted a new arrival with gusto. 'That is most impeccable timing. I was about to leave, but now I can introduce you to Mr Lark before I depart.' He was beaming with pleasure. 'Mr Lark, this is my niece, Anna. Anna, this is Mr Lark, a member of Colonel Stanton's staff. I am endeavouring to convince him to join our expedition.'

'I heard you talking, Uncle, I was wondering who to.' Anna smiled politely at Jack, but made no move towards him. 'I am delighted to meet you, Mr Lark.'

'Good morning, Miss Baker.' Jack hazarded a guess at Anna's surname. He would never dare say the number aloud, but he reckoned Sir Sam's niece was in her early thirties. She wore a day dress of a gentle lavender that sat well against her pale skin. Her dark brown hair was bound behind her head in a neat bun held in place by a series of golden clips decorated with pearls. Her features were slim, and she had the same quick blue eyes as her uncle. But even though he had only just met her, Jack could tell she possessed a certain frosty reserve.

She gave him no more than a cursory glance before directing her attention back to Sir Sam.

'Uncle, we are late. I should not have to remind you that we are due to meet the prince and princess at nine.'

'I apologise, my dear.' Sir Sam took the rebuke in his stride. 'Gentlemen, I shall speak to you both later.' He walked quickly to the door, his niece beating him to it by a good yard, and they left without another word.

'Well, Mr Lark. Now you have met the family.' Julian broke the silence that had fallen. 'And once dear Aunt Florence arrives, you will have met the whole clan.' There was an acerbic undertone to his words.

'Will she join the expedition?' Jack ignored Julian's inflection, but he marked it nonetheless. He would do well to learn more of the relationships between the members of the Baker family.

'Sadly, yes.' Julian pulled a face at his own words.

'You don't like her?'

'Why would you say that?' he replied with mock surprise. 'I do not think there is a man alive who does not like dear Aunt Florence.'

Jack did not try to understand, but he did try to push away his immediate dislike of the Royal Navy officer he would be spending the day with. 'I shall look forward to meeting her.'

'I am sure you will.' Julian rolled his eyes. 'Now, if you are quite finished with your tea, perhaps we can make a start on the day.'

'Oh, I am more than done. It was as weak as piss and tasted just as bad.' Jack did not care that he had revealed just a hint of his true self to Sir Sam's nephew. There would be no hiding it, not when the expedition started in earnest, so it was best that Julian learned something of the man his uncle wanted to hire. He had spent half his life pretending to be someone he was not. Now he was himself, nothing more and nothing less.

Chapter Eight

———◆———

The Baker warehouse was not far from the library of the Egyptian Society, deep in the back streets of the Copt quarter. Julian had led the way there without saying a word, Jack left to follow him through the heaving streets.

As they arrived, he spotted a finely dressed Egyptian with exuberant waxed whiskers waiting near the double doors at the front of the warehouse.

'Mr Julian! *Sabā il khayr*! Good morning!' The man walked briskly towards the Royal Navy officer.

'Calm yourself, Mr Marcopolo, calm yourself.' Julian shook his head at a greeting clearly far too enthusiastic for his taste.

'Excuse me, Mr Julian.' Marcopolo grinned from ear to ear. 'And I see a new face this morning. *Ahlan wa sahlan*.' He bowed towards Jack, hands clasped together in front of his chest. 'Welcome, my new friend, welcome.'

'*Shukrān*.' Jack found it almost impossible to hazard a guess at the man's age. Somewhere between forty and fifty was the best he could do. 'My name is Lark, Jack Lark. It seems I may be joining your expedition.'

'Let's see what my uncle says about that first, shall we, Lark?' Julian stepped in swiftly. 'We should take care not to get ahead of ourselves.'

'Why don't you call me Jack?' Jack was quick with his own reply. 'Seeing as how it appears we shall be working together very soon.' He would not let Julian nettle him; he suspected that failure would rankle with the younger man more than his presence alone appeared to be doing.

'Oh, how lovely. Perhaps we can become chums,' Julian sneered.

'You never know. Stranger things have happened.' Jack had met plenty of well-bred young men like Julian Baker. He had killed a few too. 'Now, Mr Marcopolo. Sir Sam tells me the preparations for his expedition are well under way. Perhaps you would do me the honour of showing me around your supplies.'

'Oh, Mr Lark, that would be my most absolute pleasure.' Marcopolo's smile grew even wider, but Jack caught a fleeting glimpse of something else in the dragoman's eyes. Something shrewder. Darker, even.

'Thank you.' He nodded his gratitude and returned the warm expression. But he made a mental note to watch the Egyptian closely. He had the sense that the man was playing a part, the genial, laughing display nothing more than a facade. It made sense. Sir Sam was trusting Marcopolo with a small fortune as the dragoman sourced the supplies for his expedition. He would not trust a fool.

Marcopolo clapped his hands together, then turned to the double doors behind him, fishing deep inside his galabia as he did so to produce an enormous iron key.

Jack stood back until the doors were fully open before

following the Egyptian inside. The sight that awaited him took his breath away.

The warehouse was huge. And it was filled almost to capacity.

'Good grief.' He breathed the words as he walked towards the nearest pile of wooden packing crates. He had not expected anything on such a scale. To his eye, there looked to be enough supplies to keep an army on campaign for a year. The vast amount of stock in the warehouse told him more about the gamut of Sir Sam's expedition than words ever could. Moreover, it gave him the first indication of the time period envisaged. This was no short-term operation. From what he was seeing in front of him, it was abundantly clear that he would be joining something that was expected to last for years.

'There are four years' worth of supplies for the Europeans in the party, plus trade goods and stores to last us for at least the first two.' Julian seemed to have read Jack's mind. 'The English goods came from Silber and Fleming of Wood Street in London. They are not the cheapest, but they do not penny-pinch like Fortnum's and my uncle has never found them wanting. However, we still managed to spend some nine thousand pounds on the articles necessary for the expedition. And that is before we paid out for the supplies we have sourced locally or else had shipped here.'

'You've worked hard,' Jack remarked. He was genuinely impressed.

'We have another warehouse like this one and will likely need more storage space before we depart.' Julian walked past Jack and approached a stack of hessian sacks near the entrance. The one uppermost in the pile was open, and he pulled back the sacking to reveal a tightly bound bundle of scarlet woollen blankets. 'I have lost count of how much we have spent on Manchester goods. My uncle tells me the locals adore them.'

'We have blankets in blue, scarlet and white,' Marcopolo hovered at Jack's elbow, 'as well as rolls of plain calico. Then there are at least four-score bundles of cotton sheeting. But that is just the tip of the iceberg.' His English had barely a trace of an accent and it was clear he was fluent. 'There are flannel shirts in both scarlet and navy, along with serge jackets, Indian scarves in the most vibrant colours I could find and five hundred of the finest handkerchiefs in every colour of the rainbow.'

'We are in the process of getting everything stored away.' Julian walked to another pile. 'Uncle insists everything be repacked into these tin boxes.' He pointed to a tower of hinged metal storage crates. Each one was numbered and labelled with precise white stencilled lettering. 'They are soldered shut to keep out the damp and the insects.'

'What are in those ones?' Jack gestured at the boxes.

'Mr Marcopolo?' Julian directed the question to the Egyptian.

'Those contain hammers, chisels and other tools. The ones next to them hold pocket watches from London, along with fifty musical boxes with bells and drums that play "God Save the Queen". We have also purchased a number of magic lanterns. There are fourteen boxes of children's toys, the mechanical ones that move if you do the winding.' The dragoman listed the items from memory. 'We also have six-inch silver balls that can be suspended from the branches of a tree. Sir Sam has found them to be the greatest wonder to the locals.'

'He knows what is in every single box, don't you, old boy?'

Julian clapped a hand on Marcopolo's shoulder. 'The man is a damned marvel.'

'It is my job to know.' Marcopolo shrugged away the praise, and Jack noticed how he prickled at Julian's touch.

'So where is the most important item of all?' Jack made a play of looking around him. He was watching Marcopolo carefully and saw the hint of a scowl form, a moment's true emotion revealed as the Egyptian tried to fathom what he meant.

'Yes, the most important. Without it the expedition will surely fail.' Jack's tone was teasing.

Marcopolo's face became composed once again, the calm veneer firmly back in place. '*Ana miš faahim*, Mr Lark, I do not understand. What is this thing you speak of?'

'Tea, Mr Marcopolo.' Jack made sure his own expression was serious. 'Where's the bloody tea!'

Julian guffawed.

'Tea! Of course, tea!' Marcopolo exclaimed with relief. 'Where would we be without a nice cup of the good old Rosie Lee?'

Jack made sure to grin as Marcopolo realised what he had been alluding to. But he had learned a lot in the short exchange. It would be easy to underestimate the dragoman, but there was clearly more to the man than met the eye. All the same, it was an important question. Years spent wandering across the United States of America fuelled by nothing more than coffee had taught him the importance of a sufficient supply of tea leaves.

'Oh, we have tea. There will be plenty, I promise you, Mr Lark.' Marcopolo clapped a hand to Jack's forearm and steered him deeper into the warehouse. 'We had it sent across from

Malta. Look, there.' He stopped and pointed to a huge stack of tea chests.

'That does look like it will be enough.' Jack pulled a face as he grudgingly agreed.

'Here, Lark, you might be interested to see this,' Julian called across.

It was not lost on Jack that the aide still addressed him by his surname, but still he walked across to join the younger man at the head of another row of neatly piled metal storage crates, interspersed with teak cases that appeared to have been sealed with soldered tin.

'This is just a fraction of our military stores.' Julian indicated the long aisle.

Jack noted the change in the naval officer's demeanour. His former supercilious attitude had gone.

'We have fifty brand-new Snider rifles straight from the Royal Small Arms Factory in Enfield,' Julian continued, 'along with some fifty thousand cartridges.'

'Sniders?' Jack was immediately interested. He had witnessed the power of the Snider rifles at first hand. Unlike a rifled musket such as the British Enfield or the American Springfield, the Snider was a breech loader. Converted from the 1853 pattern Enfield Rifled Musket, it had been given a unique mechanism, so that the whole process of loading, firing and unloading took just a few seconds, and troops well practised with the weapon could fire something close to ten rounds a minute. He had seen Sniders used on the battlefield against the warriors of the Abyssinian emperor, and the slaughter that day had been quite unlike anything he had experienced before, even at Solferino or Shiloh. Advances in manufacturing were making killing more efficient, and he did not know where it would end. But he knew that war was changing. Technology was now paying attention to the battlefield. The same notion of progress that had invented steam-powered engines to improve manufacturing and industry was now being diverted into creating ever more efficient ways of killing.

'There's more.' Julian's enthusiasm was evident as he moved towards another stack of metal crates. 'We have two hundred Hale rockets, and if that's not enough firepower, we are also being trusted with a number of bronze mountain guns that fire eight-and-a-quarter-pound shells.' He was more serious now as he detailed the armaments the expedition would be taking.

'Blow me tight.' Jack could not hold back the exclamation. One thing was clear. Sir Sam was not just going on an expedition. He was embarking on a military campaign.

'We must be prepared for all eventualities.' Julian clapped a hand on top of the nearest tin box. 'Who knows what challenges we will face.'

'How many men will be coming with us?'

'Over a thousand. Two regiments of infantry are to be attached to the expedition. One Sudanese, one Egyptian. There is also talk of some cavalry.'

'What are they like?' Jack had never heard much about the local forces, but he had fought alongside the native infantry regiments in the service of the East India Company, and against those same men during the mutiny back in '58. If the Egyptian and Sudanese units given over to Sir Sam's command were even half as good, the expedition would be a fully fledged small army.

'The Sudanese are said to be the better of the two.' Julian offered a teasing smile towards Marcopolo. 'But the Egyptians are not too shabby, although their officers leave a little to be desired, I am told.'

'Perhaps my countrymen will surprise you, Mr Baker.' Marcopolo hid any rancour behind a broad smile as he dared to gainsay the opinion.

'No offence meant, old boy.' Julian waved away the remark, clearly paying it no heed.

Jack noted the byplay, but he wanted to know more. 'So you expect to have to fight?'

'It is certainly possible.' Julian looked deadly serious.

'Go on.' Jack was intrigued. It was a reminder how little he knew about the area far to the south of Cairo.

'Well, we shall run into interference for certain; the whole of the area to the south of Khartoum is plagued with men who will do whatever it takes to retain control of their personal fiefdoms. If we try to do anything whatsoever to curtail their trade, whatever it might be, they will fight us. That is not a threat to take lightly.'

'Surely they will be no match for you? Not with arms like this?' Jack gestured towards the great piles of munitions.

'Do not underestimate them. We will be entering some dangerous lands. The men there think nothing of killing to hold on to the areas they control. And they are not as ragtag as you may imagine. They move in groups that number as many as one hundred, sometimes even more. They are involved in lucrative trades, and they are not shy about spending whatever it takes to protect their activities. They will be well armed and well supplied, and I guarantee they will not do as we tell them. It may very well be that we have to fight if the expedition is to succeed.'

'Does that not concern you?'

'It does not.'

'It should.'

'Perhaps.' Julian inclined his head. 'But I do not think it will be the type of fighting you are used to either. It will not be battle as you know it.'

'Oh, you'd be surprised.' Jack had fought on a dozen front lines, that was true, but he had been more than just a soldier. His battles had come thick and fast over the years. Not all had been in war, and not all had been on the battlefield.

And from what Julian was saying, he would soon be heading back into the wild lands where the rule of law meant nothing.

That suited him just fine.

Chapter Nine

———◆———

The garden at Shepheard's Hotel was bathed in sunlight. The warmer hours of early afternoon had passed, and so the terrace was quiet, the chilly early-evening air persuading all but the hardiest souls to take their afternoon tea indoors.

Jack sipped at his Indian tea, savouring the peace, watching a waiter in a flowing white galabia as he walked forlornly around the empty tables overlooking the busy street to the front of the hotel, the lack of guests leaving him with little to do. Another waiter delivered a silver pot of coffee to an old couple sitting on the far side of the terrace. Yet another followed, carrying a multi-layered cake stand filled with a beguiling collection of miniature confections and sweet creations. Both men moved with confident panache, smiles fixed firmly in place beneath the fezzes perched on their heads.

It had been an interesting day. Jack had stayed with Julian and Marcopolo until his mind had been unable to retain any more details of the massive quantity of supplies laid in for the expedition. They had gone their separate ways shortly after noon. He had been back at his rooms in the Hotel d'Albion for

no more than an hour before a note had been delivered requesting that he attend on Sir Sam at four that afternoon. He had
made sure to get there early, but it was now close to five o'clock
and he was on his third tea. Clearly Sir Sam did not stick to his
own schedule. But Jack did not mind the delay. It felt good to
have some purpose. His work for Colonel Stanton had been
sporadic at best, and he was tired of kicking his heels waiting
for the consul general to send him a summons.

'Good afternoon, Mr Lark.' Sir Sam was striding briskly
across the terrace.

Jack rose respectfully to his feet. 'Good afternoon, sir.'

'Sit down, sit down.' The explorer gestured impatiently.
'I apologise for keeping you waiting. I do hope it was not too
disagreeable.'

'Not at all. I have been more than content. There are worse
places to pass a little time.'

'That is good of you, Lark. The prince kept me engaged,
and I confess I lost track of time. Ah, good.' He broke off as a
waiter arrived at his shoulder. 'Coffee for me. Mr Lark, can I
offer you something?'

'A tea, please.' Jack ordered his fourth without hesitation.

'And some of those baklavas the chef makes, if you please,'
Sir Sam added to the order. 'Florence tells me I should not eat
them, but I confess I find them rather irresistible.' He spoke in
a conspiratorial whisper, as if frightened his wife would
somehow hear him. 'I trust you will not dob me in.'

'Your secret is safe with me, sir.'

'So, what think you of our preparations?' Sir Sam settled
into his chair as the waiter left with their order.

'They are impressive,' Jack replied honestly. 'I confess I had
not fully appreciated the scale of the operation.'

'The success of the expedition will depend greatly on our organisation. As you have seen, Mr Marcopolo has worked tirelessly to collect together a great deal of the equipment and supplies we will need. Cairo is not London, and yet he has been able to procure nearly everything necessary.' Sir Sam was quick to give credit to his dragoman.

'He has done a fine job.' Jack could only agree. 'I take it that once you have departed, there will be few chances for resupply.' He thought back to the long march across Abyssinia. Napier had refused to advance his army until he was certain that sufficient supplies had been laid in to support the men as they marched across the inhospitable and mountainous terrain. Jack had been impressed by such preparations, preparations that had been severely lacking years before when he had served with the British Army in the Crimea. Napier had constructed a series of supply depots a day's march apart, along with wells to extract fresh water from deep within the ground. The army would not have been able to cross the four hundred miles without them, and the success of the campaign against the Abyssinian emperor was due in large part to the impeccable planning. Sir Sam had clearly learned from the same rulebook and was making sure that his own expedition would not fail due to a lack of supply.

'You have it, Mr Lark.' The explorer nodded in agreement. 'There can be no doubt that once we have departed, we shall very much be out of sight and out of mind. We must be prepared to be completely independent, and if we are lacking in any regard, we shall have no choice but to carry on as best we can, for there will be no resupply save for the most basic of essentials.' He paused. 'I noted you said *you*, not *we*. Does that tell me you are not interested in joining us?'

'Not at all.' Jack was impressed with Sir Sam's perceptiveness. He was clearly not all cheery bonhomie, a sharp mind behind the genial facade. 'Are you still of a mind to offer me employment?'

Sir Sam leaned forward. 'I have spoken to Colonel Stanton. It appears your tenure with the consul general's office is perhaps a little unusual. It is off the books, as it were. Stanton understands the situation. He will give his blessing if you choose to take a more proper form of employment with me.'

Jack felt his hackles rise slightly. He did not like his business being discussed behind his back. And he did not need Stanton's blessing. No man controlled his destiny. 'I am not sure I am glad to hear that Colonel Stanton is so quick to dispense with my services.'

Sir Sam scowled. 'I will not apologise. Things must be done a certain way.' He fixed Jack with a fierce stare. 'My way. There can be no other. It is important you grasp that from the get-go, as it were.' He paused. 'Do you understand me, Mr Lark?'

'Yes.' Jack did not shirk from the other man's searching gaze. 'I understand.'

'Then I have an offer for you. I would like you to join the expedition as my aide.'

'I thought your nephew occupied that role?'

'He does. You will be his second. He will most certainly be in need of assistance. There is much still to be done while I am away in England.'

'I am to be an assistant to an aide?' There was a touch of scorn in the reply, but Jack laughed at himself almost as soon as he had said it. He had commanded a company of redcoats in battle, and he had once even been a maharajah's general.

It appeared his career was going downhill.

'You care for titles, Mr Lark?' Sir Sam's eyes narrowed as he made the remark.

'No. We have a saying where I come from. You can call me a prick so long as you pay me.' Jack laughed again. He could not help it. He was being arrogant, and he did not care. Sir Sam had made it clear that he was in command. Now Jack was making it clear just what manner of man he was hiring.

'Two hundred and fifty pounds per annum, plus I will cover your expenses.' Sir Sam delivered the offer in a clipped tone.

'No.' Jack knew his worth. Sir Sam was being paid ten thousand pounds a year by the khedive. There was money to be made here. He might be a long way from his old home in Whitechapel, but he would always be a boy from the back streets, and he knew how to tally a profit. 'Five hundred pounds.' He smiled. 'Plus expenses and payment of the bill I have run up this past month.'

'Three hundred and your debt paid.'

'Three hundred and fifty.'

'Done.' Sir Sam sat back in his chair and clapped his hands. 'I am glad you have made this choice, Mr Lark. I am pleased to have you on board.'

'As am I.' Jack spoke honestly. 'And now that I am employed, please call me Jack.' He felt the fingers of a cold hand brush across the back of his neck. The choice had been easy to make; it had always just been a matter of price. He was not even really sure he had made it for himself. In the end, everything was down to Fate.

The conversation had come to a natural pause. It was filled by the return of the waiter with a silver platter bearing a fresh teapot for Jack, a silver coffee pot for Sir Sam, two white porcelain cups and a small plate covered with a number of delicate pastries.

Sir Sam took one and bit into it. 'I fear we will soon have to forget about such luxuries as this. I would urge you not to underestimate the difficulties we will soon be facing.'

'I won't.' Jack reached for one of the sweet pastries. 'And you don't have to worry about me. I've survived in worse places.'

'I know but a little of your history. You have mentioned the mutiny and the recent campaign against the Gorilla King. Were those your only campaigns?'

'No.' Jack paused. He would not reveal all of his past, not to anyone. 'I was at the Alma. After that I was in India for a time. Then Persia.'

'I arrived too late to see action in the Crimea.' Sir Sam looked away as he spoke, as if to hide any trace of disappointment in his expression. 'I understand the Alma was a hard-won victory.'

For a moment, Jack could not reply. He had led his company of men against the Russians' Great Redoubt along with the rest of the Light Division. The Russian gunners had stood their ground and the slaughter had been prodigious.

Sir Sam was watching him closely. 'I have a notion that there is a particular task for which you are most ideally suited, but let us talk of that later. I would like you to join me tomorrow afternoon at the same time. Come up to my rooms. I can go over the outline of my plan for the expedition.' He dusted his hands on a napkin, then drained his coffee in one go. Clearly the meeting was over.

'Very good, sir.' Jack rose to his feet.

'It is good to have you with us, Jack.' Sir Sam stood too,

then reached to shake Jack's hand. 'I think we shall become firm friends, you and I.'

Jack watched the explorer depart, then reached for another pastry. Sir Sam's wife was right. A man could indeed eat too many of the sweet treats. Jack was nearly forty now, and he knew that he had to take care not to pile on the weight. At least the expedition would be good in that regard. He suspected it would be no different to being on campaign, and that meant he would be worked hard. At the very least, he would not get fat.

Chapter Ten

———◆◆◆———

'Mr Lark! *Misa' il khayr*!' Marcopolo greeted Jack warmly as he ushered him through the door to Sir Sam's suite of rooms.

'Good afternoon, Mr Marcopolo.'

The room was much changed from Jack's previous visit. The pale green sofas had been pushed to one side. In their place stood a large dining table covered with maps, lists and ledgers. A sense of purpose flavoured with expectation hung heavy in the air.

'Good afternoon, Jack.' Sir Sam was leaning over the table, scribbling notes onto a map with a pencil. 'Thank you for being on time.'

'And thank you for agreeing to be my second.' Julian Baker stood at his uncle's shoulder. He delivered the remark with both eyebrows raised high, as if he were astonished that Jack should have accepted.

'My pleasure. I am looking forward to working with you.' Jack had yet to get Julian's measure. When they had been discussing the expedition's military supplies, the younger man had proven to be both knowledgeable and professional, just as

Jack would expect from a serving naval officer. Yet there was this other side to the man, a crass upper-class haughtiness that grated on Jack's nerves. Time would tell which of the two aspects would be dominant. One thing Jack knew for sure was that he would not be able to hold his tongue for long. If Julian proved to be nothing but a silver-spoon-fed cock, the two of them would soon be at loggerheads.

'I am sure you will work well together.' If Sir Sam sensed anything brewing between the two men, he did a very good job of ignoring it. 'Now, if you please, Jack. Step over here, and I will show you the outline of what we hope to achieve.'

Jack did as he was told, coming to stand at Sir Sam's left-hand side, whilst Julian remained on his uncle's right.

'There are few maps for us to rely on.' Sir Sam rifled through the papers until he found the sheet he was looking for. 'But we must make do with what we can find.'

Jack leaned forward, his eyes taking in the detail on the map, or rather the lack of it. To his eye, it looked little more than a rough outline of a great expanse of land, the area mainly left blank.

'The initial staging post for the expedition will be here, at Khartoum in the Sudan.' Sir Sam's index finger pointed to a city marked on the northern periphery of the map. 'From there we travel south on the White Nile. Our first objective is here.' The finger traced a path southward, then jabbed at a small dot on the map. 'Gondokoro, a journey of some one thousand four hundred and fifty miles. There we shall establish a headquarters. I am of a mind to name this new station Ismailia, after the khedive, but we shall see.

'The establishment of this headquarters will be key to the success of the expedition, and so we will take every precaution to ensure we have it secured and supplied before we attempt anything more, no matter how long that takes. To achieve that aim, we will most likely have to deal with the local tribes, who will no doubt resent our presence in their land. I know the main tribes well enough from my earlier travels. The Bari in this area are led by a chief called Alleron. I am told he cannot be trusted, no matter what he says. The Bari's main adversaries are the Loquia. The two are great rivals and will do anything they can to get one over on the other; however, we must remain wary of their uniting, for together they would form a considerable force.

'Once we are fully established, we will attempt to reach the Albert N'yanza by way of Labore, Afuddo and Fatiko. From there we will journey to the region known as Unyoro. Its capital is here at Masini,' Sir Sam's finger traced south, following the route he planned to take, 'and we shall most certainly establish a presence there. Unyoro is ruled by King Kabba Rega, a young man recently ascended to the throne. It is said that he is fully in the thrall of the Arab traders, and so we shall no doubt have to persuade him of the right path to take before we annex the region in the name of the khedive. With that in hand, we will be able to turn our attention further afield, as we work to establish government in the region whilst opening it to trade and navigation.'

Jack listened carefully to Sir Sam's description of the journey ahead. The place names meant nothing to him, but that did not faze him. He had travelled halfway across the globe, and more often than not he had little more than the vaguest notion of where he was, let alone where he was going.

'Now, you must be under no misunderstanding about the challenge that lies ahead of us.' Sir Sam gave Jack his fullest attention, fixing him with a steely glare. 'We shall be entering into a veritable hornets' nest. That I, an Englishman, should be given command of this mission is nothing short of remarkable. I will be met with hatred, malice and suspicion every step of the way, and I have no doubt whatsoever that you will receive the same as you work on my behalf.'

'Do you expect to fight?' Jack repeated the question he had posed to Julian. It would be interesting to see if he got the same answer from the expedition's leader.

'Yes.' Sir Sam did not so much as blink as he gave the resolute answer. 'I fully expect it will become necessary, and I shall not shirk from the challenge. Now perhaps you can understand why I was so keen for you to join us. We shall have need of your experience, Jack. I wish it were not so, but I must ensure we are prepared. We shall have a formidable force, but to have a man of your experience could prove to be invaluable.'

Jack nodded. He did not bother to show a more modest response. 'What can you tell me of the forces at our disposal? I understand there are two regiments of infantry alongside artillery.'

'There are indeed. One is Egyptian. Its ranks are filled with convicted felons, and I confess I do not expect much from them.'

Jack's eyebrows rose. Thieves and murderers were not his idea of reliable troops. 'And the other?'

'The other is Sudanese. I have heard good things about them, and I must admit I have high hopes for them. They are known as Jihadiyya in these parts, and are led by Turco-Egyptian officers, some of whom served with the French army in Mexico. They have been trained on European lines, which bodes well, I believe.'

Jack absorbed the information, but paid Sir Sam's expect-
ations no heed. He would make up his own mind about the
quality of the men. Over the years, he had fought alongside
soldiers from a number of different armies. In his experience,
all were a mix of the bad and the good.

'I shall also have around two hundred irregular cavalry at
my disposal.'

'Irregular is the word.' Julian joined the conversation. 'I had
the pleasure of reading a report about them last week. I would
say they are rather too irregular to be useful.'

'We shall see, Julian, we shall see.' Sir Sam did not mind the
interruption. 'As you will have discovered today, we shall also
have artillery. We have been given ten rifled mountain guns,
which I have organised into two batteries. The good men
of Woolwich have also provided us with some two hundred of
their three-pound Hale rockets, which I have arranged into a
single rocket battery. We also have fifty Snider rifles.' He smiled
rather wolfishly. 'We shall be a force to be reckoned with.'

'Indeed.' Jack was impressed. It was abundantly clear that
Sir Sam would be commanding a veritable army.

'Now, allow me to tell you more about our organisation.'
Sir Sam was clearly relishing the chance to talk through his
plan. 'I have decided to divide our number into three distinct
parties for the journey from Cairo to Khartoum. If we attempt
to travel as one, the difficulties of supply will be magnified. The
first division will set sail from Cairo in June whilst the waters
of the Nile are still sufficient to allow them to traverse the
cataracts. This division will comprise six local steamers, fifteen
sloops, and fifteen dahabiyas, and it will carry all our merchandise and the greater amount of our supplies, along with the
bulk of the infantry. Once at Khartoum, it will rendezvous

with another three steamers and twenty-five other vessels that are to be provided by the governor there, a fellow called Djiaffer Pasha. I have sent him full instructions. I know him well enough, and I have no doubt that he will do as he is told. That will give us a total of nine steamers and fifty-five sailing vessels ready for the journey beyond Khartoum. I would like both of you to travel with the first division, so that you will be among the first to arrive.'

Julian nodded, clearly familiar with the plan.

'The second column will be under the command of Edwin Higginbotham,' Sir Sam continued. 'Edwin is one of the finest engineers I have ever known and we are fortunate indeed to have secured his services. He holds one of the keys to the success of the expedition, as it is he who has the task of constructing the steel-hulled steamers that we shall need to open up communication within the region. Only with these can we establish a legitimate trade that will supplant and replace the current reliance on slavery and all manner of destructive industries. To that end, I have ordered the components for five steel steamers. I trusted the task to the Samuda Brothers of London, and I have no doubt they will be ready on time. The engines are to be provided by Penn & Co., and I do not think we shall find better. All are to be made ready to be transported in plates and sections to Khartoum. Edwin will leave Cairo with these dismantled steamers and travel by flotilla as far as Korosko. From there, he will transport them across the Nubian Desert via camel train. I have ordered one thousand camels to be held ready at Korosko, along with as many gun carriages as can be provided.'

'Why can they not travel down the Nile?' Jack asked.

'By the time they are ready, the river's levels will have fallen, making the cataracts impossible to traverse, especially with such a heavy load. No, the desert route is the only practical option.'

Jack noted the information. It was clear Sir Sam knew what he was about.

'I shall lead the third column. We shall voyage to Suez then on to Souakim. From there we will cross the desert to Berber, then make our way to Khartoum. I expect to arrive there early in January. If you quit Cairo as planned in June, you should have several months to ensure all is in order for our departure, which I anticipate will take place shortly after I arrive.'

Jack tried not to baulk at the timescale of the expedition. It was becoming even more clear that he had not made a short-term commitment. The initial movement of the expedition to Khartoum would occupy the rest of the year, and God alone knew how long it would take to reach their first objective from there, let alone secure the rest of Sir Sam's ambitious goals. Yet the notion did not deter him too much. There was nowhere he had to be.

'Good afternoon, gentlemen.' The briefing was brought to a halt by the arrival of Anna Baker. She came to stand at the table, her eyes scanning the documents and maps scattered across its surface. 'Uncle, you must look to store these away. We leave with the prince and princess on the morrow.'

'You are right to remind me.' Sir Sam turned to his aides. 'I'll leave that to you two.'

'Very well, sir.' Julian nodded, then glanced at Jack, a sly smirk sliding onto his face.

Jack read the expression easily enough. The task would be delegated to him as Julian's assistant. This job might yet prove more challenging than he had first thought.

'Anna, you remember Mr Lark.' Sir Sam smiled at his niece. 'I am pleased to say he has agreed to join our expedition.'

'How delightful. I trust you know what you have got yourself into, Mr Lark.' Anna sounded anything but delighted.

'Yes, ma'am.' Jack tried not to be put off by the cool reception. Anna was prim and proper in the well-groomed, elegant fashion of a girl used to both money and attention. But once again he was struck by her icy reserve. No matter. He was too old to even consider attempting to get involved with another woman. Or at least that was what he told himself.

'There is no need to *ma'am* me, Mr Lark. A simple Miss Baker will suffice, I assure you. There can be no airs and graces where we are going, or so my aunt tells me.' Anna was as cool as a cucumber.

'I will remember that, thank you.' Jack turned to Sir Sam. 'Will your wife be coming with you in the third party, sir?'

'She will indeed.' Sir Sam beamed at the thought. 'I look forward to introducing her to you, Jack. She is a remarkable woman.'

'I shall look forward to it.' Jack gave the polite reply and avoided looking at Anna as she swept out of the room, leaving the three men alone once again.

'Indeed.' Sir Sam seemed well pleased with the answer. 'But before that can happen, there is much to be done. Which reminds me. I have a special task for you, Jack, one to which I think you are eminently suited.'

'Go on.' Jack felt the first stirrings of something in his gut. Senior officers with special tasks generally spelt trouble for those given responsibility for delivering whatever pet project needed to be completed.

'When you reach Khartoum, I want you to select a cadre to

work with. A special force, as it were, one that we can rely on utterly, no matter the circumstances. There must be no more than fifty men. Pick the very best from both regiments; that way we will breed a true *esprit de corps*. I want you to work with them, bring them up to standard and make sure they are the very best they can be.'

Jack's fears died in an instant. This was a task he would undertake willingly. He had not officially commanded men since his time with the First Boston, the regiment he had joined at the very outset of the war between the American states. Leading men, no matter where they came from, was one of the few things from his past that he truly missed. Sir Sam was giving him a precious gift. He was granting him the right of command.

'Fifty men. So they are to be armed with the Sniders.' Jack made the link quickly.

Sir Sam grinned. 'Precisely my idea. But they must be capable of using them effectively. We cannot know how these regiments will perform when they are put to the test. We *must* have men we can rely on, no matter what we face. That is why this is such an important role.' His smile died as he became completely serious. 'I will hold you accountable for their performance, Jack. Do not let me down.'

'I won't.' Jack tried to keep his expression neutral and hide his delight at the task he was being set. Commanding soldiers was a precious responsibility. It came with authority, power and status, but there was so much more to being a true leader than that. He had begun his career as an impostor to prove that he could be a better officer than any fool born with enough money to purchase a commission. That desire had led him to the battlefield, and it had been there, amidst the bloodshed and the slaughter, that he had learned what it truly meant to be a commander. Officers served their men, not the other way around. Only the best leaders understood that, and in his experience they were few and far between.

'The men are commanded by Lieutenant Colonel Abd-el-Kader. He is a fine officer and I have no doubt that he will give you every assistance. But make no mistake, Jack. This command is yours and yours alone.'

'Very good, sir.' Jack felt himself standing a little straighter as he absorbed the news. He had accepted Sir Sam's offer of employment to find the purpose he needed in his life. It appeared Fate was rewarding him for that decision.

Chapter Eleven

Khartoum, 15 December 1869

ack stood at the sloop's rail to get his first good look at Khartoum. It was not an impressive sight; in fact he was not sure he could remember ever seeing such a shithole as the one that hove into view a mile or so ahead.

The town sat to the south of the junction of the White and Blue Niles like a fat and ancient slug that had long since been desiccated to little more than a husk by the relentless Sudanese sun. He had listened with interest to Marcopolo's many tales of the great city and the wild lands that surrounded it. He had learned that the area had been known to the first Arabs to visit the area as al-Khartoum, which Marcopolo had translated as 'the elephant's trunk', in a nod to the shape of the land between the two rivers. The name had stuck, yet now Jack could think of a dozen other names that would better describe the decrepit, decaying town that was to be his home for the next weeks and months. Certainly something must have happened to reduce the fabulous city of Marcopolo's description to the sorry state it was in now. He had seen something similar before in India. Decay came fast. Plague, war or a simple lack of money could reduce even the most splendid town to a ruin in the span of a few short years. He wondered which fate had befallen Khartoum.

From what he could see, the palm-shaded waterfront was abandoned and near derelict, though there were signs of former industry. Great wooden water wheels lined the bank of the river on the city side, one every hundred yards. He had seen similar wheels before and their design had been unchanged for centuries. They were used to draw water from the river, which was then fed into a large number of irrigation channels that carried it far into the city. All now stood silent, and he could see that they had started to fall apart. Interspersed with the water wheels were a number of steam pumps, the modern replacement for the wooden machinery standing forlorn, the once-noisy machines left to rust in silence. Between the river and the city were the remains of what might once have been well-tended and handsome gardens, now overgrown, or else scorched and barren.

Yet the waterfront was not bereft of all life. The stone embankment was dotted with people, a slow stream of women coming down to the river to collect water, which they carried away in clay pots balanced on their heads. A number of landing jetties were occupied with vessels of one type or another. He had no idea what the different craft were called, and to be honest he didn't much care. He was pretty sure Julian Baker would be able to give him a detailed description and a name for them all, but he was of no mind to find the aide and ask. Baker was often waspish, and he favoured a sharp word over a kind one, but there was nothing mean or nasty in his character. Once Jack had understood that, he had begun to actually like the young man, even finding his ability to be snarky at all times rather amusing.

Beyond the waterfront, he could see something of Khartoum itself. An impressive structure dominated the waterfront; a large U-shaped two-storey construction made of red bricks. Seemingly devoid of life, it had the air of an abandoned palace. The city beyond was filled with palm trees, the bright green fronds standing high above the earth-coloured rooftops. Jack had been told that Khartoum was protected to the south and east by a high parapet and ditch. To the west and north, it was flanked by the two great branches of the Nile, the Blue Nile to the north, the White Nile to the west. To support the mix of man-made and natural defences, there were three forts. He could name them all, thanks to the many lectures he had been given by Julian. Fort Omdurman stood to the right of the junction between the two rivers. Far to the east was Fort Moghran, the bank between the two lined with a great number of palm trees. To the west was Fort Burri. None of the three seemed to be in a good state of repair, signs of abandonment and decay obvious even from a distance.

Away from the waterfront was a wide-open space dotted with small pits that separated the main town from what looked to Jack to be the native quarter. The latter appeared to be made up of a tangled labyrinth of tiny alleys and passageways that meandered through a mix of mud-brick houses and make-shift native huts. A cone-shaped minaret stood proud of the lowly housing, a reminder of the religion that dominated the area. Beyond the native quarter, the surrounding country-side stretched away for miles. There was little to see; just a great expanse of scrub, baobab trees and the black thorn shrubs that the locals called the wait-a-bit, or *kitr*, thanks to the pairs of hooked black thorns that decorated every branch. It gave the feeling of a city perched in the midst of a great scruffy wilderness. Not for the first time, it felt like he was voyaging to the ends of the earth.

His sense of dislocation had been enhanced by the array of strange beasts he had watched coming to the banks of the river during the long journey down from Cairo. He had spotted dozens of enormous hippopotami, the huge beasts most often seen lying under the cooling water or wandering along the riverbed, their great pink backs just about visible through the murk. He had seen a brace of rhinoceroses, the great armoured animals standing like a pair of statues on the riverbank as the ships sailed by. Once they had even caught a glimpse of a lion, a large male, though it had run long before the sloop was near, giving Jack little more than the impression of a shadow. Yet not even the king of beasts terrified him as much as the crocodiles he saw on a daily basis. The reptiles were ever present, their gaping mouths often held wide open as they lay basking in the sun. His fear was made worse by the many stories the sloop's crew had of shipmates taken and devoured by the ferocious-looking creatures. If just a handful of the gruesome tales were true, it was clear that the crocodiles killed in large numbers, and he knew that the dread would linger in his mind as they pressed south and the risk of a face-to-face meeting with one of the horrible beasts became ever more likely.

The thought made him look down at the water that swirled around the sloop's sides. It flowed fast, churning and kicking up spray as the sloop cut a path through it. For once, he couldn't see any of the dreadful creatures, but it was still not a pleasant sight. It also smelt foul, the stink so bad that he wondered if the sloop was in fact ploughing through the town's sewer. The water was the colour of shit and as thick as soup, the surface littered with debris. Large and small tree trunks floated past, along with a thousand smaller branches, and wide mounds of matted brown and green vegetation formed small floating islands that surged along, propelled by the current.

'Good grief.' Jack pulled up the bandana he wore around his neck so that it covered his mouth and nose. It did little to spare him from the stench as the corpse of a long-dead cow surfaced near the sloop, the animal's bloated and putrid flesh bobbing above the water before being sucked down by the wake of the small sailing ship.

'What on earth is upsetting your delicate constitution this morning, Lark?'

Jack turned from the rail to see Julian Baker approaching.

'You look like you are about to part company with your breakfast.' Julian moved adeptly across the deck, his body moving to the sway and pitch of the sloop with practised ease.

'It's not the only company I wish to part with.' Jack pulled a face as he gave the pithy retort.

'How rude.' Julian came to stand at the rail next to him. 'Goodness, that is rather foul.' He had caught sight of the putrid bovine remains.

'It's not a pretty sight.' Jack took another look. The carcass was not improved by a second glimpse.

'I expect you have seen worse.'

'Depends what you mean by worse.'

'I expect a battlefield looks a fair sight more gruesome than that.'

'True.' Jack looked closely at Julian. It was a perceptive remark.

'We never see anything like that at sea. Of course, some of our chaps get hurt, but I don't think that can compare. For us, death is more often than not delivered and received at a distance. For you, it's up front and personal.' Julian paused. 'Do you miss it?'

'No.' Jack's answer was quick. It was the truth. He did not miss battle, not any more. Yet he was thrilled to have been given command of Sir Sam's cadre. The paradox was not lost on him. He wanted to be a commander, but that did not mean he wanted a return to the bloody, chaotic maelstrom of war. If it did come to it, he would not shirk from the fight, or from leading his men into battle. Yet he would not seek it out. He did not have anything left to prove. At least not to himself.

'But we may have to fight before this expedition is done.'

'We might.'

'And what then?'

'Then we fight. I may wish otherwise, but we will do what has to be done.'

'You sound damned dour.' Julian goaded him. 'I thought soldiers like you wanted to get onto the battlefield as quickly and often as possible.'

'Not me. At least not any more.' Jack looked down over the side of the sloop. The dead cow had sunk beneath the waves again. He could see nothing more than the murky brown water. 'I did want to once. I thought it was all I had. All I was good for. But then I learned that was only so much bullshit.'

'Goodness. Is that you being wise?' Julian grinned. 'You are showing your age, Lark.'

Jack snorted. Julian might have been joking, but it was the truth. He was nearing forty now. He had left his old life behind some fifteen years before. Those fifteen years had seen him journey across continents and fight more battles than he could even recall. And he had changed, he knew that. Once he had sought out battle, thinking he could only be his true self in war. He had learned the truth at Shiloh. But that did not mean he wanted a quiet life. Far from it.

'You should be taking notes. I don't want my wise words to be forgotten.'

'I rather think I have forgotten them already. What was it you said again?'

'Stow it.' Jack sighed. 'When do we disembark?'

'As soon as the captain can find us a mooring. I don't know about you, but I have had my fill of this bloody sloop.'

'Amen to that.' Jack could only agree. It had been a long journey and an even longer summer, as they worked tirelessly to prepare for the expedition's departure. Yet they had been hampered at every turn. Delay had followed delay. The first target date for their departure had slipped past, then the second and the third, Sir Sam's expedition paling into insignificance against the grand opening of the Suez Canal that was being planned for the end of the year. The khedive had left for Europe, and the expedition to claim the lands to the south of the Sudan had been overlooked. It had taken all their limited powers of persuasion to gather the last supplies, and the permissions and bona fides they would need to travel south. They had eventually departed Cairo on 29 August, some three months late.

Yet even once on their way, their problems had not been put behind them. The first column was made up of six steamers, fifteen sloops and fifteen dahabiyas, and they were carrying the bulk of the expedition's merchandise. They had passed Asyut and Aswan without problem, descending the First Cataract then sailing past Korosko, the start of the main caravan route that headed directly south across the great empty expanse of the Nubian Desert to Abu Hamad. From there, the Nile meandered in a wide C-shaped bend to the west. At that stage of the journey, the waters had been calm, making for easy sailing, and Julian had even been hopeful of making up some of the time lost in Cairo. Then they reached Wadi Halfa, and the journey ground to a halt.

The waters beyond were now too shallow for the draught of the steamers. Had the column departed on time, the Nile would easily have been deep enough, but now Julian had no choice but to order the steamers to turn back and return to Cairo, thus abandoning a good portion of the expedition's merchandise.

The reduced column had pressed on. They had traversed the Second and Third Cataracts without delay, passing Old Dongola before reaching Korti, the starting point for the caravan route that went directly south east across the Bayuda Desert, thereby cutting the corner as the Nile took a great loop to the east. Julian had held them at Korti, replenishing supplies and allowing the crews time to rest.

The remainder of the journey had passed without incident. Jack had even begun to enjoy himself. There was a simplicity to the days. He had awoken with the dawn, breaking his fast in the cool morning air on deck, then spent time with Julian going over the details of the next stage of the journey, or else planning for their eventual departure from Khartoum. He had learned much, his knowledge of the land that would be his home for the coming months growing with every day. As the sun set, they had dined on deck then spent the evenings alone, both men content in their own company.

The days had passed swiftly. They had sailed by Merowe,

then crossed over the surging waters of the Fourth Cataract. Abu Hamad, the southern end of the caravan route that started at Korosko, had slipped past serenely, and not even the wilder waters of the Fifth Cataract had caused them delay. They had held the column for a day of rest at Berber, the start of the great caravan route to the east that cut across the thousand miles of rolling steppe known as the *goz* out to Souakim on the Red Sea, then sailed on, passing Ad-Damar, where the Atbara river joined the Nile. The last cataract, the Sixth, had been traversed a few days previously, and now they had reached their destination, the great city of Khartoum in the Sudan.

Jack stood away from the rail. He had seen enough. Khartoum might not look like much, but the initial stage of their journey was now complete. The first months had been a huge challenge, but he had a feeling that they were merely a taste of what was to come.

They had only just made it to the stepping-off point.

They had much, much further to go.

Chapter Twelve

———◆·◆·◆———

'I suggest we take care with our pocket books, Lark.' Julian gave the advice as the two men left the waterfront behind. They had been the first ashore, and both were keen to see something of the town where they would have to prepare for the next stage of the journey that lay ahead.

'I will.' For once, Jack did not snap at the unnecessary advice. He was relishing the chance to stretch his legs. After so long incarcerated on the sloop, he felt the first flicker of freedom.

Not that he was walking in pleasant surroundings. The ground underfoot was littered with detritus, mounds of discarded paper and heaps of rotting refuse piled high against the walls of every building. As he passed a darkened town house, the face of an old woman pressed against a window on the lowest level, staring out with an expression etched with misery. For a moment, she looked at the two new arrivals, her flat gaze unchanged, then she turned away, resuming her miserable inspection of the world outside.

'Marcopolo told me this place was a thriving trading centre,' Jack said. 'But look at it. I wonder why it is so damned quiet?'

It was late in the afternoon. He would have expected the town's thoroughfares to be filled with life at this cooler time of day, just as they were in Cairo. But there were few people abroad. Those he had seen appeared to be servants, either carrying water or on some kind of hurried errand. The only figure to have stood out was a well-presented young male hurrying past on the back of a large white donkey, his right hand clamped to the tarboosh perched precariously on the very back of his head.

'Maybe it's too grim even for those that live here,' Julian answered, his tone betraying his unease. 'It hasn't always been like this. This place is the centre for all trade in the region. Ivory, slaves, gum arabic, hides; it all comes through here. It is connected to the south and north by the Nile, whilst caravans come in from Darfur to the west, or from Abyssinia to the east. They say all roads lead to Rome; well, in these parts all roads lead to Khartoum. Although if that is true, I must say I too wonder where everyone might be hiding.'

'Maybe they've all buggered off. I can see why. Look at that.' Jack pointed at a pulsating mound on the far side of the street. It was the corpse of a dog, or what was left of it. The dead animal had been dumped against a wall. Now it was a feast for the millions of flies that swarmed over the putrid remains like a dark, swirling cloud. Jack could smell the rotting flesh even from yards away.

'For heaven's sake.' Julian lifted a hand to cover his mouth and nose.

'Suck it up.' Jack could not help smiling at his companion's distaste.

'It is disgusting.'

'It's life and you'll have to get used to it.' Jack stated the bald fact.

'Well, let us find the post office. I need to send a message to my uncle to let him know we've arrived. Then we must present ourselves to the governor. He should have our preparations well in hand; my uncle gave him clear instructions as to our needs. When that is done, we can disembark the men and set up our lines.'

'Fine with me.' Jack would not argue. He felt a strange sense of discombobulation. They had arrived at their first destination and he felt as out of place as he ever had. It had been too easy. He had fallen into the expedition, and now he found himself far from any notion of civilisation without really knowing how he had got there. It left him with a sense of unease and a knot of trepidation deep in his belly.

They walked on, neither man speaking but both drinking in the sights, such as they were. A few more people were abroad as they ventured further into town, but all seemed reluctant to linger for long on the filthy streets. Not one person caught their eye.

They passed a fine building standing in its own walled and gated courtyard. Jack peered in through the chained and locked wrought-iron gates. Behind them was a garden, an oasis compared to the grotty streets outside. From what he could see, it was filled with trees. He recognised some, like the jasmine and the mimosa that would infuse the garden with a gentle scent. The rest he could not identify, but it was nice to see that not all of Khartoum was a dump.

A group of men swaggered into view. They walked in a tight knot, voices loud and brash, confidence filling the street.

'Watch yourself.' Jack reached out to place a guiding hand on Julian's forearm, stopping him then leading him to one side. The group carried themselves with the air of conquering soldiers, their presence taking ownership of the space they occupied. It was clear these men were certain of their power in the forgotten streets of Khartoum.

'Who the devil are those fellows?' Julian breathed the words as he came to stand next to Jack.

'No idea, but keep your bloody head down.' Jack gave the instruction as he saw Julian staring at the group.

'They won't trouble us.' Julian was certain. 'If they do, I am sure we will be fine. We have the best bona fides, after all.'

'Are you certain about that? They don't look like the kind of folk that will want to read some bits of bloody paper.'

Already heads were turning their way. There were about ten men in the group. Several had become aware of the two new arrivals. Jack eased Julian further from the centre of the street, taking up a position with the mud wall of a tall building behind them.

'Nonsense.' Julian spoke confidently. 'It's not as if we don't have permission to be here. The governor himself knows we are due to arrive. And I will not doff my cap to a bunch of damned ruffians. After all, I am an Englishman.'

'You won't be for much longer if you keep spouting crap like that.' Jack glanced at the men. They were a polyglot lot. Two were black, whilst one was Oriental in appearance. Three others looked Arabian, to his eyes at least, and the rest appeared to be either European or American. They slowed their pace as they came closer.

'Good afternoon, gentlemen,' Julian called out in greeting as the leading men approached.

'For fuck's sake,' Jack hissed. He could not believe his ears. Julian was acting like they were strolling down Pall Mall.

One of the men, a swarthy European, seemed to be their

leader. As he stepped forward, Jack ran his eyes over him. He was not tall, perhaps three or four inches shy of six foot, but he had the burly build of a brawler, with powerful shoulders and a squat frame. Jack was not good at guessing ages, but he reckoned the man to be in his forties, his craggy face well lined with wrinkles, and he possessed the red-rimmed eyes, bulbous nose and veined flushed cheeks of a heavy drinker. He was roughly shaven, a heavy growth of stubble smothering his cheeks and neck, whilst his black hair was flecked with grey.

'English?' He spoke the single word in a heavy, guttural accent.

'We are. We've just arrived.' Julian replied for them both.

The leader contemplated the answer. He looked from one to the other, expression betraying nothing.

'Don't say another fucking thing,' Jack muttered out of the side of his mouth. For his part, he would keep quiet. No good could come of this meeting.

The group's leader checked on his followers. They had arranged themselves around him, forming a flattened U shape facing the two Englishmen.

Jack took a half-step away from Julian. It was not to distance himself from the fool, but rather to give himself space. He sensed violence was not far away. He could feel it in the air, and he could see it in the way the group in front of him had positioned themselves ready to pin the two of them against the wall at their backs. It was subtly done, but he knew what it might mean, even if Julian did not.

'Would you be able to direct us to the post office?' Julian addressed the leader.

The man placed his hands on his hips as he contemplated the question.

'Or perhaps to the governor's offices? He is expecting us.'

The man grunted in acknowledgement of the remark. 'You have money?'

Julian scowled. 'What's that you say?'

'You pay now.' The leader took a step forward and held out a hand.

'What the devil? Are you expecting us to pay some form of toll just for bally well being here?'

The man thrust his fat hand out further. 'Sovereigns. Thalers. Piastres. You pay now.'

'Now look here, my man. We don't want any trouble, but I have no idea why you think we would pay you. I assure you we shall not give you a penny, and when the governor hears of this—'

'That's enough.' Jack cut Julian off in mid flow. He sighed. He did not want this confrontation, but he would not avoid it. He took a small step forward, making sure the group's leader saw him. From his accent, Jack reckoned the man was Russian. He had no idea whether he spoke English, but it did not matter. He reckoned he would understand the message he was about to deliver well enough. It was somewhat universal.

The Russian was not impressed. 'You. Money.'

Jack moved his head from side to side, freeing the muscles. 'Not how it goes, chum.' He raised a finger and pointed over the Russian's shoulder, then stepped forward, closing the gap between them. 'Fuck off.' He gave the instruction slowly and clearly.

The Russian laughed, then said something to his gang in a guttural language Jack did not understand. When he turned back, all trace of mirth was gone, his expression set in stone.

Jack gave him no chance to say anything further. He

snapped his head forward, straight into the centre of the Russian's face. It was a fine headbutt and it connected splendidly, pulping the Russian's bulbous nose. Blood came fast, both nostrils releasing a torrent of claret-coloured liquid.

Jack was not done. He had planned his moves with care the moment the group had come close. Even as his own head rang from the vicious impact, he swung his right fist upwards. It was a good punch, one of his best, a fast, rising blow that connected with the point of the Russian's chin with enough force to rock the heavy man back on his heels.

'Let's fucking dance,' Jack cried out as he darted forward. The Russian would be hurting, but he was far from beaten, and Jack knew he could not give the man a moment to recover. He punched again, left hand swinging into the Russian's stomach with enough force to double him over, upper body falling forward as he absorbed the blow. As his head came down, so Jack lifted his right knee. It connected with the Russian's face, slamming his head up and away so that blood sprayed into the air.

Still Jack was not done. As the Russian staggered back, Jack went after him. His fists moved fast, the left following the right, landing two more blows to the man's battered head. It was enough. For one long moment the Russian tottered from side to side, then he fell, landing heavily on his backside, dust flung high as he hit the filthy ground.

He sat there, face running with blood, eyes fixed on the man who had just knocked him on his arse.

'My goodness me.'

Jack heard Julian utter the words in a hushed, almost reverential tone, but he paid them no heed. He kept his eyes on the Russian, waiting to see if the man would stand.

'You had enough, chum?' He did his best to keep his tone level and calm, even though he could feel his heart pumping nineteen to the dozen.

The Russian spoke quickly, a torrent of unintelligible words of command directed at his men. Orders given, he raised an arm so that he could be helped to his feet. Two of the group hurried to obey, hauling the heavy man upright. He stood there for a moment, blowing like a spent bull. Then he charged.

Jack saw him coming, but he was slow. He could do nothing as the Russian grabbed him around the waist, driving him backwards and into the wall behind. The contact was brutal. Every scrap of breath was driven from his body, and the pain in his back was almost more than he could bear as his spine crunched into the stone. Yet the Russian gave him no time to recover, stepping back then launching a punch of his own.

This time Jack saw the blow coming. He was older now, reactions dulled, but he still managed to duck. The Russian's fist missed his head by no more than an inch before smashing into the wall behind him, the sickening sound of bones breaking following the crunch of impact.

The Russian howled in pain. He recoiled, the broken fingers of his right hand dangling at sickening angles.

Jack heard the cry of pain but paid it no heed. The Russian's gut was in front of him, so he lashed out as hard as he could. The blow hurt him, his hands on fire from the punches he had already landed, but it hurt the Russian more, and he staggered away, head hanging down as he struggled to stay on his feet.

Jack saw his chance. He stood straight, then reached out with his left hand and grabbed the Russian's right, taking the broken, twisted fingers in a remorseless grip. Then he squeezed.

The Russian yelped, dropping to his knees in agony, good hand clawing at Jack's in a fruitless attempt to force it to release his broken fingers.

Jack squeezed harder, feeling bones grate in his grip.

The Russian babbled at him then, face twisted in agony. Jack lifted the hand higher, maintaining the pressure. The Russian's cries increased in intensity, the man begging with Jack to let him go.

Jack lowered his head so his face was no more than an inch from the Russian's own. He could see the pain in the man's eyes, the tiny beads of sweat on a face smothered with blood. 'You need to learn some fucking manners, chum.' He squeezed harder, one last reminder of his power. Then he let go.

The Russian cried out in relief, cradling his injured hand as he rose to his feet and backed away.

Jack returned to his place at Julian's side, holding himself tight, revealing nothing of the pain that he himself felt. The Russian's men had not moved. Yet. He could only suppose they had been ordered to stay out of the fight. But that could change quickly, and so he took as deep a breath as he could manage. His hands burned and his back felt like it had been snapped in two. If the Russian ordered his men to carry on the fisticuffs, he knew he would not last long.

But the Russian had more pressing matters to concern him.

'Vladimir?' A tall, dark-haired man was walking towards the Russian, ignoring the rest of the group, who immediately backed away, their respect and fear obvious.

The Russian hung his head. He still held his broken right hand carefully in his left. He said nothing, but he seemed to visibly crumple.

'Go away.' The newcomer gave the terse command.

He was obeyed instantly, the group turning and moving off without a second's delay.

'I am sorry you had problems here.' The remark was addressed to both Jack and Julian.

Jack noted a French accent colouring the apology. 'Are those your men?'

'Yes.'

'Then you need to keep them on a shorter leash.' Jack was scathing. He studied the Frenchman. He was taller than Jack, leaner too, with not a scrap of spare flesh on his body. His face was partially covered by a neatly trimmed black beard, and he wore his hair long enough for it to fall over his ears and down to the collar of his shirt. He was dressed simply, in calf-length brown boots with tan trousers below a white shirt. The only oddity was a single black glove that covered his left hand.

'Perhaps.' The Frenchman held Jack's stare. His expression betrayed nothing but confidence. 'Although you seem to have survived.'

'No thanks to that Russian piece of shit.' Jack's back was hurting more by the minute. Pain added sharpness to his tongue.

'Vladimir learned a lesson here today, I think.' The Frenchman smiled.

'He did indeed.' Julian stepped past Jack. 'You would do well to heed my friend's advice and keep those men of yours under control.'

The Frenchman inclined his head. 'You are both English?'

'We are.'

'That explains it. Vladimir hates the English. But then don't we all.' The Frenchman flashed a smile. 'Now let me make amends. Perhaps I can escort you to your destination?'

'We can manage perfectly well by ourselves,' Julian replied airily. 'Are you all right?' He hissed the question at Jack, as if to prevent the Frenchman from hearing.

'I'm fine.' Jack glowered. He would not reveal his own pain. 'The post office. Then to the offices of the governor.' He spoke loudly, directing the instructions to the Frenchman as he overruled his superior.

'Very well.' The Frenchman gave a half-bow in acknowledgment. 'I will show you. This way, if you please.' He gestured for them to proceed.

Julian pushed past Jack, shooting him an icy glare as he did so. But he still did as the Frenchman suggested.

For better or worse, they had found themselves a guide.

Chapter Thirteen

———◆———

'You have just arrived in Khartoum?' the Frenchman asked as they started to walk.

'Yes.' Julian chose to answer for the pair. 'And no sooner had we set foot in this damnable place than your thugs set upon us.'

The Frenchman gave a very Gallic shrug. '*C'est normal.* Especially here. You are not in jolly old England now, old bean,' he mocked.

Jack laughed. He did not mean to, but the look on Julian's face was enough to set him off.

'You speak very good English, for a Frenchman.' Julian spoke sharply.

'My mother was English.'

'And your father?'

'Was a bastard who disappeared long before I was born.' The Frenchman glanced back over his shoulder at Jack, who trailed behind. He showed no shyness in revealing his past. 'My mother came to Paris for love. She did not find it, but she stayed after I was born. It was not easy for her, but she kept me alive.'

'And she is there still?' Julian tried to steer a course towards polite conversation.

'No, she died. I was twelve.'

'What did you do?'

'I survived.'

It was clear that Julian was unsure what to say. But he rallied quickly. 'So, what brings you to Khartoum?'

'Business.'

'What sort of business?'

'I trade ivory.'

'Ah yes.' Julian's eyes narrowed. 'That is still a thriving trade, I am told. Although it can be a dangerous profession, if the accounts are true. Ruthless, too.'

'At times.' The Frenchman was evasive as he brought them to a halt. They had walked no more than a quarter of a mile and now stood on what appeared to be a major thoroughfare. A few locals were around, but it was far from bustling. 'The post office.' He pointed to a small building ahead. A dilapidated sign hung on the wall above the door, the painted wording so faded and peeling it was quite illegible.

'Ah, good. Why don't you two wait here. I shall not be long.' Julian did not wait for an answer and strode across the road before disappearing into the dark interior of the building.

'You don't say much,' the Frenchman observed.

Jack stayed silent. An old man came past leading a scruffy-looking donkey that had more bald patches than fur.

'You don't say much, yet you beat Vladimir.' The Frenchman tried again. 'Not many can say that.'

'It was nothing.' Jack did not bother to hide his testy tone. His back was still hurting. The pain dogged him most days, the persistent nagging ache the legacy of a childhood humping barrels of watered-down gin and over a decade of soldiering. The impact with the brick wall during the fight with the Russian had set it off so that it now felt like the devil himself was digging out the small of his back with a very blunt spoon.

'You were a soldier?'

'For a time.' Jack met the Frenchman's stare. 'You?'

'For a time.' The Frenchman borrowed Jack's reply.

'Where?'

'Everywhere.' He inclined his head, then lifted a thick finger and drew an imaginary line down the left-hand side of his own face to replicate the scar he saw on Jack's. 'Where did you get that?'

'Delhi.' For a reason he did not fully understand, Jack answered honestly. He had been outside the walls of the city when he had been attacked by a party of mutinous sawars. The fight had been short and sharp, and it had cost him more than the wound to his face.

The Frenchman considered the answer. 'That was your first fight?'

'No.' Jack gave a bitter laugh. There had been many battles before the long siege.

'And it was not your last?'

'No.'

The Frenchman nodded, but he was spared saying more as Julian emerged back into the late-afternoon sunlight.

'We are all done here,' he called out breezily as he came towards them. 'Now perhaps you will be so kind as to show us to the government offices.'

'Very well.' The Frenchman looked once more at Jack, then turned to do as Julian had asked.

Julian smiled his thanks, but he hung back as the Frenchman

began to walk off. 'Can we trust this man?' he whispered. 'If he trades in ivory as he says, he may very well be just the sort of man whose activities we will have to curtail.'

'So don't trust him.'

'Then what the devil are we doing with him?'

'He's showing us where to go.' Jack shrugged the question away, then answered it by following the Frenchman.

None of the three spoke again as they made their way back towards the waterfront. They passed a dozen more dead animals, the poor creatures left to rot where they lay. Decaying vegetation was everywhere, and worse, the citizens of Khartoum were not above dumping their own waste wherever they saw fit. Stagnant pools of piss collected in every depression in the rutted streets, the noxious mixture steaming in the afternoon heat. The collection of filth created a heady miasma, the smell of decaying flesh mixing with shit and the sour stink of rotten fruit to produce an aroma that caught at the back of the throat. Yet the few denizens around paid the squalor no heed. A man stood forlorn behind a simple stall selling bread, whilst a water carrier ambled around in ever-decreasing circles, his metal cups clanging despondently as they bounced against the tank on his back. Two young men with painted faces sauntered past, bodies swaying as if they moved to a secret music, their hooded stares and coquettish smiles directed at the three men as they walked by.

The Frenchman came to a halt in a small square. The buildings around pressed close, giving the place an oppressive feel. On the far side was the two-storey red-brick building Jack had seen from the sloop. It was the kind of building that should have bustled with life, its proximity to the waterfront making it almost certainly one of the most significant government buildings in town. Instead, it appeared half abandoned. On the upper storey, at least half a dozen windows were broken, and one swung back and forth on snapped hinges, the now empty frame banging as it repeatedly hit the wall.

'That is the governor's palace. His offices are on the upper storey. Go through the gate and ask there.'

'Excellent.' For the first time since they had arrived, Julian seemed pleased. 'Jack, perhaps you should stay here whilst I present our letters of introduction.' He did not wait for a reaction and headed directly for the arched gateway the Frenchman had pointed out.

Jack contemplated disobeying the instruction, if only to irk his superior, but before he could move, the Frenchman held out an arm to hold him in place.

'Let him go, *mon ami*. They will keep him waiting for hours. Spare yourself that.'

Jack heard the sense in the warning. His back hurt and he could feel his knuckles beginning to swell. A tedious wait for some government official was the last thing he needed.

'Let's get a beer instead,' the Frenchman suggested. 'I owe you that, I would say.'

'You do.' Jack felt no need to be gracious.

The Frenchman laughed. 'There is a place nearby. You can wait for your friend there.'

'Very well.' Jack stood back and let the Frenchman lead him.

'What brings a pair of *rosbifs* to Khartoum?' The Frenchman settled onto the bench opposite Jack and made himself comfortable.

Jack did not answer. He was arranging the many cushions

on his own bench so that they rested against his spine. It took a while, but he found a position that was as comfortable as he could make it.

The baladi bar the Frenchman had chosen was pleasant enough. The interior of the building was dark and not particularly hospitable, but the owner had shown them to a small courtyard to the rear. It was a tranquil oasis compared to the squalid streets beyond. A fountain filled one corner, the rectangular pool at its base lined with pale blue and orange tiles. The sound of moving water added a peaceful air to the scene. There were just five tables, all set low on the ground, the benches on either side covered with thick woven blankets and fat square cushions in a colourful array of patterned fabrics. The walls of the courtyard were decorated with rusted mirrors and handwritten bills of fare that were so faded they were almost completely illegible. A pair of hookah pipes stood ready near each table, but not one was in use, the courtyard deserted save for the Frenchman and his guest.

'You came here for business?' the Frenchman probed as his question was left unanswered.

'An expedition,' Jack replied succinctly.

The Frenchman chuckled. 'Ah yes, you English and your explorers.'

'Someone has to do it.'

'Do they?' The Frenchman raised an eyebrow. 'Why?'

'Knowledge.'

'And that matters why?'

'Do you not think it is important to know what lies out there?' Jack waved an arm to encompass the world beyond Khartoum.

'*Je m'en fous, mon ami.*' The Frenchman laughed the idea

away. 'I care only for business. You English, you seek know-ledge so you can come back and take over the damned place. That I do not want to see. You would ruin me.'

'Perhaps.' Jack did not gainsay an idea that might very well prove to be close to the truth if Sir Sam's expedition was to achieve all its aims.

The conversation was interrupted by the bar's owner arriving with a silver tray on which stood two ancient-looking glasses and two very large bottles of beer. He carefully placed a glass in front of each of them, then poured the beer, the amber liquid sloshing and foaming as he filled each glass to the brim.

'Here. Wash the dust from your throat.' The Frenchman lifted his glass as the bar's owner backed away. 'Chin chin.' He drank deeply, draining half the glass in his first few mouthfuls.

Jack did not need to be told twice. He lifted his own glass, savouring the taste of the bitter beer as it slid down this throat.

'So, your friend. He is on this expedition of yours?' The Frenchman refilled his glass.

'He is. He is the nephew of the man running the show.'

'Ah yes, that explains it.'

'Explains what?'

'Why he acts like he has a dick up his arse.'

Jack laughed. He probably shouldn't have, but he couldn't help it. It was hard to dislike the man sitting opposite him.

'You say you have business here,' he said, 'yet this place is hardly thriving. It looks like a ghost town.'

The Frenchman pulled a sad face. 'That is true. It was not always so. When I first came here five years ago, the place was thriving. Many men made their fortune here.'

'Ivory?' Jack remembered what the Frenchman had said earlier.

'*Exactement*. Ivory was much in vogue even then. All of Europe wants its billiard balls. It was easy and a man could make a fortune for a year's work. Back then, the local tribes would trade ivory for a handful of glass beads that cost no more than a few sous. Oh man, those must have been good days.' The Frenchman sounded wistful as he thought of the easy money that had been made in the years before he had arrived. 'And of course there was the other trade.'

'Slaves?'

'Indeed. The two are connected.' He crossed two fingers to reinforce what he was saying. 'The slaves, they come from the same places as the ivory. And they are useful. They carry the ivory here, and then *voilà*, you have two things to sell.'

'And this place was the centre for all that?'

'Yes. Men came here from all over the world. Caravans arrived from every direction, bringing not just slaves and ivory but ostrich feathers, gum arabic too. But then the plague came.'

Jack nodded slowly. 'You were here then?'

'I had just arrived.' The Frenchman drank more beer. 'It was bad. Very bad. Half the town died. More left afterwards, including the residents from both our countries and others besides. It has never recovered.'

That explained the ghostly feel of the place. Jack knew what it was to live with ghosts, and Khartoum was full of them.

'Now there are just a handful of us left.' The Frenchman pulled a wry expression that could have been a smile but looked more like a grimace. 'Life is hard here. Very hard.' He shrugged. 'But we survive.'

'Harder than being in the army?'

'No.'

'Do you miss it? Being in the army?'

He looked at Jack for several long seconds before he replied. 'Yes.' He smiled. 'And no.'

Jack understood the answer. It matched his own feelings. There was much of his life as a soldier that he missed. And much that he didn't.

'It is funny, is it not.' The Frenchman broke the silence. 'I have fought alongside you British. Yet if I had been born forty years before, I would have fought against you. It is strange how the world turns.'

The answer intrigued Jack. It also revealed where the Frenchman might have served. 'You were in the Crimea?'

The Frenchman nodded.

'The Alma?'

Again a nod.

Jack said nothing more. He had been an impostor then, stealing a rank and a place that was not his. It was there that he had first seen what it meant to lead men in battle. The French army had formed the allies' right flank, scaling the cliffs that secured the Russian general's left. It was meant to be a feint, a diversion from the main British assault over the river, but no one had told the French soldiers that, and they had somehow found a way to scale the heights then drive back the Russians' left flank.

'You were there too?' The Frenchman had read Jack easily enough.

'With the Light Division. We attacked the redoubts.'

'It was a hard day. But it got worse afterwards.'

'I wasn't there then.' Jack had left the Crimea after the Alma, but he had heard of the bitter fighting that had followed. 'I was lucky.'

'Not if you attacked the redoubts. I saw the field the next day.'

'What regiment were you with?' Jack asked the question of veterans the world over.

'I was half English so I went where they would take me.' He paused. 'I joined la Légion.'

The answer was enough to almost make Jack choke on his beer.

The Frenchman read his reaction. 'You have heard of us, I take it.'

'Something like that.' This time Jack held back the truth. He had temporarily joined the ranks of the French Foreign Legion on the battlefield of Solferino. He had not seen bloodshed like it since, even though the fight at Shiloh came close. 'First or Second?' He probed deeper.

'La Deuxième.'

He hid his reaction by concentrating on pouring the last of his beer from the bottle. It was the Second Regiment of the Legion that he had fought alongside, first on the slopes around San Cassiano, then down on the plain where the regiment had been broken by the rampaging Austrian cavalry. He still dreamt of that dreadful afternoon, the Austrians on their great horses coming for him in his nightmares. Now the Frenchman was revealing that they had fought in the same regiment on that fateful, bloody day.

'I know the Second.' He drank his beer. 'You were good.'

The Frenchman inclined his head to acknowledge the comment. 'We learned the hard way. I was in Algeria at Zaatcha. That's where I first killed a man. In the Crimea I learned to suffer and at Solferino I learned what it was to come close to death. And in Mexico I got this.'

Jack watched transfixed as the Frenchman pulled back the
left sleeve of his shirt. At first it revealed nothing more than
the black glove he wore on his left hand, but as the shirt was
pulled back further, a long black leather sheath was exposed.
He tucked the sleeve above his elbow then slowly removed the
glove.

Jack stared at the wooden hand that was revealed. It was
carved from deep brown wood, scuffed with dozens of
scratches, but it seemed to be well made, the fingers articulated
so that they could be moved and held in different positions.

'My friend made it for me whilst I recovered from the
butchery of the surgeons.' The Frenchman laid his right hand
on the wood, his fingers tracing a pattern over the battered
surface. 'We were guarding the supply line between the front at
Puebla and the coast when I was hit. And that was that.' He
carefully replaced his glove. 'I could have gone back to Paris,
but there was nothing for me there. Fate led me here. It wasn't
easy, but I found work. Now here I am.'

Jack listened to the abbreviated history of the man sitting
opposite him. It was not so different to his own. They had both
been born poor and had done what they could to escape the
lives Fate had allotted to them. And now here they were, sitting
together in a back-street baladi bar in Khartoum.

'You listen, but you do not say much.' The Frenchman was
still watching him closely.

Jack grunted. 'There is not much to tell.'

'I do not believe you.'

'Believe all you want.' Jack downed his beer.

'Another?'

'Why not.' He had no idea how long Julian would be kept
waiting by the governor. He might as well make himself at

home. He was sitting back, moving into a slightly more comfortable position, when a thought struck him. 'What's your name?' They had spoken for a while and had shared a beer, yet he did not know the name of the man sitting opposite him.

'Dubois. Emile Dubois. And you?'

'Jack Lark.' He reached a hand out across the table.

'Well met, Jack Lark.' Dubois shook Jack's hand then signalled to the bar's owner. 'How long until you and your friend depart?' he asked as he settled back on his couch.

'A couple of weeks, I think. The leader of the expedition is expected to arrive in early January. If all is prepared, I expect we will depart almost immediately he gets here.'

'I wish you luck with that.'

Jack saw the smirk on Dubois' face. 'What do you mean?'

'Let us just say that things do not happen easily down here. Minds can be easily distracted.' He rubbed his fingers together, as if feeling money.

'I see.' Jack said nothing more as two fresh bottles of beer were placed on the table. He only spoke again when the bar's owner had left them in peace once more.

'Perhaps I should offer you employment.' Dubois grinned at the notion.

'I have employment.' Jack waved the offer away.

'Such things change quickly in these parts. People are not who they claim to be, and they rarely do what you ask. Trust no one here, Jack. And I mean no one.' Dubois leaned back. 'If you change your mind, come and find me.'

Jack raised his glass. 'You never know.'

Dubois raised his own and clashed it against Jack's, slopping beer in every direction. 'But do not wait too long, *mon ami*. I leave in a week.'

'Where are you headed?'

'Bahr Gazal. There are copper mines there. I think it will be a good place to settle for a while.'

'Whilst you trade for ivory?'

'Precisely. I have the backing of the governor. He is supplying me with the ships I need.'

'How many is that?' Jack tried to get a sense of the scale of Dubois' enterprise.

'Eleven.'

'That's a lot of men and supplies.'

'We will need the space. We shall not return empty-handed.' Dubois banged his wooden hand on the table to turn the remark into a joke.

Jack laughed. The Frenchman was proving to be good company. And they shared a history. For a moment, he contemplated taking him up on his offer. A part of him was drawn to the idea of trading for ivory more than he was to months of toil slogging south as a part of Sir Sam's expedition. Yet even as he felt the first flicker of temptation, he knew he would never walk away. He had given his word, and so he would be true to his salt, no matter the temptation. But that didn't mean he couldn't spend a few hours with the former legionnaire. After all, they both had tales to tell.

And the beer was pretty good.

Chapter Fourteen

*J*ack stood in front of the sixty men parading on the dusty parade square outside their temporary barracks and tried to remember a time when he had seen a body of men that looked less like soldiers.

The sixty were formed up in four ranks. Not one was armed, and they were standing any old how, some with hands deep in pockets, others picking noses or scratching behinds. The spacings between the ranks and files were anything from a couple of inches to a good two feet, and at least half the men were chatting easily with their neighbours.

The soldiers on the left-hand half of the formation wore loose-fitting white tunics with a single row of brass buttons down the front, paired with baggy white Zouave trousers and bright white gaiters over black boots. To Jack's eye, it was a smart uniform, set off nicely by the splash of colour provided by the red of their fezzes. But not one jacket was buttoned properly, and every tunic was stained and crumpled. He knew these to be the men from the First Egyptian Regiment. Sir Sam had told him the ranks of the regiment were filled with convicts, but to Jack's eye they were no different from any other soldiers he had ever seen. At that moment, they had the guarded look of troops confronted with a strange new officer. A commander controlled the fate of his soldiers, even holding their continued survival in his hand. Such a man was never regarded with anything other than trepidation, at least until he had proved himself, something that would take time. Jack knew it and understood it. He could not force the issue, no matter how much he wished otherwise.

The right-hand half of the ranks was formed by the men from the First Sudan Regiment. The contrast between the two groups was stark. The Sudanese were larger to a man and broader of beam. They wore dark blue jackets trimmed with yellow and matching trousers. Red sashes were cinched tight around their waists and their red fezzes were similar to those of the Egyptians. The uniform was more gaudy than smart, and Jack could see it was neither well made nor well fitted, the baggy tunics threadbare and worn. Yet the men themselves seemed hale and hardy enough, even if they regarded him with exactly the same degree of suspicion as their Egyptian comrades.

At least the men had paraded as he had ordered. Each one carried a black leather backpack containing all his kit and belongings, with a blanket rolled and tied tight over the top. Around their waists were thick black leather belts from which hung an ammunition pouch and bayonet scabbard. Both pouch and scabbard were empty, the men unarmed during the journey from Cairo. It had been done deliberately and according to Sir Sam's exacting instructions. The journey was too long and tiresome for the soldiers to be trusted with weapons. Incarcerated on the small ships, they had soon grown fractious, and barely a day had passed without some sort of fight being reported. Had they been armed, those fights would likely have turned deadly. As it was, they had disembarked in Khartoum tired, grouchy and heartily sick of being on board ship, but otherwise largely intact.

It was the one meagre ray of sunlight amidst a shit storm. Julian had emerged from the governor's office in a rage. He had been unable to discover which, if any, of Sir Sam's requested preparations had been completed. He had been told to come back the following day, a delay that had sent him into a funk that had lasted all afternoon and far into the night. Jack had been glad to leave him to return to the governor's offices alone that morning, whilst he himself concentrated on forming the select cadre of men Sir Sam had ordered. He was determined he would not be the one to let the expedition down. No matter what it took.

'Good morning, sir.'

An elegantly dressed officer came to stand at his side, the greeting given in a respectful tone and in barely accented English.

'Good morning, Colonel.' Jack had only met Colonel Abd-el-Kader, the commander of Sir Sam's native troops, a few times before they had left Cairo. For the duration of the journey south, they had been on different ships, and so they had yet to form any sort of working relationship. According to Julian, Abd-el-Kader came with a good reputation, and Sir Sam had been well pleased when he had learned the Egyptian was to command his forces. Jack had resolved to form his own impression, trusting to instinct rather than relying on hearsay. Yet he had to admit the colonel looked the part. He was well over six feet tall, and slight of build. His long face sported a small and perfectly formed moustache that matched his immaculate appearance. His uniform was made from dark blue cloth. The long jacket hung below his waist, but was well cut so that it fell perfectly. Its facings and collar were dark red, and three tapes of gold braid formed a bold chevron with a knot above on his cuffs, the markings of his rank bright in the early-morning sunlight. Along with tight-fitting white trousers and tall black leather boots, it made for a smart ensemble, presented immaculately despite the hour.

'What think you of your new command?' Abd-el-Kader smiled as he made the remark.

Jack looked at the colonel sharply, trying to read the man's expression. He failed, quite unable to perceive anything from the composed countenance.

'They need a little work.' He spoke as tactfully as he could manage. 'These are your best men?' It was the question that had formed the moment he had first clapped eyes on the sixty soldiers.

'They are. They will surprise you, I think.'

'Good.' Jack ran his eyes up and down the ranks. He had requested the early parade the day before, asking the colonel to present his best sixty men. He had deliberately asked for a mix from the two regiments, just as Sir Sam had suggested. Not that he disagreed with the notion. It made sense to form a cadre made up from both. Over the next few days, he would pick the best, forming the small unit that Sir Sam wanted; the elite heart of the forces at his disposal.

'I must introduce you to Lieutenant Fattah el-Sisi. He is to be your second-in-command.' Abd-el-Kader beckoned a young officer to come closer. 'You will be pleased to hear that he speaks perfect English.'

Unlike the colonel, the lieutenant wore an all-blue uniform. His cuffs bore a solitary band of braid that was formed into a chevron just above the red facing of his blue jacket. To Jack's eyes he looked impossibly young, more a schoolboy playing dress-up than an officer ready to lead his men into battle.

'I am pleased to meet you, sir.' El-Sisi bowed as he presented himself to his new commander.

'Likewise, I'm sure.' Jack did his best to look friendly. He felt no joy at assuming responsibility for el-Sisi. He had taken young officers under his wing before. Some had thrived. Some had died. 'Shall we inspect the men?' He made the suggestion to hurry the morning along. He had never been good with small talk.

'I shall leave you to it.' Abd-el-Kader made his excuse to leave.

'Thank you.' Jack nodded. It was tactfully done. These were not to be the colonel's men. They were Jack's and his alone, and his assumption of that command would be made easier if he were left alone. He appreciated Abd-el-Kader recognising that.

'So, Lieutenant,' he addressed his second in command, 'let's get on with it, shall we?'

'Yes, sir.' The young officer could not help straightening to attention as he received his first instruction.

Jack did his best not to sigh. He could practically smell el-Sisi's eagerness.

Leaving the lieutenant to follow, he walked towards the ranks. The men were supposed to be standing to attention, but most had remained slouched whilst the short conversation between the officers had been going on. Not one straightened up as the two men approached.

A drummer and a bugler stood together just in front of the foremost rank, the two men charged with relaying Jack's orders choosing to stare at their boots rather than lift their heads to greet him. The men behind were paying him the same level of attention. He could feel their animosity in the air as if it were a physical thing. He understood it. He was an unfamiliar officer and he was taking command. That alone was no easy thing and few soldiers would take it without a degree of distrust. Yet there was something else, something more that he did not understand. He did not know if it was simple resentment at being paraded early, but it was a sour undercurrent that washed around him as he approached the front rank. One thing was certain. These soldiers did not want to be there.

'What's your name?' He paused before one young soldier. The lad looked barely old enough to have taken the khedive's shilling, or whatever passed for a soldier's attestation in these parts.

The lad stared back at him, expression flat and uncomprehending.

El-Sisi repeated the question in a language Jack did not understand.

'Habib.'

'How long has Habib been a soldier?' This time Jack looked to el-Sisi to translate.

An answer came back, two words delivered without any trace of emotion.

'One year,' the lieutenant told him.

Jack kept his eyes fixed on Habib. 'He has served one year and yet he is one of the best men in the regiment?'

'He is.' El-Sisi smiled anxiously.

Jack nodded. It was not the time to question his new subaltern.

He moved on, turning as he passed the last man in the front rank. The files behind looked little different. Hooded, distrustful eyes stared his way, sullen faces betraying nothing but disdain for the white-faced *ajnabi* standing in front of them.

He had seen enough, but he went through with the charade. It did not take long to walk along the rear rank, surveying the men and their equipment. They were no smarter for the closer inspection. He quickly lost count of how many buttons were undone, and every leather article needed a good clean and polish. He could not bring himself to even look at the condition of their boots.

He finally came to a stand in front of the middle of the foremost rank. Some of the men looked his way. Most did not.

'Translate for me.' He made the request of el-Sisi, who still trailed behind him, a look of concern plastered across his young features.

'My name is Jack Lark.' He paused to let his subaltern translate his words.

'I've been a soldier a long time. Maybe since some of you were still having your arses wiped.' Again he waited as his words were repeated.

'I know how to fight.' He kept it simple. 'And I am here to make sure you do too.'

The slightest murmur followed el-Sisi's translation. Jack could not tell if it was a positive reaction to his words, or something darker.

'We do not have long. So you will need to work hard.' He paused, every sense tuned to the men in front of him. 'Tomorrow we will start our preparations. Tomorrow we start getting ready to fight.'

He stood straight as el-Sisi relayed his message. He had no more to say. He did not care if the men liked his words. He was not there to be popular.

They were soldiers.

His soldiers.

'No.'

'Don't be bottle-head stupid.' Jack tried to hold onto his
temper. It was not easy. It had been a long day and he was
worn out, both physically and mentally. He had worked his
men hard, taking them through some simple drills whilst also
trying to commit to memory as many of their names as he
could, a task he found inordinately difficult, the unfamiliar
pronunciations refusing to stick in his mind. Communication
had been both laborious and slow, his need to rely on el-Sisi to
translate just an extra frustration he had to bear. He had
dismissed the men only when the sun had begun to set, allowing
them to return to their barracks with a strict instruction to
parade again at first light. He would have liked to have gone to
find some rest himself, but instead he was now faced with an
irked and exhausted Julian, who was refusing to listen to his
request.

'It is not I who is being stupid.' Julian sat on the far side of
a rough plank tabletop that had been set up on a pair of trestles
as a makeshift desk. He had taken over a small room in the
barracks the men had been given by the governor, turning it
into a temporary office with a space for him to sleep just behind.
The barracks, not far from the waterfront, was clean and tidy.
It was pretty much the only preparation that had been made
for them. The governor was still giving Julian the run-around,
but it was becoming abundantly clear that nothing at all was
ready for the expedition's next leg. But at least the men had a
place to sleep, and the storerooms were filled with dhurra,
wheat, rice and lentils, so they would not go hungry.

'Giving those men the Sniders now is nothing short of folly.' Julian shook his head vehemently, as if Jack were proposing something preposterous.

Jack ground his teeth. 'They need to learn how to use them.'

'And they will. Look, Lark, we have enough to worry about already. The damned governor has let us down badly. Nothing is ready, and I mean *nothing*. My uncle is going to be apoplectic. I would have telegraphed him, so at least he is aware of the situation, but I have no idea where he will be at this point in time and so we cannot know if the message will even reach him.'

'He'll be here soon enough.' Jack stood opposite Julian. There was just the one chair in the room. The rest was nothing but bare walls and flaking plaster, with a small window that overlooked the dusty parade square at the centre of the barracks.

'And the last thing he will need to discover is that those bloody convicts of yours have run off with his best rifles.'

Jack took a deep breath. 'They won't run off with them.'

'You do not know that, Lark. Give them those weapons and I would wager they'll be for sale in the nearest souk within the hour.'

'You have a low opinion of our men.'

'Our men?' Julian scoffed. 'These are not *our men*. They belong to the khedive and are here under sufferance. If you think you can command their loyalty, you are deluding yourself. These are not redcoats, or even native infantry. You would do well to remember that.'

Jack could understand the younger man's frustration. None of the ships Sir Sam had requested were ready, and from what Julian had told him, there was no knowing how they could be found at this stage in the season. But it was not his problem.

He had been tasked with forming a cadre for exactly the reasons Julian was propounding. Sir Sam had to have a unit he could rely on no matter what. It was his job to get that unit ready for whatever it might face, and he would be damned if he would let anyone prevent him from leading them as he saw fit.

'Thank you for the advice.' He did his best to keep his tone civil as he turned away.

'Where the devil are you going at this time of day?'

'I'm going out.'

'Who with?'

'Dubois.'

'Dubois? You mean that French fellow we met the other day?'

'Yes.' Jack was tiring of the questions.

'You won't be joining me for dinner?'

'No.'

Julian sat back heavily in his chair, making it creak alarmingly. 'You should not associate yourself with such men.'

Jack could not help pulling a face.

'They are not good for the reputation of the expedition,' Julian continued.

'Don't be daft.'

'He is not one of us. What on earth will my uncle say when he discovers you have been cavorting with such riff-raff?'

'Riff-raff?' Jack mocked Julian's choice of words.

'He is most certainly not a gentleman.' Julian half rose up from his chair as he became more animated.

'No, he's not. But then again, neither am I.' Jack had had enough.

'No, you are not, as I am learning.' Julian stood, coming around his desk as if to physically prevent Jack from leaving. 'My aunt and sister will be arriving soon. Despite what you may have heard of them, my uncle will expect us all to act with propriety when they are here. If they see you cavorting around town with a man like that bloody Frenchman . . .' he sucked in a breath as he struggled to find the words with which to rebuke Jack, 'well, it will not be seemly.'

'Seemly?' Jack made a play of looking around him. 'You think being *seemly* matters one jot here?'

'Of course it matters. Just because we live amongst the uncivilised does not mean that we should lower our own standards. How are these people supposed to learn how to behave unless we set an example?'

For a moment, Jack could not form any words as he absorbed the crassness that was spewing out of Julian's mouth.

'Must I also remind you that I am your superior?' Julian changed tack. 'I forbid you from associating with that Frenchman.'

Jack laughed. He did not mean to, but it escaped before he could hold it back.

'Do not mock me.' Julian's tone changed. Stung pride and hurt, layered with anger.

'And don't take me for a fool.' Jack's laughter died. He looked at Julian, seeing the way the younger man was vibrating with barely suppressed frustration. Then he turned sharply on his heel.

'Do not disobey me, Jack. You hear me?' Julian shouted after him. 'You will do as I say.'

Jack continued to walk. He did not look back.

He would do as he saw fit, no matter what. It had taken him a long time to become his own man, and he would not stop now. Not for Julian. Not for anyone.

Chapter Fifteen

———◆•◆———

'Call them to attention, please, Lieutenant.' Jack gave his first order of the morning. He had marched his small command to an area of open land outside the city walls where they could be away from the prying eyes of the rest of the men in the barracks. There was not much to see. The Blue Nile was away to the north, the waters far enough distant for their unpleasant smell not to reach them. Around them was little more than the same featureless scrub that seemed to stretch on uninterrupted for hundreds of miles. Everything appeared to be made from pinky-orange sand, even the dusty soil beneath their boots coloured to the same hue.

The men stood waiting for their new officer to reveal what he had planned. Their level of discontent did not appear to have altered after their first experience of Jack's style. It was obvious in the way they stood, or rather slouched, and he could hear it in the muttered comments and see it in the looks shared between the files.

Lieutenant el-Sisi took a few steps forward as he prepared to relay the command. His nerves were obvious, and he had to clear his throat noisily before he translated the simple order into Arabic.

Jack watched closely as the men straightened and stiffened their posture. Some made a fair job of it. Most did little more than shuffle on the spot, and he marked their faces. It was time to start to work on these men, and that meant selecting those he would keep and those he would send away.

He walked forward to take up a spot in front of them.

'Stand next to me, Lieutenant.' He summoned el-Sisi to his side. Only when he had arrived did Jack look at his men.

They stood in four ranks, just as they had the previous day, and just as before, the Egyptians formed the left-hand side of the formation, with the Sudanese standing to their right. A few clearly resented the early start, their petulant expressions making it obvious to all that they wanted no part in the proceedings.

Jack took a breath, then turned to his lieutenant. It was time.

'Third man from the left, front rank, and then the sixth from the same rank. Tell them to go back to the barracks. I don't want them.' Jack selected two of the men who seemed most disgruntled.

'Sir?' El-Sisi looked at his officer, surprise on his face.

'If we are to get along, I suggest you learn not to question my orders.' Jack snapped the reply.

'Yes, sir.' El-Sisi almost jumped to attention before he hurried to obey.

Jack stood as still as a statue as his message was delivered. He did not so much as twitch even as the two men reacted to the command the lieutenant relayed. One shouted, his face betraying nothing but anger, whilst his compatriot laughed, reacting with scorn rather than rage. It took el-Sisi a good two minutes to usher the pair away from the ranks, two long, protracted minutes, every part of the exchange watched by the men who remained. Jack hoped it would be enough to make them understand that they were there under his sufferance. He could send any of them away at any time.

El-Sisi scurried back to his side.

'Thank you. Now close the ranks.' Jack did not look at his subordinate.

An order followed and the front rank shuffled together.

Jack waited for the men to stop moving. Only when they were still did he take a quarter-turn to the right and wave to the local waiting patiently on the seat of a donkey cart not far from where his small command was standing.

As soon as the signal was given, the man flicked his reins and set his cart into motion. Three others were queued behind him, and they followed his lead before drawing up near where the fifty-eight men were standing.

'Lieutenant, I want you to walk to the nearest of those carts. Open up the first box you see and bring me one of the items it contains.' Jack gave his instructions slowly and clearly.

This time el-Sisi did not need to be told twice. He double-timed across to the closest cart. Every man watched him as he went around to the back, disappearing from sight.

A few seconds passed, then he reappeared.

A low moan of pleasure came from the watching ranks. They had spotted what the young subaltern now carried.

Jack heard the sound and it pleased him. The soldiers had seen his gift and their desire for it was obvious. It had taken all his powers of persuasion to convince Mr Marcopolo to release the Sniders from the expedition's stores. But he was convinced that it was necessary. Now he saw the effect his decision was having on his new command, and he was pleased he had gone against Julian's order.

He stood motionless, expression neutral, as he waited for el-Sisi to return. Only when his lieutenant was close did he hold out a hand for the rifle the junior officer carried. He nodded his thanks, then took two paces towards his men.

He held the rifle high in his right hand, making sure every man could see it. He had their full attention.

'This is the Mark Two Snider Long Rifle produced by the Royal Small Arms Factory in Enfield.' His arm felt the strain of holding the heavy weapon in the air, but he kept it still, wanting the men to see the modern rifle they would be using if they remained under his command.

'Shall I translate, sir?' Lieutenant el-Sisi hissed the question.

'Yes.' Jack did not take his eyes off his men. He did not want anyone to misunderstand.

He waited as his words were translated. Only then did he lower the rifle.

'Tell them to fall out and form a half-circle in front of me.'

They came quickly, eager to see. It did not take them long to form a rough semicircle just a few paces in front of him. He was pleased to notice some men jostling with one another as they made sure they had a good view of his demonstration.

'The Snider.' He held the rifle in both hands, walking around the half-circle, letting the men see it. He knew the weapon well enough. He had seen it in use on the battlefield. He knew its power. 'It's a breech loader.' He indicated the heavy metal breech as el-Sisi did his best to translate. 'If you are any good, you will be able to fire ten rounds a minute with this. Ten rounds.' He repeated the statement and heard a few whispers ripple around the men as they absorbed what he was telling them. Ten rounds a minute was unheard of in the world of rifled muskets that could only manage two or three shots in the same time span.

'Now, to load it. First, put the rifle at half-cock. Then the breech opens like this.' He moved the rifle's side-hinged breech-block to the right, then held the rifle up again. 'Next, push in the cartridge.' He reached into a pocket and pulled out a single stubby metal-cased cartridge, which he slid into the open breech, holding the Snider at an angle so the men could see exactly what he was doing. 'There is no need for a percussion cap.'

He paused, letting el-Sisi catch up on his translation. Only when the lieutenant had finished did he carry on.

'Now close the breech and make sure it is locked tight.' The breechblock was moved to the left, locking into position with a satisfyingly loud click. He glanced up. The men were watching intently. 'The rifle is now ready to fire.'

He turned away. Standing still, he moved the hammer back to the fully cocked position before settling the rifle into his shoulder. A moment later, he squeezed the trigger.

The Snider fired sharply, the faintest puff of smoke erupting from the end of the barrel.

He faced the men once again. Most were smiling, something pleasing in the crisp retort of the rifle firing. It boded well. Their reaction told him these men were soldiers.

'To reload, we put it back to half-cock.' He waited for el-Sisi, then continued. 'Open the breechblock, then pull it firmly to the rear.' He followed his own instructions, tugging the breechblock sharply, engaging the casing extractor. With the spent cartridge casing now sitting in the breech, he once more lifted the rifle, showing it to the men. 'Now all you need to do is turn the weapon to the right and tip the cartridge out.' He twisted the Snider and let the empty metal casing drop to the ground.

Demonstration complete, he looked around the circle of faces. The atmosphere had changed. With the men huddled around him, it felt more intimate. He sensed he had made a good impression, but he had no idea whether it was his skill or simply their fascination with the Snider. Either way, it would do for now.

'Lieutenant, fall them in. Tell them it's their turn.'

Jack stood waiting behind the two-man line. In front of him, the men shifted ever so slightly, excitement building.

'They are ready, sir.' Lieutenant el-Sisi saluted as he approached, face flushed.

'Thank you.' Jack acknowledged his subaltern, then turned to his guest. 'Let's see what your boys can do, shall we, Colonel? Do you think they are up to it?'

Colonel Abd-el-Kader had joined them late in the morning. From their brief conversation, it was clear the Egyptian officer was keen to see the Snider demonstration.

'Of course.' The colonel scowled.

'Let's see.' Jack took a single step forward. He had shown the men a dozen times how to load the Snider, repeating the sequence over and over to make sure it was ingrained in their minds. Then they had practised for themselves whilst their sergeants and corporals learned the sequence of commands they would give in battle to control the pace of the line's volleys.

Now they would fire the rifles for the first time.

Jack filled his lungs. 'Load!' he shouted.

The men obeyed, the air filled with a series of clicks as every rifle was half cocked.

Jack could feel his heart beating that little bit faster. He could not deny the feelings that had surged through him as he had given the order. It had been a long time since he had commanded a body of men. The mixed bunch of Egyptian and Sudanese infantrymen could not be further from the column of Confederate soldiers he had led into the Hornet's Nest on the battlefield of Shiloh, or the Texan cavalrymen who had stood at his side when the Mexican bandoleros had swarmed around the abandoned hacienda where they had made their final stand, but they were still his men, and taking command had filled a hole he had not realised existed in his soul.

A man in the rear rank, a Sudanese whose name he had learned was Suliman and who possessed the tiniest yet brightest eyes he had ever seen, fumbled his cartridge. He cursed, then ducked down to retrieve it, knocking the man to his right hard enough to make him stagger forward. That man, a tall and rangy Sudanese called Osman, swore then turned on his clumsy comrade, right hand coming away from the rifle to thump an open hand into Suliman's shoulder. Men in the front rank twisted around to see what was happening and joined the fracas, some shouting, others jostling as they sought a better view.

An Egyptian soldier named Gamal, a handsome fellow with a perfectly symmetrical beard that clung to the very edge of his jaw, dropped his rifle as he turned to see what was going on. It smacked against the leg of another Egyptian, a native of Cairo whose name was Ali and who had either eight or nine children; el-Sisi had said the number was a matter of debate. Gamal immediately dived forward to pick up the fallen Snider, his screech of frustration earning him a clip around the ear from the man it had hit. The blow stung enough for Gamal to turn on his comrade, threats and invective spewing forth.

Jack looked at the colonel. To his credit, Abd-el-Kader's expression was unchanged, even as Gamal and Ali both dropped their rifles and started to wrestle with one another.

'What do you think now, Colonel?' Jack asked, tone mild.

'I think they have much to learn.'

He thought on the answer for a moment before he replied. 'You don't think they are hopeless, then?'

'No.'

'But what if I order them to fight and they end up doing that?' He pointed to the melee, which was starting to get out of hand as more and more men started to push and shove.

'They know how to fight.' Abd-el-Kader met Jack's gaze. 'They are killers.'

'I need more than killers. I need men who will take orders. I need soldiers.'

'Then teach them. They will learn.'

Jack said nothing for a moment. Then he nodded. 'Fine.'

He turned back to his troops. The fracas was dying out. Most of the men had managed to load their rifles. Those who hadn't were doing their best to finish. It had taken well over a minute to load the single round.

'Lieutenant.' Jack called to el-Sisi.

'Sir?'

'Have them unload. We will do it again.'

'Sir.' El-Sisi relayed the instructions.

Jack stood calmly, even as he heard some of the men groan with displeasure. Murmurs of discontent rippled along the ranks, heads turning this way and that as the order was debated.

'Lieutenant.' Jack bit back his frustration at the language barrier. 'Tell them to shut up. Now.'

'Sir.' El-Sisi glanced once at his officer, face creasing with concern, then spoke to the men. He was ignored.

One man in the white uniform of the First Egyptian Regiment had had enough. He sat down, Snider dropped carelessly into the dust at his side, and protested to his comrades, arms waving this way and that as he encouraged others to follow his lead.

Jack strode forward, holding his anger in check as best he could. The man swivelled around, face twisted with scorn as he saw who it was that had come to berate him.

Jack's hands balled into fists. He had forgotten the man's name, but that did not matter now. His time in Jack's cadre was done.

'Get up.' The words came out wrapped in iron.

The man's mouth curled into a look of utter disdain and he made no move to obey. He started to speak, a babble of unintelligible words spewing forth.

'Get up.' Jack growled the order. Again he was disobeyed.

The men around them were quietening down, every one of them watching the confrontation.

Jack repeated the command for a third time, motioning with his hand to make sure the man knew what he was being told to do.

He was rewarded with nothing but more protest. The soldier remained on the ground, arms crossed over his chest, mouth moving nineteen to the dozen as he complained to his fellows.

'For fuck's sake.' Jack had seen enough. He stepped forward, grabbed the man under his arms and hauled him to his feet.

For a single moment, the soldier's mouth gaped open as he was manhandled. Then he cried out, protest and abuse spewing forth.

'Shut the fuck up.' Jack pushed him in the chest as forcefully as he could, causing the soldier to stumble away as he fought to stay on his feet.

'Tell him to go back to the barracks,' Jack shouted to el-Sisi, then bent down and picked up the man's Snider.

El-Sisi did his best, but the soldier was having none of it. He stepped forward, finger jabbing towards Jack. The lieutenant was forced to block his path, putting his body between his officer and the disgruntled man. Even then, the fellow kept up his protest, pushing at the young subaltern.

It took the colonel's intervention to stop the affair getting out of hand. He snapped a single word of command, and the soldier stopped shouting and hung his head. Abd-el-Kader spoke quickly and quietly, then the disgruntled Egyptian nodded and began the long walk back to the barracks.

'El-Sisi.' Jack snapped at his lieutenant. The burn of frustration was painful. 'Tell the men to put the Sniders back on the cart. I've seen enough for one day.' He kept his tone level, despite the emotions that were raging inside. This was not the start he had hoped for.

It had been a long time since he had commanded soldiers, and it appeared his leadership skills had quite deserted him.

Chapter Sixteen

J ack slunk into a corner seat in the quiet courtyard towards the rear of the baladi bar, breathing a deep sigh of relief as he settled into the soft cushions. But no matter how badly his back was hurting, it was as nothing next to the pain of that day's failure with his new command.

He had left his men to return to their barracks after the failed attempt to demonstrate the Snider. But he had not left them in peace, insisting they parade again in the afternoon. There had been no improvement in their mood, the men just as hostile as they had been at the beginning of the day. That resentment had only grown when Jack ordered them on a march, though at least they had followed him. He had set a fast pace, leading them on a route he guessed was approaching six miles long. It had certainly been far enough to leave every one of them sweating hard. But they all needed the physical exertion, him most of all, and the completion of a hard march had at least ended the day on some sort of positive footing. Not that he was deluding himself. Following a new officer on a march was one thing. Following him into battle was a very different prospect, and he had no false hopes that anything had changed. For now, he had to recognise that his supposedly elite cadre was about as reliable as a priest in a whorehouse.

'Hurry up with that beer!' Dubois shouted to the bar's owner as he thumped heavily into the seat opposite. He paused and made a play of inspecting Jack's face. 'Hard day?' He chuckled as he asked the question, reading Jack's pained expression with ease.

'Something like that.' Jack squirmed, trying to ease his aches as best he could. Life in Cairo had left him soft.

'Beer will help.' Dubois smacked his wooden hand into the table, then laughed at Jack's grimace.

The beers duly arrived. There were five.

'You expecting someone else?' Jack asked as he reached for a bottle and a glass.

'Some of my men. Do you mind?' Dubois poured his beer fast and carelessly, the froth surging up to fill the glass then spilling over the lip.

'No,' Jack answered honestly. He poured his own beer more slowly, tipping the glass and taking care to let only the smallest head build. After his first encounter with some of Dubois' men, he felt a little wary of meeting more, but he was keen to learn more about the ivory trade from Dubois and the men he employed. When the glass was nicely full, he raised it. 'Cheers.'

'Santé.'

Jack closed his eyes, savouring the taste of the beer. When he opened them again, he saw the same look of pleasure on Dubois' face. 'How are your preparations going?' he asked.

Dubois placed his glass on the table, then wiped his good hand across his face, smearing away the froth that had stuck to his beard. He shrugged. 'Things move slowly here. But we are getting there.'

'When do you leave?'

'In six days. At least, that is what I hope.'

'And your ships are ready?'

'They are. I am just waiting on more ammunition. It is still on its way from Cairo. They say it will be here tomorrow, or perhaps the day after, or the day after that.' The Frenchman shook his head. '*Ça me fait chier.*' He spoke the words softly to himself. 'But never mind. Such talk is not for today. Today we drink.'

'Works for me, chum.' Jack lifted his glass to acknowledge the remark.

Their conversation was halted as three more men made a noisy arrival. They swarmed towards the corner table, burly bodies filling the small space.

'*Guten Abend.*' The first to reach the table gave the greeting then flopped down heavily. He was a big man, well over six feet tall and broad of shoulder. His hair was cropped close to his skull, and unlike most men of his age, he was clean-shaven, although his cheeks and jaw sported a heavy growth of stubble that was almost as long as what little hair was left on his head. He grinned at Jack, then thrust out a hand. 'Herman.'

'Jack.' Jack shook the hand, noting the heavy German accent. He liked the short introduction. Nothing more was needed.

'That is Khan. He won't say much.' The German waved a hand at another tall man taking a seat next to Jack. He was olive-skinned and slender, with long black hair that curled around the sides of his head and fell almost to his shoulders. 'And I think you already know my good friend Vladimir.'

Jack quickly shook the hand Khan offered, then turned to the last man to join the group. The squat, heavy-set figure was indeed familiar.

'I would shake your hand, my friend . . .' the newcomer paused, 'if I could.' He slipped onto the couch opposite Jack. His right hand was heavily bandaged.

Jack studied him carefully, watching for any sign of impending violence.

Then the Russian grinned from ear to ear and held out his left hand. 'It was a good fight, my friend.'

Jack half rose from his seat as he shook the man's hand. He saw nothing he could perceive as a threat.

All three of the new arrivals busied themselves pouring beers. It gave Jack a chance to settle back. He had done his best not to reveal even a trace of his discomfort, but the pain in his back was a bastard and it was showing no sign of relenting. It would take many more beers to ease it, but at least he was in the right place for that. And in the right company.

'So, my friend.' Herman spoke first. 'Where did you learn to fight?'

'The Alma.' Jack looked pointedly at the Russian, watching for a reaction.

Vladimir stared back over the rim of his beer glass. His dark eyes revealed nothing. 'You were there?'

Jack nodded.

The Russian burped softly. 'That was a hard day.'

'It was.' Jack glanced at Dubois, who offered a tight-lipped smile. Clearly he knew what was to come.

'I was in the redoubt. Near the river.' Vladimir drained his beer. 'You red-coated bastards did not know when you were beaten.'

Jack closed his eyes as the hairs on the back of his neck stood on end. For a moment he was back on the bloody slopes of the Alma river, the ground around him carpeted with the dead and the dying, his mind echoing to the sound of the Russian cannon and the heart-rending cries of those hit by the storm of shot and shell that had torn through the British ranks. Once again he tasted the fear of those bloody moments. His terror had been all-consuming. There had been nothing else to do save to press forward and keep putting one foot in front of the other, no matter that he walked into the jaws of death. Around him, men had bent double, as if they were walking into the teeth of a gale. And they had kept going, even as their friends and comrades were butchered by the Russian gunners, who had poured on the fire without mercy.

'It was a hard day.' He opened his eyes as he used the Russian's own choice of words. Vladimir was looking directly at him.

There was a moment of silence, then the Russian raised his empty glass. 'We need more beer.'

'That is the most sensible thing I have ever heard you say.' Herman had seen the byplay between two men who had once stood on opposite sides of the same battlefield, and now did his best to help them. 'More beer!' he shouted, waving at the bar's owner. 'More beer now!' He guffawed, his face flushed from the heat of the bar.

'You all speak good English,' Jack observed.

'He insists.' Vladimir answered for the group, gesturing towards Dubois.

'It is the only way.' Dubois pulled a wry expression. 'I suggested French, but blockheads like Herman cannot speak it.'

'Blockhead, you say?' Herman was affronted. 'What is that?'

Dubois grinned. 'We speak different languages, that is true, but they all understand when I give them an order. And they obey. That is enough.'

The comment resonated with Jack. His failure with the Egyptian and Sudanese troops still rankled. 'Where were you when I needed you?' He spoke quietly, the words meant for himself.

'You have a problem, *mon ami*?' Dubois raised his eyebrows.

Jack took a breath. 'The soldiers we have been given for the expedition. Let's just say they are not quite what I had hoped.'

The Frenchman grinned in sympathy. 'I have a few locals with me. Do not underestimate them. They can be difficult, that is true. But you need to remember they are not legionnaires. Or redcoats, for that matter. But that does not mean they cannot be good soldiers. They are just different, and they need to be handled differently.'

Jack sat forward. 'How so?'

'At first you need to show them nothing but strength. If they think you are weak, they will ignore you.'

Jack thought back to the Egyptian soldier he had dismissed that day. That man had sat down when he had had enough. It had taken the intervention of Abd-el-Kader to get him to move, the recalcitrant soldier ignoring Jack completely. He understood now that the display had done nothing to improve his standing with his new command. He had not resolved the situation for himself. That had been a mistake.

'Go on.' He urged Dubois to continue. He did not mind seeking advice from the Frenchman. He needed it.

'Beat them if you have to. It is not what we are used to, perhaps, but you need to show them that you are tough. Only then will they begin to hear you.'

Jack absorbed the advice. He was not too proud to accept that much of the fault lay with himself. He had turned up and taken command without a thought, as if it were his right. He had not given his men any reason to follow him. He had not shown them anything other than a white face. He did not even speak their language. The failure was not down to his men. It was down to him.

'And you need to bond them to you.' Dubois used his glass to gesture towards the three men who had joined them. 'My men come from all over the world, yet we stand together. And we are bloody good.' He grinned at his own lack of modesty. 'You should see us. I would wager no one could stand against us.' He lifted his glass and toasted them.

Jack saw the look of appreciation on the three faces. Dubois was right to be proud. It was no small thing to unite and then lead a group of disparate individuals from a range of countries. Yet from what he could see, the Frenchman had done it. He could feel the bond between the four of them, and for a moment he felt a spark of jealousy. He was an outsider here, just as he was with his own men. Just as he had been since the moment he had first taken an officer's scarlet coatee for himself. He had set himself apart from others, and there were times when he regretted it with every fibre of his being. He had chosen a lonely path.

'Give them something.'

'What do you mean?' Jack looked at Dubois questioningly.

'Give your men something to bind them to you. And to each other.'

'Like what?'

'What first bonded you to your redcoats?'

Jack thought for a moment. 'The uniform, I suppose.' He smiled. He remembered how badly he had once wanted a red coat for himself. The uniform of a British soldier set the men apart. The coat itself might not have been worth much, monetarily at least, but to the men who wore it, it was priceless.

It showed the world who they were. It did not matter where they came from, or what they had done before, the red coat united them all. It was the same the world over. Whether it was young soldiers putting on their blue uniform for the first time before Bull Run, or the disparate group who had worn the dusty khaki of Hodson's Horse, the men's uniform defined them. It united them.

The notion set him thinking. His men came from two very different regiments and wore very different uniforms. Perhaps dealing with that would be a good start and set him on the path to earning their respect.

'You talk a lot of sense,' he admitted, 'for a *crapaud*.'

Dubois laughed. 'Of course.' He spread his hands wide in an expansive gesture. 'And for sure you are a *rosbif* and so you won't listen to my wise advice, but heh, what can I do?'

The bar's owner arrived with more beers. As he set them down, Herman tugged at his sleeve then whispered in his ear.

The owner nodded and scurried off to obey whatever instruction he had been given.

'I propose a toast.' Dubois filled his glass then raised it once more.

The others did the same, and the five beers came together over the table.

'To men like us. May we all find what we are looking for.'

As he drank, Jack realised that he was starting to feel part of the group. He had only known them for a short while, had recently fought one of them, but for a reason he did not fully understand, he felt like he fitted. It was a strange sensation, one that he had not felt for many years. Yet it was there nonetheless. He was with men who were like him. They were not fit for the drawing rooms of the elite, or for a gentlemen's club on

London's fashionable streets. They would never fit into polite society, or be the sort of men any civilised family would want to join them at their dinner table. Yet here, far from that world, they had found their place. Here they belonged.

His musing ended when five new arrivals made their way to the table. It was what Herman had requested, the German giving his order as if he had been requesting just another round of drinks.

The five women were dressed simply. Not that any of them had a great deal on. The whispers of silk and gauze barely covered their decency. All jangled as they sat down, their forearms covered with dozens of thin gold and silver bangles, and small shiny discs decorating their meagre clothing. Not one of them spoke as they seamlessly split up, each taking a place next to one of the beer-drinking men. They knew what they were there for.

Jack sat down his glass and looked at the woman who had appeared at his side. She was young, to his eyes at least. Her dark hair was pulled back from her face and decorated with small gold pins that flickered in the bar's lights. Large dark brown eyes stared back at him as a smile formed on lips rouged red. She was skinny, her arms and legs long and slender; thin enough for him to be able to see her ribs beneath the thin film of wispy silk that barely covered her.

'Good evening.' He greeted her politely, offering a smile. He could smell her now she was close, her skin fragranced with jasmine and rose water.

Around him, Dubois' men roared with approval. They jested with one another, ribald comments coming thick and fast. Jack tuned them out, concentrating his attention on his new companion.

She spoke to him then, but he heard little of her words over the shouts of the men at the table, and those he did hear he did not understand. So he drank his beer and smiled at the young woman who sat so close that he could feel her warmth soaking into his leg.

The Russian staggered to his feet. He drained his beer, then took his companion's hand and stumbled away. Khan and Herman followed moments later.

Only the Frenchman was left.

'She is beautiful.' He spoke to Jack.

'She is.' Jack could only agree.

'I think we are the same, you and I.' Dubois glanced once at the girl who sat patiently at his side, then looked back to Jack. 'Cut from the same cloth, isn't that what the English say? We are both looking for something that we never find. Even here. Even with such beauty within our grasp, we are not where we want to be. Or *who* we want to be.' He offered a wry smile. 'Take comfort where you can, Jack. Who knows what tomorrow holds?'

He got to his feet, holding out his good hand to his companion. 'Don't worry. These ladies are on me. Just try to enjoy yourself, *mon ami*. The world can fuck off for one night at least.'

Jack said nothing. But he nodded.

Left alone with the woman, he thought about what the Frenchman had said. Dubois was correct. The two of them were alike. There was only one place where they belonged, but it was not where most men were comfortable. Yet it was where they were meant to be. For only in the dangerous wild lands could they be their true selves. Only in chaos could they release what dwelt inside them both.

The woman at his side reached forward to take his hand.

He looked at her then, really looked at her. He did not know her name. He did not know her story. He did not know what had led to a life spent in a place like this, with men like him. It would likely be a sad tale, he knew that much. No young girl dreamed of the life this woman now led, but Fate had led her to him, just as she had led him to this place and put him into this moment where he had a choice and the woman at his side likely had none.

She stood, as if to lead him away.

Jack hesitated. He was tempted. It would be so easy to give in and go with her. A night of sex held many temptations. As Dubois had said, he should look to take his comfort where he could. It had been a long time since there had been someone in his bed. But he had spent too much of his life living amongst whores, first in his mother's gin palace and then in his own place. He knew their tales, where they had come from and where they hoped to go. Worst of all, he had heard their stories of the men who paid them to lie on their backs. And he knew it was not for him, just as it never had been. It might leave him lonely and cold in his bed, but he would not give in.

He smiled at the woman, then let go of her hand.

'Go.' He dismissed her with the single word, then twisted away to summon the bar's owner, who was loitering nearby. 'Beer.'

He settled in to wait for his new friends to return. The beer would dull the ache of his loneliness, just as it would dull the pain in his back.

For a while, at least.

Chapter Seventeen

Jack stood on the same patch of dusty ground near the river, waiting patiently for his men to arrive. His head was throbbing and his mouth felt as if a tramp had lodged there for the night. Neither affliction was helped by the blindingly bright morning sunlight, or the heat he could already feel building in the air. It promised to be another fine day, the sky already clearing of early cloud and the breeze clean and dry, the gentle wind doing something to scour away the sheen of sweat from his face. Yet it was doing nothing to improve his foul mood.

He had sat alone in the bar for the best part of an hour before Dubois and his men had returned. Their overly loud and boisterous mood had helped buoy his spirits, and they had drunk long into the night. At some point, he did not remember when, they had switched from beer to arrack, the local spirit getting every one of them drunk with indecent haste. After that, he did not remember much. From the stains on his shirt, it was clear they had eaten something at some point, but quite what it had been, or where they had eaten it, was lost in the fog of his memory. He did know that Dubois had escorted him back to

the barracks when the sky had already been brightening with
the first trace of dawn.

The sound of troops marching reached his ears. A small
column of soldiers was approaching, the men doing a poor job
of keeping the ranks and files neat as they traversed the scrub
that bordered the main road out of town. Lieutenant el-Sisi led
them, the young officer completely out of step with his men and
blithely oblivious to the fact.

Jack let them come close. He did not move even as they
halted and faced him. He said nothing, his mouth dry and his
throat claggy and sore. Instead, he waited, his head turning to
the right as a single cart came along the road, just as he had
ordered.

Despite his hangover, he had still been up before anyone
else in the barracks. It had not taken long to find Mr Marcopolo
and deliver the request that had been inspired by his conversation with Dubois the night before. He might not be able to
issue Sir Sam's cadre with the red coat that had so motivated
his younger self, but he had an idea for something that could at
least start to unify his small command.

The donkey and cart came to a halt a short distance
from the formed ranks of the fifty-seven men who waited
patiently for the first order of the day. A few glanced hopefully
towards it to see if the Sniders had been brought back, but
the single cart held nothing more interesting than a dozen cloth
sacks.

'Lieutenant.' Jack summoned his subaltern.

'Good morning, sir.' El-Sisi rushed forward then came to
attention, flashing a sketchy salute. He was smiling.

'Have the men remove their tunics and shirts.'

'Sir?' The smile faded fast.

'Have you got cloth ears, Lieutenant?' Jack snapped. He was in no mood to have to repeat his every command.

'Sir!' El-Sisi's mouth turned down at the corners, but nonetheless he relayed the strange order.

The men looked at one another, a low murmur spreading fast, yet they did what he asked. It took a while, but eventually every man stood bare-chested, shirts and tunics piled on the ground in front of them.

Jack scanned the ranks. He could see the discontent on nearly every face, yet he did not doubt what he was doing. It was the right thing. The men just didn't know it yet.

'Lieutenant, I want you to go to that cart. You will find a number of sacks there. Open one and bring me a single item from inside.' He spoke slowly and clearly. 'Did you hear that correctly?'

The young officer licked his lips, his nervousness obvious, then nodded.

'Carry on, Lieutenant.'

Every one of the fifty-seven half-naked soldiers watched as the subaltern ran to the cart and reached up to pull open the nearest sack. He pulled something out, a fleeting flash of scarlet quickly hidden as the young officer bundled the item into his arms then ran back with it, his pace increasing as he saw his officer waiting for his return.

'Thank you, Lieutenant.' Jack nodded once, then came forward to take the single item. He ran his fingers over the cloth, feeling the fibres, then paused, eyes scanning the soldiers watching his every move. Then he held up the scarlet shirt, making sure every man could see it.

'You will all now wear one of these.' He held the shirt higher. 'I don't care where you come from, or what you have done before this day. From now on, you are a red-shirt and you belong to me.' He stopped there, falling silent as El-Sisi translated.

The reaction was immediate. Murmurs became full-blown conversations, the men looking this way and that as they voiced a mix of emotions. Surprise, distrust, disdain, Jack heard them all. And he did not care about any of them.

'Lieutenant, have the men form a line by the cart.' He gave the clipped instruction, then walked towards the vehicle himself. The driver sat quietly eating a pastry as he watched the display, a sly smile on his face. Jack ignored him and jumped up onto the back. He was pleased to see that Marcopolo had done exactly as he had asked, and there were a dozen of the large sackcloth sacks, all holding more of the red shirts raided from Sir Sam's expedition supplies.

A line formed behind the cart, the men obeying his instructions thus far. He paused, making sure they were ready, then squatted down and held out the first shirt.

The lead man in the line reached for it, already turning away.

Jack held the shirt fast. Waiting.

The soldier stopped as he realised the shirt was not being released. Only then did he look at Jack.

Jack held his stare. 'What is your name?'

'Samir.' The man understood enough English to know what he was being asked. He grinned as he replied.

Jack did his best to commit the man's name and smiling face to memory. He did remember that el-Sisi had told him that this man was renowned for beating his wife and children without thought of mercy. The information belied the cherubic features.

He released the shirt, letting the wife-beater go. The next man stepped forward. Once again Jack held out the shirt then asked the man's name, making sure to look the soldier dead in the eyes before releasing it.

It took time for every man to receive a shirt directly from his hand. He did not rush it, even as his knees began to creak. Every man received the same attention, as did Lieutenant el-Sisi, the subaltern unable to hide from his expression the conviction that he was serving a madman.

Only when the last man was on his way back to join his fellows did Jack stand. Most of the soldiers had already dressed in the new shirts. A few were swapping garments, trying to get one that fitted better. He had only taken the larger shirts Marcopolo had brought from Cairo. It meant that the smaller, slimmer soldiers were slightly swamped by the red fabric, whilst two of the largest Sudanese wore shirts that were stretched tight over their broad chests, but in the main they fitted well enough.

It was his turn. He jumped down from the cart, doing his best not to wince as his back and his knees protested at the impact, then removed his own shirt. He could feel the wind whispering across his skin, the dry, fast-moving air making the fine hairs on the back of his neck stand to attention. He shivered, then slipped one of the shirts over his head. The fabric was coarser than his own shirt, but it would do, and he took a moment to tuck it neatly into his trousers. Only when it was settled to his satisfaction did he walk back towards his men.

'Fall them in,' he called across to el-Sisi.

The command was relayed. Jack took his place in front of the middle of the foremost rank and ran his eye over his soldiers. They looked different now. No longer did they wear two contrasting uniforms. But it was still clear that the Sudanese regiment formed the right half of the formation, whilst those from the First Egyptian stood on the left. So there was something else he wanted to do.

'Have every other man step out of the line.' He gave the order to his lieutenant.

El-Sisi shouted the command, and Jack was pleased to see the men obey the instruction correctly.

'Have them form a new line, then dress the ranks.'

He stood and watched as the men moved sharply, forming two new lines then straightening them up.

'Tell rank one and three to form on the right.'

It did not take long for the men to obey. He was left facing two ranks once again, but now the two regiments were well mixed. It would do for now.

It was a start.

'I damn well hope you are not wasting my time, Lark.' Julian snapped the waspish remark as he walked at Jack's side.

'I am making progress.' Jack did his best not to bite back.

Julian had insisted on the demonstration, demanding to see how Jack was getting on with the task Sir Sam had set him. It was late afternoon, and he had worked with his new red-shirted unit all day. He had made progress, but there was still a long way to go. The men knew their drill well enough, but they lacked any sort of sharpness, shambling through the routines and often wandering this way and that as they carried them out. He knew he could never make them guardsmen, but they still needed to do better. That fact had been ably demonstrated when he had ordered them to form a skirmish line. The result had been nothing short of a disaster, the men clearly having no idea what he wanted them to do. It had taken the best part of an hour to get them to understand the commands, and even by that hour's end, it was still the roughest line Jack had ever seen. He would persevere with that drill above all others. Where they were going, it was highly likely that the rigid, tight ranks of the usual line and column formations would be wholly unsuitable, but the dispersed, widely spaced skirmish line would work perfectly. If they could only master it.

'What the devil?' Julian caught his first glimpse of the small formation of red-shirted soldiers.

'They look smart, don't they just?' Jack tried not to grin at the reaction. He was pleased with what he saw. The men were sitting on the dusty field where he had drilled them all day. They had fallen out and were enjoying a rest and a drink. Their red shirts were sweaty now and all were covered with a liberal layer of dust from a day spent in the field, but he did not mind the grime. Now at least they looked like a single body of men rather than a gathering from several different regiments.

'Those shirts were meant for the expedition!' Julian's anger was swift.

'Where the hell do you think those men are going?' Jack fought the urge to laugh.

'But those were for trade. Not for anyone who fancied a cheap change of wardrobe.'

'I am sure your uncle will understand.'

'Really. You know him that well, do you?' Julian shook his head.

Jack did not care that his supposed superior was peeved. He would justify the use of the shirts to Sir Sam if he had to.

He did not wait to see what else Julian had to say. Instead he led him towards the men, who were hurriedly forming two lines now that their commander was approaching. As he drew closer, he could see that they looked tired. They had most likely not been worked this hard for a long time, but that did not mean he would let them finish the day. Not yet. He wanted to show Julian that he was beginning to shape the small unit into one Sir Sam could indeed rely on.

They did not have long. They had received a letter informing them that the expedition's leader was on his way to join them. It had been dated some weeks previously, but at least they now knew that Sir Sam, his wife and his niece were expected to arrive early in the new year.

'Sir.' Jack's arrival was greeted by el-Sisi, the young officer's dusty, grime-streaked face wreathed with concern.

'Good afternoon, Lieutenant. Have you met Mr Baker?' Jack watched his subaltern closely as he made the required introduction.

'No, sir. Good afternoon, sir.' El-Sisi hurried through the pleasantries, then looked to his commander. 'There is a problem, sir.' He spoke quietly, as if Julian would suddenly be unable to hear.

'What?' Jack could see the lieutenant looked about ready to burst into tears.

'There was trouble when you left.'

'What sort of trouble?' Jack glanced at Julian, checking his reaction to the news. From the pinched and peevish expression on his face, he was not impressed.

'We had a visit.'

'Who from?'

'A group of men.'

'What sort of men?'

'Slavers, sir.'

'What the hell did they want?' Jack tried not to snap, but drawing information from the young officer was like pulling teeth out of his arse, and just as painful.

'They offered the men employment.'

'They did what?' He had not expected that answer.

'And they are offering more money, I'll wager,' Julian interjected.

'What did the men say?' Jack tried to cut to the heart of the matter.

'Five men went with them.' El-Sisi's head dropped, and he stared down at his dust-shrouded boots.

'Did you not stop them?'

'I tried.' He would not meet Jack's eyes.

'Bollocks.' Jack spat out the single word.

'They deserted?' Julian sounded outraged. 'Goddammit! They will bally well be flogged when we find them. The black-guards.'

'We won't find them.' Jack's reply was desperately tired. 'They'll be long gone.'

'But we cannot just let them go.'

'We have no choice.' He brushed Julian's anger aside. It would serve no purpose, not now. All that mattered was the men who had chosen to stay. 'What about the rest?'

'They are not happy, sir.'

'They are not meant to be fucking happy!' For the first time, Jack revealed some of his own anger. 'Goddam it all to hell.'

'So much for your highly trained cadre.' Julian's fury had turned to a cruel mockery. 'It's a wonder any of them are still damn well here. Just imagine if they had the Sniders, as you had suggested . . .'

It took all of Jack's self-restraint to hold back the choice words that sprang to his tongue. 'I'll deal with it.'

'And how do you propose doing that?' Julian sneered. 'You have been in command for no more than a couple of days, and already a tenth of your men have deserted. How many will be left by the week's end?'

Jack balled his fists. 'I'll deal with it,' he repeated. 'Call the men to attention, Lieutenant.' He fired off the instruction, then stomped to his position in front of the ranks, leaving Julian where he was.

The men fell in, but he could see their discontent. It was written in every sullen expression.

'On my command, we will about-turn then form a skirmish line. Just like we practised.'

El-Sisi relayed the instructions.

'Now.' Jack snapped the single word.

El-Sisi shouted the order.

It was greeted by silence.

'Tell them again.' Jack felt his anger burn bright, yet he refused to let it show in his face.

El-Sisi repeated the order, but this time his voice lacked conviction, the instructions sounding like a request, not a command.

And not one man moved.

'Shit.' Jack could feel his heart pounding faster as the emotions surged through him. Frustration. Anger. Impotence. He felt sick. This was not how it was meant to be. But he had to deal with it, just as he had told Julian he would. It was a crucial moment. If he lost the men now, he would never get them back.

He gritted his teeth. He would not give an inch. There

was another way to show them what manner of man now commanded them.

He told el-Sisi to move aside, then stalked forward. He took his time, his eyes moving from one man to the next, meeting their discontent with icy calm.

'Who's the ringleader?' He fired the question at el-Sisi over his shoulder.

'Sir?'

'Who leads them?' Jack growled. He knew these men. One of them would be the soldiers' mouthpiece – a barrack-room lawyer – the one who fanned the flames and shouted the loudest.

'Corporal Monsoor, sir.' Jack could hear the tremor in the young officer's voice as he named the man.

'Where is he?' Jack remembered the name, but could not put a face to it.

'At the end of the front rank, sir,' el-Sisi replied.

Jack kept moving slowly, making sure every man saw him. Eventually he reached the end of the rank.

Corporal Monsoor had heard his name called out. If it worried or concerned him, not a trace of it showed on his pugnacious features. Instead, he glowered at Jack, his face contorting with barely controlled fury.

Monsoor was no more than five and a half feet tall. Yet he was powerfully built, with heavy shoulders and a broad barrel chest. Underneath his fez, his face was dark, with hooded eyes and a hooked nose so large it was almost comical, totally out of place on such a small man.

'Do you have a problem, Corporal?' Jack drew himself up to his full height as he addressed him.

'You want me to translate, sir?' El-Sisi was shuffling

awkwardly towards his officer, clearly reluctant to come any closer.

Jack kept his eyes fixed on the corporal. 'No, thank you, Lieutenant. The corporal and I understand each other well enough.'

Monsoor's mouth moved, as if to form a smile in reaction to Jack's claim. That smile was still no more than half formed when Jack hit him.

He had known he would do it the moment he left the lieutenant's side. He remembered the Frenchman's claim that the local soldiers respected only strength. It was time to see if that was true.

It was not fair, hitting a man who was not prepared for it, but at that moment, Jack did not care, and it felt wonderful to slam his fist straight into the centre of Monsoor's sneering face. It was a good punch, one that snapped the corporal's head backwards, his fez thrown away by the force of the impact, and rocked him back on his heels, so that he staggered away from Jack. He might have fallen had the men in the rank behind not stepped forward to hold him up.

Monsoor found his balance. He lifted a hand to his face and stared at the blood on his fingers. Then he snorted like a boar and took a pace forward, fists raised like a pugilist stepping into the centre of the ring.

The men roared with approval and began to cheer for their man, goading him on.

'Come on then.' There was time for Jack to hiss the words under his breath before he skipped to one side, twisting his body around so that Monsoor slipped past his hip. It was almost too easy. His timing was perfect, and he linked his hands together and brought them down sharply on the back of

Monsoor's neck. It was a blow that would have felled an ox, but somehow the corporal kept his footing as he blundered past, the merest hint of a stagger his only reaction. He turned fast, breathing hard. Then he came at Jack, fists swinging.

Jack tried to twist away, just as he had done the first time, yet he was not quick enough. Monsoor led with his shoulder and thumped into Jack's side, then pumped with his legs, driving him backwards.

It was all Jack could do to keep from falling. He raised his fists and punched down, striking them against Monsoor's back. Yet Monsoor pushed on, lifting Jack's legs so that for a second he was suspended in the air. His balance gone, he was powerless to do anything at all as Monsoor rose up, arms wrapped tight around his midriff, then lurched forward, flinging them both to the earth. They hit the ground brutally hard, bodies intertwined.

The men bayed and cheered as they saw their new officer go down. It was a feral sound, wild and filled with violence, the wall of sound deafening.

Jack felt the breath driven from his lungs as he hit the sun-baked soil on his back, with Monsoor on top of him. The pain came then, hot and fierce, a fiery lance of pure agony shooting down his spine. He cried out, the squawk escaping with the rush of air forced from his lungs.

Monsoor pushed himself up, and straddled Jack's body. There was a moment's pause, just long enough for the corporal to look down into Jack's face. Then he punched.

Jack saw the blow coming, yet he could do nothing to avoid it. It struck him on the jaw, knocking his head to one side. Then the second punch landed, hitting hard on the other side, and his world turned grey. His ears were ringing, and his jaw felt like it had been shattered. Yet Monsoor was not done. His fists moved faster than Jack's floundering senses could track. Again they cracked into either side of his head, flinging it from side to side.

It was all Jack could do to stave off the darkness. Pain was filling his head and blood was flowing freely down his face. Monsoor was sitting on his stomach, knees pressing down and crushing his lungs. He could feel the man's weight shift as he swung this way and that with the power of his punches.

He knew he could not take much more. Another punch would send him into the dark. And Monsoor would not stop. He would carry on bludgeoning his fists into Jack's unprotected head until he was battered half to death, or even all the way. He had to stop it. And he had to stop it now.

He reached forward, hand cupped. He found his target and grabbed hold, fingers like claws. He dug them deep, cruel and relentless, grasping and twisting with every scrap of force he could exert.

Monsoor shrieked as he felt Jack grab hold of his balls. That shriek went up another octave as Jack twisted his hand around, wrenching the testicles as if about to tear them away from Monsoor's body.

The watching crowd of soldiers winced collectively as they saw Jack's vicious counter-attack. Some even cried out in sympathy, their exclamations of shared pain coming loud and clear.

Monsoor leapt up, fists swinging against Jack's arm to force him to release his hold. Jack had no choice but to let go, but Monsoor was off his chest and it gave him the chance to scrabble onto his side, then up and onto his feet, facing his foe. He was in time to see Monsoor curl forward, both hands held cupped around his damaged vitals. Jack barked a short, bitter laugh. Then he attacked.

Monsoor saw him coming and tried to face him, but his body was still wrapped around his damaged balls and he just could not react in time.

Jack saw his chance. He grabbed hold of Monsoor by the collar with his left hand, whilst his right grabbed the back of the man's trousers. He held him like that, forcing his head low, then raised his own knee as sharply as he could, driving it directly into Monsoor's face. It struck just as he'd planned, accompanied by the grotesque yet satisfying sound of bony knee meeting soft face.

Monsoor went limp, and Jack released his hold. The corporal landed face first in the dirt, senses gone.

Jack sucked down a breath. Everything hurt, and he could taste blood on his lips. But he did not care. 'Anyone else got a fucking problem?' The words came out between gasps for breath.

His men stared back at him, stunned into silence by the short scrap that had seen their ringleader left in the dirt.

And in that moment, he knew he had them.

They were his.

Chapter Eighteen

Khartoum, 6 January 1870

‘As the sun rose, it spread a beguiling palette of orange and yellow across the horizon. The scene was benign, tranquil, the warm light casting the Nile and the embankment on the northern flank of Khartoum in orange-toned shadows that marched across the land as the sun made its languid process into the sky. Yet the beauty of the dawn could do nothing to disguise the rotting aroma that wafted up from the river, the vegetation that floated along in compact matted islands casting an evil miasma across the waterfront.

Jack stood in front of the two ranks formed by his small command. Lieutenant el-Sisi was on the right of the front rank, whilst the place at the left of the rear rank was taken by the newly promoted Sergeant Monsoor. Every man was dressed in the red shirt Jack had issued, paired with baggy white Zouave trousers, white gaiters and freshly polished black leather belts, boots and packs. All carried a brand-new Snider rifle, the ammunition kept in a smart black leather pouch attached to the front of the belt, whilst the rifle's bayonet was kept in a white leather scabbard that hung over the right buttock. On their heads, they wore a red fez, a fitting finish to the uniform. They might look nothing like the redcoats he had once led, but Jack could not recall a sense of pride as deep or profound as the one he felt that morning, his unit forming an honour guard to welcome the expedition's leader.

A group of local women sauntered past on their way to the river. All wore the simple but colourful tob that covered them from neck to ankle, with a long hijab over their heads on which they balanced the heavy clay pots that they would soon fill with water. Every one of the women looked across at the smartly dressed soldiers. From the low murmur Jack heard behind him, the men had noticed the attention they were receiving. He was pleased to hear it. The more pride they felt in their appearance, the easier his task became. He wanted that pride, just as he wanted the unity he had worked hard to create. The men needed to be bonded to one another. It was that bond that would make them an effective fighting unit, more than drill or even practice with the powerful Sniders. They had to fight for one another. They had to fight for him.

Every day since Jack had issued the scarlet shirts had been filled with drill and rifle practice. He had worked the men hard. All were now proficient with the Snider, even if they still could not quite manage ten rounds a minute. At first they had struggled to learn the commands that he insisted on shouting in English, but with time they had picked up enough to know what he wanted them to do. They were fitter and stronger, but they were still not true soldiers, not as he knew them. But they were getting there. He had whittled down the ranks. Three men had been injured. Another nine he had dismissed when they had not reached the standard he had required. He was left with forty men, two musicians and the single keen young lieutenant. He had formed the cadre Sir Sam had requested, and he looked forward to being able to present them to him. They would be the one ray of light in what would likely prove to be a gloomy morning.

'Here they come.'

Jack saw the dahabiya at once. It was sailing towards the embankment, where the landing jetty had been kept free so that it was ready for the arrival of the expedition's leadership.

'God help us.' Julian Baker stood near Jack, staring at the sailing ship that carried his uncle. The words echoed the look of concern on his face.

'It's not your fault.' Jack did his best to be pleasant.

'I do hope you will tell Uncle that.'

'I might.' Jack could not resist the barb. Julian was right to be worried. Little was ready for Sir Sam's arrival. Practically all his orders and requests had been ignored, with the governor insisting that it was impossible to supply the number of vessels he had demanded. Julian had protested and argued, but his words had fallen on deaf ears. The governor's only concession had been to provide Sir Sam with a fine town house on the best street in Khartoum, where he could rest for the remainder of the season. It would fall to Julian to give his uncle the depressing news that morning, and Jack could well understand why the naval officer was dreading the moment when Sir Sam realised his expedition had suffered yet another delay.

'That's him.' Julian was watching the dahabiya closely. No sooner had the ship moored and the gangplank been set into place than the first passenger raced ashore, followed by a small group of other Europeans trailing at a more leisurely pace.

Sir Sam walked briskly towards the small welcoming party.

He was dressed in long cotton shorts that fell to the knee, over gazelle-skin gaiters that had been tanned with the skin left on and tied tight around the top to seal them off. His shirt was made of the same native cotton as the shorts, with sleeves that reached to his elbows and a turned-down collar. In place of buttons, it had a simple drawstring that ran from the collar to the bottom of the shirt front, and the cotton had been dyed a muted earthy brown colour. Around his waist he wore a thick brown leather belt lined with a number of small leather pouches of the same colour. On his feet were a pair of lightweight moccasins, whilst on his head he sported a hunting cap made from the same animal skin as his gaiters. The slightly bizarre-looking outfit was completed by the thick shank bone from a gazelle that hung on a string around his neck and bounced up and down as he approached his nephew.

To Jack's eyes, Sir Sam's clothing gave him a wild appearance, the contrast to the sophisticated gentleman he had met in Cairo stark. Yet he got the impression that the explorer was in his element here, far from civilisation, and he reckoned every part of the strange outfit was based on hard-earned experience.

He considered his own choice of dress, wondering whether he would have to effect a large number of changes to make it suitable for the journey into the wilds that would follow. He'd stolen his supremely comfortable army boots from an unfortunate officer at the climax of the march on Magdala, the man likely still cursing their loss. He wore pale grey cotton trousers and the same style of loose red shirt that he had issued to his men. Around his neck was a blue neckerchief; he had learned the value of the simple square of cotton from the Texan cavalrymen he had fought alongside in Mexico. Around his waist was a British army officer's belt, with a Beaumont–Adams five-shot revolver snug in a matching brown leather holster on his right hip, the weapon taken from the last man who had tried to kill him. On the back left-hand side of his belt was a knife about eight inches long, safely stowed in a brown leather sheath, sourced from a back-street smith in Cairo who specialised in blades so sharp they would cut at the lightest touch. Unlike his men, he wore a solar topee in place of a fez, wrapped in a pale blue pagdi, which could be unwound then used to cover his whole head if needed, protecting him from both sun and dust, the trick one he had picked up in India.

'Well, there you are!' Sir Sam cried out in greeting when he was still a dozen yards away.

'It is good to see you, Uncle.' Julian could not help wincing as he greeted the expedition's commander.

'And is that you, Jack?' Sir Sam beamed from ear to ear as he spotted him. 'Why, I hardly recognise you in that garb.'

'Good morning, sir.' Jack held his place.

Sir Sam came up to his nephew, clasping him in a giant bear hug, right hand slapping his back enthusiastically. 'It really is good to see you both.' He grinned at Jack over Julian's shoulder.

Jack could not help smiling. He had forgotten the force of the man's personality. Sir Sam exuded energy.

'And that is our cadre on parade?' Sir Sam released his nephew and addressed the question to Jack as he strode towards him, hand outstretched.

'Yes, sir.' Jack shook Sir Sam's hand then gestured towards his soldiers.

'They look fine, indeed they do.' Sir Sam walked on until he finally came to stand in front of Jack's small command.

Jack ran his eyes over the ranks, noticing the way the men straightened just a touch as they saw the expedition's leader for the first time. There were no sullen looks or pouts of disdain, just the blank, expressionless masks of soldiers the world over as they were inspected by a senior officer.

'If they fight as well as they look, then we shall be in safe hands.' Sir Sam clapped his hand onto Jack's shoulder and gave an overly firm squeeze. 'Are you proud of them, Jack?'

'Yes, sir.'

'They look fine indeed, and I would say dangerous to boot. Why, I should not want to face them on the field of battle!' Sir Sam grinned from ear to ear as he contemplated the cadre. 'They have an air about them, don't you think?' He gave Jack no time to answer. 'They look like a band of rogues, or perhaps thieves. How many are there?'

'Forty, sir.'

'Then they shall be known as the Forty Thieves!' Sir Sam clapped his hands with glee as he came up with the epithet.

Jack was not so pleased to hear his men called thieves. But Sir Sam was happy, and that was enough.

'Jack has worked hard, Uncle.' Julian was never one to stay out of a conversation for long. 'As have we all.'

'I never doubted it for one moment.' Sir Sam beamed with pleasure. 'I have a feeling we have turned a corner, gentlemen. We can now put the delay in Cairo behind us once and for all. Why, it has taken us just thirty-two days to reach you, can you credit it? And that is all the way from Suez, mind, via Souakim, then across the desert to Berber before sailing here. Thirty-two days! We could have taken twice as long and still been pleased with our progress.'

Jack and Julian shared a look. Neither was keen to be the one to reveal the truth to the ebullient expedition leader.

'Good morning, Julian. How lovely to see you.'

They were spared sharing the bitter news of the current situation as the rest of Sir Sam's party arrived. Jack saw an attractive woman smiling with pleasure as she walked towards them. She was strong-looking, he saw that immediately, just as he noted her German accent. She was not tall, and if pressed, he would guess she was in her mid to late thirties.

'Good morning, Aunt.' Julian returned the greeting, then walked forward to take careful hold of the woman's arms before kissing her on each cheek.

Jack was surprised as he realised this had to be Florence, Sir Sam's wife. She was much younger than he would have thought, prettier too. Sir Sam had clearly been batting above his average the day he had wooed her.

'This is Mr Lark.' Julian waved an arm as he introduced Jack.

'Good morning, ma'am.' Jack stepped forward, then hesitated. He was not sure if he should kiss Sir Sam's wife as Julian had done, simply shake her hand, or just nod in greeting.

Florence saw his confusion and immediately offered a hand. 'I am pleased to meet you, Mr Lark. My husband has told me much about you.'

Jack was surprised by the strength of her grip, just as he was surprised by the way she held his hand for longer than was comfortable whilst she looked him deep in the eye. The greeting, as uncomfortable as it was, at least allowed him to notice that Florence possessed deep brown eyes and a suntanned complexion that he was sure would have been shocking amidst the pallid complexions favoured by the women of London's elite.

'I am glad my husband had the sense to bring a military man with us.'

Jack was relieved as she finally let go of his hand. 'I was happy to be employed, ma'am.' As soon as the words left his mouth, he cursed the clumsy choice. It sounded like he was there simply because he needed a job.

Florence's eyes narrowed a fraction. 'Just as I think we shall be glad to have secured your services.'

It was graciously done, but Jack had no doubt that she had seen his discomfort.

'You have met my niece, I believe, Mr Lark?' She artfully brought Anna Baker into the conversation.

'I have indeed. Good morning, Miss Baker.'

'Good morning, Mr Lark.' As ever, Anna Baker's reply was cool, and she immediately turned away to talk to her brother.

Jack kept his expression neutral, even as he was snubbed.

'Come now, Flooey, leave poor Jack alone. We have work to do!' Sir Sam interrupted the polite introductions.

'Nonsense.' Florence did not hesitate to disagree. She smiled warmly at Jack. 'You must learn to ignore my husband, Mr Lark. He can be a little impatient at times.'

'As I am learning.' Jack found himself captivated by Florence's voice. Her English was faultless, yet the German accent coloured her words, giving them a unique tone and sound that was quite mesmerising. Now that she was closer, he could see the slightest hint of freckles on skin that was otherwise flawless. There was strength in her face too, something in the set of her jaw and the purposeful line of her lips that denoted a determined character.

He realised he was staring, so he deliberately turned from Florence to look towards Anna. Her choice of clothes suited her well, the long trousers and long-sleeved shirt of the same earthy brown cotton as Sir Sam's shirt fitting closely around her lean frame. She appeared to be comfortable here. There was less polish to her, for sure. He did his best to form a welcoming expression, yet before his features could move, he saw that Sir Sam's niece was watching him closely and the half-formed expression died. He had a feeling that both women could read him as easily as they could a map.

'May I present the men to you, sir?'

'Very good, Jack.' Sir Sam gave no appearance of having noticed Jack's reaction to his wife, and he positively stamped the ground at the suggestion like a horse before a hunt.

Jack nodded briskly at the two women, then began to walk towards his men. It would be a relief to get onto a safer footing. He knew where he was with soldiers. Women were quite a different matter. The thought led to a dangerous notion, one that tantalised. He glanced over his shoulder. Florence and Anna were standing together. They were talking, faces turned to one another so neither saw him look their way. They were two sides of the same coin. Both attracted him.

But no good would come from such idle fancy.

It never had.

'It is simply not good enough.' Sir Sam slammed a fist into the makeshift desktop. 'Goddammit all to hell!'

Jack noticed Julian flinch. They were in the small room Julian had taken for his office. Sir Sam was sitting in the only chair, whilst Jack and Julian stood on the other side of the desk like a pair of errant schoolboys summoned to the head-master's office.

'I gave every necessary instruction, and I had every expect-ation that the fleet and the supplies would be ready.' Sir Sam gave full vent to his fury. 'Yet it appears my instructions have been neglected!'

'I tried, Uncle. I swear. The governor would not be swayed.'

'I do not doubt you, Julian, nor do I doubt your efforts.' Sir Sam slumped back in the chair, right hand folded over his face as he tried to hide his rage from view. 'Goddammit.' The oath was delivered with less gusto than before.

'We believe the governor is lying, sir.' Jack spoke for the first time.

'What's that you say?' Sir Sam's hand moved away. The full force of his attention was directed at Jack alone.

'We believe it's nothing more than a bucketful of horseshit. A squadron of eleven vessels has been supplied to a man called Dubois. He leaves tomorrow.'

'Jack speaks the truth, sir.' Julian took a half-step forward and spoke before Jack could say anything more. 'The governor tells us one thing whilst he clearly carries on with his own agenda with no thought to the orders of either the khedive or yourself.'

'Of course. The damned man is well known for supporting the very trades the khedive requires me to suppress. But to do so openly – why, it quite beggars belief!' Sir Sam shook his head as he considered the full scale of the governor's failure to heed the instructions he had been given. 'You will have to get used to this duplicity, Jack. These fellows will smile at your face whilst holding a serpent to your throat. I knew our expedition would be unpopular, but this, this is too much! Too much indeed!' He rose to his feet. 'We shall not allow it to delay us. I will show them what an Englishman can arrange, with or without their damned assistance. Procrastination and delay be damned!'

Jack felt the passion emanating from the man. It was impressive. It was as if the shackles of polite behaviour had been cast aside now they were far from Cairo and Sir Sam was revealing his true colours. This was the man who had found the Albert N'yanza and who had earned himself a knighthood in the process. The man who had been made the first European pasha of Egypt, and who had been entrusted by the khedive himself to eradicate the slave trade and bring the rule of law and legal commerce to the Nile basin.

'What do we do?' Julian pressed his uncle.

'Do?' Sir Sam smiled wolfishly. 'I am a pasha, am I not? I outrank the damned governor. I shall requisition everything we need and damn anyone who tries to stop us.'

'It won't be easy, Uncle.'

'Of course it won't be easy.' For the first time, Sir Sam snapped. 'Nothing worthwhile ever is. That is why it takes men like us to do it.' He leaned forward, supporting his weight on his arms as he stared at his two aides. 'And we shall do it, even if I have to turn this place upside down to find all that we need. I will not be denied.'

Jack heard the force behind the words. He could feel it emanating from the man and filling the room. He did not doubt Sir Sam's ability to make good on the claim he was making.

They would move heaven and earth to get the expedition back on track. And God help anyone who tried to stop them.

Chapter Nineteen

———————◆———————

Jack stood on the waterfront and marvelled at what he saw in front of him. Every jetty was occupied, the fleet that Sir Sam had assembled stretching along the embankment. The expedition's leader had achieved the near impossible. Thirty-three vessels were now in the final stages of preparation to set off down the Nile. Despite every obstacle, the next stage of the great expedition was about to begin.

It was a mismatched flotilla. Nile dahabiyas made up the bulk of the small fleet, the simple flat-bottomed, sailing-ships-cum-barges that ploughed up and down the great river assembled here in every size and variation. Each sported two masts, one mounted near the bow, the other near the stern, and there was a single main deck that contained the cabins. All sat low in the water, and were perfectly designed for the shallow waters of the Nile. Julian had told Jack that the sailing ships had changed little for hundreds of years, and he could well believe it. There was something timeless about the dahabiyas, and their simplicity was quite captivating.

In addition, Sir Sam had managed to procure two small Nile steamers. Jack looked at the larger of the two and did his best not to worry. He had been allocated a tiny seven-foot-square cabin on the steamer that would also house Sir Sam, his wife and his niece. Julian and Marcopolo would be berthed on the second, smaller steamer. Even from a distance, Jack could tell that the larger vessel had seen better days. The iron hull was spotted with red and black blotches where the crew had done their best to patch up the damage, and the side-mounted paddle wheels were encased in metal sponsons scabbed with great patches of rust. The steamer boasted two decks, with the single tall smokestack positioned amidships. It belched a great plume of smoke into the early-morning air, the dirty grey-white cloud streaming back from the stack like a filthy ribbon, the grimy colour out of place in the clear pale blue sky.

It would not be the first steamer he had travelled on, but the contrast to the fine specimen that had taken him up the Cumberland river was obvious. This one sat lower in the water, and it was flatter too, the two decks much smaller than those on the large American steamers that had conveyed the Confederate troops to the garrison at Fort Donelson. It lacked the polish and the well-cared-for sheen of the handsome American boats. For the first time, he wondered whether the vessel he would call home for the coming months was actually capable of withstanding the rigours of the journey that lay ahead.

Each one of the thirty-three vessels had a number painted in bright white paint on both sides, and on the sails if it had them, so that the men would know which one to board. It was just one indication of the level of organisation involved in preparing the fleet for the expedition that would set sail the following day.

It had taken Sir Sam just one month. One month filled with

fighting, manoeuvring and tireless endeavour. The governor had not known what had hit him. Sir Sam had worked day and night, requisitioning every vessel he could find. It had cost him dearly, or at least it had cost the khedive. With ships in such short supply, Sir Sam had been forced to buy aged vessels at the price of new. Indeed, he had been forced to pay the highest prices for everything, and he had spent money like water. Yet there was nothing else for it. He knew he was being taken for a ride, and there was no doubt a large number of officials from the governor downwards had profited, but he would not be denied, no matter the cost.

Julian had played his part. He had worked as hard as his uncle, his naval experience proving invaluable. Jack could not help but be impressed by the young officer, who had excelled as he prepared the vessels and their crews. Yet despite the two men's best efforts, they had still struggled to find enough sailors to man the fleet. They had been forced to use the local police force to press-gang men into service, a choice neither was comfortable with. Where they were going, they would need every man to pull his weight, and there would be no place for malcontents or shirkers. Sir Sam had done what he could. Every press-ganged crewman was offered pay far in excess of anything he could hope to earn from any other form of employment, along with the promise of handsome bonuses in the years to come. Only time would tell if the financial incentives would be enough.

It was not just the flotilla that had taken up Sir Sam's time. The irregular cavalry he had been given had been dismissed the day after he had inspected them for the first time. To his eyes, they had been far from fit for purpose. Getting rid of the cavalry had also removed the problem of transporting a couple of hundred horses, something that might have been possible had the fleet been assembled as he had requested, but that now, with the mismatched and patchwork flotilla at his disposal, was quite impractical. He had also reduced the size of his infantry contingent. There was room now for just six hundred and fifty of the men the khedive had passed into his command. The rest were to remain at Khartoum and wait for the arrival of the second column under the command of the expedition's chief engineer, which was still lumbering its way south on the overland route from Cairo. It would mean Sir Sam would have to rely on Jack's Forty Thieves more than ever, something he had impressed on him at their last briefing.

'Do I take it from your expression that you are not overly impressed by our new home, Mr Lark?'

Jack stood up straighter as he realised that Anna Baker was standing at his side. He had not heard her arrive, and he wondered how long she had been standing there before she had spoken. As ever, he felt a moment's discomfort being in her presence. He had not spoken to her many times since she had arrived in Khartoum, but every conversation, no matter how short, had proven her to be too sharp and quick-witted for an easy exchange, and he felt his guard come up as she spoke to him.

'So long as it stays afloat, I'll be happy.' He glanced down. Her hair was arranged in braids that were laid across her scalp then tied behind her head with black ribbons. The choice of hairstyle left her face open, and he saw for the first time that there was a spark of amusement in her eyes that he had not noticed before, as if she was privy to a joke no one else had been told. She was also much shorter than he was, perhaps only just over five feet tall in her walking boots.

'I doubt my brother would engage the vessel if it were not seaworthy.'

He did his best not to wince as she reacted to what she had clearly understood as thinly veiled censure of her brother's nautical ability. 'I'm sure it'll be fine.'

'I am glad you are sure, Mr Lark. Have you stowed away your baggage?'

'I have.' He had to clear his throat as he answered.

'I hope you have not over-packed. It will be cramped conditions for us all.'

'I have not.' He wished he could say something that would change the tone of the conversation. Yet he could not think of a single thing. He had never lost his awkwardness at being in a world far removed from the one he had been born into. He would never be smooth in polite society like Julian Baker, or as confident as Sir Sam, and he was too old and too battered by the life he had led to be able to change what he was. There was just one place where he knew he belonged, and it was as far removed from a polite conversation with an educated young woman as could be.

'Ah, so speaks the experienced soldier.'

Jack tried to work out if he was being mocked. He could no more read Anna's expression than he could decipher the charts of the rivers they would follow that Julian had pored over as he planned their route south.

'I do believe you are the first soldier I have ever met who does not speak of his experiences of battle.' The remark was made rather pointedly. 'Usually I have to ask them to stop regaling me with their accounts of derring-do. Yet you, Mr Lark, you say nothing much at all. Does that mean you are quite bereft of such stories?'

'No.' Jack kept his eyes on the steamer, doing his best to hide his discomfort. 'I have a few.' He tried to sound glib, but the words came out deadpan. The truth was that he had more tales than he could tell in a lifetime of chit-chat. Few were suitable for a lady's ears.

'Will you tell me one?'

'Perhaps another time.'

'But you served for many years?'

'Yes.' From the corner of his eye he could see Anna looking up at him, yet he stared resolutely ahead. He was not enjoying the probing conversation, but a part of him still did not want it to end.

'And you have fought?'

'I was just a soldier. I did what I was told.' He tried to answer as briefly as he could.

'I do not think you are telling me the truth. I can see you have been in the wars.'

To his surprise, she reached out then, and her fingers brushed across the top of his hand, her touch gossamer light. It lasted no more than a moment before her hand retreated.

'I have a few scars, that is true.' Jack looked at Sir Sam's niece then. He did not shirk from her searching gaze. Her touch lingered.

Anna smiled for the first time. It was a warm smile and her eyes sparked with devilment. 'I can see. The one on your face is displayed to the world. You rather hide behind it.'

Jack opened his mouth, a quick retort half formed in his brain. And there it remained, the words quite unable to emerge.

'Does it hurt?'

'No.' He could not read the emotions he saw reflected in her eyes.

'Yet it pains you.' It was a statement, not a question.

'Yes.'

'I can see it.' Anna reached out once again and took hold of his wrist. Her hand was chill against skin that felt on fire.

'Are you cold?' he asked.

'No, I am fine.' The answer was given quickly. 'It is nice to be outside. I confess I felt a little too confined when we journeyed here. Cabin fever, I think they call it.'

'I know what you mean.'

The conversation paused, both content to stand there. It was Anna who broke the silence.

'You are a quiet man, Mr Lark. You hold yourself close.'

Jack absorbed the perceptive remark. Of all of the ladies he had met in the last few months, she was the first to venture past the polite conversation of strangers.

'Sometimes I don't think I have much worth saying.'

'I doubt that very much.'

'You're wrong. There's not a lot to tell, at least nothing interesting. As you said, who wants to hear a soldier's tales of wars fought and battles won and lost.'

'You are being evasive, Mr Lark.'

'No. Truly, I have nothing to tell that is worth hearing.' Jack was not lying. He did not believe there was anything in his past that would offer entertainment.

'I do not think that is true.' Anna squeezed his wrist, then let go. 'Perhaps this expedition will provide you with a tale that will be fit for conversation.'

'Perhaps.' Jack's skin felt cold now that her hand had left it.

'Or perhaps it will be so dull and tiresome that you will wish you had never accepted my uncle's offer of employment.'

'Perhaps.'

'Perhaps!' This time Anna mocked him openly. 'Which do you hope for, Mr Lark? Even a man who holds himself as close as you must have a desire for something more than a life that is quite dull.'

'No. I am content with dull.' Jack lied easily enough. He would never reveal what truly dwelt in his soul.

'You sound just like my husband. He was always too busy for adventure.'

'You are married?' Jack could not hold back the question. The revelation surprised him. He was not sure quite why.

'I was. He died. Influenza. We were married for less than a year.'

'I'm sorry.'

'Don't be. It is far in the past. And if truth be told, he was a dull man. He had few ambitions beyond burying himself away in a house in the country with a dozen dogs to take out shooting. The rest of his time he spent with his nose in his accounts or in his books. He was a good man, I suppose. But he lacked spark. He would certainly have hated it here. He was not a man for an expedition and he would never have come to a place like this. He was too busy doing nothing.' Jack heard little sadness in her tone. She was matter-of-fact, nothing more.

'Perhaps he was just sensible,' he said. 'It sounds like he had a good life and knew it. There are plenty who would be envious.'

'I am sure there are.' For the first time, Anna's voice rose, her deadpan facade cracking open just a fraction. 'I know I sound spoiled. Or arrogant, perhaps. I am very aware that there are many women who would enjoy the life I was given, who would relish the chance to run a household and have their husband's children.' She stopped talking rather abruptly, as if she had steered a course into a dangerous area, the oblique reference to procreation some sort of terrible faux pas.

'Yes. There are.' Jack did not hold back the needling comment. He had known women with no choice but to sell themselves to feed their families, and others who had near starved to death before being condemned to the workhouse. They could only have dreamed of the life Anna had led, a life she had clearly hated. Yet he did not feel she was wrong, or guilty of some heinous selfish crime. He could no more despise her for having walked away from the life Fate had allocated to her than he could hate himself for having done exactly the same thing.

'It was just not for me.' The words were spoken quietly, as much to herself as to Jack. 'There is more to this world than ledgers and accounts. You cannot measure your life as if it is no more than profit and loss.'

Jack heard the trace of a long-felt frustration in her words. He did not want to probe deeper. He sensed there were demons in her past. Of all people, he knew not to stir such creatures into life.

'My husband died without ever having lived. Does that make sense to you, Mr Lark? He lived his life with such caution that he forgot to enjoy a single moment of it. He was just . . .' she paused as she struggled to find the right word, 'he was just dull.' She settled on the word she had used earlier.

Jack noted the information. 'I think he was a lucky man.'

'To be dull?'

'He was lucky that his life was so safe that it allowed him to be dull.'

'Is it not better to live, just a little?'

'Perhaps. But if you live your life on the edge, you are

handing yourself to Fate. She won't let you go, not when she
has taken hold. And once you take that first step, your life is
no longer yours to control. Sometimes you slip off that edge.
Your adventures come to a rather grisly end and there is
nothing you can do to prevent it. So yes, I think your husband
was a lucky man.'

'He still died.'

'We all die. None of us knows when or how it will happen.
It doesn't matter if it is on some dumb-fool adventure or sitting
in your armchair by the fire. Death will find you whenever
Fate decides that it's your time. There's really bugger-all you
can do about it.'

'You make it sound like we have no choice in the manner of
the life we live.' Anna did not react to his language.

'We don't. Not really. We like to think we do. We like to
think we choose what risks we take, what dangers we face
and which we avoid. We believe we can change our fate by
being bolder, or stronger, or quicker-witted. But the fact of
the matter is that no matter what we do, no matter what we
strive for, there is nothing we can do to change whatever is
ordained.' Jack answered her honestly. Once he had lived on
his wits, hiding his true self from others and trying to make
his own future, one far removed from the life allotted to him.
He no longer bothered. He faced the world as himself, without
hope or ambition. He was Jack Lark. Nothing more. Nothing
less.

'How very fatalistic.' Anna's eyes were moist and brimming
with tears. He did not quite know why.

'It's just what I've seen.' He tutted to himself as he acknowledged how he sounded. 'I apologise. I can be rather dour
at times.'

'Do not apologise to me. I expect your opinion is based on experience.'

He nodded. It was another perceptive response. 'Perhaps I'm wrong. I wouldn't be surprised. I've been wrong about a lot of things in my time.' He paused, taking a deep breath then holding the warm air in his lungs until it burned. He exhaled slowly. 'I'm sure I'm right about one thing, though.' He wanted to change tack. There were times when sticking to the trivial and mundane had its advantages.

'What is that?' Anna arched an eyebrow at the shift in his tone.

'Your husband was indeed a lucky man.'

'Why?'

'Because he was married to you.' Jack grinned as he cast the line.

Anna laughed. 'How very gallant of you.'

He enjoyed the sound of her laughter. She pressed closer, reaching out to hold on to his arm for a moment. It promised more, much more, but he did not know if he wanted more.

She pulled away, then lifted a hand to tuck an errant strand of hair behind her ear. 'I have enjoyed our conversation, Mr Lark. Thank you for being so very kind.'

Jack grimaced at her choice of words. He was not kind. Not really. He was a selfish bastard who lived life as he found it, taking what he wanted and discarding anything that did not interest him. He knew what he was. And what he wasn't.

'It was my pleasure. Now I am afraid I must return to the barracks. Your brother will wonder where I am.' He heard the coldness in the words as he spoke them.

'Of course.' Anna stepped away from him, breaking the

connection that had somehow formed between them. 'I am sure you have much to do.'

'Indeed.' Jack nodded his head in lieu of a farewell, then turned away. The conversation would linger, he knew that, as would the touch of her hand on his.

Yet he was not the man he had once been, the man who would have pursued his desire no matter the cost. Coldness was buried deep in the very core of his being where no one could reach it. Not even someone like Anna Baker.

Chapter Twenty

Outside Khartoum, 8 February 1870

The battery of cannon mounted on Fort Omdurman fired their salute, four puffs of smoke billowing from the embrasures and lingering in the still, lifeless air. Jack stood at the rail of the steamer, looking at the fort and following the streaks of mucky grey that sullied what was yet another beautiful morning. Sir Sam was close by with his wife and niece, yet Jack had done his best to sidle away from the family group so that he could stand alone as the flotilla set sail. They might be departing many months late, but there was a sense of anticipation in the air. Jack could feel it, like the tension in the sky before a summer thunderstorm. The expedition was finally setting sail on the second leg of its long journey, one that would see it sail south and into the remote lands beyond Khartoum.

The steamer's paddle wheel dug hard at the murky waters of the Blue Nile as the plucky vessel churned its way west. The flotilla would turn south when they rounded Fort Omdurman, breaking into the clearer waters of the White Nile. They would then follow the river south, their first destination the town of

Gondokoro, one and a half thousand miles away. Sir Sam estimated that that leg of the journey would take the best part of a month. It sounded an inordinate amount of time, yet the prospect did not do anything to quell the rising excitement Jack could feel squirming deep in his gut. He was heading back to the lands where the rule of law meant nothing.

A crisp volley of musket fire roared out. He flinched. He had heard the sound a thousand times, yet it never lost the power to thrill. It resonated in the depths of his being, a reminder of how he had arrived where he was that day.

He looked across to the two battalions of infantry lined up along the embankment, barely able to see them now that the cloud of powder smoke created by the discharge of their muskets lingered over them like a cloud. It was a decent enough send-off. The governor might have frustrated Sir Sam and delayed their departure by several weeks, but at least he was giving them a fitting farewell. Jack couldn't help wondering if it was inspired by an overwhelming sense of relief as he finally removed a thorn from his side.

The faintest taint of rotten eggs reached Jack's nostrils. The smell of powder was barely discernible, but still it brought alive memories of the battlefield, a place he had come to love and fear in equal measure. He gripped the steamer's rail tightly, replaying the moment of going into action. Lost in that moment, he was no longer watching the city of Khartoum sail past, but instead was riding with the Bombay Lights as they charged the Persian square at Khoosh-Ab, remembering the surge of joy as the Persian Fars broke in front of him. An intoxicating mix of exhilaration and horror surged through him once again – the chaos of the battlefield, his horse's hooves crushing the bodies of the dead and the dying, the slaughter as men ran for their lives. The British light cavalrymen had been unstoppable that day, the troopers butchering hundreds of enemy soldiers, so the ground was carpeted with the broken bodies of the men who had dared to stand against the might of the British Empire. It had been a moment when revulsion and elation had intertwined, the gruesome and the glorious woven so tightly together that he could not discern which was which, neither then nor now. Yet he knew that he had felt alive, even in the midst of such butchery, just as he had only felt truly himself when he had stormed into the chaos of the breach at Delhi, or when he had dared the Confederate soldiers to follow him as they charged the Union defenders hiding behind the thicket hedge at Shiloh. He was no warrior, he had learned that the hard way. His ability to survive was not down to talent, to being a better soldier or a stronger fighter than any other man on the field of battle. He owed his survival to the capricious whim of Fate and nothing more. Yet even knowing that did not stop him from wanting to go back there. It did not stop him wanting to be what he was meant to be.

'It feels good to be leaving, does it not, Mr Lark?'

Jack started as he heard someone address him. It was Florence.

'Yes.' The word came out somewhat gruffly, so he cleared his throat and tried again. 'It is a relief to be on our way.' He wondered how long Sir Sam's wife had been standing there. Had she seen something of his thoughts reflected on his face? Could she somehow discern the darkness in his soul that craved the chance to return to the field of battle? The thoughts flittered across his mind, as skittish as a newly hatched butterfly.

'My husband was not sure this day would come. But here it is.' Florence stepped to the rail.

Jack smiled at the colour her German accent gave her English. He also caught a whiff of her perfume as she came closer, the delicate fragrance chasing away the lingering smell of spent powder.

They stood in silence watching the waterfront slide past. The steamer was far from quiet, the metallic grumble of its engine and the thrashing of the paddle wheel creating a cacophony of sound. Yet Jack did not mind it. There was a wonderful rhythm to the twin noises, a pulsating, hypnotic score that spoke of power and purpose. It was as if someone had imprisoned an elemental beast deep in the bowels of the steamer and were channelling its strength so that they could push against the waters of the Nile and go wherever they wanted, irrespective of wind or tide.

'My husband tells me your men are in fine fettle.' Florence had to raise her voice to be heard.

'They still have a lot to learn.'

'I am sure you will be able to teach them. We have a long journey ahead. The first weeks should be easy enough, I think. It will only get harder later.'

'You have been this way before, ma'am?'

'Yes. My husband and I were here back in sixty-five. Of course, it was very different then.'

'How so?' Jack felt inclined to draw Sir Sam's wife into a longer conversation than she perhaps had sought. A few rogue hairs had escaped her braids and now whispered across her face. He found himself captivated by the movement as they flitted back and forth in the breeze. He also saw that Florence had added a necklace to her outfit, one that appeared to be made from a number of large animal claws.

'Khartoum was a wild place then. My husband apprehended

a slaver the moment we arrived. Mahomed Her, his name was.' Florence looked across the waters of the Nile as she remembered. 'He was a devil, that one. My husband had him charged, tried and bastinadoed.'

'Bastinadoed?'

'It means flogged, Mr Lark. On the sole of the foot. One hundred and fifty lashes.'

Jack winced. He had seen a number of punishments in his time. Men flogged until the skin of their backs resembled offal. Others who had been buried in the sand up to their necks, then left as food for any hungry animal that passed by. Yet something about the idea of being whipped on one's bare feet felt inordinately cruel. A man punished in such a way would be unable to walk properly ever again.

'I watched, Mr Lark. It took a long time.'

Jack sensed Florence was observing him closely, so he kept his face neutral. 'I am sure he deserved it.'

'He did. I would have hanged him there and then. I would even have tied the rope around his neck myself.'

Jack glanced at her. Her face was set firm. There was no doubt in his mind that she meant what she said. It appeared it was not just her necklace that had claws.

'This whole area looks to have changed a great deal since I was here last.' She stood a step forward and held fast to the rail. 'They call the area to the south of Khartoum the Jazira. For many years it was thought to be impenetrable, at least for a white man.'

'Or woman.' Jack was quick to interject.

Florence giggled. 'Ha, yes, Mr Lark, or a woman.'

He was pleased to have made her laugh. She had a generous mouth that was well suited to it. There were fine lines around her eyes, as if she laughed a great deal. The flaws added to her attraction, the lack of perfection somehow making her seem more real. Anna was different. Her skin was flawless, and he had barely ever seen a single hair out of place on any of the occasions he had met her. But apart from that, and their respective ages, the two women were very similar. They were not related by blood, yet there was something that connected them. He was seeing it here for the first time in Florence, just as he had seen it in Anna the previous day. Perhaps it was that they had both escaped the confines of polite society, and that now Fate would let them be who they were meant to be.

'The Jazira is not a kind place,' Florence continued. 'There are clouds of tsetse flies and mosquitoes so dense that you cannot see what is directly in front of your face. Then there is the Sudd. It blocks the river for months at a time and makes all travel impossible.'

'What is the Sudd?' Jack was enjoying the lecture.

'It is the name given by the locals to the great islands of vegetation that form in the river. They are matted together so tightly that not even a steamer can get through.'

'So people do live there?'

'Of course. The Nilotic tribes once thrived in those lands. There are the Bongo, the Bari and the Loquia, among many others. They were once so numerous that the first Arabs to come to the area called it *bilad-as-sudan*. The land of the blacks.' Florence translated for him.

'You said they once thrived. What happened?'

Florence nodded in approval at his perceptive question. 'The Egyptians happened. They first came here in the twenties. The khedive of those times, Mohammad Ali Pasha, conquered the Sudan, beating the Funj sultanate that had assumed some vestige of control over the tribes. They created two new provinces in the forties, with capitals at Fashoda and Gondokoro. Then they set about trying to modernise the country. They brought in new crops, settled some of the nomadic tribes, built hospitals in both capitals, and tried to link the land with railways and telegraph lines. They set up schools for the children of the tribes, established a postal system and opened up the southern reaches of the Nile with steamers. They tried to emulate you British, I think.'

Jack nodded at the remark. He had spent time in India and had seen the efforts of the British to force their version of civilisation on the country. He had also lived with a maharajah and seen the effect of that modernisation from the other side.

'But they failed. Little of what they did lasted. Then came the slavers and the traders. They own these lands now.' The tone of Florence's voice changed, becoming laden with sadness. 'The tribes here have been decimated, and nearly all the wildlife has gone. Within ten years, the area around Khartoum was emptied, and so these ruthless souls have pressed further and further south and west, searching far and wide for slaves to sell and animals to kill.'

'But not for much longer.'

Florence looked at him sharply, her right hand lifting to shield her eyes from the morning sun. 'No, Mr Lark, not for long now. My husband loathes these men as much as I do. He will not rest until they have been scoured from this land.'

Jack noticed that her eyes were moist. It was a reminder that this woman had once been a slave herself, or at least had found herself as a commodity for sale in a slave market.

He stayed silent, letting her words settle. He did not want to cause her any more pain.

Together they looked out across the river. The steamer was thrashing along at a steady rate, and already they were not far from the junction with the White Nile.

Jack watched an odd-looking black and white stork skim across the water and haul itself into the air. It was one of the ugliest birds he had ever seen. It had what appeared to be a half-red, half-black naked head above a grotesque pink neck the colour of raw pork.

'The poor marabou.' Florence watched the bird as it spread its wings and soared up and away from the waters of the Blue Nile. 'It is not a handsome bird.'

'No.' Jack could only agree.

'But look there.' She pointed out another group of birds gathered together in shallow water near the bank. 'The proud crest crane.'

These birds were far more handsome than the maligned marabou. Standing on long, skinny black legs, they did indeed look proud, even slightly noble, at least to Jack's eyes. He was no ornithologist, but there was much to be admired in the crescent of feathers the colour of fresh straw that stuck bolt upright on the bird's head, whilst the front of its wattle was a bright shock of red. Its forehead was decorated with stumpy dark feathers that shimmered as it moved. The rest of the plumage was just as fine, with long black feathers across the back whilst the rest was coloured red and yellow.

'It is said that the local tribes rely on the crest crane to tell them the time of day, as its call changes from morning to night. It is even said to dance.' Florence started to clap, then began to sing.

Sah ein Knab' ein Röslein stehn,
Röslein auf der Heiden,
War so jung und morgenschön,
Lief er schnell es nah zu sehn,
Sag's mit vielen Freuden,
Röslein, Röslein, Röslein rot,
Röslein auf der Heiden.

The cranes located the source of the singing and started to bob their heads as if in time to the song.

'See!' Florence laughed loudly. 'They dance!'

Jack couldn't help but laugh too. Florence had an infectious personality.

'I see you two are getting on famously.'

He turned to see that Sir Sam had come to join them.

'We are. Mr Lark is a good student. He is learning the names of all the birds.' Florence patted Jack's arm as she delivered the praise, giving it a quick squeeze as she did so.

'That is capital indeed. And I am sure you make for a fine teacher, Flooey.' Sir Sam reached out and slipped an arm around his wife's waist.

Jack watched his new commander closely. Sir Sam smiled warmly enough, but there was something else in his gaze. A warning perhaps? Or just a trace of displeasure at seeing his wife with another man, no matter how innocent the occasion. Jack noted it, and understood. He was impressed by Florence. Sir Sam was right to be worried. Jack found his wife captivating. He pushed the thought away as soon as it popped into his mind. He was not there to chase another man's wife. Or his niece, for that matter.

He did his best to smile and nod as Sir Sam pointed out

another wading bird that had emerged from the rushes at the river's edge. It was safer to take an interest in the wildlife. It was less likely to get him into trouble.

Chapter Twenty-one

———◆◆◆———

*J*ack marched at the head of his men, looking ahead at the government station of Fashoda. The fortified town looked sturdy enough, with a high wall with tall flanking towers stationed at regular intervals. The town stood at the centre of a wide swathe of flat ground surrounded by interminable marshes, and it dominated the river, its situation giving it the power to control the traffic journeying to and from Khartoum.

Sir Sam led the column with his wife, niece and nephew, whilst Mr Marcopolo brought up the rear, where he led a party of thirty men carrying gifts for the governor of Fashoda, as well as the sacks and water barrels that Sir Sam hoped would soon be filled. The main body of the column was made up of Jack and his Forty Thieves, his men happy to have been given the opportunity to stretch their legs and get off the ships for a time. The journey from Khartoum had taken just over four days, the one hundred and eighteen miles passing quite without incident. They had arrived early that morning, and Sir Sam had dispatched a messenger to let the town's officials know of their arrival. The main column had set off as soon as it was light enough to safely follow the narrow path through the marsh.

They were drawing a crowd. Children pranced and capered along the sides of the embankment. All were naked, yet they showed no shame, some even bravely stepping onto the causeway and doing their best to mimic the marching soldiers. A few adults stood in silence and watched as the armed column approached, their expressions carved from granite. Thanks to Sir Sam's briefing that morning, Jack knew that most of the locals came from the Shilluk tribe, which was related to the much larger Dinka tribe. They had long ago been subdued by the Egyptian forces and now lived in peaceful co-existence with the occupying soldiers.

As they reached the end of the causeway, Jack saw that the main gate to the town was wide open. A party of officials waited there. Some wore the dark blue of officers in the Egyptian army, whilst others were dressed in the ubiquitous cream linen suits that seemed to be the unofficial uniform of officials throughout North Africa. At least two wore bright white galabia, the local dress somehow out of place amidst the uniforms and suits.

'Welcome! Welcome!' A tall figure stepped forward as the Europeans leading the column came close to the gateway. Jack watched as the man swept towards Sir Sam, his arms outstretched in an exaggerated gesture of welcome.

'Ali Bey!' Sir Sam called out as the two came together, embracing in a warm bear hug. 'It is good to see you, my friend.' He released the man, then held him at arm's length as he studied his face. 'It has been too long.'

'Too long indeed.' The official beamed. 'And now you bring friends.' His English was flawless, with just a trace of an accent colouring the words. 'But wait, do my eyes deceive me, or do I see that your beautiful wife has once again accompanied you on your expedition.'

'I would not be without her.' Sir Sam gestured Florence forward. 'My dear, you remember Ali Bey.'

'Of course.' Florence kissed the tall official demurely on both cheeks. 'It is good to see you again.'

'I also have the pleasure of presenting my nephew, Julian, and my niece, Anna.' Sir Sam was positively glowing with a mix of pride and happiness as he introduced his family.

Jack lifted an arm and signalled to his men to halt well short of the greetings. It gave him the chance to inspect the man Sir Sam was so pleased to meet. The governor was well over six feet tall, and handsome in an ascetic, gaunt fashion. He was certainly suave and charming, two traits he demonstrated most admirably as he greeted the rest of Sir Sam's family with fulsome delight.

'And I must introduce you to one more person, Ali Bey.'

To Jack's chagrin, Sir Sam beckoned him over. 'Jack! Please do come and meet the governor.'

Doing his best to keep his face neutral, Jack stepped forward.

'This is Mr Jack Lark. He commands my best men.' Sir Sam made the generous introduction.

'Then I am pleased to meet you, Mr Lark.' The governor came at Jack, hand outstretched.

His handshake was firm to the point of being painful, his long, bony fingers holding on far too long for Jack's liking. Despite the tight grip, Jack made sure to study the other man closely. The governor's eyes were so dark they appeared almost black, and he saw no spark or light there. Whatever Ali Bey was saying, and no matter how widely he smiled, none of that friendliness was reflected in his eyes. For a moment, Jack was reminded of the eyes of a Texan rattlesnake. Ali Bey's had the same flatness to them, as if he regarded the whole world as either prey or threat.

'So.' He finally released Jack's hand, then addressed the group as a whole. 'Welcome to you all.'

'I trust all is well here?' Sir Sam posed the question as the introductions ended.

'Of course. My town thrives.'

'I am pleased to hear it. I cannot say the same of Khartoum. The place is almost a ghost town. It seems the khedive's efforts to eradicate the slave trade from his domain are having an effect. I am glad to hear that Fashoda is not suffering the same fate.'

'No, no, no. We are doing very nicely here, very nicely indeed.' Ali Bey's smile never faltered.

'But what of the slave trade? Fashoda was once an important staging post on the route to Khartoum. Is that no longer so?' Sir Sam spoke innocently enough, but his eyes narrowed.

'No, no. I will always follow most faithfully the instructions and orders of my master the khedive.' Ali Bey was suitably scandalised at the very notion. 'I assure you there are no slaves passing through my station.'

'None at all?'

'None!' He laughed. 'We are simple traders here now. Ivory and gum arabic. But we also have a new trade, one that you will not quite believe.' He steered the conversation towards firmer ground. It was slickly done. 'Ostrich feathers! Can you believe that? I tell you, the traders here cannot find enough of them.' He gave an exaggerated shrug. 'I suppose it must be the fashion in Europe now, although why such beautiful women would feel the need to distract with fanciful items is quite beyond me.' He offered a half-bow towards the two ladies. 'But enough of this for the moment. I think perhaps we should continue these most fascinating discussions somewhere a little more comfortable. I have prepared refreshments that I hope will be to your taste. Your men can retire to the barracks, where I have ordered food and drink to be prepared for them also, and I have ordered water and supplies to be prepared for you to take back to your ships. Never shall it be said that Fashoda does not know how to welcome its friends!' He preened as he made the claim, clearly enjoying being the centre of attention.

'That is very good of you.' Sir Sam could not have looked happier.

'Then follow me!' Ali Bey turned and led the way towards the town's open gate.

Jack hung back to let the others go first. Ali Bey was too slick for his liking. There was an oiliness to his charm. His earlier comparison to a snake seemed to sit rather well; he would no more trust Ali Bey than he would a cornered rattle-snake.

'Do come along, Mr Lark.' Anna had turned back, and now chivvied Jack to hurry. She pitched her voice low so that her words would not carry.

'I thought I might stay with my men.' Jack glanced over his shoulder. The Forty Thieves stood in formation, the men still and silent, just as they should be.

Anna shook her head at the idea. 'I think my uncle would want you with him.'

Jack grimaced. He would be far happier in the barracks with his men than he would be enduring the polite chit-chat and hobnobbing that would surely be the order of the day if he accompanied Sir Sam and the governor.

'I see that idea does not appeal.' She read his expression easily enough.

'No,' he replied sulkily. He really did not want to go.

'But you cannot just slip away, not now you have been introduced.'

'No one will miss me.'

'Do not be so childish,' she rebuked him.

'Childish?' Jack was a little taken aback.

'Yes, childish. You are pouting like a petulant schoolboy.'

His eyes widened.

'Oh, don't look all innocent.' Anna gave him no time to reply. 'You are terrible at concealing your thoughts, Mr Lark. At least in this regard.'

'What do you mean?'

'I mean that normally you hide your every emotion away. Yet today your expression makes it very clear that you do not like the governor.'

'I don't.'

'And on what do you base that opinion? You have only just met him.'

'I don't trust him. He's more slippery than a snake-oil salesman.'

Anna pulled a face. 'You are very quick to form an opinion.'

'I'm a good judge of character.'

'And oh so modest.' She shook her head in exasperation.

Jack laughed. He knew he shouldn't, but he could not hold it back. He was being arrogant. But he was also right. He knew it. Ali Bey was good at putting on a show, but that was all that it was, a show.

'Mr Lark, please,' Anna chided.

'Oh, come on. You must see it.' Jack said nothing more, instead turning towards his cadre and el-Sisi, who stood in front of the first rank with the drummer and bugler either side of him. 'Take the men inside. Make sure they behave themselves. I'll join you as soon as I can.'

'Sir.' El-Sisi saluted.

Jack turned back to Anna. 'You are too quick to trust, Miss Baker.'

Anna's brow furrowed. 'I do not believe that is the case.'

'I do. You asked me why I don't like that slimy shit. So now I ask you. Why do you trust him?'

Anna blushed at his choice of words, but she did not dodge the question. 'I have faith in my uncle's judgement.'

'That's not what I asked.'

'But that is enough for me. As it should be for you.'

'No.'

'No?'

'It is never enough to hide behind someone else's view. I'll make my own mind up about people.'

'You have a high opinion of yourself, Mr Lark.'

'And yours is too low of yourself,' Jack replied with a snap in his voice. 'You are clever and intelligent and yet you follow your uncle like a hound.'

Anna's eyebrows shot up in surprise at being addressed in such a way. 'I do not,' she huffed.

'Think for yourself, Anna.' Jack used her given name without thinking. He was speaking the truth. It was why he was no good at polite chit-chat. In the end, he got either bored or annoyed, and that loosened the lashings that should have held his tongue in check. No good had ever come of his speaking his mind.

'I trust my uncle.'

'Good. Trust him. But do not follow blindly.'

'And what of you, Mr Lark? Here you are, following my uncle just as I do.' Anna turned the tables. 'Why are you here?'

'I chose to be here.'

'Did you?' Anna regarded him questioningly. 'There were many bidders for your services then?'

Jack barked a short laugh. 'No.'

'Then why are you here?' She repeated the question.

'Because I had nowhere else to go.' He answered honestly. 'And I believe your uncle will give me what I want.'

'Which is?'

For the first time, he hesitated. Anna was right: he held himself close, revealing as little of himself as he could. Yet now he felt something shift. 'I crave to be free, Anna. I have learned that I do not fit in. Not in Cairo. Not in London. Not anywhere there are nice, polite, civilised people. There is just one place I can be me.'

'And where is that?' she probed.

He could feel her gaze boring into him. Yet like her, he did not shirk from the question. 'Here.'

'Here?' The answer surprised her. 'In Shilluk country?'

'Yes. And no.' Jack wanted to be clear, to make her understand. 'I don't want to be *here*.' He pointed at the dusty soil under his boots. 'I want to be *here*.' He held out his arms, gesturing around him.

'Why?'

'Because there are no constraints here. It doesn't matter

where I was born, or who my father was. It doesn't matter about all the bad things I've done. None of that matters. Not here. Here I can just be me.' His arms dropped to his sides as he finished speaking. 'I suspect that doesn't make a whole lot of sense.'

'No.' Anna shook her head forcefully 'It makes perfect sense.' She paused, suddenly quiet. 'I feel the same.'

'Have you done bad things then?' Jack tried to sound glib, but the words came out rather flat. It was rare for him to be so candid. He did not fully understand why he had chosen to reveal the truth to her. But he did not regret it.

'I rather think we need to go inside. That young man over there is going to have a fit if we stay out here much longer.' Anna diverted the question away.

'Yes. You are probably right.' Jack glanced at the young official, who was hopping from foot to foot as he waited for them to enter the town. 'It looks like the poor fellow is about to explode.' He gestured towards the gate. 'After you.'

'No.' Anna smiled. It lit up her face. 'We can go in together.'

Chapter Twenty-two

―――――•‡•―――――

17 February 1870

*J*ack stood at Sir Sam's side at the bow of the steamer. He had never seen a sight like the one that confronted them.

'The Sudd.' Sir Sam breathed the words.

'Is there another way?' Jack saw creases of concern on the other man's face.

The great mass of floating vegetation stretched from one bank of the White Nile to the other. It stank, the air filled with the rich, heady aroma of rotting weeds and foul sludge. The islands of the Sudd had matted together to form one pulsating morass of putrid, decaying gloop, the dense, spongy mass forming a solid dam that appeared to have changed the entire river into little more than one enormous marshland. There was no sight of the Nile itself amidst the mounds of muck, its waters completely smothered.

'Perhaps.' Sir Sam stared ahead, his mind clearly elsewhere.

'You summoned me, my pasha,' Marcopolo called out as he scurried towards them.

'Have you seen this?' Sir Sam threw out an arm and pointed at the Sudd.

'Yes, my pasha.' Marcopolo's face fell. 'It is not good. Not good at all.'

'No.' Sir Sam gritted his teeth. 'God damn those delays.' He hissed the words with genuine venom. Then he sighed. 'I apologise for my language. But if only we could have been here earlier.' He offered a tight smile to Jack.

Jack waved away the apology. 'Is there another way through, Mr Marcopolo?' He was no sailor, but he could see there was no way the flotilla could just sail on down the river.

'I have been speaking to our guides, Mr Lark. There is another way.'

'The Bahr Giraffe?' Sir Sam spoke before Mr Marcopolo could draw breath.

'Yes, my pasha.'

'What's the Bahr Giraffe?' Jack wanted to know more. Sir Sam had spoken the name of the alternative route in the tone of voice men reserved for a path they did not want to take.

'It is a tributary of the White Nile.' Sir Sam once again looked ahead, as if he hoped to find a route through the choking morass if he just searched hard enough.

'But it is not a good route?' Jack pressed.

'No. At best the Bahr Giraffe is seventy yards wide, but for most of its length it is no more than fifty. And it is shallow, perhaps too shallow.'

'But we can get through?'

'Perhaps.' Sir Sam grimaced. 'I have heard conflicting accounts concerning the possibility of navigating it. Although many traders are said to favour it this season, I doubt any have a steamer even half the size of ours. The waters will be dreadfully low at this time of year. We may find ourselves marooned, and there will be no turning back. We will be stuck there for the rest of the season until the rains come.'

'What is the alternative? Turn back and wait at Khartoum?'

'That would be the prudent approach.'

'But?'

'But it would mean a delay of many more months.'

Jack could see Sir Sam was wrestling with the decision. It was not an easy one. If they changed course and entered the Bahr Giraffe, it sounded like there was every chance they could find themselves stuck in the middle of nowhere for months. It was not a palatable option, but neither was turning tail and heading back to Khartoum to wait for the rivers to clear.

For once, Jack was glad he was not in command. These were the decisions that could cost men their lives. Ordering a return to Khartoum was the safe course of action, but it would achieve nothing. If they tried the Bahr Giraffe and became marooned, they would be in a perilous situation, far from any assistance. Yet if they could get through, then the mission could continue. It was not easy balancing the risks against the chance of success. Yet few decisions were easy, not once you reached a position of command. It was why leaders like Sir Sam were paid more and given the respect of their rank.

Thus far, the going had been good. The previous day they had reached the junction with the Sobat river, which according to Julian's calculation meant they had covered some six hundred and eighty-four miles from Khartoum.

The Sobat had a very different appearance to the clear waters of the White Nile. It was yellow in colour, filled with sediment that had created long, dirty streaks. Sir Sam had told him that its source was unknown, even though it was a great river and much bigger than the White Nile at this point. He had claimed the source must lie far away in some distant mountains. Jack had seen the gleam in his eyes as he had talked. It was an unknown, and to an explorer like Sir Sam, it offered another challenge, one that clearly appealed.

After the junction with the Sobat, the expedition had carried on down the White Nile as they headed ever further south. It had been a dull journey. The view from the steamer had been monotonous, the banks of the river at this point flat and ugly, the ground a sickening yellowish colour. The only splash of interest had been the odd palm tree, or an occasional native village, the small square huts made from earth with a simple hole for a door.

The character of the White Nile had changed after its junction with the Sobat, entering an area of immense flats and boundless marsh. The river had started to wind and turn as it cut through the marsh, often doubling back on itself so they seemed to spend as much time going north, east and west as they did south. Progress felt very slow. They still had some seven hundred and fifty miles to cover before they would reach Gondokoro, a journey that had begun to feel like it would take forever.

'The Bahr Giraffe it is.' Sir Sam made his decision, looking from Jack to Marcopolo, his jaw set firm. 'We shall split the flotilla. I will take a party ahead, leaving you, Mr Marcopolo, in command of the main flotilla. Jack, I want you and your men with me. We shall take one of the steamers and six dahabiyas; that should be sufficient. Let us discover if the Bahr Giraffe will suit our purposes.'

Jack nodded. Only time would tell if Sir Sam had made the right call. Or if he had just committed the expedition to disaster.

Chapter Twenty-three

———◦•◦———

'God damn it to hell.' Jack spat as yet another mosquito dived into his mouth. 'Will these little fuckers never give up.' He wiped a hand across his lips. A tiny black body came away with it. 'Fucking things.'

'You'll have to get used to them.' Julian laughed at Jack's tirade against the insects. 'They will only get worse, I am told.'

'You would say that.' Jack waved away another crowd of mosquitoes attempting to land on his face.

'You'll see.' Julian laughed again, then turned to his uncle, who was walking towards them.

The first few days of their journey along the Bahr Giraffe had been hard going to say the least. They had been travelling against a strong current that had slowed the pace of even the steamer to little more than a crawl. For now, the water level was sufficient, perhaps as much as nineteen feet, but it had been dropping every day, and Sir Sam had the steamer's crew measuring the depth constantly. The river had also started to wind this way and that. They had quickly lost sight of the main body of the flotilla that was following them. It was as if they had entered a great marshy labyrinth, one that seemed to have no end.

Sir Sam had called a halt after yet another day of aimless meandering back and forth. It was becoming clear that the expedition was worryingly short of the small boats that were so vital to its progress. The little craft were in use almost constantly, scouting ahead or slipping ashore to drop off a party who would range far and wide gathering firewood for the insatiable steamer, or else hunting for food to supplement the rations carried in the ships' holds. At times they would haul the dahabiyas along, the crews forced to row for hours on end when the wind or the current meant that the sailboats could make no progress alone. With so few of the small boats available, Sir Sam had set up a temporary encampment where he had challenged the flotilla's shipwrights to build him some more. Thus far, it had proven to be hard work. Wood was scarce, the only trees that could be found a species of mimosa that the Arabs had named *kook*. The shipwrights were doing their best, and Jack had been astonished to see the outline structure of a boat emerge from the piles of scruffy misshapen wood that was all the craftsmen had been given to work with.

'Are you sure you wish to come with us?' Julian asked rather pointedly.

'Yes.'

'Just don't get in the way.'

'I won't.' He meant it. Julian and Sir Sam went hunting at every opportunity. The pair killed wildfowl by the dozen, the expedition's rations supplemented by duck, geese and even the odd pelican. Two crocodiles had been slain the previous week, much to the delight of the Sudanese soldiers, for whom the creatures were a much-sought-after feast. Sir Sam had even managed to kill a bull hippopotamus. The dead animal's head had been boiled in a great cauldron with salt, cayenne pepper, chopped onions and gallons of vinegar. During cooking, the skin dissolved into fat and produced a thick soup that Sir Sam had devoured with great relish. Jack had eaten it – he was too long a soldier to be fussy – but it tasted grim.

Not every animal the pair hunted was for food. They talked incessantly of both elephant and lion, the two beasts spoken of in the same reverential tone Jack had heard used by men discussing their vices in church. Thus far, the opportunity to hunt either creature had been denied them, but both hungered for the chance to register another trophy on their tally.

At times, Jack wondered whether Sir Sam's claim that they needed more of the little boats was nothing but an excuse to go on shooting trips whilst the shipwrights worked. Not that he minded the delay himself. It had afforded him the chance to give his men some exercise, and he had even organised a shooting range for them. Every man had been given five rounds to fire, something that had cheered them up no end, and the air had been filled with shouts and laughter as they competed with one another to hit the simple targets he had set up for them. Now he was going to have some fun of his own: he had asked to join Julian and Sir Sam on one of their hunting trips.

'Are you ready, Jack?' Sir Sam approached with a spring in his step. Four gun bearers followed, each one carrying a pair of rifles and a bewildering array of ammunition pouches.

Sir Sam had come equipped for the hunt. He had brought nine different rifles, made by Tatham, Reilly, Manton, Beattie and Purdey. He also had a revolver and a brace of double-barrelled pistols. His favourite of them all was a double-barrelled breech-loading rifle he called the Dutchman. It was made by Holland of Bond Street, and he claimed it was accurate to three hundred yards. Jack doubted that was the case, but he had still handled the rifle with reverence. It fired heavy black-powder centrefire cartridges that contained the primer in a metal cup inserted into the very centre of the cartridge's base that was struck by the firing pin mounted on the gun's hammers. Sir Sam had told him that they were Boxer primers, patented by Colonel Edward Mounier Boxer whilst working at the Royal Arsenal at Woolwich.

Unlike the rimfire cartridges Jack had used in the past, which contained the primer across the bottom of the cartridge, these newer centrefire cartridges were much more robust, and the smaller area covered by the primer made them less likely to be fired by accident. He was looking forward to seeing the weapon in action, although a part of him felt there was some-thing rather gratuitous in the hunt. Certainly some of the animals they shot went to feed the soldiers and crewmen of the flotilla, but he had often heard Julian boast of the day's bag, the tally of animals and birds shot seemingly of much greater import than the fate of the creatures themselves.

'I am ready.' He nodded, then followed Sir Sam as he walked past, taking a place just in front of the bearers.

None of the men spoke as they walked away from the river. Sir Sam set an eager pace, and they covered the ground quickly, following raised pathways that led through the marsh. At all times they were surrounded by channels and lagoons, the water choked with vegetation so that barely a clear patch of water could be seen. There was little to look at. Jack kept his head up, his eyes roving the barren landscape for a flicker of life, his hands moving constantly around his face to wave away the million insects that were intent on landing there. Tall papyrus grass stuck up in clumps here and there, whilst some of the channels were lined with thin, wispy reeds. Smaller, stubbier cumbungi plants formed great clumps around the reeds, whilst heaps of thick-leaved plants that to Jack resembled cabbage floated amidst the cloying mats of tangled greenery. It was clear that to step off the pathways would be to sink into a stinking morass.

'There!' Sir Sam pitched his voice low so his words would not carry.

At once, both Sir Sam and Julian crouched down.

Jack glanced around. He saw the four gun bearers sink onto their haunches, but that was all he saw. There was no sign of any other living creature.

'Get down, Lark,' Julian hissed, glowering in his direction.

Jack did as he was told, then crept forward until he was next to Julian.

'What is it?'

'Did you not see it?' Julian was scathing.

'No.'

'It's a damn bull elephant. As big as the queen's Thames barge.' He shook his head in exasperation.

'Jack!' Sir Sam was beckoning him forward.

'Don't mess this up, Lark.'

Jack eased past Julian, ignoring the warning, and moved as quickly as he could along the narrow pathway.

'Fortune smiles upon us.' Sir Sam greeted him with a broad grin of obvious delight. 'Come.' He gestured for Jack to step around him. 'There, do you see?' He leaned forward, his arm resting on Jack's back as he pointed ahead.

Jack followed the direction of Sir Sam's finger. At first he saw nothing but more of the same endless swamp.

And then he saw the beast.

'Fuck me,' he breathed.

Sir Sam snorted, not in the least offended by the choice language. 'He's a beauty.'

The bull elephant faced half away from them as he fed, snapping branches from a thorny-looking tree, then stripping away the leaves and shoots with his trunk and shoving them deep into his mouth, the action almost mechanical in the way it was repeated over and over, the bull working hard to fill his enormous belly. To Jack's eye, he was magnificent, huge, imposing. He had never seen another animal its like.

He stayed perfectly still, totally mesmerised. The bull looked old, to his eyes anyway. The creature's two enormous tusks were streaked with brown, and even from a distance he could see cracks and fissures running along their length. He wondered what struggles the great beast had endured, how many times it had fought for the right to exist. The thought captivated him. The bull fought for itself, nothing more. It fought because that was what it was destined to do. And it would continue to fight until it collapsed into the dirt. Then it would be no more, its victories and its defeats lost to the winds of time. The thought was enough to make him shiver.

The sight of the animal reminded him of the last time he had seen an elephant. He had been fleeing the Maharajah of Sawad's fortress, his loyalty to the British Crown pulling him from the court where he had been accepted as one of the maharajah's trusted advisers. He had been a general then, for whatever the title was worth, and he had found a home amongst the people the British government thought only to subdue. Yet still he had left. He had done what he thought was right. And it had cost him dear.

On that fateful day, the maharajah had addressed his army from the back of an elephant, though the creature bore little comparison to the fearsome beast standing a few hundred yards away now. From his howdah high on the elephant's back, he had dared his men to launch an attack on the British cantonment at Bhundapore. Jack had never seen a sight to match it. Yet now he looked across at the bull and wondered if the local tribes had found a way to corral the power of such an enormous beast. If they had, they would surely be unstoppable.

'He is magnificent, is he not?' Sir Sam whispered directly into Jack's ear, mouth so close that his lips touched the soft flesh of his lobe.

'Yes.' Jack had no more words. He was lost in awe.

'The wind is in our faces. He won't smell us.' Sir Sam reached to squeeze Jack's shoulder. 'I wager those tusks will weigh one hundred and twenty pounds each. They will be a fitting trophy for your first hunt.'

He paused, both men staring reverently at the mammoth creature they had discovered.

'You have the shot, Jack.' Sir Sam gave the gift then slipped away.

Jack's back felt cold where the other man's arm had laid across it. He half turned to see Sir Sam signalling to one of the bearers, who was already scuttling forward with the Dutchman held ready. Sir Sam took it, then held out a hand for the pair of centrefire cartridges that followed a few moments later. As Jack watched, he broke the rifle open, slid in the cartridges, then snapped the weapon shut.

'It's all yours, Jack.' He held out the loaded weapon.

Jack took the Dutchman then faced the bull once again. The animal stood just as it had when he had last looked, its long trunk never still, its mouth moving constantly as it chewed on its fibrous breakfast, its great ears flapping to and fro like loose sails caught in a crosswind, so certain of its power that it could stand in the open and feed without a care in the world.

'Aim just behind the eye.' Sir Sam hissed a last word of advice then eased away, leaving Jack alone once again.

Jack maintained his position. He could smell the weapon now that he held it, the tang of gun oil with the merest whiff of spent gunpowder. He could feel its power. It was heavy, far heavier than a Snider or a rifled musket. That weight felt good.

He settled into a more comfortable position, dropping one knee to the ground so he could brace himself better. He rested his left elbow on his thigh whilst his right pressed tight against his chest.

He lifted the rifle for the first time, the metal cold where it brushed against his cheek as he sighted down the barrel. The bull was about eighty yards away and he let the beast fill the shallow V-shaped iron sights at the end of the Dutchman's barrel. There was a thin white line marking the bottom of the V, and he lined it up on the elephant's eye then moved it a fraction, finding the spot just behind that Sir Sam had advised him to target.

He held the pose. Around him everything was perfectly still. Only the rifle moved, the sights swaying ever so slightly from side to side.

It was time. He slowed his breathing, letting his mind settle. He felt his muscles relax and breathed slowly, one measured breath after another.

He took one last breath that was deeper than the others, and held it, feeling it fill his chest. Then, slowly, he let half of it out.

Everything went still. The rifle steadied. He was ready.

Then the bull turned and looked directly at him.

There was no drama. No sudden explosion of alarm, or fear. The bull continued to feed, as calm and serene as it had been when they had first spotted it. Yet everything had changed. With that one simple action, the animal had reminded him that it was a living, breathing creature. It was not a target. A trophy. It was alive. And it had every right to that life.

He let out the half-breath he had been holding. Slowly and carefully, he lowered the Dutchman.

He stayed like that then, watching the silent animal. Over the years, he had held the power of life and death in his hands too many times to count. What mattered today was that he had not killed. He could have slain the beast, and yet he had chosen not to.

He turned slowly on his heel. Sir Sam was watching him intently.

'What the hell is going on up there?' Julian hissed. 'If you aren't going to bally well shoot, then let someone else have a pop.'

'Be quiet,' Sir Sam snapped without taking his eyes from Jack.

'But Uncle—'

'I said be quiet, goddammit.' There was venom in his tone. Julian fell silent.

Jack took a deep breath, then moved back to his commander, holding out the double-barrelled rifle. 'Do you want to take the shot, sir?'

'No.' Sir Sam smiled. 'It was yours to take. Not mine.'

He gently took the rifle from Jack's hands. There had been no censure in his tone. No anger. No recrimination. Just understanding.

'It is time we headed back.' He gave the simple instruction then gestured for the bearers to move.

Jack glanced over his shoulder. The elephant had turned around, its attention diverted by another tree still resplendent with fresh green growth.

It would go on with its life without ever knowing how close to death it had come.

Chapter Twenty-four

———◆•◆•◆———

Bahr Giraffe, 23 February 1870

'Make ready!' Jack gave the order to Lieutenant el-Sisi. He stood at the bow of the steamer looking out at the tangled, matted foliage that blocked their path, his men gathered behind him, every one of them stripped to the waist.

They were deep in the marshland now, the horizon stretching away for miles in every direction with nothing to be seen save for more of the shit-coloured mushy terrain. In the swamp, the only dry spots were a scattering of high white ant hills. The chaotic waterway itself was half-choked with tangled islands of vegetation, whilst beyond, the ground was little more than a wide swathe of marshland where nothing appeared to grow save for clumps of tall reeds and papyrus grass. For the last dozen miles or more, the Bahr Giraffe had broken up into hundreds of tiny, narrow channels, most little more than a yard wide. Jack had no idea how Sir Sam was navigating a path through the confusing tangle. Direction had no meaning here, or at least there was little sense of it. Following a compass bearing was impossible, but at least they could still make progress, no matter how slow, and the small flotilla was picking its way through, the steamer leading the way as best it could, its engine working at full power for hour after hour so that it screamed as if in agony from the heavy workload.

Now, even that was not enough, the river impassable even to the steam-powered vessel, and Sir Sam had had no choice but to order his soldiers into the water. There they worked in muck up to their waists, cutting a path through the tangled vegetation with sword and axe. When the weapons were blunted, more were sent down, along with a fresh party of men, the effort kept up from first light until last. It was a near impossible task. At times, the grass that clogged the water was tall and immensely thick, with tangled nests of roots that were completely matted together. The men had to hack it apart then bundle it into great bales that other men could haul away. Only then could they attack the smaller knots of vegetation, the green, slimy morass hewn apart then dragged to one side to create a narrow channel just wide enough for the steamer's bow.

Progress was painfully slow.

Jack took a deep breath. Like his men, he had stripped to the waist, so that he wore just trousers and boots. There was no breeze in the marsh, and he could feel sweat running down his spine.

The Forty Thieves had not been happy when he had ordered them to make ready to take their place in the water. They had believed they would be spared the exhausting task, their role as the elite cadre of the expedition's forces affording them the freedom to sit back and watch as the men from Sir Sam's two infantry regiments cut their way through the marsh. Jack had quickly disabused them of that notion, ordering them to take their place in the queue of men waiting to be sent into the foul stinking marsh.

'Let's go.' Jack saw the last of the current working party hauled onto one of the small boats that were supporting the effort. It was time for the Forty to start their shift.

He lowered himself over the side of the steamer, holding his weight on his hands then dropping down. He hit the marsh with an obscene squelch.

'Shit.' Water splashed across his bare chest. It was warm and thick, so that it felt as if he had jumped into soup. The smell was appalling, a claggy, rotten stink filling his mouth and nose.

He moved away from the steamer, forcing his way through the Sudd. It was hard to take even a step, the matted islands barely yielding as he pushed forward.

More splashes followed as his men came down after him. Oaths and curses accompanied them.

'Let's get on with it,' Jack shouted. There was nothing else for it save to suck it up and do what had to be done.

'Heave!' Jack spat out the word then hauled on the rope that was looped over his shoulder. His hands burned with the effort and his shoulder was on fire where the coarse hemp dragged across his skin. 'Heave!'

The five men working with him did their best. The mound of grass and reeds had been hacked away from the floor of the swamp and bundled together. Now Jack and his little group were hauling it away.

He had lost count of how many times he had repeated the same task. He was splattered with mud and mush up to his neck. His world had shrunk around him so he saw only the morass, and thought only of the task at hand.

'Come on, you bastards, heave!' he exhorted his tired men as he felt the bundle's movement slow. If they let it sink, the task would become twice as difficult, something they had learned the hard way. Once below the surface, it would suck up the liquid, doubling in weight and snagging on any roots still buried beneath the water. There would be nothing else to do save to hack it free once again, then somehow drag it away from the cloying grasp of the swamp.

The five men with him did their best. As one they bent their backs and heaved. Jack pulled with them, even as he felt the skin on the palms of his hands split open. Somehow they got the bundle moving. They dragged it on, boots slipping and sliding, the murky water of the marsh slick on their chests. It took all of their strength to force it through the fibrous morass, the tangled vegetation clinging at the bundle, making them fight to move it even a single foot.

'Here.' At last they reached the side of the channel they were cutting. 'Get it up!' The order came breathlessly, the sheer effort of forcing a passage through the gloop stealing Jack's strength.

As one they grabbed at the bundle, getting lower in the water as they tried to heave it up. Jack ducked down, water, mud and dank greenery sliding over his shoulder as he pushed from beneath.

'Up!' He gave the order, then had to spit as one of the million insects that swarmed around them slipped into his mouth. He had lost count of the number of mosquitoes and midges he had swallowed that day, the tiny insects doing their best to add to the men's misery by constantly attacking their faces, tirelessly going for the eyes, nose and mouth.

The bundle moved a couple of inches. 'Come on, you bastards, push!' Jack hissed the encouragement, and together they rolled the bundled grasses up and onto the mound of vegetation that had already been cut and hauled away from the channel.

He stepped back. To his relief, the bundle of grass stayed in place, and he readied himself for the slog back to the centre of the channel, where the rest of the Forty were cutting a path in front of the steamer. Another bundle would be waiting for them when they got there. The back-breaking task would have to be repeated.

He looked up at the steamer as he began to push through the muddy water. He reckoned they had covered a hundred and fifty yards since the Forty had jumped down into the waters. It was scant reward for the amount of effort it had taken.

He saw Anna standing at the bow of the vessel with Florence at her side. Both were looking down at him. Anna waved half-heartedly, the instinctive gesture dying an awkward death as she saw the look on his face.

Jack ignored them both, though he could feel their gaze. They would be able to see the network of scars he carried, the thick weals that were the legacy of the life he had led. He felt no shame at the thought, partly because he was too damn tired to care, but also because he wanted Anna to know him for what he was. There was little spare flesh on him, and there was barely an inch that was not scarred. Over the years, he had been shot more than once. He had fought other men, sometimes with his bare hands, sometimes with a blade, and he had come close to death on more than one occasion. His body carried the tale of those fights, the welts and marks a map of his past.

'That's enough, Jack.' Sir Sam had come to stand at the ladies' side. He too looked down at Jack as he called out the instruction. 'Bring your men in.'

Jack found enough strength to nod. From where he stood, Sir Sam looked impossibly clean. For a moment, he felt a hint of anger. But it was not the expedition leader's place to be down in the mud with the men. It was his.

He sucked in a breath, then spat, clearing his throat. 'Stop.' The single word came out crabby.

Faces turned his way. All were covered with grime, great streaks of the mould and scum that infested the water caked over every inch of skin. All bore the same look of exhaustion.

'Out!' He pointed at the steamer.

Not one man had the strength to smile. They turned and pushed their way through the marsh, heading for the rope ladders that had been slung over the steamer's side.

Jack went with them, forcing his aching legs to find the strength to push through the matted skin of vegetation that remained even after his men had cleared the channel. Already he could see the larger islands of vegetation starting to creep forward as the Sudd reclaimed the waters. He knew that within the hour there would not be a single clear patch of water left, the Sudd once again wrapping itself around the steamer, so that the first team into the water the next day would spend hours clearing it away from the hull.

His men hauled themselves up the ladder whilst he waited in the water, waist deep in mire, letting them go ahead. Only when the last one had climbed up did he take hold of the thick ropes and start to ascend.

Hands burning, he hauled himself up one painful rung after another. For one grim moment, he thought he might actually fall, his shaking legs slipping from the rope caked with clods of stinky river mud and all manner of green debris. Somehow he recovered his balance and pulled himself up and over the steamer's side.

There he stayed, muscles cramping, able to do nothing but bend double and wait for his body to recover.

'Here.'

He looked up to see Anna coming towards him, a blanket held out in front of her, as if she were a mother greeting a toddler after a paddle in the sea. He did not move away as she wrapped it around his body.

'Thank you.'

'You are very welcome.' She regarded him with concern. 'You look done in.'

'I am.' Jack groaned, then straightened up, one hand coming up to clasp the blanket together. 'I'm getting too old for this.'

She smiled. 'You should let the men do it. The *younger* men.'

He grimaced at the barb. In that moment, he reckoned she was right. Already the Forty Thieves were dispersing and heading below. The first peals of laughter came as one man, a huge, broad-chested Sudanese called Abdallah, who possessed a bald head shaped just like a roundshot, pulled a long strand of creeper from the inside of his drawers. It was a good sign. The men were tired, but they were still in good spirits.

'Tea?'

Jack saw Florence approaching, her hands cradling a sailor's tin mug from which a thick cloud of steam was emerging.

'Thank you.' He reached for it gratefully, one hand still keeping the blanket tight around him. The mug was fiercely hot, the metal scalding his bloodied and scratched hands, but he did not care. The tea was as dark as the muddy waters he had spent hours fighting. It was perfect.

'How long can we keep this up?' Anna asked.

Jack sipped at his tea before he replied, the liquid scalding his lips and burning as it slid down his throat. It was too sweet for his taste – Florence must have added sugar – but it still tasted divine.

'As long as it takes.' He cradled the mug against his chest.

'You sound like my husband.' Florence laughed.

'Do we have a choice then?' Jack heard crabbiness in his tone, but was too tired to care.

'No. We don't.' Another voice entered the conversation. Sir Sam was striding across the deck towards the small gathering, brow furrowed. 'We press on. No matter how long it takes.' The slow progress was clearly irking him.

'How long will the river be like this?' Jack felt a shiver run through him. It was warm on the deck, but the long immersion in the marsh had left him chilled. It would take hours for the cold to seep out of his bones.

'There is no way of knowing,' Sir Sam replied, a hint of pepper in his tone, as if he considered the question either needless or foolish, or perhaps both. 'My apologies, Jack.' He corrected his tone. 'I should not be short with you of all people.' He offered a tight smile. 'You and your men have worked like Trojans. I can ask no more of you.'

'We're just doing our job.'

'I thought you were a soldier, Jack?' Anna interjected. 'Your enemy should not be vegetation.' She offered a teasing smile.

Jack grunted. He was not in the mood for mockery, however well intended. 'There's more to soldiering than fighting.'

'Ha!' Sir Sam pounced on the answer. 'I like that, indeed.

And you are correct, of course. Still, I thank you for your efforts.'

'My pleasure.' Jack sipped at his tea. It was a little cooler now, and he drank deeply, savouring the taste.

'And I believe you will get your chance to demonstrate your other skills before long. This is wild country, after all.' Sir Sam gestured around him. 'If we are to bring the rule of law to these lands, I am certain your men will have to show what they are about before long.'

'Good.' Jack meant it. He might readily take his place in the swamp, sharing his men's hardships and setting the example they needed to keep them working in the foulest of conditions. Yet that did not mean he did not relish the chance to do more.

And to show them all that he was a true commander.

Chapter Twenty-five

4 March 1870

The crocodile lay half in and half out of the water. Jack stood at the steamer's rail, staring at the enormous creature, hands wrapped tight around the wooden barrier.

The beast had to be at least twenty feet long, perhaps more. It was lying completely motionless, its mouth wide open as if it had been frozen in a permanent yawn. From where Jack looked on with a mix of fear and fascination, he could see rows and rows of bright white teeth, just as he could see a single fat, round eye. There was something very sinister in the way it was just lazing in the sun as though it hadn't a care in the world.

He felt a moment's fear, his revulsion instinctive and strong. Yet as he studied the enormous creature, he felt some of that fear shift. The crocodile was another living being. It had every right to its life. It might be a killer. One that was merciless, and quite without compassion. That did not mean it deserved to die.

His musings were interrupted as a cloud of mosquitoes swarmed towards him. He slapped them away, but a dozen or more landed on his face, the delicate touch of their tiny legs tickling across his skin.

'Fucking hell.' He swore, ducking down, shaking his head vigorously and blowing hard to drive the annoying pests away. It took several long seconds, the tiny insects clinging tenaciously on to his skin. When his face was clear, he looked up again. The crocodile was gone.

He turned away, the beast forgotten, the prospect of another day toiling through the seemingly endless marsh weighing heavily. The soldiers were in the water all day, cutting a path through the stinking morass that choked the river, or else hauling the flotilla along by their own strength alone, hands ripped by the coarse hemp ropes attached to the bows of the ships. He took his place with the Forty, refusing to stay on the steamer whilst his men worked. It was back-breaking toil, the long, miserable hours spent half buried in the swamp sapping every ounce of strength from his body. Yet it had to be done. The only alternatives were either to sit marooned, or else to turn tail and go back the way they had come. Neither was a palatable option to any of them.

'Jack?'

He turned to see Anna emerge from the stairwell that led below deck.

'Good morning.'

She came towards him, hands busy behind her head as she used pins to hold her braids in place. There was something engaging in the act, something very feminine. He liked it, probably more than he should. The expedition was no place for such thoughts.

'How are your men holding up?' she asked as she approached.

'They're tired.'

'We are all tired.'

Jack heard a hint of censure in her tone. It was true enough. The men slogged their guts out hauling the fleet through the morass. Yet Anna and Florence were working just as hard, the men coming back onto the boats with dozens of cuts, welts and sores that needed attention from the two women, who were now the expedition's de facto surgeons and care-givers.

'Maybe we should ask your uncle to give us all a day off.'

Anna snorted at the idea. 'I think we both know what he would say to that.' She came to stand at his side, staring out at the surrounding terrain. There was little to see, save for more of the same swampy terrain that had filled the horizon for days now.

'Damn it.' Jack hissed the oath as another mosquito landed on his neck. He slapped a hand down, crushing the insect into oblivion.

Anna laughed at his reaction. 'Do you need more ointment?'

'No.' He grimaced as he scratched at the spot where the insect had landed. 'Little bastard got me.' He saw Anna's eyes widen a fraction at his choice of words. 'I apologise for my language.'

'There is no need.' She brushed the apology away. 'I will not faint away in shock simply at hearing an oath.'

Jack liked the answer. Anna was not like many of her class. She was proving to be tough and resolute, no matter what was asked of her.

'Look at that!'

He saw her point down at the water. The enormous crocodile had returned and was swimming down the side of the steamer, the top of its back just about visible through the crust of vegetation that smothered the murky water. It was moving slowly, easily, its long tail sweeping languidly from side to side.

'It is a magnificent creature, is it not?' She could not take her eyes off the crocodile as it passed their position on the steamer.

'No. It's bloody terrifying,' Jack grunted as he acknowledged his fear of the giant reptile. Like Anna, he followed the creature as it swam by. Unlike her, he looked up to see where it was headed.

'Oh shit.' He breathed the words. One of the Egyptian soldiers on the dahabiya following the steamer was sitting on the foredeck, his legs dangling over the side and hanging down towards the water.

'What?' Anna looked up sharply.

But there was no time to explain. 'Heh!' Jack shouted. His voice had been trained on a dozen battlefields and it carried with ease. 'You! Get up! Now!' He waved his arms as he bellowed for all he was worth.

The Egyptian soldier looked up in surprise at the sudden loud shouts. He saw Jack, just as he heard him; he would have had to be both blind and deaf not to. But he did not understand and he stayed where he was, legs bouncing gently up and down against the side of the boat.

'Get up!' Jack ran along the deck of the steamer, one hand on the rail, the other waving wildly. 'Get away from the water, damn you!'

The Egyptian soldier looked back at him. Jack could see the concern alongside the lack of comprehension on the man's face. Yet neither emotion was enough to make him move.

Jack had opened his mouth to shout one more time, his mind racing as he tried to conjure some method of making the man understand the danger he was in, when the crocodile rose out of the water.

It moved at an incredible speed, surging up like a kraken erupting from the depths of the sea, its tail thrashing the water into a frenzy, its mouth gaping wide.

Jack saw the Egyptian's own mouth widen in a moment's pure horror. Then the crocodile struck. Jaws snapping together, it tore both legs clean away from the soldier's body, then fell away, hitting the water with an enormous splash. Blood fountained from the remains of the legs, the bright red liquid spraying the bow of the dahabiya and staining the swirling water crimson.

'Good God.' Jack came to a breathless halt. He had seen men dismembered on the battlefield; bodies torn apart by cannon fire. Yet there was something grotesque in the sight of the poor soldier sitting there, his legs ripped away in the blink of an eye.

The soldier screamed. The sound came clear and loud. Then he slumped to the deck.

Jack could do nothing. He stood there impotently as more men emerged near the dahabiya's rail, drawn by the dreadful sound the man had made before he collapsed.

There was no sign of the crocodile. It had disappeared, lost from sight beneath the crust of vegetation, its gory breakfast surely held fast in its mouth.

A man's life had been taken in the span of a few seconds.

'Jack, I need to get over there.'

Jack turned to see Anna at his side, her face the colour of old milk as she registered what had just happened.

'Yes.' He nodded his understanding. It would take time, but they could use one of the steamer's small boats to ferry her over to the dahabiya so that she could tend to the unfortunate Egyptian. He looked at her as she turned away to run along the deck. For a moment, he thought to call her back, the soldier almost certain to be dead long before they could reach him. But he checked himself. He knew her well enough now to be aware she would not heed his words, no matter whether she knew them to be the truth or not.

'Come on! We need to get my medical chest,' she snapped over her shoulder as she saw him still standing there.

Jack did not wait to be told again. He rushed after her, obedient and willing. It was only as he reached the steamer's bow that he had the feeling it would not be the last time he would be running to do her bidding.

Chapter Twenty-six

———◆———

Jack came on deck, hair still wet from a quick dunk in a bucket, the expedition's rudimentary capacity for ablutions not allowing for anything more.

An odd sound caught his attention immediately. He cocked an ear, straining his hearing. It was hard to make out anything over the constant pounding from the steamer's engine, but the strange sound came again. It was one he recognised; he had heard it too many times for it not to register for what it was.

'You hear that, Jack?' Sir Sam strode energetically towards him.

The sound came again, louder this time.

'Gunfire.' Sir Sam made the first identification.

'Yes.'

'How far?' He deferred to Jack's hearing.

'Two, maybe three miles. It's hard to tell.' Jack closed his eyes and concentrated on the sound. 'It's not close, but someone is having a high time of it. There's a good number fighting.' The gunshots came almost constantly, the sound carrying well enough for him to pick out several different weapons firing.

'We should investigate.' Sir Sam smiled wolfishly. 'Are your men ready?'

Jack smiled. 'Yes.'

'Then go.' Sir Sam's face was cast into a serious expression. They had endured days of painfully slow progress.

But now Fate had intervened.

'How far?' Jack hissed the question between heavy breaths.

'A mile,' Sergeant Monsoor answered immediately. Unlike his officer, his breathing was even. They had followed any sort of path they could find, but still for most of the first mile they had been forced to slog through knee-deep marsh water.

'Good.' Jack was glad to have the short Egyptian with him, something reassuring in the calm, competent manner with which he faced every challenge. Monsoor had been at his side since the moment they had disembarked from the steamers. The Forty's young lieutenant, el-Sisi, brought up the rear of the small column.

'There!' Monsoor pointed a few dozen yards ahead. 'You see it?'

'Yes.' Jack had seen the dry land at the same moment as his sergeant. 'Thank God.'

Monsoor glanced at his officer, his face serious. 'God is with us, I think.'

'Let's hope.' Jack had no time for the thought of a beneficent God leading them to drier land. But like more than half his men, Monsoor was a Coptic Christian and took his faith seriously. Most of the rest were Muslims. Thus far, Jack had seen no sign of tension between the two religions. It seemed they were well used to living alongside one another, and for that Jack would happily offer a prayer of thanks. He had seen the effect of religious strife at first hand in India, and knew how devastating it could be.

The column moved on. It wasn't long until they were able to climb up onto the drier land.

'Let the men have five minutes' rest.' Jack gave the instruction to his sergeant. It felt wonderful to be on a surface that did not yield to the pressure of every step.

Monsoor nodded, then waved at them to spread out.

The Forty needed little encouragement. All were filthy, trousers caked in swamp mud and green gunk. They broke ranks and sank to the dry ground with relief. Every man was breathing hard, chests heaving with the exertion of the fast pace Jack had set.

Jack alone stayed on his feet, looking at every man as he came past. He was pleased to see that not one of the Snider rifles was dirty, and the ammunition pouches were all dry and clean, the men carrying them wrapped over one shoulder to keep them out of the gloop.

'Five minutes.' He held up a hand showing the men his four fingers and thumb. 'Just five, you hear me.' In the distance, he could still hear the sounds of gunfire. They could not delay for long, but he knew his men needed a moment to catch their breath and drink something after the hard going. If they arrived into a fight breathless and exhausted, they would be at a disadvantage.

Lieutenant el-Sisi was the last to arrive. Like the men, he was covered in grime, his once blue uniform now so sodden and streaked with mud that it looked almost black.

'El-Sisi, choose four men to go ahead. Have them ready to move out first.'

The lieutenant nodded to acknowledge the order. Overall,

Jack had been impressed with his subaltern. What el-Sisi lacked in experience, he made up for in energy. Even when they had been neck deep in the swamp, he had encouraged the men around him. It boded well.

'*Afandi.*' Monsoor had returned to Jack's side, and now offered a canteen.

'Thank you.' Jack lifted the vessel. Monsoor was taking good care of him. He drank deeply, then almost choked as he gagged on the arrack it contained. Eyes watering, he swallowed the mouthful then handed the canteen back to his sergeant. 'Jesus Christ.' He hissed the word as the local spirit burned his throat on its way down.

Monsoor saw the look on his officer's face and laughed. 'You should not take the Lord's name in vain, *afandi.*'

'Then don't bloody well try to poison me.' Jack cuffed the tears away. 'Hell's teeth.' He saw Monsoor's face crease into a smile at the more fitting expression.

'It is the very best arrack.' The sergeant's grin stayed in place as he took a fast swig from the canteen. 'At least, the best I could find in a shit-hole like Khartoum.'

Jack laughed, just as he was meant to.

'You want more?'

'No,' he answered sharply. He needed his wits about him. 'We need to get going.'

He turned to check on el-Sisi. The young officer was doing as he had been told, and already four men were grouped together.

He waved at the lieutenant. 'Send them forward. Tell them they need to keep us in sight at all times.'

He left el-Sisi to translate the more detailed order and gestured for the rest of the men to fall in. 'Form column!' he shouted, words rasping in his arrack-scoured throat.

The men understood the order well enough. They formed up into a tight marching column four files wide, just as he had made them practise. As soon as they were ready, Jack took his place at their head, with Monsoor taking station at his left-hand side.

'Forward, march!' He called out the command, then started forward.

The ground was wonderfully firm underfoot as they set off once again. After so long in the marsh, Jack's legs almost buckled with every step, his muscles unable to adjust to not sinking down several inches. Still, he set a face pace, his eyes moving from the scouts ahead to the ground around him.

The sounds of gunfire were getting louder with every passing minute. The shots came sporadically now, the change in sound telling him that the skirmish, or whatever it was, had slackened off, the men firing taking the time to aim.

The column pressed on, settling into the rhythm of a fast march. He could feel his body becoming accustomed to the pace. If felt good to be moving.

He was back on dry land.

Back where he belonged.

And he was marching to the sound of the guns.

'Halt!' Jack raised an arm and brought the column to a sharp stop. Ahead, he could see that his four scouts had gone to ground.

'Wait here.' He gave the command to the lead rank, reinforcing the instruction by holding his palm out so that it faced towards the men. 'You too.' He repeated the gesture, this time for Monsoor alone, then began jogging forward, keen to see what the scouts had found.

He double-timed, holstered revolver banging up and down against his hip as he ran. As he left the head of the column, the sound of gunfire intensified once again. What had been sporadic single shots turned into every gun firing as fast as it could, the shots coming so closely together that the sounds blurred into one. For the first time, Jack heard men shouting, loud voices calling out over the gunfire. Then screaming, the dreadful, horrified wail that men gave when they were hit.

'What is it?' Jack sank to his haunches as he reached the scouts. A moment later and Monsoor joined him, the sergeant ignoring the order to stay with the men.

One of the scouts was Gamal, the handsome Egyptian soldier who had dropped his Snider the first time he had tried to load the weapon. Now he gestured to the ground at his side, his face set into a grim expression.

Jack saw the corpse almost immediately. And then he smelt it.

The elephant was lying on its side. At first it was hard to see its wounds, so dense was the cloud of flies feasting on its flesh. Then the tiny creatures shifted and the full horror was revealed.

'Fucking hell.' He could not hold back the exclamation, just as he could not hold back the rush of vomit that surged up into his throat. Its acrid touch burned as he swallowed it down, holding on to his horror.

The elephant's skull had been blown apart. Blood, bone and brain smothered the ground, the ruined head a feast for the millions of flies they had disturbed. Yet the wound that had killed the enormous beast was not the only grotesque horror to have been wrought on what had once been a proud, majestic animal. Two great cavities had been dug in its face, each one now little more than a gruesome pit of offal festooned with flies and maggots. The beast's tusks had been hacked from its body, the men who had done it caring nothing for the animal they had killed save for removing the only items that had value.

'There.' Gamal lifted his hand.

Jack followed his finger. Another elephant lay sprawled on the ground, not far from the path they had been following, the soil around it darkened to a deep brown by the blood that had long since soaked away.

'And there.' Gamal was pointing out to his other side. The corpse of another much larger elephant lay a short distance away. Like the others, its tusks had been removed.

Jack turned to Monsoor. 'They look fresh?'

The sergeant nodded. 'They were killed yesterday. Not before.'

'Shit.' Jack studied the position of the bodies. Most lay close together, with just one further out. The hunters had been ruthlessly efficient.

'Right.' He had seen enough. Someone had slaughtered the herd. From what he could see, they had done a good job of it. Only time would tell if the fighting he could hear was somehow connected to this carnage.

He reached out to pat Gamal on the shoulder. 'Good job. Now move out. Stay in line of sight.' He gestured to his eyes to reinforce the order.

It was time to close on the firefight and see just who was fighting who.

Chapter Twenty-seven

———◆●◆———

Jack led the column forward. They covered the ground quickly, every step underscored by the sound of gunfire.

Ahead, the scouts went to ground for a second time.

'Halt.' Jack stopped the column.

The men obeyed. He could hear them breathing hard, but he did not turn to check on them. He had eyes only for the scouts.

Gamal waved back at him, then gestured with both hands before pointing ahead.

Jack understood. They had reached the fight.

It was time.

'Form skirmish line. Move!' He signalled to the men to re-form. He wanted them in the loose, widely spaced formation. He did not know what they faced, but he was sure it would not be an organised enemy. The skirmish line would spread them out and give them the flexibility to respond to whatever they encountered. Stalking along the line as it formed, he hissed commands, urging the men into place. They were doing well. They had practised the evolution, forming the skirmish line over and over on the dusty field outside Khartoum. Now they were doing it for real.

'You two, stay there,' he snapped at a pair of brothers called Taha, who were moving too close to the pair on their right. He pressed on, checking the spacings between the men. The skirmish line required them to fight in twos. Each pair would spread out from their neighbours, maintaining a spacing of twenty paces. When they came into contact with the enemy, one of the pair would aim, then shoot, whilst the other covered them. As soon as the first man had fired, the second would step forward and be ready to offer covering fire whilst his partner reloaded. They would work like that in tandem, and would carry on until ordered to cease.

Jack had done his best to train the men to find cover as they advanced, yet neither on the practice field outside Khartoum nor here in the marsh was there much for them to use to screen their movements. They were in open ground, swamp giving way to wide dusty plain. There were clumps of grass in every direction, some as tall as a man, others no more than knee height. They offered the only cover available, save for a few folds and dips in the ground that could perhaps screen a single man from sight if he stayed low enough. It was a world of pale yellows and greens, the grass mostly the colour of straw. Above, the sky was clear, a great sheet of blue that stretched from horizon to horizon.

'Ready!' He gave the command from the centre of the line. Some of the men, especially those on the far edges, were still moving, but he was fast running out of patience. He wanted them advancing before anyone realised they were there.

He held back the next command, biting his tongue a moment longer. Monsoor settled at his side, ready to cover his officer as they moved forward. El-Sisi was on the far right of the line with the enormous Sudanese, Abdallah, whom Jack had selected for the task of protecting the junior officer. The Forty's other sergeant, an Egyptian called Hassan, who thus far had failed to impress, held the left flank. Jack just hoped the man was up to the task.

He waited, counting to ten, letting the men settle. The line was a little rough and ready, some of the spacings too wide, whilst others were too narrow. But it would do.

'Forward!' He waved his arm, giving the signal.

As one, the line moved briskly, the men scurrying forward half crouched. Some weaved left and right as they advanced, using what little cover there was, yet they kept up a good pace, the line covering the ground fast.

Jack darted ahead, slipping around the thickest stands of grass. He kept his eyes moving, waiting for his first glimpse of the firefight.

He got it no more than half a minute later.

One side was arranged in a defensive position at the edge of what looked to be a long-term encampment, some men crouched down behind water barrels or stacks of wooden packing crates, others behind an overturned handcart that had been forced into action as a rough and ready rampart. The rest lay on the ground, heads low. All looked to be European, with a dozen or so local tribesmen keeping well to the rear and away from the gunfire.

Their enemy was a group of men no more than fifty to a hundred yards away. Like the men defending the encampment, all were Europeans. Unlike the defenders, these men were never still. They moved fast, using what cover was available to them, keeping as low as they could in the flat, featureless terrain.

Only when they fired off a shot did they pause, the action completed in the blink of an eye. As soon as the shot was away, they displaced.

Yet they were paying a price for facing the defenders. Jack counted at least three bodies on the ground. The closest was no more than a dozen yards from the overturned cart. It was all the evidence he needed that the men attacking the encampment had come close to rushing the rough defences at least once.

For now, the battle had descended into a long-range firefight. From a quick tally, he reckoned the attackers outnumbered the defenders at least three to one, perhaps more, but for now, neither side could turn the tide to their advantage, the attackers unable to rush the defensive line but still too numerous to be driven away completely. With neither side backing down, the fight had reached a stalemate.

But one that would not last much longer.

Even as he watched, the attackers rushed forward.

They fired as they charged, bullets whizzing around the ears of the defenders. Nearly all thumped into the temporary defences, either ricocheting away, or else burying themselves into wood. Just a single shot found a target, and Jack saw one defender rise up, a bullet bored deep into his shoulder, his shouts and curses of pain loud and clear.

The defenders poured on the fire as best they could. Yet a revolver held five rounds, six at most. The men using them could fire fast, but they could not fire forever.

Jack was close enough to hear the curses as the first men ran out of rounds. At least half the defenders ducked down out of sight, hands busily ramming home fresh cartridges. It would take many seconds to complete the process. Vital seconds.

The attackers ran hard. They came forward at different

angles, darting this way and that, using cover if it was there, or else dancing from side to side so that they never ran straight. They had learned what it took to survive, or at least what gave them a chance.

The defenders with rounds left in their revolvers fired. Yet hitting the fast-moving targets was not easy, and many bullets flashed past the attackers, stinging the air around them but still missing.

The distance between the two sides closed fast. One of the leading attackers went down, his body crumpling over itself as a bullet buried itself in his gut. A moment later, another fell, his despairing cry clearly audible even over the war cries of his fellows and the sound of revolvers firing. Yet the rest rushed on.

With so many defenders reloading, there was not enough volume of fire to stop them.

The attackers were finally close to snatching victory.

One defender rose from his cover, freshly reloaded revolver outstretched in front of him. He showed himself to his men, demonstrating the courage they would need to stand their ground. His mouth opened wide as he stood there, a defiant command leaving his lips. Then he fired a heavy black revolver saved for this moment.

Jack recognised him in an instant.

He had found his friend.

He had found the Frenchman.

'Halt!' Jack shouted the command at his skirmishers. It was time to bring them into action. And he knew what they would do.

At first he had not been sure which of the sides was his

enemy. The sight of the Frenchman killed off any doubt in his mind. He was not certain of the dynamic between the two groups of Europeans, but he knew Dubois and his men were here to trade ivory. Jack might not approve of the slaughter that involved, but he knew that the khedive's ambition was to open these lands to legitimate commerce. And that included traders like the Frenchman. The attackers were clearly trying to curtail Dubois' enterprise, and so Jack and his Thieves would intervene to stop them. He did not know it all, he was sure of that, but he was certain that he was doing the right thing and that it would please Sir Sam. It was a golden opportunity to bring the power of law into these dangerous lands, just as the khedive had ordered.

Around him, his men stopped moving and braced themselves.

'Prepare to fire!' A rush of excitement surged through Jack as he bellowed the order. It had been a long time since he had fought on the battlefield. The open grassland was nothing like the field at Solferino, or the woods at Shiloh, and the battle, such as it was, was between a handful of men, not tens of thousands. But he was still leading men into combat, and deeply buried emotions surged up, powerful, overwhelming, intoxicating.

'Hold your damn ground!' Two pairs to his right rushed too far ahead of the line, and he called them back. 'Your target is the men in the open.' He pointed towards those rushing the encampment as he shouted the instruction, making sure his soldiers knew what he was asking of them.

The attackers saw the Forty.

From his position in the centre of the line, Jack could see the confusion that swept through them. Their forward rush stopped immediately, and they turned to face the line of red-shirted men who had suddenly arrived on their flank.

But it was too late.

'Fire!' Jack roared the command.

The Sniders made a deep-throated roar as every other man fired, just as he had trained them to do.

Twenty rounds tore into the attackers. Half a dozen of them were cut down, bodies thrown backwards from the impact of the heavy Snider bullets.

The defenders saw the unknown force coming to their aid, and they stood and fired, adding their own firepower to the Forty's first volley.

'Fire!' Jack bellowed.

Twenty more rounds ripped through the dispersed ranks of the men attacking the encampment, scything them down.

The attackers had been hit hard, the fire against them now coming from two directions. They went to ground, diving behind whatever cover they could find. But they were brave and filled with the madness of the battle. They did not stay down for long. Moments later, the first of them rose back up, rifles and revolvers now aimed at Jack and his men.

But Jack would give them no respite.

'Fire!' The first of the Forty to fire should be reloaded. Now he called on them to shoot again.

More bullets struck the attackers. Men who had been ready to return fire fell away. Others ducked down, the storm of bullets driving them into the dirt.

Yet some stood their ground, even with Snider bullets zipping past them. It was bravely done. Jack knew what courage it took to remain still as death stalked the battlefield.

'Reload!' There was time for him to shout the encouragement. Then the attackers fired.

No more than a dozen bullets zipped towards the skirmish line. If Jack had formed his men into the normal line of battle, the tightly packed ranks would have offered an easy target. But in the dispersed formation, they were much harder to hit. Yet still one of his men shrieked in shock as a bullet struck home.

Jack's head whipped around to see who had been hit.

It was Samir, the man with the face of a cherub who was said to beat his family so cruelly. For once, there was justice in war. And Samir shrieked as the bullet drove deep into his chest. It was a short but terrible sound, cut off abruptly as he crumpled to the ground.

Jack tore his eyes away. He had known the risk when he had ordered his men to attack, had known there could be losses.

'Fire!' He shouted the command, demanding his men keep firing. Nothing else mattered. Not now that the fighting had begun. Not even death.

No more than five or six men obeyed. Not one hit a target. The rest stared in shock at their comrade, who lay completely still, blood pumping into the dirt.

'Fire, goddammit! Fire!' Jack pulled his revolver from his holster and snapped off a shot at the men attacking the Frenchman's encampment, not even bothering to aim. He had to get his men fighting.

Another flurry of bullets zipped past the skirmishers. Mercifully, none hit, the fast-moving missiles burying themselves in the dirt or else snapping by, the air filled with the sharp whip and crack of bullets stinging the air. Yet they still had an effect.

Some of the Forty dived to the ground. Others ran left and right, or else turned and scampered away from the line, their only thought to escape the fire coming against them.

'Stand fast!' Jack did his best. 'Stay where you fucking are!'

He was ignored, the men paying more heed to the bullets whistling past them than to their officer.

It was chaos.

Over half of his small command were running. Barely a dozen remained in place, the scattered pairs all that were left of what had been a fully formed skirmish line.

He glanced at the men attacking the encampment. Six or seven were in view. The rest were there; he just could not see them. The defenders were back behind cover, any relief they might have felt at the arrival of Jack's force forgotten as they once again had to fight on alone.

'Get up.' Jack reached the nearest of his men, who were trying to shelter behind the same clump of grass. It was the Taha brothers. He hauled them to their feet, not caring that he was rough. 'Fire at the bloody enemy!'

To their credit, they did as they were told. Both knelt, then fired, one after the other.

Jack stalked further down the line. 'Come on! Stand up and fire!' he bellowed. More bullets zipped by, some clearly directed at him. He could hear them making a strange hum as they cracked past, like a fat hornet buzzing around his head. The thought of a bullet striking him down filled his mind, his arsehole clenching tight, and he could not help flinching at every near miss. But there was nothing else to be done. He had to show himself to his men. He had to set the example they needed to see.

'Stand up and fire!' He reached another pair on the left of the line who were lying on the ground, heads buried beneath their arms. 'You hear me, you bastards? Stand up and fire!' Frightened faces with wide eyes stared back at him. Gamal, the scout, and Habib, the fresh-faced soldier who looked like he should still be in short trousers, were clearly panicked. But he would not let them stay where they were, and he manhandled both to their feet, forcing them to obey.

'Now fire, goddammit!'

To his relief, both obeyed, Snider rifles raised then fired.

They were not alone. All along the line, those who had stayed fired at the enemy. It was nothing like the ordered firing of a skirmish line, but it would do. He had got them fighting.

'That's it, you two! Pour it on!' He roared the encouragement at Gamal and Habib, then made his way back up the line, making sure he walked in front of the men who remained, showing them that he did not fear the fire that came against them almost constantly. 'Shoot the bastards! You hear me? Shoot them!'

The formation was little more than a ragtag line of men loosely grouped together. He counted five pairs. El-Sisi was still there, the young officer standing over the pair on the far right of the line, Suliman and Osman. Abdallah was at el-Sisi's side, sticking to his task of protecting the young officer even as the air around him was punched repeatedly by enemy bullets.

'Form on me!' Jack bellowed the order. There was nothing else for it. He had to gather what he had.

The men began to run in. Monsoor came first, leading in two pairs, followed by the young lieutenant, whilst the four men Jack had forced to stand came towards him from the left.

'Hold here. Form up and fire! Look lively now!' Jack stood in the centre of the pitifully small group. The men understood well enough. They took up positions, aiming their rifles at the enemy.

'Fire!'

The first men fired. Jack saw an attacker go down with a Snider bullet buried in his gut.

'That's it! Faster! Come on!' he urged. They were pouring on the fire now, creating a storm that drove even the bravest attacker to the ground. No amount of courage was enough to keep men standing in the face of the modern weaponry.

'Fire! Fire! Fire!'

This was the time for the Sniders to show their worth. There were just a few of the Forty left, but they were spewing out a rate of fire that was almost impossible to comprehend. When Jack had fought with the Union Army at Bull Run, his skirmishers could fire no more than two shots a minute. But with the Sniders, his men could manage close to five times as many.

'Fire!'

There was joy in this moment, something powerful and fulfilling. He raised his revolver, aiming at the shadowy form of a grey-bearded attacker he spotted lying in a shallow depression in the ground. The bullet struck the man in the side, twisting him around, body curling round the great gouge opened in his flesh.

'Fire!' he shouted again, then drew a bead on a man he could see squirming around a clump of tall grass. He fired, the bullet smacking into the ground near his target's head. The man looked up, startled surprise registering on his face, as he realised that his attempt to find cover had failed. Jack's second bullet caught him in the forehead, tearing back the top of his skull like a knife taking the top off a boiled egg. For one dreadful second he lay still, his eyes wide as the horror of the moment filled his soul. Then he slumped forward.

'Keep firing.'

Then suddenly the attackers could take no more. One minute they were little more than shadows on the ground, then they were up and running, the open terrain suddenly filled with dozens of men fleeing for their lives.

'Fire!' Jack shouted the command one more time. There was a taste of madness then, the moment filling a gap in his soul. Three more attackers fell, bullets buried in their backs. It was an unfitting reward for men who had shown such bravery, but this was war, and he would show no mercy. Not until it was done.

Still the Sniders fired, shots blurring, the sound of gunfire intoxicating, overwhelming.

Then the surviving attackers finally got beyond the effective range of the weapons and it was over.

'Cease fire!' Jack gave his final command.

His men stopped firing. Then they cheered.

They had fought for the first time.

Over half of them had run. But enough had stayed in the fight.

The Forty Thieves had their first victory.

Chapter Twenty-eight

———◆———

'Jack Lark! *Mon ami*, is that really you?'

Jack saw the Frenchman striding towards him. It had not taken Dubois long to discover who had come to his aid.

Jack was alone now, Monsoor, el-Sisi and the men who had stood sent to check the bodies of the fallen attackers for any left alive. With them were the first of those who had fled and who had now returned. Those men walked with heads down, shame obvious even from a distance. Jack did not know if he was pleased to see them return or not, but the failure of all his men to stand stung his pride. There would have to be a reckoning for those who had run.

'You're lucky I was here, chum.' His tone was flat as he greeted the Frenchman, his disappointment at his men running leaving no room for any other emotion.

'I am!' Dubois engulfed him in a tight bear hug, then stepped back, keeping firm hold of his upper arms. 'I am glad to see you, my friend.'

'You had better be.' Jack was uncomfortable at the other man's touch. It felt decidedly odd as the Frenchman's wooden hand thumped painfully into his shoulder blade. His discomfort doubled when Dubois came towards him again and landed a loud smacking kiss on each cheek.

'I am in your debt.' The Frenchman whispered the words, then released him.

'You are.'

'Did you take many casualties?'

'One.' An image of the dying Samir came into Jack's mind. There had been a price to pay for saving the Frenchman and his cohort. He had ordered the Taha brothers to carry the body of the fallen soldier to a patch of clear ground. He would make sure the man was buried, not left as carrion like the elephants they had found.

'The dead animals, back there.' He thumbed back the way his men had come. 'Were they your doing?'

'Yes, my friend.' Dubois nodded, a sly smile creeping across his face. 'We found the herd yesterday.'

'And you took the tusks then just left them there to rot?'

Dubois gave a very Gallic shrug. 'It is how things are here. We have no need of the meat.'

Jack grappled with the notion. 'It seems a waste.'

'And deny the animals a feast?' Dubois showed no shame as Jack called him out. 'This is Africa, my friend.' He spread his hands wide. 'It is a different world to the one you are used to.'

'Perhaps.' Jack remained unconvinced. In that moment, a part of him disliked the Frenchman for such a callous decision, but Dubois was right about one thing. This was not his world.

'Who were they?' He asked the question as he watched two of his men drag one of the dead attackers from behind a tall stand of grass. It was the man he had shot in the head.

'Does it matter?' Dubois turned and spat out a thick wad of

phlegm. Then he sighed. 'This is their land, or at least they believe it to be so.' He came to stand at Jack's side. Together they watched the pile of corpses grow as the Forty gathered in more of the dead.

'Why were they attacking you?' Jack tore his eyes away from the grisly sight.

'This is their territory. They do not like the fact that we are here.'

'Why? What have you done?' Jack wanted to understand what his men had fought for, what Samir had *died* for. It would help him explain the affair to Sir Sam. Not that he expected the expedition's leader to be anything but delighted. Establishing law and order was a key part of their mission. The group that had been attacking Dubois' men had just learned that they no longer had control over this domain. They would now know that there was an army that would come to the aid of anyone who had a legitimate reason to be there.

'We have done nothing!' Dubois played to the moment, feigning surprise. Then he smiled wolfishly. 'Well, perhaps they are mad because we took what is theirs. They wanted it back.' The smile died and he met Jack's gaze calmly.

'The ivory?'

Dubois shrugged. 'Yes. Among other things.'

'Such as?'

'You will see, *mon ami*.'

Jack let the matter lie. He was beginning to feel the weariness that came after a fight.

The Frenchman clapped his wooden hand onto Jack's shoulder again. 'Now, I think we could all use a drink.'

Jack looked over towards his men. The gruesome task he had set them was almost done, the last of the dead attackers gathered in and laid together ready to be buried. 'That sounds good to me. Although you had better have something half decent to drink.'

Dubois barked a short laugh. 'Don't worry. I have brandy. The best.' He winked at Jack. 'It's French. Now, come.' He turned and led Jack further into the encampment.

His men had already left their defences, such as they were. Some were already digging graves. Dubois had had three men killed and the same number wounded. Jack saw the Russian Vladimir amongst those working on the dusty soil. His former foe waved, acknowledging his presence.

'You got off lightly,' Jack remarked as they approached the fresh graves.

'Thanks to you and your men.' Dubois barely looked at the three bodies laid out near the graves. 'We will bury the man you lost.'

'Thank you.' Jack acknowledged the offer.

They walked into the encampment proper. It was clear that Dubois and his men had been there for some time. A neat row of bell tents was arranged towards the eastern side of the encampment. To their front was a series of fire pits, each lined with a circle of stones. Far to one side of the tents, two great tarpaulin sheets were stretched over a large number of wooden supply boxes, whilst next to those were four handcarts that were presumably used to haul goods to and from the river. The encampment had the organised air of a military camp, reflecting Dubois' time with the French Foreign Legion, but it was not that that captured Jack's attention.

It was the ivory.

He had never seen so much of it. It had been gathered together in one enormous heap, the top of the pile covered with a blue tarpaulin sheet that did little to hide the sheer number of tusks that Dubois and his men had accumulated. Jack did his best to tally them up. He could see at least forty of the fat, creamy tusks, and he was certain there were more behind and beneath those that were visible. It was a fine haul. One that would make Dubois a rich man.

'You've done well here.' He stopped to point at the ivory.

'It is good, yes.' Dubois placed his hands on his hips as he considered his success. 'But that is just the start.'

'The start?'

'Of course. I will need much more than that if I am to repay the men who lent me the money for this expedition. Ten times as much. At least.'

'Blimey.' Jack exhaled. For the first time he was beginning to understand the scale of Dubois' operation.

'You seem surprised.'

'I am.' He answered honestly.

'Ha! Then I am glad. Perhaps you underestimated me.'

'Maybe I did.'

'But that is not all. We have been busy.' Dubois reached out to take hold of Jack's upper arm, then twisted him around and pointed at a neatly arranged group of wooden barrels. 'Gum arabic. For coach wax. I have ten barrels so far, but I aim to have at least fifty by the time we are done. Then there are the animal hides.' He pointed to a heap not far from the barrels. 'They are not worth so much, but they will help pay my men. I will have at least twenty times as many before the season is done.'

Jack took in the goods Dubois had already accumulated. He knew he was looking at a small fortune, every one of the items the Frenchman had pointed out worth a pretty penny once it reached the traders in Khartoum.

A thought struck him. He looked around, counting the men in Dubois' small force. There were no more than twenty. He tried to conjure an image of what the encampment would be like in a few months' time. If Dubois was even half as successful as he hoped to be, there would be a mountain of goods to shift to the river. The manpower needed to move such a horde would be far beyond the capabilities of twenty men. 'How the hell are you going to get all that to the river? It will take you days, even with those carts.'

'You think we will carry it ourselves?' Dubois laughed as he answered.

'How else will you do it?' Jack did not understand the hilarity.

'With those, of course.' Dubois pointed to the far side of the encampment.

At first Jack could not work out what he was seeing. Beyond the ivory was a stockade, the kind used to contain livestock, made from wooden stakes with pointed ends that had been driven deep into the ground. The walls were high, perhaps as tall as four feet, and there was just a single gate, guarded by two of Dubois' men, who stood staring into the stockade with revolvers held low in their hands. The height of the staked walls made it hard to see inside, but Jack could make out some movement – perhaps asses or donkeys, he thought, the beasts perfect for transporting heavy burdens.

Then he realised what was truly in the stockade and his heart sank into his guts.

'I have been busy!' The Frenchman was beaming with pride. He reached out to once again clap Jack on the shoulder with his wooden hand. 'I took them just a week ago. They will carry my ivory. Then I will kill them, or let them loose, I have not decided yet. In the meantime, at least the *putains* provide my men with some comfort. It's a lonely place all the way out here. What man doesn't want a woman to warm his bed, even if they are not so willing, eh?' He nudged Jack with his elbow, a knowing expression on his face.

Jack could not find the words to answer. He was staring at the stockade and the people he saw held inside, hoping against all hope that his eyes were deceiving him.

They weren't.

The stockade was filled with women and children.

'What the fuck is this?' He nearly choked on the question. The feeling of dread was subsiding, replaced by something colder. Something darker.

'So now you know why those *branleurs* were attacking me.' Dubois grinned. 'I am not the only one who has come south for the ivory. Those others, they got here before me. They tried to drive me away, killing my men and keeping all the ivory for themselves. So I went to their encampment and I waited there. I waited for two whole days and nights. Then when they left to track down a herd, I took what is most precious to them. Now we will see how tough they are without their women and children. We will see if they still think they rule these fucking lands now.'

Jack tore his eyes from the stockade to look at the Frenchman. Dubois met his stare calmly. There was no shame in his eyes.

'What else am I to do?' He shrugged. 'I told you before. People here only understand strength. I have to show those others I am stronger than they are. Only then will I get what I want. It is how things are done here, Jack. There are no rules. No laws, nothing. You take what you want and then you fight to hold on to it, no matter what it takes.' He paused. 'You have a lot to learn, I think.'

'You bastard.' Jack could barely form the words. Abhorrence

rushed through him. He had done bad things in his time. He had killed and he had murdered. He had left people behind without a qualm, abandoning them to face whatever fate had in store for them. But he had never waged war on women and children. His wars had rules. Rules that clearly meant nothing to Dubois.

'Where do you think you are, Jack?' For the first time, Dubois' expression became more guarded. He even stepped away from Jack, putting distance between them. 'This isn't jolly old England. Those other traders, they are just like you and me. They know I will fight for what I want, just as they will fight to stop me. They will not let me come here and just take away ivory they believe belongs to them. So I have to make them see I am stronger than they are. Only then will they fuck off and leave me alone. Either they do that, or I kill them and their women and children.'

Jack could find no more words. Instead, he walked towards the stockade. It drew him in. He needed to see more. He sensed Dubois following, but he did not care. He had eyes only for the faces he saw behind the wall.

The stockade stank. The prisoners were filthy, the bare feet and legs of the children and the simple dresses of the women stained with grime. All looked worn out, faces drawn and the colour of week-old whey. Jack took in the beaten countenances of the women before him, lips cut and bruised, eyes blackened. Most of the children bore their own wounds, their small bodies and faces covered with bruises and freshly scabbed-over cuts. Their clothing was ripped and torn, the women's skirts bearing the evidence of the assaults they had endured at the hands of Dubois and his men.

It was clear that Dubois was starving the families he had

captured. There was no food or water, just an empty wooden trough, the kind used for pigs, and one corner of the stockade had been left as an open latrine, the shallow pit now full of shit and piss attracting a great cloud of flies that swarmed over the ordure. The women and children sat huddled together like frightened sheep penned in the slaughterman's yard.

Never had Jack seen such misery on so many faces at once. He turned away, unable to bear it, hands balling into fists as the first flicker of madness ran through him. Like a drowning man tossed into the wildest storm, he tried to keep his head above water, lest he sink beneath the waves forever.

Dubois had followed him to the stockade. Now he kept his distance, a guarded expression on his face as he saw Jack's reaction.

'How did you think it works here, *mon ami*?' He laughed. It was a dry, humourless sound, no trace of pleasure in his expression. 'You did not know who you saved, I think.'

'No.' Jack spat out the single bitter word, then glanced back behind him. One of the prisoners was standing up. She couldn't have been more than twenty years old. The ruins of her filthy dress hung over her emaciated frame. Her long blonde hair was lank and matted with grime, and there was a wide bald patch where a great hank of hair had clearly been torn from her scalp. She had been severely beaten, both eyes sporting shiners whilst her lips and cheeks were puffy and bruised.

She walked forward slowly, expression blank, until she came to the wall of the stockade. There she stood still, swaying like a sapling in the breeze, her eyes locking onto Jack's own.

Jack met her stare. It took all he had not to look away.

'Help us.' She spoke in English, her words barely louder than a whisper.

He felt something twist deep inside him.

'Shut your filthy fucking mouth,' Dubois bellowed, voice loud and strident.

'Help us.' The woman lifted her hand, holding it towards Jack, reaching out to him.

'Shut her up,' Dubois shouted to the men guarding the entrance to the stockade.

'No.' Jack gave a command of his own. 'Leave her alone.'

'You think you are in charge here?' Dubois spat out the words, then gestured to his men. Without fuss, they entered the stockade, both brandishing their revolvers, as if fearful of being attacked. But there was no fight left in any of those they had taken prisoner. Nobody did anything but stare as one of the guards came up behind the woman pleading for help. He did not hesitate, his revolver turned around in his hand before it was brought down sharply on the back of the woman's head.

She fell like a stone.

Jack turned to stare in accusation at Dubois. 'What the hell are you doing?'

'Whatever it takes.' Dubois' expression was set in stone. There was not even a flicker of emotion.

'But they're people.' He forced the words out. 'They're innocent *people*!'

'What is wrong with you, Jack?' Dubois did not understand. 'We are at war here. Us against them. Those,' he waved his wooden hand towards the stockade, where his two guards were already closing the gate, their vicious response to their leader's command completed. 'They do not matter. Who cares about the fate of some fucking women and their bastard children?'

'I thought you traded ivory.' The words came out in little

more than a whisper. They sounded pathetic even to Jack's own ears.

'I do, Jack. This is just what it takes.' Dubois pointed at the prisoners. 'You saved us. You know that, Jack. *You* saved us. If you had not arrived when you did, right now those *putains* would be running free.' He laughed again. This time it was a rich sound, one laced with mockery and scorn. 'You are as guilty as I, *mon ami*. You saw those bastards attacking your friend and so you intervened. Now why did you do that if it was not the right thing to do?'

Jack swallowed with difficulty. His mind was in turmoil.

Dubois smiled, reaching out to touch his arm. 'Come now, such things are not worth fighting over. I am in your debt. Now let us drink and talk about other things. Things that matter.'

'I don't think so.' Jack's right hand dropped to his revolver. His revulsion at the man standing in front of him was complete.

Dubois looked at Jack's hand, then back to his face, fixing his eyes with his own. 'So that is how it is to be?'

'Yes.' For one moment, Jack contemplated drawing the revolver and gunning Dubois down there and then.

Dubois sighed with disappointment. 'Think on this, Jack. As I said before, you are alike, you and I. We are cut from the same cloth.' He held Jack's glare. 'You know it could be you standing in my shoes, don't you?' He shook his head slowly, as if he were a schoolmaster confounded by a slow-witted student. 'Men like you and me, we are different. We have seen the worst of this world. Jesus, we *are* the worst of this world. We are not to be held to account, not like other men. We take what we want. We do not wait for it to be handed to us on a fucking plate.'

'No.'

'No?' He mocked Jack's reply. 'Tell me you have not done

bad things then. Tell me that and I will let those pathetic creatures go.'

Jack stood silent. Emotions raged through him. Dubois was right. He *had* done bad things. He was no better than the man standing in front of him.

'You see?' Dubois smiled, then came closer until he was in arm's reach of Jack. 'You know what you are,' he whispered. 'Just as I know what I am. We made our choices a long time ago, my friend.'

Jack pulled in a long breath. He had never felt hatred as strong as this before. One thought and one thought alone filled his mind.

'Shoot me and your men die.' Dubois shrugged as he read Jack's intention. 'If that is to be your choice.'

Jack's fingers tensed. But he had long ago learned when not to fight. No matter how strong the temptation.

But that did not mean he would go quietly.

'Next time I see you, Dubois, I'll kill you.' He spoke the words deadpan, then balled his right hand into a fist. He punched hard and straight. The blow came fast and clipped the Frenchman on the chin, throwing his head to one side. He fell like a sack of horseshit, landing on his arse in the dust.

Jack looked down on the man he had just made his enemy. 'I'll be back. When I do, you'll die.'

He did not linger. There was nothing else to be said. He had made his vow.

He stalked away, hatred burning bright. Yet it was not Dubois he hated.

It was himself.

For he had saved the Frenchman, and nothing would ever be the same again.

Chapter Twenty-nine

---•◦•---

5 March 1870

*J*ack stood in the darkness, staring up at the stars. They were present in legions, filling the sky from horizon to horizon and casting a pure white light over the land. He liked the stars. Normally there was something in their serenity he found comforting. They had never abandoned him. No matter where he was in the world, he could look up into the night sky and for a moment he would not feel so alone.

Yet that had been before.

He tried to trace patterns across the brightest points of light. He knew that cleverer men than he had fixed drawings into the night sky. No one had ever shown him what they were, so now he tried for himself, sketching patterns across the heavens. Yet no matter how many times he tried to draw something, he found himself staring into the blank, lifeless eyes of those who had lost all hope. Here, alone in the dark, they came to him with the utmost clarity, their stares boring deep into his soul. There was no accusation in those stares, no hatred or fear. What he saw was worse. For he saw eyes filled with nothing.

They were the eyes of the dead fixed into the skulls of the living. And they tormented him.

The evening air was warm and muggy, yet still he shivered. He could sense Fate's presence. She was mocking him. Everything he had ever done had led him to this point. Hope, ambition and pride had sustained him, his desire to be a commander pushing to the fore so he could show an uncaring world what he could do. And yet no matter what he had done, and what he had been, Fate had brought him to the moment where he had ordered the deaths of men fighting to save their families. He had given that order without thought, fighting just as he had always fought, leading his men into battle to vanquish the foe in front of him and to save his friends. Except this time he had been utterly and completely wrong.

He replayed the events that had followed his striking of Dubois. The Frenchman had let him go, sitting in silence, nursing his jaw. He had not spoken again, not even to summon his men to hold Jack to account. For his part, Jack had walked away without looking back. He had gathered his men, keeping them far from the stockade and its pitiful contents. As soon as they were ready, they had left, taking Samir's body with them. None of the Forty had seen the prisoners. Their presence was a burden Jack would carry alone.

As he stood there staring up at the stars, Dubois' words echoed in his mind. The Frenchman was correct. The two of them were indeed the same. Jack was no better than the man who had taken the women and children. For he had not hesitated to save a man he had believed to be his friend, and that act had condemned those Dubois had imprisoned to a destiny that no man, woman or child should ever face. Worst of all, he had found joy in that moment. For when he had led his men onto the field of battle, he had been complete. In that moment, he had been happy. Dubois was right. He had made his choices a long time ago. He had not become this man, this killer of men, this supposed commander, overnight.

It had taken time to condemn his soul to the darkness.

'Jack?'

He closed his eyes. He did not want to be disturbed. Not now.

'They are beautiful, aren't they just? On a night such as this, I think I shall never be able to live in a city again.'

Reluctantly Jack opened his eyes. Anna Baker moved closer, a shawl wrapped around her shoulders. Anger came then, fiery and hot. She would never be able to understand this. Not now. Not ever. He found that he resented her for it. Her mind was clean. Unsullied. And that was unfair.

He did not want to be so alone.

She came to his side. He tried to find words to return her greeting. But there was no room left in his head for a mundane comment, it was too full of the revulsion at the man he had become. He had told Sir Sam of the fight, the loss of Samir and the presence of Dubois and his men. Of the Forty's inability to stand and fight he had revealed nothing, just as he had done nothing to punish or chastise those who had fled, his own shame leaving no scope to castigate men who had merely run for their lives. And he had said nothing whatsoever of the prisoners, painting a picture of the Frenchman as an innocent ivory trader who had been the victim of unprovoked aggression. Sir Sam had swallowed the tale without question, even going so far as to praise Jack for his intervention, before regaling him with tales of previous encounters with the gangs who tried to control Sudan. Jack had listened, but not a single word had registered. Even when Sir Sam was done, he had not said a word more. He had kept to himself since, holding himself close and praying that the memory of the day would fade, so that he could bury it away with the other dark memories in the recess of his mind where they could be contained and corralled. For now, he just had to wait. For he knew that even the most evil memories would lose their power if he only gave them time.

'I heard there was something of a battle.' Anna stood close, eyes roving across the heavens.

'Yes.' He managed the single word, but no more.

'Monsoor told me. He said you were one of the bravest men he has ever seen.' She looked up at him, brow furrowed as she tried and failed to read his expression. 'He said you stood up and showed the men what you wanted them to do, even when the battle was at its most dangerous. He said he had never seen anyone do that before.'

'No.' Jack wanted to summon more words, but they would not come to him.

'Jack, are you quite all right?' Anna reached out a hand, placing it on his forearm.

Jack found he could not speak. Emotions bubbled through him. Hot, raw, potent. Stronger than anything he had felt before. They surged against the barriers he had erected to keep them at bay. Like floodwaters surging against a dam, they threatened to break through. He knew that once they were released, they could never again be contained. If the dam broke, it could not be repaired. It would be broken forever.

He would be broken forever.

Anna would have had to be made of stone not to see the emotion raging through him. Yet she stayed silent. Instead of speaking, she looked up at the stars. But she left her hand in place.

Jack focused every one of his senses on the touch of her hand on his arm. It was warm and it was small, fragile even. He could feel it trembling against his skin, as if she were cold and was shivering. The slightest movement flickered through her fingers, and for one dreadful moment he thought she was going to take her hand away. Then they settled and stayed still.

'I am here, Jack.' The words were spoken softly. 'If you would like to talk.'

He swallowed with difficulty. Yet the raw feelings were subsiding. His barriers had held. For now.

'It cannot be easy. To have to kill.' She kept her face towards the sky as she spoke, giving him the space he needed.

'No.'

'No?'

'No. It is too easy to kill.' Jack sighed. 'Far too bloody easy.'

'I do not believe that.'

He reached across to remove her hand from his arm, then stepped away from the rail. He felt coldness return to his soul. It was a relief, and he relished its arrival, holding it close, cherishing its icy touch. Without it, he did not think he could hold on.

'Believe it or not as you will.' He heard the coolness in his tone. But he could no more change it than he could draw patterns in the sky.

Anna's eyes registered hurt, but before she could utter another word, the steamer gave an almighty lurch to one side.

'Shit!' Jack could not hold back the oath as he was thrown from his feet. He went down hard, the breath driven from his body.

For a moment, all he could do was lie there, absorbing the pain.

The steamer lurched again. Shouts followed, panicked voices bellowing.

Anna had clung to the rail as the ship pitched back and forth. Now she called to Jack, reaching out her hand.

Jack ignored it. He pushed down on the deck, levering himself to his feet. As he found his footing, the steamer bucked again, the deck rising and falling as if they had been caught in a terrible storm. Yet the air was heavy and still, just as it had been before the vessel started to move so erratically.

'We are under attack!' A new voice cut through the babble of frightened shouts. It belonged to Sir Sam, who came striding across the deck with Florence trailing in his wake.

'What?' Jack didn't understand. He was forced to spread his arms wide as he tried to hold on to his balance. The ship was rocking from side to side as if it were being shaken from beneath.

'Goddammit, Jack,' Sir Sam snapped as he staggered to one side. Behind him Florence danced across the deck, then grabbed hold of the rail next to Anna. 'Something is attacking us.'

The steamer gave another great lurch.

'The hull is breached! We are taking on water!' This time the voice belonged to one of the crewmen.

'All hands below decks. Man the pumps!' Sir Sam bellowed the orders, then looked to Jack and the two women. 'I need your help. We have precious supplies below. We must save what we can. We cannot risk them being spoiled as we take on water.' The command was given staccato, then Sir Sam rushed away, heading for the door that led below decks.

'What can have done this?' Jack fired the question at Florence. He had to know what was happening.

'A hippopotamus has attacked us.' Florence grabbed at Anna's arm to hold herself steady.

'Shit.' Jack swore again as he skidded across the angled deck until he reached the side of the steamer. The waters below were churning, the normally placid, murky river thrown into a frothing frenzy. A quick glance down the side of the ship showed where the hippo had hit. The starboard paddle wheel had been twisted out of shape, and at least two paddles had been torn away from the steel framework.

No sooner had he taken in the damage than the steamer gave an almighty groan. Moments later, the bow sank down, the whole front of the ship dropping a good ten degrees.

He looked at the two women. 'We need to be bloody quick about this.'

'We will.' Florence stepped away from the rail. 'The medicines are in the forward hold. We must get those out first.'

'Fine.' Jack didn't care what they aimed to save, so long as they moved quickly.

The sense of danger was very real. Although they were in the shallower waters of the Bahr Giraffe, the steamer could still sink to the bottom, something that would certainly flood the entire lower deck and make the upper deck a dangerous place to be. The water was plenty deep enough to drown in.

He looked up and down the river, trying to find somewhere they could take the supplies they needed to rescue from the hold before it flooded. They were in the middle of the channel. As always, the steamer was surrounded by the Sudd, the vegetation forming a carpet around it. He knew from the miserable hours he had spent in the water hacking a path through it that it was never going to be firm enough to stand on. All they could do was jump into the water then wade away. That thought did not sit well in his mind. Not with some deranged animal attacking the ship, one plainly powerful enough to punch great gashes in the iron-clad hull.

He ran to the port rail, his eyes scanning for better ground. There was just enough light from the stars to show the opposite bank. Yet he saw nothing but more of the tangled vegetation.

'Jack!' Anna shouted to him. 'Jack, over there!'

He whirled around. She was pointing out over the rail towards the stern.

'Where?' He made his way towards her across the canted deck. Just as he reached her, the steamer heaved up, the bow rising a good five feet in the air before crashing back down, the impact sending a dreadful shudder along the length of the ship that threw him forward, all balance lost. He would have fallen for a second time had not both Anna and Florence grabbed at him, each taking firm hold of an arm and hauling him sideways until he slammed into the rail.

'There. You see it?' Anna was clutching at his arm. She jabbed her finger forward as she saw his head turning this way and that as he tried and failed to spot what she had noticed.

'I see it.' Finally Jack clapped eyes on what she had found: a patch of dry land no more than half a dozen yards from the starboard side of the steamer. It would have to do.

The steamer crabbed from side to side as it sank further into the water. Jack was no sailor, but he knew it must be taking on water fast.

'Right, come on.' There was nothing else to be said. He reached out, grabbing Anna's hand. 'You lead, I'll follow.'

He fired off the instructions, then took firm hold of Florence's outstretched hand too.

Anna nodded and set off, moving quickly, Jack following, with Florence at the rear, the three linked together. Jack skidded as they made for the entrance that led below. Somehow he kept his footing as they scrambled through.

It was brighter inside, a gas lamp positioned over the tight stairwell that led to the levels below the main deck. The steamer was not a big ship, but there was still something horribly daunting about going down below. As they made for the stairs, the vessel rolled sickeningly to port, and this time it stayed there, canted at nearly forty-five degrees.

'Quickly now.' It was Florence who encouraged them on.

Anna plunged down the stairs. Jack did his best to follow, staggering from side to side so that he ricocheted painfully off the wooden walls of the stairwell.

They reached the lower level. There was a good six inches of water sloshing across the deck. As they came off the stairs, Anna slipped, boots skidding, and fell to one side. Jack grabbed her arm, breaking her fall, then hauled her up.

'Let's go!' He urged her on, no time to waste. The feeling of being below decks as the steamer took on water was simply awful, like willingly lying down in a coffin before it was lowered into the ground. Water swilled around his boots. It was getting deeper by the second.

No sooner had Anna found her feet than the ship twisted on its keel, lurching back so that it was flat in the water once again. It would make for easier going, but the movement caused a tidal wave of water to sweep across the deck. More water followed, rising fast; it was now nearly ten inches deep.

'Come on.' Anna moved forward, boots kicking up spray

as she splashed her way through. They passed two forward storerooms before she stopped by a closed door. 'This is it.'

'Right, stand back.' Jack let go of the women's hands and reached for the door. With so much water already in the hold, it took all his strength to haul it open.

The storeroom beyond was flooding fast, the water swirling around the stacks of crates. With the steamer lurching so dramatically, the tin boxes were being thrown this way and that. It was only a matter of time before their seals broke open. Once water got inside, the medical supplies would surely be ruined.

'Which ones?' He turned to look at Anna.

'Those!' She pointed at some boxes that were mercifully close to the door.

Jack assessed them quickly. He reckoned he could carry two, which left one each for Anna and Florence.

'Right, take this.' He reached for the uppermost box, grabbing hold then swinging it around before shoving it towards Florence. As soon as she had taken it, he picked up the next, thrusting it at Anna, then turned for the last two. 'This had better be bloody worth it,' he hissed, then gasped in pain, the weight of the crates pulling at his back and sending a single jolt of pain shooting down both his legs.

The women turned to go back the way they had come, and Jack was about to follow when he saw a rifle case propped up on the other side of the cabin. He recognised it at once. It was the Dutchman, Sir Sam's beloved rifle.

'Go! Go!' He saw Anna hesitate, so shouted at her to move before dumping the tin boxes he had picked up back onto the floor.

'What are you doing?' Anna called back at him.

'I'm coming. Now bloody move.' Jack was already moving further into the cabin. It felt like he was stepping into his own grave. The water was getting deeper by the second, so that he could feel it cold on his legs as it slopped over the top of his boots. He could taste his own fear. It surged through him, icy and sickening. Yet it did not stop him reaching out for the rifle. It took no time to sling it over his shoulder, then he was on his way back to the door.

Yet as he picked up the two crates, the door swung shut, and he was plunged into darkness.

At first, he could do nothing but stand there. He could see nothing, the blackness now complete. His breathing stopped as the cold, remorseless hand of terror took hold of his soul.

He was trapped.

Chapter Thirty

*J*ack tried to calm his breathing as he felt the water lap up over his shins. He failed. Every instinct screamed at him to move, but his body refused to obey. In the darkness, he could do nothing.

The fear had him completely.

The walls of the storeroom seemed to be closing in around him. It felt as if they were rushing forward, pressing in, the space getting smaller and smaller by the second. Before long it would squeeze him tight, and he would be fixed in place, unable to move, unable to breathe.

Water swirled around his calves. He could sense it getting deeper. Yet still he could not move.

Faces filled his mind. Some he knew. People he had loved alongside those he had lost. Then came the dead, comrades who had fallen parading with the nameless faces of those he had killed. They filed past in his mind, one after the other. Then came the faces of Dubois' prisoners. They laughed at him, mouths opening and closing whilst their eyes remained blank. They beckoned him towards them, the faces of the dead and the lifeless calling for him to join them in the darkness.

He knew he should move, that he should hammer on the door and fight his way free. Just as he had always fought. Yet for a reason he could not fully understand, he did not move so much as a single inch, for Fate had led him there. And so he would let her lead him out. If she wanted to punish him for what he had done, he would not fight her. Not now. If this was to be his fate, it was one he deserved.

Light rushed into the storeroom. Bright. Warm. Alive.

'Jack! Come on!' Anna stood in the doorway, tin box held across her front whilst she fought to hold the door open with her shoulder.

For one long moment, Jack could do nothing but stare at her, his mind quite unable to process what his eyes were seeing. Then his body moved of its own accord, lurching into an awkward, jerking motion. He reached the open door in no more than three strides.

'Thank you.' The words exploded out of him.

'Come on, you fool.' Anna was already moving away from the door.

'Where's Florence?' Jack's senses were coming back to him. Fear contained. Terror banished.

'She's gone. She'll be fine.' Anna waded forward. On her shorter legs, the water reached to just below her knee. Jack followed her, back the way they had come.

The steamer was creaking, the sound alarming and strange, the stricken ship groaning. Cries and shouts came constantly, as the crew battled to keep as much water out as they could. Jack paid none of it any heed as he trailed after Anna, eyes fixed on her back.

The stairs came closer. Nothing could be seen of the lower treads, all now submerged. But it did not slow them, and both climbed fast, staggering from side to side with the motion of the steamer as it wallowed and pitched.

Jack tasted a moment's elation as he clambered up the last step then broke out into the night-time air. The feeling of suffocation that had gripped him ever since he had gone below blew away. He was free.

'This way.' Anna shouted at him to follow. She lurched across the awkwardly canted deck, making for the starboard rail. The steamer was dreadfully low in the water now, the river little more than a yard below the upper deck.

Jack caught sight of Florence. One of the dahabiyas had come alongside the steamer and she was being helped across, whilst a stream of Sudanese infantrymen were jumping aboard the ship and heading below to join the fight to pump out the water surging in through the holes in the hull.

Anna was already near the starboard rail and was heading towards the stern. He thought of calling after her, telling her to change direction and follow Florence onto the dahabiya. But he could see the other ship was already pulling away, its captain anxious to keep his distance in case the steamer dragged his vessel under as it sank ever lower into the waters of the Bahr Giraffe. It meant that avenue of escape was lost before he could even begin to think of making towards it.

There was nothing else to be done. He hefted the tin boxes and followed Anna towards the stern. Before they could reach it, though, the steamer listed once again, the deck pitching down towards the water on the starboard side. And there it stayed.

'Stop!' He called her back. They had gone far enough.

She turned to face him. Even in the darkness, he could see her face was pale with fear.

'Over the side, quickly now.' He dumped the cases on the deck, then reached towards her.

She came to him, placing her box on top of his then taking hold of his hands.

'Over you go.' He grunted with the strain as he took her weight and swung her up and over the rail.

'The cases!' Anna stood there, feet balanced on the steamer's side, her upper body resting on the rail.

'Here.' Jack handed over one of the boxes. 'Now jump.'

Her eyes met his for just a moment, then she turned and launched herself forward.

He heard the splash as she landed in the river. He picked up the other boxes and shrugged the rifle's carrying case so that it was firmly seated on his shoulder, then clambered onto the rail. It was not easy. He pushed up, getting his backside on top of it, then swung his left leg up and over. With the heavy cases in his hands, he was ungainly and unbalanced, so he threw his right leg onto the rail, thinking to balance on the other side just as Anna had done. But that night he was as agile as a decrepit crone, and he felt his balance go the moment he tried to complete the awkward manoeuvre. There was one horrible drawn-out moment when he balanced on the rail on his arse with his right leg hanging in space, then he toppled over.

He hit the water hard. It clawed him down, choking and cold, swirling around him, running into his mouth and filling his nose. He had no idea what was up and what was down, his senses overwhelmed. Then he hit the bottom, or at least the vegetation that was stuck to the riverbed. It was enough for him to understand where he was. He rolled himself around, moving his legs beneath him then pushing them down, forcing his body up and out.

He came up blowing hard, water cascading from his head and shoulders. As he found his footing, he sucked down a breath, holding it in his lungs with pure relief.

'You all right?' Anna was standing no more than a yard away, the water just below her shoulders.

'Yes.' Jack turned and spat, clearing his mouth of the crud he had swallowed. 'Move!' He jerked his head towards the island of firm ground that was close by.

She did as she was told. It was not easy, but she struggled through the water and the crust of vegetation that covered the surface. Jack followed, doing his best to keep the two tin boxes out of the water.

When Anna reached the firm ground, she stopped, heaving her own box up and out of the river and onto the solid soil. Relieved of the heavy burden, she tried to get herself out of the water, but her strength failed her and she slipped back into the murky swamp.

'Hold there.' Jack waded closer, and with a grunt and a lot of straining heaved both tin boxes he carried onto the drier ground, following them with the rifle. Then he moved next to Anna, showing her his hands, which he cradled together then slipped below the crusty water.

She understood, sliding her boot into his hands and reaching to hold his shoulder to steady herself. He pushed upwards, bunking her a good yard in the air then propelling her forward out of the water so she flopped onto the drier ground like a newly landed fish.

'Fuck me,' he groaned, his back cramping. But at least he was nearly done. With Anna free of the cloying water, he could look after himself. He reached up, getting his arms and elbows onto the dry ground, then with the last of his strength pushed down with his legs and squirmed forward, sliding himself up and out of the water.

Finally he was clear. He crawled forward on his hands and knees, then rolled onto his back. He took a deep breath, holding it in his lungs, feeling the tension leave him, then lay still. He was utterly spent.

But he would not be left in peace.

Anna's face loomed into view over his.

'You need to sit up.' Her voice was firm.

Jack looked up at her. Her skin was streaked with dirt and her hair clung to her head from the drowning it had taken in the river. Her khaki shirt and trousers were soaked and filthy, and a long strand of green creeper was stuck into her belt.

'Come on, sit up. You swallowed a lot of water.' She repeated her command.

With a groan, he levered himself up into a sitting position. He felt sick. It came on quickly, and he pushed himself onto his knees with a sudden burst of energy, his guts emptying onto the sandy ground in front of him. The vomit gushed out of him and he heaved and heaved.

Eventually the waves of nausea subsided. Still he stayed where he was, head hanging down as he panted with the effort of puking out the contents of his stomach.

'Are you done?'

Anna was crouched at his side. For the first time, he noticed she was rubbing his back in a series of comforting circles.

'Yes.' He forced out the word, then struggled to his feet, wiping his sleeve across his face to remove as much of the spit and snot as he could. As soon as he was standing, he stepped away from her, and from the foul liquid he had voided.

'Do you feel better?' She did not let him retreat, but came

after him, hand reaching for his arm, face creasing with concern.

'Yes.' Anna was close now. It would be easy to sweep her into his arms. He sensed she would not resist if he did.

The image of the prisoners' faces flooded back into his mind. They tormented him, filled his soul, leaving no room for anything else. Or anyone.

Anna took a hesitant step closer, her eyes fixed on his.

Jack held his ground for the span of one more heartbeat. The temptation was powerful, but he would not surrender to it. The defences in his mind were nowhere near strong enough to hold, and if he gave in now, they would be breached. And he would break.

He turned away and bent down, retrieving the rifle case he had dumped on the ground. Anna gasped, but he ignored the sound, just as he ignored the racing of his heart, concentrating instead on untying the clasps and buckles that held the case closed. He felt no guilt. His soul was full of it already.

'Do you not trust me, Jack?' She had wrapped her arms around her middle, holding herself tight.

'No.' Jack's fingers fumbled a clasp. Despite the warmth of the night, he was cold, his soaked clothes chilling his blood to ice.

'Why?'

He grunted as he freed the fastening. He would not answer.

'Can you not trust anyone?'

He ignored the question and pulled open another buckle. It was the last one and he drew the rifle out, dropping its leather case to the ground.

'You have been hurt.' Anna spoke gently. 'I can see that.'

He hefted the weapon in his hands. It was far heavier than a standard rifle. Even the Snider with its heavy breechblock felt like a child's toy compared to the weight of the Dutchman.

'You are so lost, Jack. But you won't find yourself. Not until you learn to trust.'

Jack glanced at her. 'Do not waste your time on me.' He spoke the cold words in a monotone. 'I know what I am. What I have become.'

'You can be more.'

'No.' He shut her down. He had tried that. For a while he had believed he had found what he had been looking for. And he had been happy. Until he realised what he had done.

'You are wrong, Jack.'

This time he did not answer. He did not have to.

'I am standing on the edge of something.' Anna spoke quietly, refusing to be driven away.

'What's that?' Jack was scathing.

'A new future. I just have to take one more step, and everything changes.' She moved closer. 'Do you want to come with me? Do you want to see what that future holds?'

Jack lifted the rifle. A part of him wanted more. But he shut it down, just as he shut away the rest of the emotions that powered through him. He would not give in. He could not give in. He pulled the weapon tight into his shoulder and sighted down the barrel as if at some imaginary enemy. It placed the rifle between them, a barrier as effective as any words he might have uttered.

'You cannot run from this, Jack. You cannot run from yourself.'

He held his pose.

Anna sighed. It was a sad sound, disappointment and regret combined. 'I will be here, Jack. If you need me . . .' She left the thought unfinished. Then she stepped away, turning her attention to the tin boxes they had rescued from the steamer.

Jack lowered the rifle. He had done as he had been asked. He had kept Anna safe and he had managed to get the precious medicines off the ship. He had even saved Sir Sam's prized rifle. Yet as he stood there, he felt his former despondency return with full force. He had not done enough. Not by a long way. Not compared to the crime he had committed.

Only one thing would assuage that guilt.

And he would not rest until it was done.

Chapter Thirty-one

—◆—

12 March 1870

'This will not do, I tell you! This will not do at all!'

Jack stood stock still as Sir Sam stormed into the cabin. He did not fear the man's anger.

'Uncle, you must reconsider.' Julian Baker had flinched as his uncle raged, but to his credit he had rallied fast. Now he lifted his chin and dared to contradict the expedition's commander.

'Damn your eyes, Julian. Are you a croaker too?' Sir Sam strode across the cabin until he stood directly in front of his nephew.

Julian visibly quailed, but he stood his ground. 'I see no other course of action, sir.'

'No, of course you damned well don't. That is why you are standing there and I am standing here! Goddammit, goddammit all to hell.' Sir Sam glowered once more at his nephew, then slumped into the cabin's only chair. 'These damned guides. They tell me it is impossible.' His anger, as swift and sure as it had been, was fading fast.

'Perhaps they are correct.' Julian half-whispered the words, then glanced towards Jack for reassurance. It was not often the two agreed, but this was a rare occasion when they were of one mind. They had talked of this before Sir Sam had arrived. Both agreed it was time to admit defeat and turn the expedition around. The going was just too difficult, their progress too slow. Both men were certain. They could not hold to the current course.

Jack could understand Julian's reticence. Sir Sam was not an easy man to contradict. But that did not mean it did not have to be done. It had been a tough few days. Very tough. They had been forced to wait forty-eight hours for the steamer to be repaired. The hippopotamus had torn two great gashes in the steel-plated hull, its tusks shredding the starboard paddle wheel. The shipwrights had done their best. They had worked on the damage day and night, repairing the hull by plastering white lead over thick felt, which was then covered with planks and secured by wedges from a cross-beam. The job was only temporary, and despite their efforts, the damaged area still let in enough water for the pumps to have to be manned at all times. But at least they had got the steamer back into action.

The same could not be said of the supplies it had been carrying, the water the ship had taken on enough to soak tonnes of rations. Sir Sam's insistence on securing the goods into the tin boxes had saved a great deal, but many of the crates had been broken open when the steamer was battered by the hippopotamus's violent attack.

Once the steamer was patched up, the flotilla had pressed on, but the Bahr Giraffe had become more impassable by the day, the river choked with thick, cloying mud that forced the men back into the water to try to hack out a channel through which the expedition's ships could sail. Progress had become dreadfully slow, the distance covered in a day measured in yards rather than miles. Finally Sir Sam had granted the exhausted men a day off. In truth he had no choice, the Muslim festival of Hadj something he could not avoid. The day's rest was a welcome respite from the never-ending toil of trying to shift tons upon tons of mud. For Julian and Jack, it had offered an opportunity to confront Sir Sam with the lack of progress made.

'Of course they are not correct.' Sir Sam harrumphed as he pooh-poohed the idea that the two local guides he had engaged could possibly know better than he. 'No, we shall hold to our course. Why, to turn tail and run at the first difficulty would be nothing short of reprehensible. The khedive would have my guts for garters.'

'Very well, sir.' Julian bowed to the inevitable.

But Jack was not so easily swayed. He took a half-step forward, making sure he had the expedition leader's fullest attention.

'I firmly believe we should turn back, sir.' He spoke slowly and formally. He did not want to be misunderstood.

'Not you too, Jack.' Sir Sam sounded disappointed.

Jack held firm. 'You must give the order to turn back.'

'Mind your tongue, sir.' Sir Sam's cheeks coloured. 'Know who you are speaking to.'

'I do. I'm speaking to you. We must turn around.'

'Must? Damn you, you are not in charge here.' Sir Sam glared at him. 'I expected more of you, Jack. Much more.'

'Then you were mistaken.' Jack's words were as hard as iron. 'How long can we carry on as we are?'

'As long as it damned well takes.' Some of Sir Sam's earlier fire returned.

Jack held his own temper in check. It would not help him. Not with a man like Sir Sam. But he had to turn the expedition around, no matter what it took. He had to go back and put things right.

'At this rate, it will take months. How much progress have we made these last days? A mile a day? Less?'

'The river will clear. We just need to persevere.'

'When? When will it clear?'

'There are lakes to the south. No more than a dozen miles distant. The Sudd will disperse.'

'And if it doesn't?'

'Then we carry on regardless.'

'What if you are wrong?'

Sir Sam scowled. 'You doubt me, Jack?'

'Not your dedication.' Jack softened his tone. 'But there are times when that dedication clouds your judgement.'

'Damn your eyes, are you saying I am deluded?'

'Yes.' Jack held Sir Sam's stare. 'We have the men in the water at first light. We work them all day. It takes everything they have to dig a channel through that stinking mud. All for what? So we can make another quarter-mile?'

'It will not last.' Sir Sam fairly hissed the words. His certainty was obvious.

Jack was less sure. They had barely made any progress for the last two days. He had been in the water with his men, the Forty taking their shifts with the other infantrymen. It was miserable, back-breaking toil. The only way to clear a path for the flotilla was to dig deep into the stinking morass. Hour after hour of hacking at the gloopy black mud, then piling it up to make artificial riverbanks. Every second of their labour was plagued by a million insects drawn to the sweating faces of the men. In the fetid quagmire, hours felt like days. It was miserable, exhausting work. And it was proving to be a killer.

'How many more men will have to die to make you see sense?'

'Jack!'

He took another half-step forward. He would not back down. The first man had died three days before. Another fifty were sick. There were so many men needing attention that Anna and Florence were hard pressed to tend to them all. He was sure more would die before the week was out. Sir Sam needed to be reminded of that. The stakes were rising by the day. Progress would soon be measured in lives spent, not yards gained, and that could not go unchallenged.

'Well?' He did not give so much as an inch.

Sir Sam rose to his feet. 'I am in command here, Jack, in case you have forgotten that. I regret that man's death, just as I regret the suffering the sick are enduring. But that will not turn me from my path.'

'You don't care how many will die?'

Sir Sam came closer. 'No.' The word emerged wrapped in fire.

Jack saw the fervour that gleamed in the expedition leader's gaze. He had seen it before. Men like Sir Sam had ambition. Ambition that cost other men their lives. It was a coin some would spend without hesitation.

'So there it is.' He breathed the words.

'Yes, there it is. It is how it has to be. We cannot achieve the aims of this expedition if we turn tail the first time we lose a man. It is regrettable, but what we are striving for here is worth the cost. I have said it before, and I will say it over and over without hesitation, because I believe it. As should you, Jack.

You were a soldier. You of all people surely understand that sometimes a sacrifice must be made to achieve a certain goal. It is no different here. What we are trying to accomplish is too important for us to give in. The stakes are too high.'

'So we carry on, no matter how many men die? No matter how bad it becomes?'

'We do.'

'And what if someone close to you dies? What if it's Julian? Or Florence? Would we stop then? Would the price be too high then?'

'You go too far.' Sir Sam took a pace towards Jack. 'You will obey my orders. We will hold to our course. Is that clear enough for you?'

Jack ground his teeth. He was getting nowhere.

'What is going on here?' Anna entered the cabin and immediately sensed the atmosphere. 'I could cut the tension with a knife.'

'Jack and your brother believe we should turn around, my dear.' Sir Sam glowered one last time at Jack before he sat back down.

Anna shot Jack a look. If Sir Sam had regarded him coldly, her stare was made from permafrost. 'I see.'

'We are making little progress and now men are dying.' Jack sighed. 'How many are sick?'

'Fifty-seven. At my last count.'

'And how many of those will die?'

'None, if I can help it.' Anna's reply was clipped and sharp. 'Since when did you care about the sick, Mr Lark?'

Jack opened his mouth to reply, then thought better of it. It was time to shut up. He knew when he could not win. He turned to Sir Sam. 'I meant no offence, sir. I merely stated the facts as I see them. I apologise if I stepped over the line. Truly.'

Sir Sam looked hard at him, then nodded. 'Thank you, Jack.' He gave a thin-lipped smile. 'I appreciate your candour. It is better such things are aired in the open rather than festering in the dark.'

'Indeed.' Jack did not try to return the smile. It was beyond him. But he was glad Sir Sam had accepted the olive branch he had offered. It would be no good for them to be at loggerheads, and so he would beat as graceful a retreat as he could. He would have to bide his time. For now, at least.

But it appeared Anna would not let him retire without one last volley for good measure.

'I do not think Mr Lark fully understands, Uncle. Perhaps it might be best if he returns to Khartoum. Alone if necessary.'

'I hardly think it has come to that.' Sir Sam scowled at the notion. 'Give me one more day, gentlemen.' He addressed himself to Jack and Julian. 'One more day, and I promise we shall see progress.'

It was clear he would not be swayed. The expedition would carry on.

Jack stood at the bow of the steamer. He could feel a brisk breeze scouring over his skin. It came from the north, buffeting against his back with enough force to make him have to hold on to the steamer's rail lest he lose his footing.

He looked out over the bow at the way ahead. The sight of open water sickened him.

Sir Sam had been proven correct. It had taken one more day of horrific toil, then the channel had opened. They had reached the lakes, just as he had predicted.

Progress was finally possible.

And if the open water had been sent by God, then he was in a beneficent mood. For then the north wind had come.

The troops on the nearby dahabiya were banging drums and singing, and the rising notes of bugles filled the air. They were delirious with happiness, the thought of no longer having to spend the day up to their waists in the foul-smelling mud enough for them to start celebrating. Sir Sam had seized on the moment, raiding the stores to issue a double ration of rum to the men. The promise of easier days to come and the immediate arrival of alcohol were two of a soldier's favourite things. If the expedition leader could have added a feast and enough willing women to the mix, his men would likely have worshipped him like a god.

Jack was glad that Sir Sam had allowed the celebration and he had taken a bottle of rum for himself. He intended to drink it all. Alone. A party for one.

Only then would he find the peace of mind he craved. He knew it would only be temporary, that it would last only as long as the hangover that would follow. But it would do.

And then he would wait. He had been forced to be patient before, and he could be so again. His moment would come. He was certain of it. Fate would not forget him.

She never did.

Chapter Thirty-two

2 April 1870

'Fucking push it!'

Jack snapped the instruction as he heaved his shoulder under the great bale of grass that had been cut from the covering of matted fibres that smothered the river. Monsoor did his best to help, an explosive grunt escaping his mouth as he strained at Jack's side. Both men were chest deep in the scummy green water, which smelt as if a thousand creatures had died in it and were now rotting away just below the surface.

The great roll of grass barely moved.

'Push!' Jack called again, the words hissing out of his mouth as he bent his legs and shoved with all his might, or at least all the might he had left after three long hours in the festering foulness of the river channel.

Slowly, reluctantly, the roll of matted fibres began to move.

Jack gritted his teeth, then pushed once more. Finally the grass came out of the water, foul black liquid cascading from the tangled fibres, and they heaved it further up the bank the men had made from other bales of the knotted foliage that blocked the river.

It had been Sir Sam's idea to try the new approach. The men now attacked the swathes of greenery that stretched across the river, creating a channel then heaving the baled foliage out of the water and forming a rudimentary bank to the meagre canal they had made. It was painfully slow work, but if pressed they would all have agreed it was better than the toil of the week before, when they had been forced to hack a path out of the thick black mud clogging the river. Yet it was still back-breaking work, and once again the progress of the flotilla had reduced to little more than a cruel crawl.

The success of the lakes had not lasted long.

There had been a single good day. The small fleet had regrouped in the clear open waters, the first time the whole flotilla had been together for many weeks. Yet no sooner had they tried to make progress south than they found themselves once again stuck in tangled vegetation that formed an almost impenetrable barrier, through which not even the powerful steamers could force passage. Within hours they had lost sight of the river itself, and Sir Sam had been forced to order the men back into the water.

Days of hard toil had followed. The water was deeper here, the terrain different from the Sudd-choked channels they had encountered earlier. The river was filled with tall grasses, and tangled green reeds and creepers lay in a thick layer on the surface. Sir Sam had ordered the ships to line up nose to tail as they tried to push through the narrow channel the men had been able to create. It was working, but it was painfully slow, and the troops were once again labouring from dawn to dusk.

And it was costing them dear.

Sickness was still spreading rapidly through the ranks of Sir Sam's small army. Exhausted, and with bodies reduced by weeks of brutally hard toil, the men had little strength left to fight it. Another man had died two days after they had left the lakes behind. Three more had followed in the last day alone. Sir Sam's command was paying a high price to grind their way south.

'Jack, look out! Snake.' Monsoor hissed the warning as the pair staggered back from the bale of grass they had just heaved out of the water.

Jack saw a lithe brown body slide through the grass he had just moved. The thought that his face had been no more than half an inch from the grass, and therefore probably the same distance from the venomous reptile, sent a shudder of cold fear running through him. He hated snakes, and the river teemed with them. Men were bitten daily, adding to the numbers of the sick. The idea was almost too grim to contemplate, and so he stepped gratefully away, even though it meant slogging back through the chest-deep water and moving another roll of grass.

'*Afandi!*'

Jack looked for the voice calling for his attention. He saw two of his men waving at him. It was the Taha brothers, the pair inseparable even here in the gloopy waters. They were proving to be amongst his very best men, but they loathed being in the river, not one of the men from the Sudan anything close to what could be called a good swimmer. This time, though, they were not trying to get his attention to beg him to let them return to the steamer. Instead, they were fighting to keep Abdallah out of the water, their huge countryman, who had so diligently protected Lieutenant el-Sisi in the recent skirmish, sagging in their arms, his head hanging so low it was almost submerged.

'Shit.' There was time for Jack to hiss the oath before he started wading towards his men. He did not need to get closer to know the powerful Sudanese was unconscious. It was a dreadful omen. Abdallah was by far the strongest of the Forty. Now even he had succumbed to the evil sickness that was decimating the ranks.

'Get him up.' Jack snapped the order as he reached the twins. 'Hold him under his arms.' He reached forward, helping the pair hold Abdallah's head out of the water.

As soon as they had firm hold of the sick man, he pointed to the steamer, which was twenty or thirty yards away. 'We need to get him on board.'

There was nothing more to be said. Jack led the pair back along the river. At least their path was clear now, after the day's work cutting the channel, but it still took several exhausting minutes to make their way to one of the rope ladders slung off the steamer's sides.

'Heh! Lend a bloody hand!' Jack shouted up. He was rewarded almost immediately by the sight of the ship's crew coming to their aid.

The large Sudanese man seemed to weigh as much as a small bull elephant, and it took all three men in the water, and another four on the steamer, to haul him up onto the deck.

No sooner was he on board than Anna leaned over the rail to peer down at Jack.

'Snake bite?'

'No.' Jack held on to the ladder with one hand whilst he swiped the other across his face, smearing away muck and sweat. 'He's just done in.' He did not care that Anna saw him as he was, half naked and covered with filth.

She nodded curtly. 'Are you coming out?'

'No.'

'You want water?'

He shook his head and started to climb back down the rope ladder. It would be another hour at least until his men would be ordered out of the water so that fresher ones could take their place. He would not quit until then. He would stay with his men no matter what it took.

The scream rang out, pure and clear.

'Again.'

The next scream came louder than the first. It was a shriek of pure agony, and it went on and on, the sound of a soul in torment.

'Goddammit. Again.'

Jack flinched as Abdallah jack-knifed on the table, and it took all his strength to pin the big man's shoulders down. Crazed by pain and fever, Abdallah thrashed and jerked, his entire body convulsing as the electric charge surged through him. Such was his strength, Jack was forced to use his full weight to keep the man from flopping onto the floor, and the thick rubber gloves he had been ordered to wear were slipping and sliding over Abdallah's sweat-slicked skin. A glance at Julian told him that the Royal Navy officer was having just as much trouble holding the man's ankles down.

'Again.'

'Fucking hell.' Jack hissed the words through gritted teeth as Sir Sam gave the hideous order. Yet he would not leave. The Sudanese was one of the Forty, one of the men who had stayed in place during the fight to save Dubois. Jack would not abandon him now in his moment of need.

The scream that followed did not last as long as the ones that had come before. It was cut short as the Sudanese disappeared into the oblivion of unconsciousness.

'Goddammit.' Sir Sam shook his head. In his hands he held two long metal probes, from which a single wire led back to the wooden box containing the magnetic battery that had produced the shocks that had driven Abdallah into fits of agony. 'We will try again when he awakes.'

'Jesus Christ.' Jack released his hold on the sick man and pulled the heavy gloves from hands covered in sweat.

'It is either that or he dies,' Sir Sam snapped. He dropped the pair of probes as if their touch revolted him. 'There is nothing else we can do for him.'

'Maybe that would be for the best.' Julian spoke the words softly. Like Jack, he was red in the face, sweat running freely across his skin.

Sir Sam nodded slowly, then pulled a handkerchief from his pocket and wiped his brow. 'Maybe you are right. This damn thing is doing no good to the poor fellow.'

'Did you think it would?' Jack could not hold back the biting comment.

'It is said to be effective.' Sir Sam looked crestfallen.

'By the man who made it?'

'Yes.' Sir Sam stepped away from the table. The cabin they were in was cramped, so he did not have much room to go further. Like all the steamer's cabins, it had been given over to the care of those who were ill. This particular one had been turned into a temporary surgery, the dining table they had once shared now used as a makeshift operating table. The rest were filled with the worst of the sick. Yet there were still too many to sleep in comfort, and the rest, the ones deemed to be less unwell, were lying on the decks of the dahabiyas. All were suffering terribly. Most had a fever that burned through day and night. With it came sickness and diarrhoea, the men quickly reduced to mere skeletons as the illness scoured through their insides.

'I'm afraid to say I think our poor patient has expired.' Julian was examining Abdallah, his hand resting on the man's neck.

'Dear God,' Sir Sam sighed.

Julian looked up. His eyes were streaked with red, and there were puffy grey sacks beneath them. He might not have taken his place in the water, but he was no less exhausted. Sir Sam was working them all hard.

Jack swallowed with difficulty. Abdallah was the first of the Forty to die since the fight. He came to the big man's side, reaching out to close eyes that now stared lifelessly up at the ceiling of the cabin.

Then he turned towards Sir Sam. 'That's six now. How many more will have to die before you are satisfied?'

'Jack!' Sir Sam recoiled from the harshness in the words.

'Ten? Twenty? Fifty? A hundred?' Jack glanced at the Sudanese. He had been one of the best amongst the Forty. He did not deserve the hand that Fate had dealt him.

'That's enough, Jack,' Julian warned.

Jack ignored him. 'We've covered barely twelve miles in as many days. The men are losing heart, surely you must see that?'

'The men or you?' Sir Sam snapped.

Jack's anger came swift and sure. 'Fuck you.'

'Jack!' Julian could not believe what he was hearing.

But Sir Sam was made of sterner stuff. 'You forget who you are speaking to.'

'No, I know very well.'

'Then I would urge you to mind your tongue before you say something you will regret.' The words were delivered shrouded in ice.

But Jack didn't care. He would not hold his tongue. Not when men were dying to satisfy Sir Sam's ambition. He realised he had read the expedition leader wrong. For the man now standing in front of him, reputation was all. It did not matter how many souls had to be sacrificed to achieve his goals.

'One hundred and fifty men are sick. Six have now died.' Jack listed the bare facts. It was all he could do not to shout the numbers into Sir Sam's face. He had to make him understand what he was doing, what price he was making others pay. 'It's been fifty-one days since we left Khartoum and how far have we come? We must turn back. We must.'

Sir Sam had held Jack's gaze as he had spoken. Only now did he look away.

'What is going on?'

Jack turned to see Anna and Florence entering the cabin.

'He's dead,' Jack replied, pointing at the body of the Sudanese on the table.

'It didn't work?' It was Florence who asked the question as she came towards her husband.

'No.' His answer emerged as barely more than a whisper. 'It didn't do a damn thing.'

Jack would not hold back, not even now the women had joined them. 'Why don't you take a long, hard look at him. All of you.' He gestured towards the dead body. 'Take a good look and ask yourself if this is worth it.'

'That's enough.' Anna was not deterred by his harsh tone. She came to stand at his side and busied herself checking over the man who had died despite Sir Sam's attempt to apply the latest science-based cure to his care.

'No, it's not enough.' Jack could smell Anna now she was standing next to him. After his hours in the dank water, she smelt clean and fresh. 'How many more will have to die until your uncle is satisfied?'

'Be quiet.' Anna hissed the words as she turned away from the dead Sudanese. 'We need to move him. There are others we must tend to.'

'What's the point?' Jack was cruel. 'You're not making any difference.'

'That does not mean we should not try.' Her expression registered the hurt his words were inflicting. 'What would you have us do, Jack?'

'I would have us turn around and go back the way we came.' He held her stare. Despite everything, he still felt an attraction to this woman. She worked as hard as any of the men, hours upon hours spent caring for the sick. He was being cruel to deny the success of her efforts, but at that moment he did not care. All that mattered was turning the flotilla around.

'That is up to my uncle, not you.'

Jack sighed. The tiredness was stealing his strength and his will to fight. 'Well, sir?' He turned to look at Sir Sam. 'What say you? Do we continue? No matter the cost?' He posed the question one last time. It was all he could do.

Silence filled the cabin. The fate of them all, and of the hundreds of men under Sir Sam's charge, hung on this moment.

The silence stretched thin.

To Jack's surprise, it was Florence who broke it.

'Jack is right. We should turn back. We can try again when the waters clear and when the men have had time to recover.'

Sir Sam lifted his gaze. He looked long and hard at his wife, his eyes searching her face.

No one spoke.

'So be it.' He said the words softly, then slumped back in his chair, as if they had exhausted him. 'We will turn the flotilla around.'

Silence greeted the pronouncement. All knew what it meant.

Jack was too knackered to smile, but he still felt a flicker of satisfaction. And of hope.

He would get his chance to make good his mistakes. Fate had not forgotten him. She was giving him his chance at redemption.

He would let nothing and no one get in his way.

Chapter Thirty-three

13 April 1870

*J*ack took his time cleaning the Beaumont–Adams five-shot revolver. The weapon had not always been his. He had taken it from the corpse of a man who had tried to kill him. He had owned finer weapons in the past, but he knew that the Beaumont would not let him down. The gun had killed before. It would do so again.

'So you're going?'

Jack was sitting on the deck not far from the steamer's bow, the tools he used to clean the revolver lying on the handkerchief he had spread out in front of him, a cardboard packet of cartridges and a new carton of percussion caps to hand. He did not relish being disturbed.

'Yes, Anna.' He answered without looking up.

'You think you will need that?'

'Yes.' He kept his voice neutral. He had endured enough arguments. The last few days had been filled with discord, every disagreement, no matter how small, becoming fractious. There was something shameful in beating a retreat, something incredibly sobering in the knowledge that men had died for nothing. Even the normally placid Marcopolo had lost his temper, the Egyptian reacting badly when Julian had suggested they cache some of their precious supplies for when they returned. He had refused to countenance abandoning even a single box from his stores, and it had taken Sir Sam's intervention to bring the argument to a close, when he had overruled Julian, backing his dragoman over his nephew.

The going had been no better when they started to head north, following the route they had taken just days before. It was as if the river was mocking them, the Sudd refilling the channel they had cut so that the men were forced back into the water once again.

'Did you seek my uncle's permission to go?'

'Yes.'

'And?'

'He forbade me.'

'So why are you getting ready to leave?'

This time Jack did not answer. He was satisfied his revolver was clean, and so reached for the first cartridge. The Beaumont–Adams only took five, unlike the Colt he had used for so long, which had capacity for six rounds. He would have to make sure he did not forget that detail in the heat of battle. For a battle was coming, of that he was certain.

Because he planned to start one.

'If you flout his orders, he will not forgive you. Not now.'

'And?' Jack glanced up as he pushed the cartridge into the chamber and forced it home with the ramrod fixed under the barrel. He took his time, making sure it was well seated. He could not afford a misfire.

'Does that not matter to you?'

'Not really.' He reached for a second cartridge. The early-morning sun was low on the horizon, and it was directly behind Anna, making it hard to look at her for long. At least that was what he told himself.

'You may be dismissed.'

Jack sighed. Anna was stating the obvious. He did not need to hear it. For he did not care. It had taken days to retrace their route back up the Bahr Giraffe. Every one of them had tested his patience to the limit. When they had finally reached the landing spot near Dubois' encampment, he had asked Sir Sam for permission to take the Forty inland. He had not said why; just that he wanted to give his men the chance to feel solid ground under their feet.

He had been refused permission. Sir Sam would not allow his men to be distracted from getting the flotilla back to a place of safety, where the sick could be treated and where they could all lick their wounds and resupply with wood and water ahead of a second attempt to push south as soon as the waters had cleared.

'Does that not concern you?' Anna persisted.

Jack loaded two more chambers as he contemplated the question. He did not mind the idea of dismissal. Fate would take care of him. She always had. The risk of unemployment meant nothing, not compared to the weight of the guilt he had carried since the moment he had walked away from the French-man's encampment on that fateful day when he had killed men who were fighting for the lives of the ones they loved.

'Jack?' she pressed.

'No, Anna. It does not concern me.' He rammed home the last cartridge, then reached for the smaller cardboard packet that contained percussion caps.

'You will be cast out.'

'I don't care.' He fished out a percussion cap and pressed it onto the first of the five nipples, pushing down with his thumb to make sure it was seated firmly.

'Why are you doing this?'

'It's important.'

'To make the men march? Why, you yourself said they were exhausted. Yet now you insist on taking them away from the ships.' Anna looked down at him shrewdly. 'Why do you really want to do this?'

Jack said nothing. He kept seating more of the percussion caps.

'Will you tell me what is going on?'

'No.'

She bit her lip, frustration growing. 'If you will not tell me, then I cannot help you.'

'I don't need your help.'

'You do. You are just too proud and too stubborn to admit it.'

'Honestly, I don't.' Jack paused and looked up. As ever, Anna was dressed in her khaki trousers and shirt, with her wide-awake hat planted firmly on her head. All had been battered by the elements, a dozen rents in the fabric of the shirt and trousers sewn together with a mismatch of coloured thread, and the dull, earthy brown of the cotton faded so it was now a light grey. She might not have been forced into the river to clear a path for the flotilla, but she had endured her fair share of hardship taking care of the many sick, and the strain of the last few weeks showed clearly on her face. Puffy grey bags sat underneath both eyes, and her lips were chafed and cracked. Like everyone in the flotilla, she looked worn out.

'This means that much to you?'

'Yes.' Jack answered honestly.

'Will you tell me why?'

He concentrated on the last of the percussion caps.

'No, of course you won't. Because you don't trust me, do you, Jack?'

He ignored the question. All five nipples were now covered with a cap. He took a moment to rotate the cylinder, so that the hammer was aligned between chambers to prevent accidental discharge. Then he stood.

'You need to learn to trust.'

He holstered the revolver, nestling the weapon on his right hip, then bent to pick up his tools and the spare ammunition. He would take as many rounds as he could ram into the pouches he would affix to his belt.

'Are we done here?' He loomed over her. She was so much shorter than he was that she had to crane her neck to look up at him.

'If your mind is made up then—'

'It is.' He cut her off.

'Then there is nothing more to say.' She looked at him, then offered something close to a smile. 'At least I understand now why you argued so hard for us to turn around.' She cocked her head to one side as she considered his face. 'Perhaps this is all to your design.'

Jack grunted. She was almost correct. Returning to Dubois' encampment had been the reason he had pressed for the flotilla to return this way. But he had not engineered the situation. He had just turned it to his advantage. It was Fate that had given him his chance at redemption.

'When do you leave?'

'When we are ready.' He gave the clipped answer.

'We?'

He shook his head. He would not be drawn.

'I would tell you to take care, Jack. But I do not think that is in your vocabulary. I think you will do as you please. It seems that is what you always do, no matter the price you may pay.'

Jack smiled. For once it was genuine. This time Anna was correct. He was no longer the servant, or the soldier, the man who would do as he was told regardless of what he believed to be right. He was his own man. That would cost him, he knew, but he would not forgo the right to stand alone. He had made a dreadful mistake in saving Dubois and his men.

Now he would put it right.

No matter the cost. To him or to anyone else.

'Ready?'

'Yes.' Monsoor stood next to Jack, Snider rifle slung over his shoulder.

'And the men?'

'Yes.'

'They know what they are doing?'

'Of course.' Monsoor grinned from ear to ear. 'Do not worry, *afandi*. We know what you are asking of us.'

'Good.' Jack tried not to smile. He had gone to Monsoor the moment the ships had stopped for the day and explained everything, telling the Egyptian sergeant of the captives and his intention to free them, no matter what it took. Anna was wrong. He did know how to trust. And who to trust. He would trust his men, at least the best of them. He had no right to ask them to come with him. But he had asked nonetheless. And they had made their decision.

The nine men stood in a rough line. They had snuck off the steamer, the exit made easier by the bottle of rum Jack had handed the sentry who was meant to prevent any of the men disappearing now the flotilla had moored for the day. He had led them a few hundred yards away from the river before he had called a halt on a small patch of dry land that stood out amidst the swamp like an island in a sea. The swamp was not improved by a second visit. Jack stared at the sodden ground, trying to pick out a path between the reeds and grasses that thrived in the damp, dank conditions. It would be a hard slog for the first mile, the men forced to wade through knee-deep marsh until they reached the drier, firmer land they had found the first time they had ventured towards Dubois' encampment. It would be tiring, but he knew they could take it. They had proved themselves time and time again now, their tireless efforts to get the flotilla south leaving him in no doubt that a march through a marsh would not exhaust them.

They no longer looked much like soldiers. The weeks spent toiling in the water had left their uniforms battered and faded. Not one man was dressed like another, all having made repairs and replaced damaged items with what they could find or barter for. It left them looking a motley crew, and nothing like any formed body of men he had ever served with before. But at the moment, he could think of no other men he would want at his side.

'Are you ready, Osman?' He asked the question of the rangy Sudanese standing at one end of the line. The nine were the men who had stood and fought the last time Jack had led them to Dubois' encampment. Only one was missing; the tall Sudanese, Abdallah, had not been replaced. These were the men he could rely on most. All were leaner now, their bodies sucked dry of any vestige of fat. But all were strong enough to handle their Sniders, and Jack had made sure Monsoor had checked each weapon to make sure it had been cared for and would be ready should they be called to use them.

'Yes, *afandi*,' Osman replied quietly, his voice so deep that the words rumbled.

'Good.' Jack was not one for speeches, and he knew these men would barely understand him if he tried. But he would not let their dedication and loyalty go ignored. So he walked the line, nodding at each in turn. The Taha brothers were there, greeting his inspection with broad identical smiles. The fourth man from the Sudan, Suliman, looked serious in the twilight, his face downcast. The five Egyptians stood together. Ali, the father of eight – or nine – waited closest to Jack, checking his Snider rifle, the same actions repeated over and over. At his side stood the baby-faced Habib, whilst Gamal, the man Jack had trusted to scout ahead the last time they came this way, was fiddling with his thin beard, his fingers running back and forth along the edge of his jaw as he waited for Jack to order him to move out. The last pair in the group, Sergeant Hassan and a private soldier called Mostafa, made up the nine. Both nodded as Jack looked at them in turn, determination reflected in their eyes.

'Ready?' Jack turned to ask the question of Monsoor.

'Not quite.'

'What do you mean?' He did not understand the answer.

'We have one more to wait for.'

'What? Who are we waiting for?'

Monsoor's grin widened. 'Her.' He nodded over Jack's shoulder.

A small figure came walking along the path that led back to the river.

'What the hell are you playing at?' Jack fired the question at the new arrival when she was still a good six yards away.

'I'm here to look after your men.' Anna came closer.

'Go back.' Jack muttered the words then turned his back on her.

He waited, hoping to hear the sound of Anna walking away. He heard nothing save the ever-present chirp of a billion insects.

'If you insist on doing this, one of your men might get hurt. I am here to take care of them should that happen, although I hope to goodness it does not. So do not be alarmed, Jack. I am not here for you.'

He bit back a quick reply and instead looked across at Monsoor. The Egyptian sergeant grinned, then shrugged. It was all the answer Jack needed from him.

'How much do you know?' He fired the question at Anna, the words coming out of his mouth staccato.

'Just what Monsoor told me.'

'Which is?'

'There is an encampment. Where you fought before. He said there was unfinished business there. That is all.'

'Fine.' He would say no more. It was clear Anna had Monsoor's ear, and he did not want an argument, not here, not now, and not one that could turn his sergeant against him. So Anna could come. But he would not take care of her. She could fend for herself.

'Monsoor. You seem to be bright and alert this afternoon. Take Gamal and scout ahead. Stay in sight.'

'Yes, *afandi*.' Monsoor turned to flash a wink at Anna. Then he moved to obey the order.

'Move out!' Jack gave the command a minute after the two men had slipped down from the little island of dry land and started to wade through the swamp once more. The eight men did as they were told without a sound, forming up behind him in a rough single-file line, with Anna in the middle.

They were off.

Chapter Thirty-four

---•◆•---

*J*ack lay alone, the field glasses he had borrowed from the expedition's supplies pressed to his eyes, his body screened by a thick swathe of down, each stem the thickness of one of his fingers. He had picked his spot with care, choosing a location far to the western flank of the encampment, where the ground was slightly raised above the surrounding area, making sure he had a good line of sight over the whole of Dubois' domain. He did not want to risk missing anything. His men were waiting four hundred yards away, hidden in a natural bowl in the ground surrounded by a dense swathe of more of the tussocks of tall grass. They would not be seen unless someone walked right up on top of them, and to reduce even that minimal risk he had ordered Monsoor to keep four men on watch at all times, one at each point of the compass.

He rested his elbows on the ground, panning slowly across the encampment. It had changed a great deal in the weeks since they had last been there. The line of bell tents on the eastern flank was twice as long as he remembered it. In front of it were stands of rifle muskets and shotguns, the weapons arranged so that they stood ready to be grabbed at a moment's notice. The encampment had taken on the air of a small town, with the bell tents now facing three larger tents, which he took to be communal, one certainly some sort of kitchen, with roughly made trestle tables lined up outside. On the far side of the tents, the tarpaulin-shrouded piles of storage crates had expanded hugely. Dubois was clearly well supplied. From the growth in the encampment, Jack could only surmise that news of the Frenchman's dominance had drawn others to him, his power now complete over the lands where he hunted.

Towards the northern flank of the encampment, the heap of ivory had quadrupled in size. Jack tried to work out how many animals must have died to produce such a vast haul, but he quickly gave up as the sheer scale of the slaughter became obvious. Sir Sam had a taste for hunting, but Dubois had embarked on the undertaking on an industrial scale. At least one hundred creamy ivory tusks were piled together, and that was just what he could see from his current vantage point. That amount of ivory was worth a fortune on its own. Jack felt wholly disgusted by the sight of so much accumulated in one place. He was no sentimentalist. He had seen more suffering than any man had a right to see in his lifetime, and there was little left in the world that would shock him. But there was something appalling about that pile of ivory. Perhaps it was jealousy at the fortune Dubois had gathered, or maybe it was the idea that so many animals had been slaughtered to harvest just those items.

Whichever it was, it had to be ignored for now. It was time to see what he faced.

It was time to plan Dubois' demise.

He scanned the field glasses from left to right, moving them slowly and carefully as he marked every man he could see. His first impression had been quite correct. Dubois' gang had certainly grown in number. So Jack took his time, noting every man's position and face, fixing them in his mind. There were thirty men that he could see, but there were too many tents for just thirty, and he had to conclude that Dubois had at least double that number, perhaps more. The rest would be out of the camp, doing whatever the Frenchman had ordered them to do that day. Not that it mattered. He had a sense of the size of the enemy force he would be facing. That was enough for now.

There was just one last thing he had to see. He squirmed on his tummy, keeping the field glasses in place as he manoeuvred around so that he could make out the far southern side of the encampment, holding his breath as he fixed his gaze on the area where he knew the prisoners' stockade was sited.

He'd known what to expect, but still a wave of revulsion pulsed through him. A rough tally told him that the stockade contained the same numbers as before, the women and children Dubois had taken now reduced to little more than living skeletons. Clearly the Frenchman had not been kind to his prisoners. He had kept them alive. Nothing more.

Jack refused to let his mind run away from him. He had to be a soldier. Emotionless. Cold. Calculating. He had to be the killer the poor wretches needed him to be. Only when they were free could he let go of the raw feelings that bubbled away deep in his mind. Only when they were free could he be free himself.

He took his time. He moved slowly, keeping an eye on the position of the sun so as not to let it glint off the field glasses. Only when he had surveyed the entire encampment for a second time, and inspected the ground that surrounded it, did he lower the glasses. Still he did not move. Instead, he lay there picturing the battle that was to come, planning the death he would bring.

He moved only when his plan was formed.

'You know what to do?'

'Of course.' Monsoor grimaced. 'It is not so difficult to understand, *afandi*.'

'But you cannot let yourselves be seen.' Jack made the salient fact clear. He did not like leaving the sergeant behind, but he had no choice.

He had returned to the patch of dead ground where he had left his men and begun outlining the details of the encampment, and passing on the orders that would see Monsoor and three of the men remain behind to keep watch, so that should anything change, Jack would know of it when he returned. He had listed the numbers of men Dubois had at his disposal, as well as his estimate of how many prisoners had been taken.

'We will not be seen,' Monsoor reassured him.

'Good.' Jack nodded to dismiss his sergeant, then turned to look at Anna, who had come to stand nearby as he passed on the instructions.

'Did you find all you need?' She had waited patiently for him to finish with Monsoor. But now she had questions of her own.

'Yes.'

'And will you now tell me why this is so important?'

Jack drew a breath. 'This man needs to be stopped.'

'So I gather. But why is that so important to *you*?'

For a moment, he hesitated. But Anna had come with them when to do so would set her at odds with her uncle. She deserved to know.

'He has taken women and children prisoner. He is abusing them most cruelly.' He phrased it carefully so as not to shock, then shook his head. He would not dissemble. Not now. Not to her. 'He is starving them. Beating them. And forcing them to whore for his men.'

Anna's face blanched, but she did not shy away. 'Why did this man take them?'

'For power. To control this land. Only then can he do what he wants here.'

'That is terrible.' She paused as she absorbed the tale. 'But I still don't understand why it means so much to you. It is more than wanting to do the right thing, isn't it? It has eaten you alive for weeks now.' She stopped speaking as she tiptoed towards his darkness.

The silence built before Jack could speak again. 'It's my fault.'

'What is?'

'All of it. The battle I spoke of. I stopped the families of the wretches Dubois has taken from setting them free.' He had to stop. He could not say more. Not even to Anna.

'Dubois? You know this man?'

'Yes.'

She took a half-step away from him. She was looking at him as if she were seeing him for the very first time. Jack searched her eyes, looking for the revulsion he expected to find there. He saw something reflected in her gaze, but he did not know what it was.

'So what now?' she asked, tone brisk and businesslike.

'We go and get more men.' Jack shook his head to clear the emotions that had come so close to the surface. Dubois had many more men than he did. Without additional soldiers, any attack on the Frenchman's encampment was doomed. He would return to the flotilla, where he would have to convince Sir Sam to give him the troops he needed.

'At least now I understand why you had to do this.'

Jack had no answer. He did not care what she thought of his actions. Only what happened next mattered.

'I want you to tell your uncle what Dubois has done.'

'I will.'

'And I want you to convince him to give me the men I need.'

'I can try.'

'No.' He offered a thin-lipped smile. 'You *have* to do this. Maybe he won't listen to me, but as sure as eggs is eggs, he'll bloody well listen to you.'

'It would be the first time.'

'No.' He shut down her protest. 'He will listen.' There could be no room for doubt. There was too much at stake.

'You sound certain.' Anna did not look so sure that her uncle would respond even to her entreaties.

'I am.' Jack reached out and took hold of her arms. 'We need more men. When I get them, I can attack. I can free those people. I can give them justice. Isn't that what we are here for?'

'You know my uncle will see it differently. He will want to help, you know he will. But he will have to consider the bigger picture. He will not let himself be distracted. He will not give you permission to attack. He will not risk the fate of the expedition, even to save the lives of the innocent.'

'No.' Jack still gripped her arms, and now he shook them forcefully. 'He must be made to see sense. We have to do this. You *will* convince him.'

Anna searched his face. 'This is it, isn't it? It's what you have been waiting for.'

He held her gaze. It was as if she could see into his very soul. 'Yes.' He breathed the single word.

She said nothing, her eyes flickering across his face. Then she nodded. 'I shall convince him.'

'*Afandi!*'

He was not given time to say more. One of Monsoor's sentries, the Egyptian Sergeant Hassan, had hissed the warning.

'Two men coming.' Hassan waved a hand, holding two fingers aloft, gesturing for Jack and the men around him to go to ground.

'Monsoor.' Jack summoned his sergeant, pitching his voice low.

'*Afandi?*'

'Are they from the encampment?'

Monsoor held up a hand, then relayed the question to the sentry.

'Yes.' Monsoor passed on the simple answer.

'Good. Tell the men to stay here and keep quiet while you and I deal with them.' Jack made his decision quickly. It was too good an opportunity to let slip. He could send a message to Dubois. One that could not be ignored and one that would show the Frenchman that his power was not as complete as he might believe.

'Anna, stay here. We won't be long.'

'Where are you going?'

But Jack gave no answer. He was already moving, Monsoor at his side.

The pair slipped out of the dead ground. They moved swiftly, keeping low as they scurried away. Jack bent his back, ignoring the pain in the pit of his spine, keeping behind a tall line of the ubiquitous grasses, using the cover as best he could.

They covered two hundred yards, then he signalled for Monsoor to go to ground. He had picked the spot with care. The trail between the river and the encampment ran past a line of tall grasses. If the two men the sentry had spotted were indeed coming this way, they would pass about ten feet in front of where he and the sergeant now waited.

The ambush was laid perfectly.

He looked at Monsoor. He was rewarded with the composed stare of a veteran. There was no smile. Not now that it was time to ply their trade.

Moving slowly and carefully, Jack eased his knife from its sheath on the back left of his belt. He left his revolver in its holster, but he undid the buckle that held the top flap in place, just in case.

He did not have to wait long.

Two men came into view. They walked easily, chatting to one another. Clearly they were well used to the route and saw no danger.

Jack turned to look at Monsoor. 'You take the one on the right.' The words were whispered softly.

Monsoor nodded. The Egyptian sergeant had drawn a thin blade just four inches long and no more than half an inch wide. It was an evil-looking knife, the weapon of a silent killer, and precisely what was needed at that moment.

For they were about to kill.

Jack eased himself into a crouch, moving with infinite slowness. Nothing could warn the two men of their presence. At his side, Monsoor did the same. No words were needed.

Jack concentrated everything on the man on the left. His

man. He was not very old, perhaps in his early twenties, a good decade younger than his partner. But his tender age did not concern Jack. He had killed men younger.

The man was armed, a revolver sitting snug in a holster on his right hip and a blade not dissimilar to the one Jack now held on the opposite side. He was wearing a white shirt under a tan leather waistcoat with black trousers and dark marching boots of brown leather laced high above his ankles. The shirt was undone to the navel, revealing pale blonde hair that matched the curly hair on his head and the thin beard that covered his jawline and neck. Around his throat he wore a tight gold chain with a golden ring strung on it. He strode along, laughing at a remark his companion had made, with seemingly not a care in the world.

The pair came on briskly. From the path they were taking, it was clear they would almost certainly stumble on Jack's men, the dead ground no cover at all if the pair got so close as to be able to see down with ease. But it was not to remove that risk that Jack tensed his muscles and prepared to spring the ambush. It was to put in place the plan he had thought of every hour since he fled the scene of his shame all those weeks before.

It was time to start the killing.

It was time to start atoning for his sins.

'Now!'

He hissed the word, then sprang through the grass. Time stood still as he threw himself forward, boots flying across the dusty ground. Ten yards passed in a blur of sudden movement.

The young man had time to look up, his mouth opening in a silent O of shock, eyes bright and wide.

Jack charged at him, picking his spot then thrusting the knife forward, driving it straight into his throat. It was a cruel blow, and the blade cut straight through the flesh and gristle of the man's gullet, the tip of the blade punching out of the back of his neck.

Even as his hands started to reach for the terrible rent in his flesh, Jack pulled back the blade then slashed it hard from right to left, gouging the sharpened edge across the man's face, striking through his eyes.

The young man tried to scream as he was blinded, but his throat was ruined and filled with blood, and no sound came out save a hideous gurgle.

Jack was not done. He grabbed hard at the man's shoulder as he came to an abrupt halt, boots skidding across the friable ground. Then he thrust the blade forward again, punching it hard and fast into his quarry's heart. He held him then, taking the weight as the dying man fell forward, staring into the ruin of his eyes as their heads came close together. He did not look away. He could feel blood on his hands, whilst more spilled hot and wet onto his shirt, yet still he did not move. He held the man upright, watching his eyes the whole time. Only when he saw the final flicker of life leave them did he step back.

The blonde man crumpled, his bloodied, torn body slumping to the ground with a soft groan as the last air left his lungs.

Jack turned. Monsoor was crouched over his victim. Unlike Jack, he had struck just the once, the killing blow taking the other man's life in the flicker of single heartbeat.

'Dead?' Still Jack asked the question, making sure.

Monsoor did not bother to answer. Instead, he stood up, removing a handkerchief from his pocket that he slid up and down his blade, cleaning away the thin sheen of blood that coated it from tip to shaft.

Jack looked down at the man he had killed. There was a lot

of blood, and more was oozing from the corpse. It was a messy kill, especially when compared to the neatness with which Monsoor had dispatched the older man, but he did not care. It was not about finesse. It was about getting the job done. It was about killing. Nothing more and nothing less.

Monsoor whistled once, summoning the rest of the men.

They came quickly, eager to see what had happened. Anna came with them.

Jack bent over and cleaned his knife on his victim's white shirt. By the time he was done, the rest of the group had arrived.

'Will you bury them?' It was Anna who asked the question.

Jack looked at her. If she was repulsed by the blood and gore that covered his hands and was splattered across his clothing, there was no sign of it in her expression.

'No. We'll leave them there.' He watched for her reaction.

Anna looked once at each of the corpses, then she nodded.

Jack turned to Monsoor. 'Take your three men. Stay and watch, but keep out of sight. If more of them come, hide away. This is enough. For now.' Then he looked at the others. 'The rest of you, with me.'

He began to head for the track that would lead back to where the flotilla was moored. He hoped Dubois would find the bodies. It would be good for the Frenchman to know what Fate had in store for him and his men.

Jack was coming for him.

Just as he had promised.

Chapter Thirty-five

———◆•◆———

'Absolutely not.' Sir Sam spoke firmly. 'I will not let you endanger the lives of so many of my men.'

'But we will save innocent women and children.' Jack stood in front of the expedition leader on the deck of the steamer. Sir Sam had been waiting for their return. The handful of soldiers with Jack had been dismissed and ordered back to their comrades. Anna had left with them. Jack knew she would bide her time until her uncle had calmed down. 'Your mission is to bring the rule of law to these lands.' He pressed his point home. 'That is what I am proposing we do.'

Sir Sam opened his mouth as if to snap a reply, but instead he took a deep breath, composing himself as best he could. 'I do not need you to tell me my mission.'

Jack could see his commander was fighting to contain his temper, but that did not mean he would back down. 'There are women and children being held prisoner in an encampment just a few miles from here. Give me two hundred men and I will set them free and bring justice to men who think they can do whatever the hell they want here.'

'This would be the encampment you found when you

disobeyed my orders to remain with the flotilla, taking a number of my men with you?'

'It is.'

'I forbade you from going, and yet you went. Now, rather than begging for my forgiveness, you are demanding that I allow you to launch an attack.'

'Yes.'

'God damn you, Jack Lark.' Sir Sam whispered the words, shaking his head.

'I am sure he does.' Jack held fast to his own temper. It would do no good to shout. There was no place for passion here. Not when there was a job to be done. 'I'll lead the attack. I've surveyed the ground. I know how to do it. This is why you brought me along, after all, to fight for you.'

Sir Sam sucked down a deep breath. 'I understand, Jack. Really I do. But there is more at stake here than a single encampment. My mission is bigger than that. Yet you ask me to risk everything so that we can launch this one attack.'

'No.' Jack shook his head vehemently. 'You are not risking it all. You have hundreds of men with you. Why bring them if not to fight?'

'But we are in no condition to fight. You told me that yourself.'

'We outnumber them.'

'And how many of my men will die?'

'Some.' Jack did not avoid the question.

'How many? A dozen? Two dozen? How many will be injured? What do we do with those? What effect will it have on the morale of the rest of the men? No, Jack. I may wish it were otherwise, but I cannot condone this. I cannot let my feelings overrule my judgement.'

Jack could not answer the questions that had been thrown at him. He knew he had argued for the expedition to turn around, that he had pressed Sir Sam, goaded him even, telling him it was not worth the cost in men's lives to press on. Yet here he was arguing for the same men to fight, knowing that some would surely die. The irony of that was not lost on him. But it was different. He was certain of that. Some things were worth the cost. And he would not debate the butcher's bill. It would be what it would be. No more and no less. It did not mean they should not attempt to hold Dubois and his men to account. That was something worth fighting for. Something worth dying for. It meant more than simply driving ships through the Sudd. If men died, they would die to save others. For him, that was enough.

'Give me the men, and I'll do all I can to make sure we take as few casualties as possible. We will hold the initiative and the advantage of surprise.' He had not mentioned the two men he and Monsoor had killed. If Dubois had found them, he would be on the alert for a bigger attack. But Sir Sam didn't need to know everything.

'And what if you lose.' Sir Sam sighed deeply. 'The men are exhausted. What if you try this and are beaten? That man has, what, fifty, sixty men? All armed. All experienced. All hard men without a notion of mercy. Do you really think our soldiers, in their current dire condition, are capable of fighting them?'

'Yes.'

'I wish I had your confidence.'

'You need to place your confidence in me.'

Sir Sam offered something that might on a better day be close to a short laugh. 'You're an arrogant son of a bitch, Jack.'

'So I've been told.'

He shook his head. 'If you lose, there is more at stake than just the lives of my men. Their morale will be shattered. We must fight only when we know we can win.'

'I know we can win.'

Sir Sam held Jack's stare, as if trying to read his mind. 'What will you do if I forbid you from going?'

Jack shrugged. He did not need to say more.

'Then I have no choice but to ask you to reconsider your position here. If you find yourself unable to obey my direct orders, you have no place on this expedition.'

Jack fought the urge to laugh. He was being dismissed. All for doing what they were there to do. But before he could say another word, he saw that Anna and Florence were approaching. It was time to change tack. 'Ask your niece. See what she says.'

'This expedition is not run by women.' Sir Sam's reply was haughty.

'Is it not?' Florence had been close enough to hear the remark, and now came towards her husband, her face creased into a scowl.

'That was not meant for your ears, Flooey.'

'But I heard it.' Her reply was clipped. She turned to address Jack. 'Anna told me what you want to attempt. You are a brave man, Jack.'

'I have yet to give him permission to go.' Sir Sam spoke before Jack could reply.

'Why is that?' Florence came to his side, resting her hand on his arm.

'We cannot risk the men tasting defeat.'

'So you are fearful?'

'Yes, I am bloody fearful.' Sir Sam hissed the admission. 'If we try this and we lose, and the devil knows that seems possible, the damage will be irreparable.'

Florence looked quizzically at her husband for a moment. 'I do not understand.'

'What do you not understand?'

'Why you say this. Why do you say we will lose?'

'My dear Flooey. We must weigh all the risks here.'

Jack opened his mouth to interject, but before he could speak, Anna flicked her hand sharply, catching his attention. One look at her face told him it would be wise to hold his tongue.

'But I think this must be done.' Florence stepped away from her husband, distancing herself from him.

'You spoke to Anna.' Sir Sam flashed a glare at his niece. 'She should know better.'

'Yes, Anna told me what Jack has found.' Florence silenced him. 'We must help those people.'

Sir Sam stalked to the steamer's starboard rail, expression set like thunder. Anna, Florence and Jack looked at one another.

'Wait.' Anna whispered the instruction to Jack.

'You told her everything?' Jack glanced at Florence, but addressed the words to Anna alone, matching her whisper.

'Yes.'

He sucked down a long breath. 'Thank you.'

'Hush.' Anna scowled away his words. 'I did it for those poor people. They do not deserve such a fate.' She kept her voice pitched low so only Jack would hear.

'No one does.'

'No.' Anna glanced at her uncle, watching him closely. 'And I am coming with you.'

'What?'

'You heard me well enough. If you insist on doing this, you will need me there.'

'To fight?' he hissed, unable to hold back the harsh retort.

'To care for the wounded. And to care for those you seek to free. Have you thought of them, Jack? Of what they will need if you succeed?'

'No.' He looked down at the deck for a moment. She was right. He had not thought of everything. But he was sure of one thing. 'You are not coming.'

'It is not your decision.'

'It will be dangerous. More than you could ever know.'

'I am not afraid, Jack.'

'You should be.'

She shook her head at the reply. 'Fear is a strange thing, Jack. I do not fear my death, but I do fear a lot of things. I fear for the safety of my family and I fear for the lives of others. But mostly I fear that I shall be left out of life. I shall not allow that to happen, not whilst there is breath in my body.' She looked up at him, eyes blazing with a barely controlled passion. 'Do not try to stop me, Jack. Do not try to stop me from living my life as I see fit.'

Jack searched her face, though he did not know what he was looking for. He did not understand, not fully. But there was nothing more to be said. At least not yet. Not until Sir Sam had come to his decision.

The silence stretched thin. The four of them waited, Jack and Anna standing together, Florence holding her ground away from her husband, who stared out across mile upon mile of marsh, his head panning slowly from side to side as he surveyed the lands he had come to open to the khedive.

No one spoke.

'I have made my decision.' Sir Sam broke the spell that had fallen over them all. He uttered the words slowly and clearly, but he did not turn to face the other three. 'Jack, I give you my permission to go. But you may only take the Forty. No more men than that.'

'Fine.' Jack seized on the answer. That gave him thirty-five men at his disposal allowing for those he knew would be too sick to join him and for the one who had died. He would also have Monsoor and el-Sisi. They would likely be outnumbered, but he did not care. He would find a way to win. He had to.

'You will take Julian with you. I must have someone there I can trust.'

'Very well.' Jack agreed readily enough. The naval officer had proved he was more than just a competent officer in the weeks since they had left Cairo. He would be no burden.

'But you will take no one else. That includes my niece.'

'Uncle—' Anna tried to interject, but she was cut dead.

'No, Anna. I shall not see you endangered.'

'She will stay here.' Jack answered for her. He did not have to look at her to know what expression would be on her face.

'When this is done, you will leave my expedition.' Now Sir Sam turned to face them. 'You hear me, Jack? When you have done this, and if you survive, you will be finished here.' He spoke the words carefully, wanting no misunderstanding.

'Fine,' Jack agreed. It was a small price to pay.

He had what he wanted.

He had his chance at redemption.

Chapter Thirty-six

I t was twilight, the time of day when the sun sat low on the western horizon, its warm orange light casting long shadows across the land. The time of day when stomachs growled and men looked forward to time around a campfire with a drink in their hand and their mates close by.

But that wouldn't happen today. For Jack intended to end it with fire and with death.

He had picked his ground with care. The fifteen men he had chosen to form the assault party were well hidden behind a swathe of tall papyrus grass around five hundred yards away from the eastern side of the encampment. They faced directly towards the rear of the line of bell tents, with the stockade and the prisoners it contained far away on the opposite side of the encampment. He would have liked to bring them directly to the stockade, but the terrain on that side was completely open and devoid of cover. The only way to get close was to come in from the east.

Keeping low, he twisted around on his stomach. His chosen men lay in a loose skirmish line behind him. All looked at him with expectant eyes as they waited for the order to move.

'Does everything look right?' Julian Baker, lying at Jack's side, broke the silence that had fallen over them.

'Yes.' Jack had scrutinised every part of Dubois' encampment. Nothing had changed.

'And your men know what they are to do?' Julian's voice trembled slightly as he asked a second question.

'Yes.' Jack fought the urge to snap. His men were ready. He had spoken at length to Monsoor, first listening to the sergeant's report of the activity he and his three men had observed that day, then explaining the plan of attack.

'But will they follow your orders?' Julian could not resist a third question, one just as pointless as the preceding pair.

'Of course.' Jack bit off a sharper retort. Monsoor had agreed to the plan that Jack had outlined, even if he had asked to accompany Jack rather than nursemaid Lieutenant el-Sisi, whom Jack had placed in command of the larger portion of his small force. Jack had forbidden it. He wanted Monsoor with the inexperienced young officer. El-Sisi had a crucial role in the attack. If he failed, Jack and the men in the assault party would almost certainly die.

'Tell me the plan again.'

'Really?' Jack sighed.

'If anything happens to you, I shall be in charge. I need to make sure I understand,' Julian explained.

'Fine.' Jack forced away any impatience he felt. It was a fair enough request and he had noticed the hint of fear in Julian's tone as he had posed the question. If Jack fell, responsibility for the fate of the men rested with Julian, and that was no small thing.

'El-Sisi has Monsoor and twenty men. They are armed with the Sniders and they have plenty of ammunition. They are currently waiting well out of sight, but when the time is right, they will take up a position just over there.' Jack pointed at a patch of raised ground that was perhaps ten to twenty feet higher than the surrounding terrain. He would have liked to have the covering fire party on higher ground, but there was nothing better for miles and so it would have to do. They would be perhaps one hundred and fifty yards from the western side of the encampment; well within the range of the Sniders, which he knew were effective at up to four times that distance. Although a few of Dubois' men had rifles, the majority were armed with revolvers or shotguns. Neither had anything like the same range as the Sniders. It was another advantage in Jack's favour. El-Sisi and his command would also have the setting sun at their backs. That too would work in their favour, the defenders of the encampment forced to look directly into the low sun when they tried to return fire, as Jack knew they surely would. He had to hope it would be enough, that all the advantages would add up to something that would balance the delicate equation of the fight and give him the victory he so desperately craved.

'And when do they fire?'

'As soon as I fire our first shot.'

'Right.' Julian nodded firmly as he absorbed the details.

'The men in the encampment won't be expecting to come under fire. That gives us the benefit of surprise. When el-Sisi and his men open fire, the men over there,' Jack gestured towards the encampment, 'won't know what's coming. They will want to fight back, and that keeps their attention directed out towards the west. That's when we will hit them. We strike hard and fast. When we reach the stockade, we release the prisoners. I'll send half our men to escort them away and back to the ships, whilst the rest of us finish off anyone left.'

'Good.'

Jack heard Julian's voice crack as he tried to look both stern and serious at the same time. To Jack's eyes, he mainly looked frightened.

He cleared his throat as quietly as he could before asking another question. 'So you believe we will have the initiative?'

'Yes. And we'll keep it.' Jack grinned. 'Those bastards over there are ready for their dinner and for swigging grog around the bloody campfire. They're not ready for a fight. But we are. We'll hit them hard, and we'll keep beating the fuckers until we're done.'

'But what happens if they do something you do not expect?'

'They won't.' Jack was quick to answer. The truth of it was that Dubois and his men could do any of a hundred things when el-Sisi and his men started to spray the encampment with Snider rounds. But no plan could account for every eventuality. He placed his faith in his men and in his plan. Beyond that, he would react as and when he had to. And that was that.

'And will your men stand?'

'They will stand.' He was firm. The truth was, he was just as concerned as Julian that el-Sisi's men would run as soon as Dubois' gang began to return fire. El-Sisi had the men Jack considered the least reliable, the soldiers who had fled from the last fight, whereas Jack had the nine he knew he could rely on, along with the best six from the rest. If any of the Forty ran, he wanted to make sure they went from the group with the lieutenant. Those men were in the least danger, their role simply to provide covering fire. He hoped that would be enough to make them stay the course of the battle he was bringing about, but he knew anything could happen once bullets started to fly. It was another reason why he had forced Monsoor to remain with el-Sisi. If anyone could hold the men to their positions, it was the pugnacious Egyptian sergeant.

'When do we move?'

'Soon.' Jack looked across at the western sky. He alone controlled the timing of the attack. He wanted to wait until the sun was lower before he fired the single shot that would see el-Sisi and his men scramble into position to fire their first volley.

'How will you know when to start?'

'I'll know,' he replied calmly. 'But we will need to get closer first.'

'It *is* a good plan.' Julian still sounded dubious. 'But so much can go wrong. What if el-Sisi doesn't hear your shot? What if someone spots us moving? What if—'

'It is a good plan.' Jack shut the naval officer down. 'It will work.'

'And if it doesn't?'

Jack shrugged. 'Then we fight anyway.'

'So you have no plan B?'

'No.'

'They say no plan survives contact with the enemy.'

'Maybe you webfoots say that.' Jack tried to sound glib as he used the British Army's nickname for all sailors. He failed, the words sounding flat. 'The men know what to do.'

'And if it all goes to hell in a basket?'

He looked deep into Julian's eyes, then grinned. 'Then at least it will be an experience you will always remember.'

'I just hope it is one I survive.'

Jack grunted. Every man facing battle thought the same thing. Yet no matter those hopes, or how hard they prayed, some would perish. And there was nothing any of them could do about it. He had once believed he had survived the field of battle on account of his skills as a warrior and a commander. He had discovered that to be a crock of shite. He lived or died on the whim of Fate. Once he had accepted that, somehow fighting, and living, had become easier.

A man could only make so many choices.

In the end, Fate held all the cards.

All a man could do was wait to see which ones she decided to play.

'Make ready.' Jack gave the order, then drew his Beaumont–Adams from its holster.

He lay with his men in a very loose skirmish line about two hundred yards from the line of bell tents. He would have liked to bring them in closer, but there were just too many men walking around the encampment. From what he could see, the place was full, those who had been out when he had scouted the encampment all now returned. He did not bother to tally their numbers. It did not matter if there were a hundred of them. He would attack no matter the odds.

Time crawled by. The sun was touching the horizon, filling the sky with a vibrant orange, so that it looked like the whole world was aflame.

It was almost time to give the signal.

Then he saw Dubois.

The Frenchman was standing with the Russian Vladimir. Both were laughing. The sight of the man he had once begun to think of as a friend brought Jack up sharply. He was not attacking a nameless, faceless foe. This time he was about to order the deaths of men he had drunk and laughed with, men he had clapped on the back and with whom he had spoken of friendship. It was no small thing that he was going to do, and for a moment he felt something shift deep inside him, a fleeting notion of betrayal and regret. These men were no different to him. Had times been different, or had Fate dealt him a different set of cards, he knew he could well be standing alongside Dubois and his followers. Yet now he was lying there, holding their lives within his grasp. It would take a single shot, one bullet, and those men would start to die. The enormity of that power surged through him. It no longer thrilled, as once it had. There was no joy. No excitement. No sense of justice. There was just a notion of sadness, of the world turning regardless of the fruitless actions of men.

But none of the thoughts crowding into his mind would turn him from the path he was on. He would not let them. He had started down this road and he would not divert from it until it was done.

He lifted the revolver, aiming it at the sky. He was too far away to bother aiming at a target. All that mattered was giving the signal that would tell el-Sisi to open fire.

It was time.

He pulled the trigger.

Chapter Thirty-seven

---◆---

The single shot shattered the peace of twilight.

It cracked out, loud, shocking, out of place. Heads turned, the experienced killers in Dubois' gang immediately reaching for holstered revolvers, or else running to retrieve other weapons, reactions honed and instant.

Jack remained still. Like the men just behind him, he held his breath and forced himself to lie low. But he kept his eyes fixed on the encampment he had thrown into confusion.

Watching. Waiting.

Seconds ticked by. Confused voices shouted this way and that as Dubois' men tried to make sense of the single gunshot. Accusations of carelessness were thrown around when no other shots followed, the sudden sense of danger dying away just as quickly as it had flared up. The first peals of laughter followed, someone amongst the group becoming the butt of a joke.

Then someone pointed directly at Jack.

Jack saw the man who did it. He was heavily bearded and wore a rough grey undershirt stained with sweat. Something had caught his eye and now he hollered for attention, right arm extended towards the small group lying in the grass close to the line of bell tents.

'Shit.' Jack winced as his plan unravelled no more than seconds after he had put it into action.

More heads turned to look their way. Loud voices shouted for information, or bellowed questions as they tried to make sense of what was happening.

Dubois strode into the confusion. Jack looked on transfixed as the Frenchman started to direct his men, his commands cutting through the clamour of voices.

'Fuck it,' he hissed. He had no idea what had happened to el-Sisi. But it did not matter. Not now. Not now they were so deeply in the shit.

The bearded man who had spotted them started to move, drawing his revolver as he came forward. Others followed, five more men dispatched by Dubois to investigate whatever the first man had seen. The closest of them was perhaps a dozen paces behind.

'Where the hell are your bloody men?' Julian sounded aghast as he grabbed at Jack's side. 'Where are they!'

Jack ignored him. His plan was done. That left him just one course of action.

'Get ready!' He lifted his head, not caring that he could now be seen.

His men obeyed. All crawled forward, taking station to the left and right of him and Julian.

Jack took a deep breath. It was time to fight.

'Kneel!' He gave the order. There was nothing else for it. The men had practised shooting both standing up and kneeling. They had never tried it lying on their bellies, and this was not the time to find out if they could manage an accurate shot from the prone position.

To their credit, they obeyed without hesitation. All fifteen rose up, settling into the kneeling firing position just as he had trained them.

Dubois and his men saw them at once. Shouts of consternation and surprise rippled across the encampment. The six men who had been rushing out to discover what was hiding in the grass skidded to a sudden halt, the emergence of a formed body of men more than they had bargained for.

Jack would give them no time to react.

'Aim!' He snapped the order, then lined up his own first shot, drawing a bead on the bearded man in the grey shirt who had spoiled his plan. The fellow would pay a heavy price for his discovery.

'Good God.'

Jack heard Julian mutter the words under his breath as the small group of men did as they were ordered, each one squinting down the barrel of his Snider.

'Fire!'

Jack shouted the glorious word. At once, fifteen Sniders roared as one. He fired at the same time, aiming at the bearded man even as he turned to flee.

The bullets cut down the men closest to Jack's skirmishers. The bearded man went down first, hit by half a dozen bullets that spun him around before he crumpled. Three more of the men coming to investigate fell as the heavy Snider bullets tore through them.

'Reload!'

Now was the time for speed. Around him his men pulled firmly back on the hinged breechblock, engaging the casing extractor. With each man performing the same actions, they tilted the rifle to the right, shaking out the now empty casing that had been pulled back into the open chamber of the breech.

'Quickly now!' Jack urged them to hasten. He himself fired in the pause, the bullet zipping past the head of one of the remaining men, who was now hurrying away from danger.

His men were doing their best. All took a fresh cartridge from the pouch on their belt. With fingers moving quickly, they slid the long round into the open chamber, then snapped the breechblock closed, locking it in place and cocking the rifle. In a matter of seconds, they were ready to fire again.

'Good! Aim!' Jack shouted, then paused. 'Fire!'

Almost instantly, another fifteen rounds were released. Julian fired with them, the naval officer shooting his own revolver.

'Reload!

The sequence of commands echoed in Jack's head. This was the moment when he came truly alive. The moment when everything he had been and everything he would ever be focused into a single moment in time.

Dubois' men were no novices. They were moving fast, at least twenty of them taking cover as they found firing positions facing Jack's men. Even as his soldiers reloaded, the first shots came against them.

The air around Jack's head was stung by fast-moving missiles. Mercifully the first return shots missed. But that could not last.

'Aim! Fire!'

Another volley roared out. But the easy targets were gone. Dubois' men knew what they were about and were using the tents and the storage crates that littered the encampment to screen themselves from sight as they shot back at the line of men kneeling in the knee-high papyrus grass.

Jack flinched as a bullet dug a groove through the ground no more than a foot from where he knelt. More zipped by, their high-pitched whine clearly audible. It was only a matter of time before the first of his men would be hit.

'Reload!'

No matter the danger, he held his men to their task. He could hear the sound of Snider breechblocks moving, followed by the impact as empty cartridge cases hit the ground. But he could see more and more of Dubois' men joining the fight. What had been around twenty men was fast becoming double that. Dubois himself was in the middle of the encampment, directing his men, pointing out the positions they needed to occupy to bring fire down on the small band of attackers. The volume of fire he could bring to bear was increasing by the minute, and his men were pouring it on, each one firing as fast as he could manage. Thus far it had been largely ineffective, the revolvers most of his men held at the very limit of their range. Some were armed with rifled muskets or hunting rifles with a much longer range, but those weapons took much longer to reload than the Sniders Jack's men possessed, and that kept the rate of return fire down. But the fight was too unequal to carry on as it was. Eventually Dubois' superior numbers would begin to tell, Jack's men would start to fall, and their own rate of fire would drop away as they took casualties.

He had to make a decision. And make it fast.

'We need to pull back.' Julian urged Jack to give the order to retreat in between aimed shots from his revolver. 'We cannot stay here.'

'Keep bloody firing,' Jack snapped back. 'Aim!' He gave the

next order to his men, holding them in place, but he knew Julian was right. Locking them into this unequal firefight would achieve nothing. Men from both sides would die, but neither side could seize the initiative. It would simply carry on until Jack had no choice but to order the retreat.

'What are you damn well waiting for!' Julian flinched as a bullet snapped past his head. 'We need to get out of here!'

Jack fired the last round in his revolver, then dug in his pouch for more of the paper-wrapped cartridges. 'Fire!' He bellowed the command even as he pushed the first of the cartridges into the chamber and rammed it home.

'Reload!'

'Jack, we must pull back. Give the order, or so help me I will!'

Jack saw the fear in Julian's eyes. He understood it, even felt it himself. Julian was right. It was time to give in to the inevitable.

It was time to retreat.

Then el-Sisi's men finally opened fire, and everything changed.

Twenty Sniders firing as one created a storm of sound louder than even the strongest peal of thunder.

A man near the stash of ivory grunted loudly as a bullet hit him in the chest. He crumpled, his body sagging then falling to the ground. The rest of the bullets hammered into the line of carts near the tents, or else flashed past the ears of Dubois' men, who suddenly found themselves under attack from another direction.

Men who had been aiming shots at Jack and his party were reeling away in confusion. In the passing of a single second, positions that had screened them from the fire coming from the east suddenly left them exposed.

El-Sisi's men fired a second time, the volley coming within moments of the first. More of Dubois' men went down, bodies ripped and shredded by the accurate Snider rounds.

'That's it!' Jack saw his opportunity. The tide of battle had turned in the blink of an eye. 'Load and fire! Come on!' he exhorted his troops as he reloaded his revolver, ramming home the cartridges as fast as his fingers could fly. 'Reload, now.' He turned his head and snapped the instruction at Julian.

They had their chance. Now they had to take it.

Dubois' men were turning this way and that as they tried to face two dangers at once. Men fell constantly, either from el-Sisi's fire or from that coming from Jack's own men. At least ten were down, some dragging themselves through the dirt towards safety, some lying still. There was no sign of Dubois himself, but Jack knew his adversary was there, trying to make sense out of the chaos.

'Reload! Aim! Fire!'

There was no time to dwell on the Frenchman. He rammed home his last cartridge, then tugged out a packet of percussion caps and pushed them into place as fast as he could, a single curse escaping his lips as he dropped two. Then the revolver was primed and loaded. He was ready.

'Stand!' He got to his feet, calling for his men to do the same.

'What the hell are you thinking?' Julian looked up, his expression showing the strain of being under fire.

'It's time.' Jack sucked down a last deep breath.

'Time to bally well get out of here. It's over, for God's sake.'

'It's never over.' Jack shook his head. He would not retreat.

He looked over his men. They stood in line, the last of them loading their Sniders, breechblocks snapping shut as they readied themselves for his next order.

There was time to look ahead. Dubois' men were scattering to all corners of the encampment as they tried to find new cover. Confusion reigned. He caught a glimpse of the French-man running for the haul of ivory with three men at his side. As Jack watched, one fell, his head shattered by a well-aimed shot from el-Sisi's position. No more than half a dozen men were still facing to the east. It was time to take advantage of the confusion.

'Ready!' He shouted the single word, then glanced at Julian. The naval officer might have begged Jack to pull out, but now, to his credit, he stood beside Jack, ready to fight.

'I told you it would be an experience.' Jack grinned as he delivered the dry line.

He saw Julian grimace just before he glanced away to check on his men. They looked steady enough, their faces set into the grim, tight expressions of men about to be ordered into hell.

Chapter Thirty-eight

———◆———

*J*ack filled his lungs. 'Charge!' He roared the order, then started to run.

His boots thumped into the sun-baked ground, the reverberation pulsing through his body. Deep in his chest, his heart was pumping hard, the sound filling his ears.

This was his moment. His moment for madness. For rage. For death.

Yards flew by, his legs covering the ground in great loping strides. He was shouting as he ran, letting the madness loose, the rebel yell screeching out just as it had all those years before on the bloody field at Shiloh. It fuelled the emotions that had taken hold, the wild, screeching sound tuned to the moment as he ran, powering along, body, mind and soul filled with nothing but the burning urge to fight.

Dubois' men saw them coming.

They stood their ground, rifled muskets and revolvers raised. It was bravely done. It was no small thing to stand against a charging enemy, yet they held their positions, then fired, bullets zipping towards the small band of red-shirted soldiers and their khaki-clad leader, who was yelling like a fiend released from hell.

Jack strained to find more speed. The moment Dubois' men fired, so time seemed too slow. The ground no longer rushed past, his legs now cast from lead.

Bullets tore past him. He heard screams as his men were hit, at least two voices crying out in horror as fast-moving bullets struck them down, but he paid them no heed. Nothing mattered now. Nothing save closing on his enemy.

He fired as he ran, shots blurring together. He saw one bullet strike a man in the face, his head snapping back as if it was on a spring.

'Come on!' He encouraged his men on, willing them to run faster.

More shots came against them.

They ran on. Shrieking like fiends. Killers unleashed.

They reached the tents.

Time sped back up, moments flashing past.

One of Dubois' men stood in Jack's path, revolver held in an outstretched hand. Before he could shoot, Julian gunned him down, the naval officer whooping in childish glee as he hit his target. Another emerged from behind a tent and began to flee. Jack saw him and shot him a moment later, his arm tracking him without conscious thought. The bullet struck the man in the small of the back, shattering his spine so he went down like a sack of shite, control of his limbs lost in the passing of a single second.

'Let's go!' Jack led his men down the line of tents, head turning this way and that as he looked for more men to kill. His pace slowed, the speed of the charge falling away.

Ahead, the encampment was nothing more than a chaotic swirl of bodies moving this way and that. Some stood and fired, aiming at el-Sisi's men or else snapping off shots in the direction of Jack and his assault group. Most just ran.

'After them!' Jack skidded to a halt and ordered his men on. It was time to regain control after the madness of the charge.

His men did as he had ordered, Sniders held ready, the fast pace of the charge slowing to that of a steady advance. Jack stalked after them, trying to get his bearings.

It was then that he saw a lad cowering beside one of the tents. The youngster looked up at him, eyes bright with terror. He could have been no more than sixteen or seventeen years old. He carried an Enfield rifled musket, the weapon's ramrod stuck half in and out of the barrel in an aborted attempt to reload. Jack was close enough to hear a whimper of fear escape his lips.

The young man tried his best. He whipped the ramrod out of the barrel and reached for a percussion cap, fingers moving with desperate haste even as Jack lifted his revolver. The cap was just emerging from the pouch when Jack fired.

At such close range, he could not miss. The bullet hit the side of the youth's head, shattering his skull and showering the side of the nearby tent with a gruesome spray of blood, bone and brain. The lad died instantly.

Jack did not look back, the killing forgotten in an instant. He was getting a better sense of the battle. El-Sisi and his men were firing briskly, their volleys tearing into the western flank of the encampment. That side was devoid of living men, the only occupants now the dead and the dying. The line of tents on the eastern edge of the encampment was now clear, the assault group shooting down any of Dubois' men who had lingered there too long.

Jack looked for Dubois. He saw him almost at once. Clearly

the Frenchman was not done. He had understood that he was under attack from two separate forces, so he was gathering his men on the northern side of the encampment, where he had his piles of stores and the mountain of ivory. At least fifteen or twenty of his men had been cut down, but he still had numbers enough to fight back, and even as Jack watched, he saw more and more running to join him. The mistimed attack had been effective, perhaps even better than his true plan. But the advantage of surprise was slipping away fast. It would not be long before the Frenchman's superior numbers would start to tell. Jack knew he had just a small window of opportunity to do what he had come to do. What happened after that, he did not care. For now, there was just one objective, and one alone.

'Let's go!' He pushed past the Taha brothers, who loitered near the last of the tents in the line. 'Follow me!'

It was time to lead, to show his men what he wanted them to do.

He began to run once more, the empty holster on his right hip thumping against his leg. Shots rushed towards him, some kicking up a puff of dirt like he was running through a field of dust devils, others zipping past.

'Come on!' He bawled the word, encouraging those who followed. He heard a despairing cry as one of his men was gunned down, the pitiful wail followed by the thump of a body hitting the ground.

He reached the stockade. As he skidded to a halt, he heard a yelp of pain as another of the assault party was hit, the man bellowing in shock and horror.

The stockade was just as he remembered it. Inside, the prisoners crouched low, children screaming and all flinching as bullets smacked into the wooden walls that kept them corralled, their terror complete. Women cradled wailing children even as they themselves wept and shrieked, trying to shield them from the bullets and fat splinters that flew through the air.

'You, get the gate open.' Jack shouted the command at the man closest to him. 'Take another man and get these poor bastards out of here!'

He stood to one side, letting the two men get on with it, his head turning this way and that as he tried to make sense of what was happening. Puffs of smoke came from the higher ground, where el-Sisi was holding his men to their task, whilst Dubois' men were scattered across the northern edge of the encampment, some firing towards Jack and the remaining men of the assault party at the stockades whilst others blazed away at el-Sisi's command.

For now, the defenders were hunkering down and firing from whatever cover they had found. That suited Jack just fine. He did not think it would be long before either Dubois or one of his lieutenants saw what he was doing and realised just how few men he had with him. When that happened, he did not expect them to remain where they were for long. They would try to drive the assault party away. With at least forty men left at his disposal, Dubois would find that easy. He just had to recognise that it was possible.

But Jack would not wait for it to happen.

Four of his assault party had fallen. That left him with just eleven. He had detailed two men to get the prisoners away, which meant there were nine men remaining to stand and fight to buy enough time for the prisoners to get clean away.

They would have to hold Dubois' men at bay for as long as that took.

He turned back to the stockade's entrance just as his

soldiers forced the gate open.

'Hurry! Go! Go! Go!' He urged those inside to flee, and they did as they were told, pouring out like water breaking through a dam.

Dubois and his men fired without pause. One of the prisoners, a middle-aged woman, was hit, her barely audible cry lost in the tumult of sound.

More shots came. Another prisoner fell, a woman carrying a child tumbling to the ground, a bullet catching her in the back of the neck. Jack stepped forward and snatched the infant from her arms. It was cruelly done, the woman crying out in despair as her child was torn from her. Yet there was nothing else for it. Jack thrust the babe into the arms of another prisoner, ignoring the pitiful wails coming from the woman who lay sprawled on the ground, blood pumping out from the huge rent torn in her neck. He had seen enough wounds to know she would be dead in less than a minute. Saving the child was all he could do.

'Go!' He stood tall, goading the prisoners on, reaching out to steady them when they stumbled. He grabbed one woman as she fell, pulling her to her feet.

The woman stopped.

She stared at him, her bloodshot eyes meeting his for a brief moment.

It was the woman who had begged for help, and who had been pistol-whipped for her trouble.

'You're free now,' Jack told her, not knowing or caring if she would understand.

'Thank you.' She spoke the words clearly. Then she ran.

As he watched her go, something shifted deep in his soul.

He was settling his account.

* * *

'Form on me!' His voice was huge. His men were scattered around outside the stockade, some kneeling and firing, others pressing close to the walls as they sheltered from the shots coming against them.

'Get inside! Look lively now!' With the last prisoner running from the entrance, Jack ordered his men inside. It was time to make their stand.

They hurried inside, each man crouching down as if they ran into the teeth of the strongest gale, then took up positions on the far wall, kneeling down as they sheltered from the constant fire coming against them.

Jack glanced back at the woman whose child he had taken. She was dead, but still she stared back at him, sightless eyes fixed forever in despair.

'Reload!' He turned away, the unbearable sight forgotten, or at least ignored. For the moment.

His men now faced towards the encampment, the walls of wooden stakes that had kept the women and children imprisoned sheltering them. Julian was there, his face streaked with blood from a graze to his forehead. Ali crouched next to him, the father of so many offspring cursing as he furiously shook his Snider to free an empty bullet casing from the open breech. Gamal and Suliman came in last, the pair taking up station on the right of the line. Jack's sergeant, Hassan, was moving from man to man, checking the cartridge count and handing over spare rounds from his own pouch to any man running low. Mostafa, Habib and Osman held the centre of the line, loaded and ready, their bodies tense as they waited for him to order them to fire. Next to them were the two Taha brothers, still inseparable even in the midst of the battle.

Jack knelt down, reaching into the pouch on his belt for a

fresh packet of cartridges for his revolver. He reloaded fast, ignoring the constant crack of bullets hitting the walls of the stockade. When he looked up, all nine men were aiming their Sniders towards targets on the northern flank of the encampment, rifles pulled tight into the shoulder as they squinted down the barrel at their choice of target.

They were doing all he could ask.

Now it was time to hold their ground and buy the prisoners enough time to get far away from Dubois and his ruthless gang.

Chapter Thirty-nine

Keeping low, Jack moved forward, pushing between Habib and Mostafa at the very centre of the line. A bullet struck the wooden stake in front of his face, showering him with splinters, one grazing his cheek and another catching his bottom lip. He ignored the bright flash of pain, just as he ignored the feeling of warm blood running over his chin.

'Make ready,' he bellowed. It was time to take charge. 'But hold your fire.'

The men around him held themselves tight. All were reloaded. All were ready.

He glanced up. He saw Dubois almost immediately. The Frenchman was standing tall, his arms waving this way and that as he too took charge of his men. It was easy enough to understand the former legionnaire's instructions. He was ordering his men into two groups, holding around half in place to return fire at el-Sisi's men. The rest he was gathering to him, screening them behind the hefty haul of ivory that was being struck constantly by Snider bullets. He had at least twenty men with him, maybe more, all crouching or kneeling as they reloaded their revolvers. They too were getting ready.

'Hold fire. Stay down.' Jack held his men in place. But he kept his head up. He had to see.

The gunfire hitting the stockade died away. Shots still came without pause, Dubois' men remaining engaged in a long-range duel with el-Sisi's party stationed on the high ground. The Frenchman's men had little to no chance of hitting any of the covering fire group. But they did not need to. They just needed to pin them in place and keep Jack and his men isolated. It was smartly done, and a part of Jack could only applaud Dubois' skill. It was exactly what he would have done were the roles reversed.

'Ready.' He gave his first order. As one, his men came up, rifles aiming over the walls of the stockade.

'Aim.' He issued the second order calmly. With no one firing against them, it was much quieter in the stockade. There was no need to bellow or roar.

On the far side of the encampment, Dubois and his men were almost ready. All but one or two had reloaded, and they were forming up into a rough line facing the stockade. They were perhaps three hundred yards away, maybe less. Certainly they were in range of the Sniders, but Jack held fire. He wanted to control the next volley, so that when it came, it would hit the attackers like a well-placed punch to the gut.

'Here they come!' Julian hissed the warning as Dubois gave one loud shout.

'Steady,' Jack reassured his men. They needed to hear his voice.

Dubois' party charged. It was bravely done. They ran fast, each man dodging left and right as they used any cover they could find, rushing from place to place, shielding themselves for as long as they could behind storage crates or barrels.

'Steady!' Jack repeated, keeping his voice calm. He could sense his men tense around him. Nine pairs of eyes squinted down the barrels of their rifles, each one moving slightly as they tracked the target they had selected.

Still he held back the order to fire.

The men coming against the stockade were running hard. They covered the first hundred yards and still they sprinted forward, each man desperately zigzagging from side to side. Every one of them knew what was coming.

Jack held his breath. He lifted his revolver, looking for a target of his own. At the front of the rush, he saw Vladimir, the heavyset Russian he had brawled with back in Khartoum. He carried a shotgun, the weapon held across his gut as he lumbered forward. Jack was close enough to see every detail of the familiar face, from the firm set of his jaw to the way his lips were pressed tightly together.

Two hundred yards became one hundred and fifty.

Jack did not so much as twitch. He was waiting. Holding his breath. Picking his moment.

One hundred and fifty yards became one hundred.

'Fire!'

He released the word. Nine rifles and two revolvers fired as one.

Bullets struck down the closest attackers, knocking half a dozen over. Others dived to the ground, twisting away in a desperate attempt to survive. Vladimir lay sprawled in the dirt, a revolver bullet buried in his ample gut. He was still moving, his hands flapping this way and that as they clutched at his stomach, trying in vain to stem the flow of blood that was gushing out of his belly.

'Reload! Quickly now!'

Jack tore his eyes from the Russian and changed his aim, snapping off a shot at a dark-haired man dashing past Vladimir's body. His shot missed, the man ducking away as it snapped past his head. The next shot didn't. It struck the man in the groin, knocking him over so that he crashed to the ground, his body rolling over and over until finally it lay still.

His men did their best. All had reloaded swiftly. Now they fired a second volley, knocking more attackers to the ground. But the range was closing fast and Dubois' men were shooting back, revolvers firing constantly, bullets cracking into the wooden wall of the stockade, razor-sharp splinters of wood cascading over the heads of Jack's party.

He tried to hold his men to the task. A storm of bullets was tearing into the wooden walls, but still they fired back. As soon as the Sniders were reloaded, they would rise up, throwing the barrel over the wall. But they paid a price for daring to return fire, the attackers shooting at any man who revealed himself.

At Jack's side, the baby-faced Habib gave an odd little moan of surprise, then fell back, a bullet buried in his brain. Hassan was hit a moment later, a bullet scoring across his forehead, the fast-moving round parting the skin with the precision of a surgeon's knife. He reeled back in shock, face covered with a mask of blood that ran down into his eyes. A second bullet hit him a moment later, a well-aimed round catching him in the throat. He fell onto his back, arms and legs thrashing this way and that. He tried to scream, but could emit nothing more than a grotesque gurgle as he drowned in his own blood.

The attackers came on, shooting without respite, the constant barrage flensing the front of the stockade. Gamal was hit, the man Jack had relied on to scout for him. He died quietly, a bullet hitting him in the eye then burying itself in his skull.

'Jack!'

Jack heard Julian cry out his name.

He turned. Sir Sam's nephew lay on his back, hand clutching at the side of his neck, blood pouring between his fingers.

For a moment, Jack held his place. He fired once more, emptying the last chamber in his revolver. Then he moved, keeping low and scurrying to Julian's side.

'Hold still.' He snapped the words as he skidded to a halt. Even as he hit the ground, he bellowed at his remaining men to keep firing. He ripped the bandana from around his neck and pressed it into Julian's hand. 'Push this into the wound. Then lie bloody still.' He fired off the advice before bending low and starting to reload his revolver.

Julian clawed at his arm with bloodied fingers. 'I'm dying.'

'Shut up!' Jack's voice was cruel as he shook off the hand, concentrating everything on reloading his revolver. He was almost out of time.

'Tell my sister I died bravely.'

'Shut the fuck up.' He pressed new percussion caps into place, then reached for Julian's revolver, which lay on the ground next to the naval officer. He rotated the cylinder, checking to see how many bullets were loaded. Two chambers were empty, so he reached for two more cartridges.

One of his men screamed as he was hit. Jack glanced around even as he rammed home a cartridge. Mostafa was crouched down behind the wall of the stockade, his Snider dropped into the dirt, his hands clasped to a deep valley scored across his scalp.

Cartridges loaded, Jack reached for two percussion caps.

The Egyptian Ali died, a well-aimed rifle bullet hitting him full in the face, the round tearing through his skull to exit in a bloody explosion from the back of his head. Children had lost a father. Jack had lost one of his last remaining men.

Just four were left.

Dubois' men were dreadfully close now. At such short range, their revolvers were much more deadly.

Jack's small command had done all they could. Now the last of them hunkered down, not even the bravest able to keep firing, the volume of fire coming against them just too much.

'Tell my uncle I—'

'You're not fucking dying, so shut the fuck up.' Jack shut Julian down. He held a revolver in each hand. Both were freshly loaded. He had ten rounds. He had to make them all count.

One final glance told him Dubois and his men were less than fifty feet from the stockade. They came in a mob, twenty or so rushing forward together.

Part of him wanted nothing more than to stay out of sight. To stand up was to draw the fire of twenty guns. It would bring death, or worse, a wound that would leave him lingering in agony for hours, or at least until Dubois came to fire a bullet into his brain.

Yet sometimes a commander just had to stand up.

No matter the cost.

'Tell your uncle he's a miserable, selfish bastard.' Jack grinned at Julian as he uttered the words. 'And tell your sister that I wish things had been different.'

Then he stood.

Time slowed as he re-entered the world. Smoke swirled across the battlefield, the taint of rotten eggs filling his nostrils as he drew what might be his last breath, the stink of spent powder billowing across an encampment littered with the bodies of the dead, the dying and the wounded.

Faces came at him in a blur. He could see every detail in the expressions of those rushing towards him, the snarls and open mouths of men summoning the courage to charge an enemy, fear etched deep into every countenance. He saw anger. Rage. Fury. The madness of battle. These were men who knew war. Who knew what it meant to fight, and what it could cost. Yet they came forward nonetheless, storming the stockade as if they were attacking hell itself, knowing that damnation or glory awaited on the other side.

He raised both revolvers, picking his targets without thought.

And he laughed.

He laughed because he was one man standing against twenty. A commander standing up to show his men what they had to do when all was lost and the only reward was death and pain.

He fired, snapping off his first shot. There was a fleeting taste of elation as a bullet took a fat man in his wide belly, knocking him over as if he had been punched hard in the gut.

It passed fast, a volatile cocktail of emotions surging through him.

Anger. Terror. Joy.

He fired again and then again, shooting fast, his hands work-ing in tandem as he picked targets then fired in a blur of action.

Bullets whipped past him.

Dubois' men saw him standing there, a single target clear above the wall of the stockade. They fired even as they rushed over the final hard yards, revolvers aiming at the last man standing against them.

Jack shot two more men down. He whooped as they crumpled over, bodies twisting, then hitting the ground. He revelled in the moment, filling his lungs then bellowing a defiant war cry as he wielded the two guns with skill honed on a dozen battlefields.

At the end, he was a fighter. Roaring his war cry and standing tall even when all was lost.

At the end, he was a soldier. A man who thrived in war.

At the end, he was a commander. The man who stood and made sure everyone knew what was to be done.

And at the end, he was a man who had set himself free.

He was himself.

He was Jack Lark.

A bullet struck him high on his left arm. It stung, the fast-moving missile searing through his flesh. He cried out, he couldn't help it, the flash of pain taking him unawares. He tried to raise the arm, attempting to aim the revolver held in that hand. It failed to obey, the revolver tumbling from fingers numb and unresponsive. He shot once more, emptying the last bullet from the revolver held in his right hand. It struck down a dark-skinned man in mid stride, taking the man in the face.

And that was that.

Jack stood there, left arm hanging uselessly against his side, right clasping an empty revolver.

He had nothing left.

He was done.

Time slowed.

He saw Dubois. The Frenchman came striding out of the smoke. He looked huge, to Jack's eyes at least, as if he were a mythical hero entering the realm of men for the first time.

Dubois spotted Jack, and for a moment, the two men stared at one another.

Time stopped.

Then Dubois' right arm lifted. It held a huge black revolver, the weapon saved for this moment.

And it was aimed directly at Jack.

Chapter Forty

—◦●◦—

The crash of dozens of rifles firing as one roared across the battlefield. Bullets seared into the encampment, taking Dubois and his men in the flank. Nearly half of them fell, bodies tumbling this way and that, the rush against the stockade halted instantly by the storm of fire. Cries rang out, surprise and terror replacing the roars of men about to seize victory. Others bellowed in fear, whilst the dying shrieked in agony.

Jack flinched as the shots rang out. Yet he stayed standing. Holding his ground.

A second volley followed the first. Then crisp orders, the shouted commands easily heard even over the chaos.

Jack saw men moving into the western side of the encampment. They advanced in a disciplined two-man-deep line of battle, the files and ranks ordered just so. He recognised them in an instant. The men from Egypt and the Sudan had come to his rescue, the regiments that had accompanied the expedition brought to the battle he had summoned.

Sir Sam led them, distinctive in his khaki. In his hands he carried the Dutchman, the rifle that had killed so many animals now aimed at a new human quarry.

Half a dozen drummers were stationed in front of the tight ranks. They beat out the pace of the advance, filling the ears of the men behind them with a mesmerising rhythm. Sir Sam had brought two full companies of men, one from each of his regiments. Nearly two hundred men had come to turn the tide of the battle, each one armed with a brand-new Enfield rifled musket.

Even as Jack watched, the line stopped its advance. As one, the men began to reload. Hands moved through the evolutions of the drill, sergeant and corporals bellowing a series of commands. Through it all the drummers beat on, hands never still, the staccato beat thumping across the field of battle.

'Aim . . . Fire!'

Jack heard Sir Sam roar the commands. A heartbeat later, his men fired, the volley thundering across the encampment. Dozens of the last surviving men in Dubois' gang were gunned down, the scattered groups flensed with fire.

The battle was over.

Jack tore his eyes from the neat line of soldiers. He did not know why Sir Sam had decided to come to his aid, or why he had risked so much of his command to fight Jack's battle. But he knew that without their arrival, there would have been a very different result. At that very moment, he would likely have been lying in the dirt, body torn and broken, lifeblood pouring into the dusty soil.

But Fate had other plans for him that day. Just as she always did.

Dubois was running. The Frenchman recognised defeat when he saw it, and now scurried away from the ruins of his encampment. He was quite alone.

Jack dropped the revolver from his right hand. There was no time to reload, not if he wanted to capture Dubois.

He drew his knife from its sheath, then began to sprint as fast as he could, rushing out of the stockade and dodging round the bodies that littered the ground. He passed the man he had shot in the face, the shattered remains of the man's head smothering the ground around his ruined skull. He jumped over another man who crawled towards the line of tents, body leaving a snail trail of bright red blood in its path.

Men cried for his attention as he ran past them. Those who only moments before had been intent on killing him now begged for his aid. The pitiful pleas fell on deaf ears as he ran on, boots kicking against the fallen rifles and revolvers that had been dropped as the fight came to its bloody conclusion. He looked only at Dubois.

Yet the Frenchman was too far away. He was going to escape.

'Dubois!' Jack found enough breath to bellow the name.

Dubois slowed, turning to look over his shoulder. He had run through the line of bell tents and was now on the very fringe of the encampment. In a matter of moments, he would be outside and close to the ground where Jack and his assault party had waited to attack. There was no way Jack would catch him.

But Dubois did not want to escape. At least, not yet.

He turned, revolver held low in his right hand.

'Fight me, you bastard!' Jack shouted the challenge, words coming in breathless gasps as he pounded after his foe. 'You hear me! Fight me!'

Dubois glanced around him. The remains of his gang had scattered, a few running for their lives, but most just lying where they had been shot down. He stood alone.

Jack ran on, careless of any danger. He did not doubt that Dubois could make the shot if he chose to take it. Yet still he pushed his legs on, straining for speed. He knew it would not end. Not here. Not now. Not with Fate on his side.

Dubois raised the revolver. It barely twitched as he aimed it at Jack.

Jack saw the weapon steady. He knew what was to come.

He threw himself down.

The shot came a heartbeat later. It snapped past him, missing him by a hair's breadth.

He hit the ground, hard, left arm jarring. Pain flared, bright white light flashing across his vision. Yet somehow he managed to roll over, his body refusing to stay down, and forced himself back to his feet, panting and hurting, then running forward once more, the knife he had drawn still clutched in his right hand.

Dubois saw him rise up. There was a moment's disbelief on his face, then he tossed the revolver to one side and drew a thick-bladed knife from his belt before settling into a fighter's stance, his weight balanced on the balls of his feet.

Jack fought the urge to whoop in victory. Fate had left the Frenchman with a single round in the revolver, and she had kept Jack safe as he desperately threw himself down to avoid that bullet. Now she spurred him on, filling his head with madness.

Dubois held his knife ready. Jack saw the blade, just as he saw the look of determination in the Frenchman's eyes.

The distance between them closed in a flash. As Jack ran forward, Dubois bent low, then lurched forward, closing the last yards so that the two men came together in a rush.

Jack saw him coming. He tried to slow his pace, but Dubois

had timed the moment to perfection and he could do nothing to avoid a brutal contact.

There was a dreadful thump as they collided. Dubois had dropped his shoulder at the last moment, hitting Jack as he rushed on at close to full speed. It drove into his chest, forcing the air from his lungs and knocking him to one side so that he fell away, legs struggling to keep him upright.

Dubois came for him at once, blade slashing through the air, razor-sharp edge darting towards Jack's eyes.

Jack ducked away, trying desperately to keep his footing. He did not know how he missed the knife, but he saw it flash past in front of his vision. He straightened, jabbing his own dagger forward, his only thought to drive Dubois away.

It worked, Dubois jerking back from the strike. It gave Jack a moment to drag a breath into his tortured lungs before the Frenchman came at him once again.

Dubois' blade moved fast, stabbing forward, tip aimed directly at Jack's throat.

Jack sidestepped, letting it go past him. Dubois recovered fast, then backhanded the blade, slashing it at Jack's head.

Somehow Jack swayed out of the way. But Dubois gave him no chance to recover. Even as he found his feet, the Frenchman lashed out with his wooden hand. The punch came hard and fast, smacking into the side of Jack's head, knocking him from his feet.

He fell hard. The pain that followed was excruciating. All-consuming. Blinding. Debilitating. He could do nothing but writhe in the dirt, agony shuddering and rippling through every fibre of his being.

Dubois came to stand over him. 'What a shame that it had to end like this, *mon ami.*'

Jack looked up. His entire left side was numb. Pain filled his brain. It left room for just a single thought. One last desperate notion.

'You really fucked me over, Jack. You know that?' Dubois reversed his grip on the knife. Readying it for the final strike.

Jack squirmed in the dust. There was no way he could rise. No way he could avoid the blade that would soon come for him. Yet he was not beaten. He would not stop fighting. Not now. Not ever.

'At least you will die for what you cost me.' Dubois hissed the words then glanced over his shoulder. Sir Sam and his two companies of soldiers were spreading out across the encampment. They were searching the dead and checking the dying. But the Frenchman still had a chance to make good his escape. And he had enough time to finish off his enemy.

Jack moved onto his left side. The pain was almost unbearable, but it had to be endured. He had to free his right hand, no matter what it took.

He saw Dubois looking away and so moved his right hand into position. He focused everything he had on the knife in his hand, holding it tight.

He was ready.

A single gunshot came loudly in the quiet that had followed the fighting. Jack caught a glimpse of a freed prisoner standing over one of Dubois' men, a smoking revolver held in both her hands. Another crouched over a dying man, six-inch blade in her hand. As Jack watched, she pushed the knife down and forward, sawing it back and forth as she hacked through the man's neck.

The prisoners had disobeyed the men he had sent with them. He had told them to flee, to get far from the men who had taken them from their families. But they had not run and now they killed. Taking their revenge on the men who had captured them.

Dubois saw what was happening. He turned his head, spat once then looked down at Jack.

'*Casse-toi, pauvre con.*' He pulled back his arm, readying the killing strike.

But Jack struck first.

He thrust his right hand forward, dragging the sharpened edge of his knife across the back of the Frenchman's ankles, pushing the blade down with every scrap of strength that he could muster so that it cut deep and straight.

Dubois cried out in shock and pain. Then he fell to the ground, tendons severed. Desperate hands reached towards his ankles, fingers grasping the torn flesh, mouth releasing hisses of pain.

Jack did not let him lie. He forced himself to his knees, then shuffled forward, dragging himself through the dust, muck and blood that covered the ground.

Dubois lay on his back. He was broken, but still his head lifted as Jack came close.

'*Fils de pute.*' He hissed the words.

'Fuck you too.' Jack stabbed his blade down, driving it deep into Dubois' stomach just above his groin. He pulled it out, blood flung from the blade, then rammed it down again, and then again, the blows coming hard and fast, one after the other, each one tearing a wide gash in Dubois' gut.

He let go of the blade, then flopped onto his backside. The knife stayed where it was, hilt pointing straight up, blade slathered in the blood that pumped from the dreadful gashes it had cut into the Frenchman's belly.

It was over.

Jack pushed down with his good arm, levering himself to his feet. He saw blood on the ground from the bullet hole in his left arm, and still more caked across that side of his shirt. But the wound could wait. He was alive. For now, that was enough.

He staggered forward, swiping a bloodied hand across his face, smearing away the exhaustion, and looked down at Dubois.

The Frenchman's eyes were open. He was staring up at the sky. They stayed like that, not once flickering across to look at Jack. They did not move even as Jack bent down and picked up Dubois' fallen revolver.

He hefted the gun in his hand. He did not recognise the make. But it felt reassuringly heavy. He would keep it.

He turned and started to walk away. He did not look back. Not even when the woman who had begged for his aid all those weeks before came past him, a bloodied machete held in her hands. More of the women, and some of the children who had been taken, followed her. All had picked up fallen weapons from the bodies of the dead and now most carried blades. Blades they would use on the man lying powerless in the dirt, the man who had led the gang that had worked such destruction on their lives.

It took everything Jack had to stay on his feet. But he kept going, boots dragging in the dust.

He spied Sir Sam. He was walking toward Lieutenant el-Sisi, who was leading the covering firing party forward. The young officer's face was creased with worry, as if he had done something wrong. It was almost enough to make Jack smile. Almost.

Then he saw Anna.

She was working near the stockade, sleeves bloodied to the elbow as she bandaged Mostafa's bloodied head.

She saw him coming.

She tied off the bandage, then stood and came towards him.

'You're hurt,' she called out as she moved briskly across the blood-splattered ground.

Jack staggered to a halt. He was swaying on his feet, strength failing him at the last.

He watched Anna as she approached. There was something perfect about her. Something he needed. Something he wanted.

He had settled his account. The future was open to him once again.

Anything was possible now.

Anything.

The thought settled in his mind.

Then he fell into the darkness.

Epilogue

---◆---

Khartoum, 1 June 1870

Jack stood on the waterfront and kicked a stone that lay near his boots, sending it skittering away until it smacked into the wall of a nearby building with a crack like a gunshot. He was thoroughly bored, but it appeared the captain of the dahabiya he had employed to take him to Cairo was in no hurry to allow his passengers onboard, leaving Jack to kick his heels on the steps cut in the stone embankment, a single carpet bag containing his possessions dumped near his feet.

He had been in Khartoum for less than a week while he arranged transport for the next leg of his journey, but to his mind it had been far too long. Khartoum was filled with ghosts, and he could not walk the quiet, almost empty streets without thinking of the time, not so long before, when he had been carousing around town in the company of Dubois, Vladimir and the Frenchman's other lieutenants.

But at least he was his own man once again. He had left Sir Sam as the expedition set up an encampment not far from

Dubois'. They planned to remain there for the foreseeable future, building up supplies and giving the men time to recuperate. When the river was clear, they would press south once again, although this time they would do so without Jack's assistance.

Colonel Abd-el-Kader had assumed control of the Forty. Jack had left his men with regret, and it had taken all his powers of persuasion to convince Monsoor to stay with the expedition.

He had left Sir Sam on good terms. The anger and disharmony that had coloured the days and weeks preceding the fight were forgotten in the thrill of the victory over Dubois. Florence had wanted him to remain, but both Jack and Sir Sam knew that for the terrible idea it was. There was room for just a single leader on such an expedition, and both men knew that Jack had to leave.

Julian had not died, despite his grand claims. He, like all the wounded, had been given over to Florence and Anna's care, and the pair had done their best to nurse him back to health, despite the fact that he was the worst patient Jack had ever seen. Both had also worked tirelessly with the women and children Jack had freed, the expedition's supplies raided ruthlessly for anything needed to tend to those who had been rescued. Sir Sam had been enlisted to help, and Florence had promised Jack that every effort would be made to reunite the prisoners with their families. If that could not be done, the women and children would be taken back to Khartoum then on to Cairo, where they would be given every assistance to rebuild the lives that Dubois had shattered.

Tired of waiting, he sat on the steps, ignoring their cold, damp touch on his backside. The embankment was busy this early in the morning. A constant stream of women and children were coming down for water, which they carried away in clay pots balanced on their heads. It was somewhat incongruous to see the citizens of Khartoum fetching water in the same way they had done for centuries, whilst they were surrounded by the steam-powered pumps and waterwheels that should have committed the ritual to the distant past. But at least it made for a diversion, and he watched them as they moved back and forth.

When watching the water carriers started to bore him, he reached for the revolver that sat in the holster on his right hip. It was heavier than he was accustomed to, but he was getting used to the weight. It would be some time before he would practise with the weapon in his left hand, the wound he had received in the battle taking its sweet time to heal. For the moment, his left arm was heavily bandaged and encased in a black silk sling. As awkward as it made everyday activities, he was pleased that the wound had not festered. With time, it would mend. Just as the ghosts that haunted him would, in time, fade into the back of his mind, where they could dwell with the other faces from his past.

He had learned from a gunsmith in Khartoum that the revolver he had taken from the Frenchman was called a Lefaucheux. The same gunsmith had sold him a dozen packets of the pinfire cartridges it required, enough, he hoped, to see him through the next weeks and months. He had fired the weapon just the once. It had proven to be accurate enough, and the pinfire cartridges were quicker and easier to load than the paper cartridges for the Beaumont–Adams he had left behind in Dubois' encampment. That the Lefaucheux held six cartridges over the Beaumont's five was an extra advantage.

He hoped he would have no cause to use it for a while, but he had loaded it that morning nevertheless. He would not be caught unprepared.

With a sigh, he returned the revolver to the holster then squirmed from one buttock to the other as he tried to make himself comfortable. His patience with the dahabiya's captain was fast running out, and he began to picture walking onto the sailing ship with the heavy French-made revolver on display to see if that encouraged the man to hurry the fuck up.

The thought reminded him of a vow he had made the day he had said goodbye to the Bakers. As he had sailed away on the dahabiya that would take him and the worst of the sick to Khartoum, he had promised himself that he would never work for anyone else ever again. From now on, he would make his own way in the world without being at any man's beck and call.

It was time to stand alone.

He smiled as he heard someone approach.

Well, perhaps not quite alone.

'You took your time,' he sang out, face creasing into a smile as he teased his tardy companion. She had been with him ever since they had left the expedition, her role as carer to the wounded who had been brought to Khartoum now complete.

She wore long trousers paired with a long-sleeved shirt made from an earthy brown cotton. Both had seen better days, the fabric dotted with coloured thread that had been used to sew up the many tears and rents in the fabric. On her head was a wide-awake hat with a long string that looped under her chin. Beneath the hat, her dark hair had been tied into a single thick braid that was laid on one shoulder. It was a fitting outfit for a wild town like Khartoum, finished off perfectly with a holstered revolver and a dark red umbrella that this particular lady was using as a walking stick.

'Perhaps you might have considered giving me a hand.' Anna Baker walked briskly to the embankment, then dumped her portmanteau down next to Jack's carpet bag.

'Heh, I'm injured,' Jack protested, gesturing to his sling.

'Then I suppose I should make some allowances.' She could not help smiling. 'Until you have recovered at least.'

'Good.' He used his good arm to push himself to his feet. 'But I warn you, that might take some time.'

'Oh, I am sure it will.' Anna came closer, her chin lifting as she looked up into Jack's face. 'But I will look after you, I promise.'

Jack grinned at the idea. He would hold her to her promise. At least for as long as he could.

Historical Note

———❖———

Had you heard of Sir Samuel White Baker? No, me neither. Unlike many of his contemporaries, Sir Sam has been rather ignored by the popular histories of this great age of explorers. Yet in my opinion, his career was no less impressive than those of his peers, nor he himself any less illustrious. However, he never gained favour at court, and his exploits, although acknowledged by such august pillars of Victorian society as the Prince of Wales, have largely been forgotten. In part, this could easily be due to his arguably surprising choice of second wife. Florence was his junior by some seventeen years. That he purchased her at a slave market whilst hunting with a maharajah is perhaps one of the strangest stories I have read of the Victorian age, and I suspect a good part of the reason why Sir Sam, although adored by the contemporary public, at least for a while, never became a fully fledged part of the most notable group of famous explorers and game hunters.

Sir Sam's career continued after we left him in this novel. Following the establishment of the camp to allow the men to recover their strength, which he named Tewfikeeyah, the expedition continued until early in 1873, when he and Florence called time and headed home. Sir Sam was lauded for having laid firm foundations on which his successors could build, and the series of garrisons he established along the Nile created a network that would begin the long and difficult process of suppressing the slave trade whilst establishing alternative sources of income, such as Britain's favourite, cotton farming. Although there was some debate as to his role in the massacre of a large number of natives, he was largely applauded for his work in the Sudan. A world tour followed, which did not conclude until early in 1882, after which Sir Sam and Florence settled down on their estate in Sandford Orleigh, Devon.

Sir Sam's adventures finally came to an end when he died in Florence's arms of a heart attack on 30 December 1893, aged seventy-two. His exploits fell out of public consciousness in the years that followed. This is not the place to debate the rights and wrongs of these Victorian hunter-explorers. There are very many reasons to laud their achievements, just as there are as many compelling reasons to damn them all as villains. For the purposes of this note, I shall sit firmly on the fence. However, there can be no doubt that men like Sir Sam played a pivotal role in the creation of the British Empire, and no matter your opinion on that, they still hold great historical interest. I find the stories of their lives compelling.

I shall leave the last words on Sir Sam to the Prince of Wales himself, who wrote of him to his mother, Queen Victoria, in February 1869, 'We find Sir Samuel Baker very agreeable, and with so much to tell me about the country, which no one knows better than he does – that I cannot say how glad I am to have him to accompany me there.'

Now it is time for me to confess to those changes I made to

the timeline of the expedition. At the start of the novel, I sped up Sir Sam's appointment as pasha, bringing it forward to March 1869 and the end of the prince and princess's visit to Egypt. In truth, the appointment took some time, and it was not in fact fully agreed until April, with the details of the mission, as listed in the firman the khedive issued to Sir Sam, not completed until 16 May. Sometimes the story has to come first, and a protracted negotiation just would not have suited the pace I needed.

Sir Sam's expedition on behalf of the Khedive of Egypt happened broadly as described in this novel. I made some alterations along the way to prevent the novel becoming as bogged down as the flotilla, and I have abbreviated or even removed some of the detail of the long journey beyond Khartoum. If you wish to read more of the expedition, or of the many others Sir Sam and Florence completed, then some excellent sources are available. Sir Sam's own account is contained in his work titled *Ismailia*. It is a fascinating read. At times, I was able to use his writing to construct the dialogue in this novel, something I think always goes a long way to establishing as much of someone's true character as is possible in a work of fiction.

I must also make reference to Dubois and his gang. Dubois is a creation of my own imagination, as is the battle to bring him and his men to justice. The Frenchman may not have existed, but I think it is true to say that all sorts of villains and miscreants were drawn to the wild, ungoverned lands in this part of Africa at this time. I needed someone for Jack to bond with, and I believed an ex-legionnaire would make the perfect foil.

I think it is worth noting here that Jack's recollections of the fighting at Solferino are based on his experiences that filled the pages of *The Last Legionnaire* and not on the true role played by the 2e Régiment de la Légion Étrangère in that battle. I should also make some note of the account of the recent campaign in Abyssinia that Sir Sam mentions early in the novel. If you have read the ninth Jack Lark novel, *Fugitive*, then you will know all about the account written by my fictional academic and reluctant hero, Horatio Watson. There is something very pleasing about being able to weave in threads from some of the other Jack Lark novels, and I hope you will allow me this conceit.

I must also make mention of the Forty Thieves. In reality, Sir Sam established this group upon his arrival in Khartoum, and so Jack rather steals his thunder. They were commanded by Colonel Abd-el-Kader and not a miscreant English rogue. Again, the needs of the story came first, and so Jack assumed the task of putting the specialist unit together then taking command in place of Abd-el-Kader. You can read more of the role of this group in Sir Sam's own writings. Corporal Monsoor existed, and Sir Sam writes of his relationship with the Egyptian, 'the best and most devoted man that I have ever seen was a corporal of the "Forty Thieves" named Monsoor . . . he accompanied me like my own shadow, he seemed to watch over me as a mother would regard an only child'. With an endorsement such as this from Sir Sam himself, I felt Monsoor had to take a place in the story, and I hope I have done him justice.

Once again, I must make note of the spellings used in the novel. Just as in *Fugitive*, there are a great variety of names given to the places and people that feature, and it can be quite confusing to know what is where, and who is who. As before, I have stuck to one version for each throughout, using the colourful names and spellings used by Sir Sam himself.

Hopefully they make sense should you read more widely on this fascinating campaign.

So that just leaves me time for a brief word about what is in store for Jack. As this novel concludes, he finds himself a long way from home in the depths of Africa. I have a feeling he may head south, but let's see. After all, it's a big continent and anything can happen.

And in Jack's case, it usually does.

Acknowledgements

Book Ten! Who would ever have thought that possible? I know I didn't. Yet here we are and there are many people who have helped me reach such an amazing milestone that I must thank.

David Headley, Frankie Edwards, Bea Grabowska and Jane Selley are due a huge amount of thanks for the guidance and assistance they have given me. More than that, I must thank them sincerely for the support they never fail to offer, no matter what. Without them, I most certainly would not have been able to write Jack's adventures for so long, and I will be forever grateful for everything they have done for me.

I would also like to thank all those who have not only read my books but taken the time out of their day to send me an email, or a message on Facebook, Twitter or Instagram. These messages mean a great deal and I am always touched when someone contacts me to tell me how much they have enjoyed reading the books.

Finally, I owe everything to my family, and most especially to my wife Deb and my children Lily, Will and Emily. They are my world.